I0691845

MASTER OF THE SKIES

Dragon Core Chronicles Book Five

LARS MACHMÜLLER

MOUNTAINDALE
PRESS

ACKNOWLEDGMENTS

Most often, readers don't know just how much they mean to us. A lot of writers are, for better or worse, often fueled by emotions and our self-worth tied intrinsically to our creations. If we get a particularly bad review, we can spend days doubting ourselves, struggling to hit our goals, or just plain ole sulking! If somebody comes with a nasty post about us on social media, the effect can be almost physical.

Does that mean we're vain creatures? Or just extremely lacking in self worth? Well... some of us. Some writers would very much disagree with my words. To me, however, it's an undeniable fact that I absolutely care about what people think about me and my writings.

Blessedly, the reverse is also true. Most readers aren't aware of just how much their positive feedback means. A simple positive comment on a post will have the writer humming, in an improved mood as they create the next chapter. A direct message saying that you loved their book can improve the result and writing of an entire day.

As such, I can only say this from the bottom of my heart: if you love their worlds? Tell them. Make a post. Share the news. They will learn. And they *will* love you for it.

As to you, user LeoD? These acknowledgements go out to you.

At a moment, where I was feeling pretty shite about myself, you brightened my day. I hope you read this. Stay awesome!

CHAPTER ONE

"It's Twelve O'clock and All's Well." - Terry Pratchett, Guards, Guards

I was on top of the world, thinking about the number three. It was a magic number, one of those you'd always see in stories. Three wishes. Three sisters. Three books, if the writer would ever get to it and finish the job. Though I guessed, with me in a different world, I was never going to read the end of that trilogy. Heh. On three important occasions, I'd stood here on top of the central fortress in Fire Peak, the capital of the Scoured Mountain.

Still, as I looked at the city, aided by my mini-map, I couldn't help but marvel at the myriad differences in the city from the first time to the third. When I first stood here, I wasn't even sure I was going to survive. At best, I was looking at a future as a prospective slave under the bonds of Selys, the majestic, bloodthirsty ruler of the mountain.

The second time, I'd been hurt, but was healing after my battle with Selys. I had been facing a capital in complete opposition, who wanted nothing to do with the promises of freedom and equality we brought. Hell, they were ready to meet our changes with blood, if need be.

Now... Now, I couldn't help but grin. I spread my wings, creating a flurry of cool air to brush along the length of my body, while I peered at different spots in the city and the crater around us. This was what success felt like.

Signs of improvement stared back at me from everywhere in the mini-map. Okay, fair. There were also a number of ruins. The human attack had been hefty and damaging. They'd dumped boulders down on the city from a mile up. How rude was that? However, the ruined buildings and signs of attack were by and large a thing of the past already, courtesy of our shamans. All told, the improvements had the ruins beat.

I glanced down on one of the poorer areas where three Urten were training in a sorcery area under the tutelage of a young Talpus shaman. They were manipulating pebbles in the air like they'd been born to it, which, for a mentally weak race, was impressive. A mile away, at the other end of the city, one of the main markets was showing newfound activity as trade and barter blossomed in the city again.

I zoomed out to gaze over one of my favorite sights. the Scoured Mountain was growing green! It had only been a month since our victory over the Dworgen and the human army of Nefren, but a full tenth of the formerly barren crater was now blooming green with freshly sown crops. That wasn't all. The eastern side of the crater was blossoming with additions, too—enclosures brimming with captured monsters to be bred for food and experience. The entire area was lit by a subtle blue glow from my Growth Boosts and Animal Boosts, magical constructions to aid the speed of growth.

I mentally reached out to the entire city and had to fight off the urge to shout, "Good morning, Fire Peak," just for the hell of it, and addressed them all. "Good morning to you all. I bring you the news of the day. Today, I share with you the wonderful sensation that there is little to report. Nothing particularly life-threatening, no invasions, and no insane monsters about to kill us all.

In the northwestern square, near the alchemist's, there has been a spill of caustic material, so stay alert until it's been cleared up. We are still looking for people interested in joining our scouts and mages, but at this moment, we have gained enough guards and fighters. Thank you all for joining up to help keep the mountain safe!

As always, if you have anything you need us to address, grab hold of a guard or go to the fortress. We are there for you! Oh, and here's a reminder: the training competition will end two days from now. Everybody who joined up and had their stats assessed should join us to get their final gains noted. I don't think I need to remind you, but the two persons with the largest improvements in attributes, mental and physical, will win a major-quality item from my hoard!"

I closed the connection and let my vision slide over random streets in the city. What I could see was wonderfully life-affirming. People of all races were going about their business, reacting to the message with smiles, and a whole lot of posturing and jibing from people who were still training. There were a lot. The citizens of Fire Peak had seen the light in the possibilities of self-improvement, and they did *not* hold back. Even Roth had to admit that a good deal of the trainees were going at it hard.

As I closed the mini-map of the capital, I opened up another mental connection. This one was newer to me and felt less tangible, more... like closing a video call on the cell phone then proceeding to call somebody on the landline. Less evolved, perhaps? Even so, the connection was solid.

The mental voice on the other end came through clearly. It was also straight to the point and not a little bit overbearing. "Onyx. You still insist on doing this on a daily basis?"

With a mental readjustment, I opened up the mini-map again, and, within seconds, had it zoomed in on the solid form of Creive. The blue Dragon was in his usual spot on the lower end of his upside-down fortress. He was cradling the half-devoured body of a Dweeler in one claw, bones and gore next to him clearly showing that it wasn't the first snack of his day. I couldn't help but smile.

"Without a doubt. While we're still building this place, we'll talk every day to ensure that everything's under control. There's no point to having perfect communications, if we don't use them." I zoomed out, trying to spot something new on his stalactite-shaped home. "So, what's the progress looking like? Are you making full use of those mana crystals I sent you?"

Satisfaction wafted from him, like from a well-fed cat resting in a sunbeam. "Oh yes. My mana regeneration has more than doubled. Constructions are growing so much faster now. I have a new construction, too: Air Control. It lets me manipulate the air inside my domain. Throw the wind any way I want to. Let any flier try to take on my domain now!"

I blinked. "That sounds excellent. And effective. Do tell me if there's something new and think about the non-combat uses of it, too!"

"What?"

"I mean, you've got, what, a mile of domain now? With the air at their backs, any of your minions should be able to fly across the domain at twice the speed, right?"

"But then I would have to focus on them all the time?"

"Sure. But, if it means that all your minions work twice as fast? Don't limit it to just that single recommendation, either. That was literally the first thing that came to mind. I'm sure you can figure out something even better. Like... being able to carry more weight while flying. Okay, that might be flawed. But think it over. I'm certain there are more uses to be discovered. Meanwhile, how are our shamans doing?"

"Huh?" Creive grumbled, still mulling over the possibilities until he collected his thoughts again. "They are... not bad. Not at all. A bit of an annoyance, since they can't fly, but they work well."

That was an understatement. Creive's fortress had grown by at least fifteen percent in size in the four weeks they'd been there. Before, it had been an old ruin with half the rooms filled with detritus and dirt and the other half open to the outside. Now, it was brimming with fortifications and new constructions, ready to take on anything and anybody.

He continued grudgingly. "In fact, since I was in a good mood, I decided to honor your request."

"Do you mean-"

"Yes. I've let one of the tiny Talpus creatures start aiding you instead of expanding my defenses further. He is out in the tunnels, extracting materials right now. According to him, you should expect the first batch of ore in a week or so."

I beamed. That *was* great news. So very, very altruistic, too. Heh. "Thank you very much, Creive. That is wonderful to hear. We can start crafting high-quality items soon, then… and then we'll be able to send it all to Ahzel for enchanting."

"Yeah, yeah. You ship that off to that white pretender. Just make sure I get my portion of the enchanted items afterward. It should do wonders for the increase of my hoard."

I promised him that he'd get his due, then went to talk with Ahzel. That talk was a lot briefer and less friendly. While our relationship had improved, we were still not exactly pals. But there was definite improvement here, and talking to him on a daily basis helped keep us cordial.

The white Dragon had also taken well to seeing the number of mana crystals I sent his way to speed up his development. That, and the aid of a shaman to help clear the area from when we'd brought the mountain down on them went far to improve his mood, especially when he realized that I'd been true to my word. Neither of us had known for sure how much would remain of my old hoard when he returned and got it cleared out. He did manage to salvage a good number of my former constructions, though, along with both of the Soul Carver's.

His constructions were springing up fast, too. Mind you, it was exceedingly weird seeing my old domain covered in a layer of frost and snow, but once he got to clearing most of the rooms of debris and soil from the cave-in, his influence started growing

5

rapidly. On top of that, he'd taken to creating enchanted items with a singleminded focus that both impressed and scared me.

As expected, he took the news that he was soon going to see high-quality items with satisfaction and renewed zeal. He promised me that he'd be done with the latest batch soon and send most of them back up to Fire Peak. Then, we had a brief discussion on technicalities about enchanting. After that, we broke the connection with little formality.

It wasn't a perfect system. Not yet. We were still ironing out the flaws, and some speed bumps impeded how fast we were able to transport items and manpower back and forth, but it was constantly improving. The best part was what my vassals didn't even fully realize. Every single interaction like this, every single cordial cooperation, however businesslike, tied my vassals closer to me, even if it worked as much in their favor as in mine, at least on the surface. In time, with enough interaction and tying ourselves closely to them, they'd find themselves a natural part of our forces, without me having to resort to coercion, bartering, or threats.

Ah. Dreams of the future. A lead role in that dream stood right next to me. My third vassal, Slither, was back up in Fire Peak, having returned from visiting his own domain moments ago. I lowered my head and looked at the spindly Stick Kin. God. Looking at his stick-thin − heh − body, it was easy to ignore exactly how powerful and dangerous the teleporting little killer was. "Good to see you, Slither. What's the news from the Aberrants?"

His smile was as disturbing as ever. He looked like a bird who'd spotted a worm and was calculating the best method to strike. But his mental message carried genuine warmth and humor. "My people are well and interested. Still, I... am not sure if you understand the magnitude of what you're asking, Onyx."

I snorted. "It's hard to fix in the mind, sure. And it's a massive scope. But, it's a worthwhile task. So, the question is whether the Aberrants are up for the challenge?"

"Let me hear this from you again. You want to tame the mountain?"

I grimaced. "Close, but no. I want to *understand* it. I want to take this insane, deadly place and learn everything we need to not be taken by surprise. I want to take the one group of people who are the best at moving unseen around the place, the Aberrants, and make you responsible for scouting the mountain and bringing any challenges to my attention. No more unanticipated monster surges. No more rabid beasts growing in strength to the point where they can suddenly roam the layers unchecked."

"But you have no plans to kill them all?"

"Heh. People in this place wouldn't take kindly to that. Live, fight, thrive, and all that? There will always be monsters to fight in this mountain. Killing all the higher-level beasts would lead to stagnation and no growth for the rest of us. But, that is no reason to let them grow unchecked and threaten to overwhelm our forces due to sheer negligence."

His head lolled as if it were loosened on his neck. "Mmmh. Still. You want us to roam the entire mountain. We can't do it, not as it stands. We're few. And weak."

I grinned. "Well, that's part of the fun of it, right? Figuring out how to do it. This isn't something that's going to take place overnight. It will be months, possibly years. You're not going to do it alone, either. I aim for there to be plenty of scouts to add to your ranks, as well."

He huffed. "I'm not sure we would love having a lot of untrained meat in our ranks. There are a lot of dangers out there. There's a reason we don't roam the tunnels more than we do."

"Oh, I completely agree. I'm truly happy you're approaching this with your eyes wide open. There are enough people-pleasers who don't dare speak up against me. So, for clarity's sake: your job would not be to take down all the monsters. We have enough fighters and mages up here by now; we can move out to eliminate any stronger gatherings of beasts.

"The important part of the job for you is traveling through

the mountain, staying safe, and finding out what's what. Oh, and if you meet any groups of intelligent humanoids we haven't talked to yet, just avoid them, and we will send out diplomats to ensure that they understand how the future in the Scoured Mountain will work. "

"That sounds... very unsafe for our people. We are not all as strong as you."

I grinned. "You will, of course, also be able to take advantage of this to take down any weaker monsters to strengthen your own forces. Your people are going to level quickly in this position. Finally, remember that, once we have treated with the largest groups of humanoids, you will only have to deal with unthinking beasts. Knowing how good the Aberrants are at taking advantage of terrain, traps and the like against enemies... I believe it would be a natural vocation for you."

He tilted his head sideways. "It still feels like we would be taking huge risks. The mountain is a dangerous place, and sometimes the only available paths forward are filled with danger. Like when you had to travel through the area that was overgrown with Veer Growths."

I nodded, conceding the point. "You're entirely right. As to that... I hope that I will have great news for you shortly. Are you staying in Fire Peak for a while?"

"I could. Do you still have any stores of human meat? I haven't eaten my fill of that. That was a truly succulent meal."

It took me a while to find a proper response for that.

CHAPTER TWO

They were gathered before me in all their dysfunctional glory. My council. My diverse band of misfits, some of them barely touching down on the shores of sanity, but all of them close to my heart.

Entering the throne room, I took a moment to take in the weirdness of it all. I had died. Real death, no fancy bright tunnels or life flashing before my eyes. My cholesterol-filled veins had finally had it and made me keel over with a heart attack. Only, instead of moving on to a generic, likely flame-filled afterlife, I'd been transported to this realm. As a bloody dragon. That in itself was weird enough that it merited another mention. So yeah, shadow dragon. Top of the world, right? Except, in this world, that only meant others would gain a boost when they *supped on your flesh*. Bloody place.

That was exactly how I met the first of my council, too. Arthor, Creziel, and Roth had all been part of the Talpus tribe who'd egg-napped me and attempted to turn me into a Dragon omelet. They'd been the lowest of the low back then, carrion eaters and worse, scrambling to eke out a living beneath the notice of the stronger beasts of the mountain. Yet, look at them now.

Arthor, my strongest shaman, stood tall—as tall as a Talpus could get, anyway—and proud, ready to challenge the world itself, if he believed he was in the right. Which was always. Lately, he'd evolved his mobile stone defense to carrying around thin sheets of stone everywhere that were tall enough to cover half his body. He had to rest from time to time, but he was getting closer and closer to going full Iron Man. Erm. With rock.

Creziel was a lot smaller and weaker-looking. He was also the less powerful shaman of the two, there was no doubt about that. Yet, his intellect was anything but weak. In fact, he might be one of the brightest on my team. When it came to construction? He excelled. In fact, he'd completely taken over the project for turning Fire Peak into a self-sufficient agricultural masterpiece.

We might not have the space for a Corn Belt, but we were definitely getting at least our very own Crop Crater. He was also working on turning the entire crater into an architectural nightmare for any attackers, improving the housing inside the city, and... yeah, he was keeping busy. Looking at him, you'd hardly be able to spot that he used to be afraid of everything and anything. He made eye contact at least half of the time now!

Roth... might be my favorite Talpus. He was simple, like me. He liked good food, a good fight, and dedicating any spare second he had to training. Okay, so maybe not that similar to me. Still, his bulk had increased to the point where, at times, you'd be hard-pressed to recognize him as a Talpus. Heh. He was definitely not the target of the mockery that sometimes still landed on the other Talpi for being one of the "lesser" species of the mountain. Dude was swole, like my daughter would say. With an eye-roll, which might mean that she was serious, was being ironic, or wanted to marry him. Hell if I knew.

Gert came later. Inducted into our forces along with a larger group of Crawls, the low-set, ugly humanoid had been an unknown to begin with. She only became their leader later on, but had taken to the role with aplomb. She had also taken a radically different approach to the leader role for a Crawl.

She didn't roll with the normal Crawl strategy, which was becoming the biggest and baddest and growing into a physical force of nature with impressive natural armor and the brain capacity of a left-handed wrench. No, she trained her mental skills and worked hard to incorporate actual learning and critical thinking into their lives. She was succeeding, too. She was one damn tenacious critter, and I couldn't be more proud of her.

Grex was another simpleton. The ugly Imp liked fighting and taking on the world, with nary a thought in consideration to tiny details like size, odds of survival or similar trivialities. He and his kind tended to live brief lives... but he lived every second of his life to the fullest. Having lost half a leg didn't slow him down in the least. He claimed it just gave him less mass to carry around when he was flying.

Dimodeus was a newcomer. He had only joined us a couple of months back, when we took on the task of reforming Fire Peak into a place worth living in. He was an Ethium, which translated into the unholy offspring of a dark elf and a humanoid insect. His long, dark-skinned arms and legs had an extra joint thrown in for good measure, and he had huge, drooping ears and too-large eyes.

He looked servile and mild-mannered—the byproduct of having survived as a former slave of Selys—and he was an excellent administrator. In fact, I was secretly planning to ladle all the responsibilities of actually running Fire Peak onto his plate. He was that good. He was also incredibly conscientious and dedicated to making the place decent for everybody. I needed to give him a token to show him my appreciation. A gift basket or a level up or something.

The entire scene was wrapped in a nice, warm glow. Not friendship or anything like that. Or, well, if you wanted to be corny about it, you might say something exactly like that. In this case, the glow gave off actual, literal boosts to our attributes. The blue glow spreading out toward our entire group stemmed from Timothy. My only fellow ex-Earthling and former-human-turned-ghost was floating in the center of the group like an apparition from some chick flick with Patrick Swayze. He was an incredible nerd, stubbornly proud of being a New Yorker, and he liked the Patriots. Despite all that, he was an amazing person.

I strode into the throne room and took in the mood. They were looking rather miffed, for some reason. Heh. Arthor always looked like he'd been hit by bad news, so that was nothing new, but some of the others also sported annoyed demeanors. I let my mental voice ring out into the room. "Soooo, who's ready for good news?"

Arthor sneered at me. "Pfah. Unless the news is that you've managed to make Timothy here finally be quiet, I am not interested."

My amused snort made Timothy's affronted look grow even worse. I smirked. "I don't think there is a force of nature in this world that has the power to succeed in that. Anything I should be involved in?"

Timothy stared me down. "Not unless you're a huge fan of slavery."

Arthor rolled his eyes. "Yes. Like your see-through friend here likes to say, repeatedly, he believes that the surviving Dworgen should be let off the hook for trying to kill and enslave us all."

Tim held up a finger. "Don't twist my words. I simply don't think that chaining them down and forcing them to slave for *us* is the right thing to do. Besides, it's not like they had any say in it, since Tellor was the one commanding them. I have been talking to them, and they want to prove themselves. I merely plan to find a decent alternative to slavery."

Ah. That topic again. I nodded thoughtfully to Timothy, then settled down, lying where I could observe them all. "We've been over this, Tim. And I agree. I'm not a huge fan of this solution, either."

"But?"

"But, it is the best solution we've come up with so far. Also, you're not improving things by trying to inflate them into something they're not. They're not chained. They're not enslaved. They're under house arrest. So, please don't try to make the council's heads explode by arguing over what's already settled. If you figure out a better idea, come to me."

He looked about to argue, but I spoke over him. "Besides, as you very well know, this isn't far off from what they'd be subjected to back on Earth. They're fed, they're hidden away, and they're kept busy. That's *exactly* what would happen back in the old prison system. We'll find a better solution in time, but for now, that's what we've got. Besides, it's not like they *want* to be let out into the streets. People aren't exactly fond of Dworgen these days, you know?"

He deflated. "Yeah. I guess. I'll stow it until I have a better alternative." He dimmed for a minute, then seemed to pull himself up mentally. "So. Good news, you said?"

"Yeah. Quite decent." I looked at them all. "Creive's about to start sending shipments of quality ore soon."

That got a warm welcome and a slurry of demands for new armors and weapons.

I laughed. "I'm sorry, all. I will have to remind you that we're still going to get everything enchanted afterward with Ahzel, unless it's something urgent. Besides, you know the drill. Tim and Dimodeus are in charge of the priorities for all of us. So, unless you haven't already, go tell Tim what you can't live without."

The blue ghost looked at all the eyes landing on him. "Joy!" he exclaimed drily. "I'll remind you all that nothing's changed. If you don't have anything *new*, new you want, and not just extra arguments for why you should be the first in line, you might as well start arguing with Grex here, for all the good it'll do you."

13

The Imp bounced in the air, looked around confused, holding up a hand, pointing at himself. "Me? Who's arguing? You want weapons? Everybody gets a weapon!"

I snorted. "All right. It's early, I know, but we've got a mountain to improve. Who's first?"

"That would be me, I believe." Dimodeus' mental voice was kind but firm. And, like that, we got down to business with the day's meetings. Heh. Killed and reincarnated, and I still had daily meetings. How was that fair?

Fortunately, our meetings were, all told, usually pretty efficient. We might get sidetracked, and sometimes they dissolved into vicious arguments, but in general, we all preferred to be elsewhere and had more interesting things to get to. Except Dimodeus, perhaps. He lived for this crap.

The updates were wonderful all across the board. Our newly created guardsmen, fighters, and scouts were deep in the process of getting outfitted, equipped, and trained to start help in and around the city. Not only that, they were improving in leaps and bounds with their training. Later on, we'd have to exchange their equipment with higher-quality enchanted gear, but for starters, the guardsmen were only getting a uniform while the fighters and scouts received weapons and armor from the hoard. Not the best stuff, though.

I'd initially been worrying about exhausting my hoard, possibly dropping down to a lower level of hoard size, what with all the items we'd been handing out left and right. However, after the loot from the recent fights and emptying out the Dworgen domain, the room around me was all aglitter with the brilliance of top-tier items. Whatever else you could say about the big brutes, they were excellent crafters. Since the items were often of a size where our people couldn't use them, they might as well boost the hoard.

Food and drink *was* a concern. However, Creziel was all over that, along with Laive. We'd have loved to have Cavinne on board for that, but they'd finally found her body, hidden in a cellar. The Culdren formerly responsible for production and crafting in the city had been brutally murdered during the battle with the Dworgen. Her replacement, a younger Urten, seemed competent enough, but was far from as decisive and savvy as her predecessor had been. That would be a work in progress. For now, however, Creziel and Laive promised that our increases in production would be enough to keep up with the city's needs.

As for our enemies, they were a thing of the past. The surviving members of the former city guard and the Gathering had stopped working against us. "People in the know," or so Dimodeus phrased it, confirmed that they were no longer on the warpath. In fact, former city guard and mage inductees were fighting to join up with us now that they could see the way the winds were blowing. We still had to keep up with vetting them properly in order to weed out those who were joining us on false pretenses, but "the times, they were a-changing" for sure.

Timothy was having a frigging ball! Or, at least, he was keeping busy enough that he didn't have a bloody chance to become introspective. He'd lost Lore, the Crawl that he'd worked closely with for a long while, and he buried himself in work to move past it. If he had a manic gleam in his eyes at times, I didn't mention it. He did clearly enjoy his work and was working wonders.

With all the new citizens, city guard inductees, and mages applying to join our forces, along with the Dworgen survivors and the Aberrants, he was doing some serious overtime to get a handle on his Quipu project and create a working overview of feats and attribute requirements. From what he said, he was getting close to where he'd have something new. He didn't elaborate, but it sounded like it would make waves, when we got that far.

Arthor and Creziel were kept incredibly busy. Not only did they have the crops project constantly keeping them out and about, suddenly they also had a ton of new mages to train and assess. Fortunately, Dimodeus handled all the administration work, but he had no talent for spellcraft, and our Talpi shamans were the craftiest ones around, after him. They had mostly divided the workload between them.

Arthor handled most of the training, delegating some of it to the newer Talpus shamans and finding others to handle the hard lifting for the irrigation system needed for the crops. Meanwhile, Creziel took care of the finer details of the canals and of trying to work out with Dimodeus how best to utilize an influx of new spellcaster talent. Gert had taken to joining them, mostly to learn more about creative thinking than anything else, I believe.

They *were* really getting creative–listening to them go on, they might either solve all our problems or kill us all. I let them go ahead, though, just asked them to check with me before they implemented any major decisions.

Roth... had never had more fun. He had a whole city to push around and train, and he was enjoying it to the fullest. According to him and the people who trained under him, he was being an absolute menace and possibly life-threatening. He was also learning new tricks around the city to use in his own training.

As for me, I stayed in the background, like a leader should, except for the occasions when I needed to be visible. Nudging them when they needed a little encouragement, challenging them if they were moving in a direction I found wrong, encouraging them to evolve and grow, and ensuring that we were, in fact, progressing where we wanted. But, all told, I didn't have to do that much. Merely be there. Because these were some damn competent underlings!

I was about to call an end to our meeting when Grex's hand shot up into the air. He had taken to sitting on my leg during these settings– it seemed that he enjoyed the elevation and the movement. I suffered the abuse quietly. I liked the little menace.

"Are we done with the boring meeting? Can I ask something? It's important!"

I smiled at the eager Imp. "Yes, Grex?"

He and his people were mostly trying to train with the other Imps and some other winged fighters of the city. They had mixed results. He was... not exactly leadership material. He sighed, then his mental voice rang out in exasperation. "I. Am. Bored. All Imps are. We need to go. Find a fight. Something new. Can we?" He fidgeted in place, tiny clawed fingers twitching.

I sighed. "I know, Grex. I know." I looked at the rest of the people assembled here and considered it... yeah, maybe it was time for another discussion on the topic. "The thing is, Grex, we need you here. The fight will come to us. We just don't know when. Same goes for everybody." I pointed out toward the city, smiled at the people gathered around me.

"There's a reason why we're not splitting up, why we're working ourselves to the bone. We are planning for the long run, but we cannot afford to split up and do whatever we feel like. The humans *will* return with a new army. We've beaten them once, but they're bound to be back. We don't know how, with how many soldiers, where they'll come from, and which kind of army we'll be facing...

"Basically, we don't know anything. This is why we are working as hard as we can to get everything on rails, build up enough of a surplus of weapons and armor, trained mages, fighters and scouts and... bloody *everything!* We have no clue what's coming, but you damn well better believe that we're going to be ready for it!"

"But... bored! What if it takes a year? I could take my Imps, get out there. Attack them. Burn them when they move." He brightened up with a huge smile. "Human villages far away, too. Easy enemies. We could burn villages. Scare them off!"

I looked at him sternly. "No. We've had this discussion. There are some avenues I will not be part of. We are not going to commit atrocities on innocent people because of what might come to pass. If they move on us, we're going to answer in kind and strike down *hard*. And we'll grow strong and prepare ourselves, so we are ready to face them."

I smiled fondly at him. "Also, if it takes a year, we will have found something for you and your kin to do. We are growing fast. If we get a year to prepare, we will be ready for anything. But I doubt that we have that long. In the meantime, we need you. What do you think would happen if the enemy arrived, and you were gone?"

He blinked, then beat his wings, slowly rising from my leg. The realization on his ugly, scrunched-up face almost made me curl up with laughter. "You would... you would all die, horribly."

I nodded earnestly, ignoring the snickering sound from Roth. "We might. So, it's really important for me and for *everybody* that you and the rest of the Imps are here, that you train as much as possible, so we are ready to take on anything. Even an entire empire! Can you do that?"

Wide-eyed, he bobbed his head vigorously up and down. "We can. I promise, we can. Imps in the city are weak, though. No good."

I grasped that and went with it. "That's it! That's your purpose. Build them *up*, Grex. Train them! Make them as tough as you are!" Poor bastards. Still, it was for their own good. Heh. If they lived.

Grex's eyes gleamed, and he floated off my leg and started murmuring to himself. With that done, we handled the last few points on the agenda and got to work.

CHAPTER THREE

"All gravy, baby." - Snoop Dogg

I planned to move to the fields and add another couple of rows of Growth Boosts, but Dimodeus intercepted me. That was normal. He often had a number of details that he deemed too unimportant for the meetings, and we would handle them quickly and efficiently before parting ways.

This time looked different, though. The normally very officious Ethium had a special look around him. I'd almost call it... smug? At the very least, very satisfied with himself. "Onyx. I have something I would like to show you."

A wide smile built on my face. "You've got my full attention. What is it?"

"A surprise. But a good one, I promise. If you would care to follow?"

Intrigued, I got up and followed him into the fortress. Of the many people who'd suffered under Selys, Dimodeus was the one who'd impressed me the most. Right from the very start, he'd shown impressive grit and defiance. Hell, he'd faced me on the very first day, challenging both me, the representatives of the city guard, and the Gathering. The balls it took to do that...

We marched through the hallways of the fortress. They were slowly being put back to normal after the Dworgen attack. Large parts of the brick hallways had been demolished by our own forces to keep the bastards from ranging straight through the halls and taking over the hoard. It was good to see the evidence of the struggles being faced out to be replaced with a normal setting. "Normal" fortunately meant that we were getting rid of some of the gaudier, red and golden settings from Selys's rule and replacing them with more earthen and subdued color palettes. Creziel was helping with that part, because my sense of colors and proper decoration was, in the words of my dear ex-wife, an absolute catastrophe. Just because I thought salmon was a fish and not a frigging color!

As the walk stretched, and Dimodeus hummed silently to himself in anticipation of whatever reveal he'd planned, I took a moment to consider the recent growth of my council. While our struggles and battles had been horrible at the time, they had also pushed our powers to new heights and resulted in some very tangible increases. My feat that gave every single minion of mine an increased fifty percent to their experience gain didn't hurt.

This time around, there was a pretty large difference between those who took part of the initial battles against the Dworgen and their old guard conspirators, and those who had the capacity to go up against the airborne human army.

My favorite lunatic, Grex, was the odd duck here, again. The poor Imp had taken an ugly scalp wound in his first battle and had been left behind early on and hadn't gained much there. However, in the fight with the humans, he'd had a frigging *ball!* He had single-handedly slain over a dozen of the hawk-like scout fliers, and that was beside his efforts against the close combat forces.

All told, he'd jumped all the way from Level 25 to 32. He'd won a new feat to make him even harder to touch in the air,

Airborne Avoidance. His Imp underlings had improved accordingly. They were starting to become a force to be reckoned with. At this point, most of them were at least Level 20. That was a lot of fiery damage.

Gert had been a part of the force who fought alongside me, all the way from the Dworgen betrayal, through several struggles with Dworgen, and up to the final clash with Tellor, the bastard who stabbed us in the back. But she couldn't help in the aerial battle against the fliers, and as such, she'd "only" gained two levels, climbing from 25 to 27. I still didn't entirely know what to make of her, but it felt like she was growing in more ways than just level-wise.

Roth had been an absolute champ. The insane nutjob had actually taken part in the airborne battle *on my back*, and if it hadn't been for him, I probably wouldn't have survived the battle alive. Unfortunately, his ability to cause damage in the air was limited. His levels increased accordingly, going from 31 to 34. Still, if there was one person who'd have my back in a fight, it would be him!

Creziel had spent the entire time defending against the Dworgen inside the fortress. On top of that, he took part in the struggle with the fliers but was knocked out right at the start, so he didn't earn that much in that conflict. Even so, he made it to Level 33.

Two of my minions outshone the rest, however. Arthor had been with me every step of the way, fought in every battle, helped face down the Dworgen - and on top of that, he'd spent the entire aerial struggle strapped to my back, tossing rocks at the enemies and keeping me safe. Every single flier he managed to force out of the skies who was later slain on the ground? Experience for him. The entire series of battles saw him explode from Level 30 to Level 38, and it won him his first Defining Feat at Level 35.

That was an eye-opener to me. I hadn't been aware that anybody but dragons got those, but... of course, they did. However, there was a difference, and it underlined the general power differences between races. I gained my first Defining Feat at Level 25 already.

Still, the possibilities were equally impressive and clearly tailored to his persona and position. He had the choice between gaining a fifty percent increase to his mental attributes, increasing the mental attribute training cap for his tribe by fifty percent or doubling his affinity with earth yet again. It came as no surprise to me that he went with Improved Mental Training. As he said, the eventual boost to his tribe on the whole would outshine the possible gains for himself after a few months, as long as he kept them training hard. The gleam in his eyes when he said that was... silently terrifying.

As for Timothy... Timothy had just been insane. He'd apparently spent half the time in the Fortress *among* the Dworgen, stunning and damaging them, leaping around fast enough that they couldn't bring their few enchanted weapons and spells to bear against him. Against the humans, he had ruled the skies. Grex took great pleasure in re-enacting the way that enemies kept dropping down inside the crater on all sides of him due to Timothy's stunning attack.

The result was overwhelming. He went all the way from Level 28 to Level 37, gaining *two* feats—one of them a Defining Feat at level 30. Clearly, the level you gained your Defining Feats at were tied to your race... so, the more powerful your race, the earlier you'd get them. Unfair, but consistent. Typical of Deyra.

Tim's earliest choices had been extremely difficult. Like me, he'd been longing for his old body, and they'd offered choices like the Poltergeist, where he'd be able to fly around and prod stuff off of shelves. There were no distracting options to choose from for Timothy this time, no lure promising added tangibility or the capability to become physically present. Seemed that ship had sailed back when he chose his specialization as an Ectoplasm – basically, a ghost with enhanced control over his ghostly body.

Still, the choices of the Defining Feat were equally

enthralling: between defensive combat efficiency, offensive combat efficiency, and out-of-combat efficiency. Basically, whichever choice he took would adapt his attributes and boosts accordingly.

Timothy did *not* choose what I'd expected. I figured that he would jump at the [Boosted Field] that would create a large permanent circle around him to boost the attributes of people surrounding him, when out of combat... but no.

In his words: "I've learned some things about myself lately. One of them is that I am in a unique position to protect those around me... but it demands that I change and learn how to become more offensive. Defending is all well and good. But I am at my most effective when I am in the middle of the enemy, stunning and debuffing them."

The [Combat Field] certainly did that. It increased his own attributes by fifty percent in combat *and* doubled the effect of the debuff he could grant enemies in battle by touching them. At this point, when he was fully focused and shrinked to his minimal size, he could debuff an enemy by a total of -20 attributes. In other words, he could make a Level 1 Dragon collapse *just by touching it.* Combined with his other new feat, Increased Stun Efficiency, which did exactly what it said on the package, he'd be even more of a terror in battle.

I had to admit, though, I was a little worried for him. I didn't want him to grow self-destructive as a result of losing Lore. Gradually, I was considering whether I might be worrying overmuch there. So far, at least, he was being very self-conscious about the whole thing and channeling it into his work.

I was just going to keep having his back and keeping an eye on him. From his reactions, the best gift from all his leveling seemed to be the fact that Timothy had gained new insight into how the feat system worked. He'd said he had a solid idea how the defining feats work, depending on race, and would incorporate that into his advice from here on. Then he chased me out so he could concentrate.

As for myself? Heh. Yeah, I wasn't complaining. The entire

string of battles, I had worked constantly to weaken as many as possible, meaning I got experience gains from every single thing I had affected that subsequently was slain. Since the effect of Deyra's Blessing was still active, I doubled those wins. All told, I earned myself a full four levels, propelling me all the way from Level 39 to Level 43.

No defining feats, not this time... but I figured the one at Level 45 would have to be.

I divided the newly gained attributes according to what I'd experienced in the battles. My Mental Power had been decent. Sure, a few large enemies were heavy enough on the Toughness that my effects took several applications to have an effect, but that was to be expected. For most enemies, a single Weakening Fog or two had them sprawled out on the ground. My Mental Control remained out of... well, control, and that was all fine and dandy. I didn't need any more than the two increases per level I got to the attribute automatically, though.

Strength was still for weaklings. Heh. Okay, I could've done with some extra Strength now and again, but the entire thing that had allowed me to get as far as I had was focusing on evasion and weakening effects, outlasting my enemies and grinding them down. I'd stick with it. My Agility had been... acceptable. Airborne, I was able to outmaneuver pretty much everybody one on one.

However, on the ground, it had been a different situation. My bulk really made it difficult for me to evade my enemies, above all in cramped situations, and that was against enemies which were typically not heavy on Agility. I would *not* want to go up against Roth with his attribute-enhancing skill, or somebody like Slither who'd made it past a hundred points in Agility. My Toughness... was a real issue.

Several times, I'd found myself close to dying from the damage, and once, I wouldn't even have been able to continue the struggles simply for lack of stamina. So, yeah. More Strength would've been nice, but less Agility or Toughness would've seen me dead.

Decision made, I split my increases equally between Agility and Toughness and observed the results.

Personal Info:
Name: Onyx
Race: Young Shadow Dragon. Level 43 – experience toward next level: 170/43000
Size: Very large

Stats and Attributes:
Health: 1340/1340
Mana: 1800/1800
Strength: 66
Toughness: 134
Agility: 180
Mental Power: 180
Mental Control: 236
Mana regeneration rate: 15072/day
Health regeneration rate: 178/hour
Attributes increased by +50% and regeneration rates by +100% due to the Blessing of Deyra.

I nodded at the sight. That would do. That would very well do. At this point, Slither might be the only person in the entire mountain who had me slightly outleveled, and that slippery critter had a lot of years on me. Also, I still had the very best decision ahead of me.

There was no doubt that the feats you were offered improved as you leveled, especially when you hit those Defining Feat levels. This wasn't one of those, but it was still an amazing range of choices. My decision was between Enhanced Shadows, Enhanced Illusions, and Enhanced Breath Attack—and having to choose was horrific!

Illusions had been game-changers more than once. However, with the mountain more or less under control, we might see more action out in the light. There, out among people without darksight, shadow manipulation had already proved itself invaluable. In short, my three choices would be useful inside the mountain, outside the mountain, or… everywhere, respectively.

Heh. Okay, maybe it wasn't that hard a choice. My Weakening Fog had already taken down more enemies than I could count. While practice helped me keep control when it came to my shadows and illusions, my breath attack was entirely based on my attributes, so any edge there would be a godsend. I selected Enhanced Breath Attack, happy with the thought that I would, once again, be ahead of the curve when it came to weakening my enemies.

[*Enhanced Breath Attack:* From now on, your Mental Control will be applied with a +50% increase, when calculating the precision of your breath weapon. The same applies for Mental Power when applying its effect.]

With a satisfied sigh, I dipped into the latest hoard size increase. Considering the level, I'd found the improvements a bit underwhelming the first time I looked at them, but I couldn't deny that they'd hit the points I really, really needed.

[Your current Hoard size: 82 Mana Crystals (Very large) grants you the following:
- Maximum Population size: 1000. (2000 with Blessing of Deyra) Current population: 2000
- Domain size: 20,000 foot radius.
- Domain detection range: 250 Miles. Domains within range: (Inside mountain: 3) (Outside mountain: 0)
- Mana regeneration rate increased by 700%. (Total current regeneration rate increase=4800%)
- The possible quality of magic abilities gained from the hoard is heavily increased. Common possibility of multiple magic abilities. Magic abilities are gained faster.
New constructions available through the hoard.

The connection and benefits will remain for as long as your Hoard is active.]

I loved the fact that my minion count had... What was the word? Octupled? Something like that. Hell, at this point, I'd say around one in four of Fire Peak's citizens were minions already, and there'd be more minions soon.

A few of my constructions had improved, some more than others. The first one was my absolute favorite.

[Construction improved:
Outpost.
With the growth of lairs, the need for guards and defensive positions increases as well. This construction allows you to define a spot where your minions will be more effective in combat.
Regardless of the name, this construction can be positioned anywhere within the domain. It adds a field, giving a slight boost to the physical attributes of all minions within range and mildly decreasing those of any hostiles.
3/4 Outposts created
Size of field: 25 x 25 yards
- Boost improved by +50%
- Debuff improved by -25%
- Number of possible outposts improved to 4.]

It was a late discovery for me and kind of embarrassing. I had learned a while ago that I could move my constructions around within my domain. But I hadn't thought to practice using it while in combat. This might change, though. The simple expedience of moving something like an Outpost on top of an active battle might swing the outcome, especially now that the boost had been increased from +25% to +50%. This could be a godsend for situations where we were outmatched, numbers or level-wise.

[Construction improved: Sorcery Chamber.
This construction transforms an area of 10 x 10 feet into a Sorcery Chamber. Inside this area, mental training will allow your peons to improve their mental prowess. If they spend enough time here, they will be able to improve selected attributes. Progress will be limited to the original attributes of the creature and dependent on the efficiency of the training.
- Your minions are now able to improve their attributes even faster. Attribute gain speed increased by +50%.
- The attribute cap of your minions has been raised. Your minions can now raise their attributes even higher.
- Chamber size increased to 20 x 20 feet.]

The only thing different here was that the attribute gain speed had increased to +50% instead of +25%. Still, it was a lovely improvement to see in a situation where we wanted gains fast, all across Fire Peak.

[Construction improved: Shadow Trap.
This human-sized construction, which attaches to walls, ceilings, or similar, resembles a patch of darkness for anybody not paying attention. Thin tendrils of shadow stretch out to touch any hostile passersby, sapping them of part of their strength. Anybody unfortunate enough to be caught by multiple tendrils may be caught and hidden away inside the pocket of the Shadow Trap. The Trap is immune to mundane damage but vulnerable to any form of magical damage.
-Increased tendril strength and length. The Shadow Trap will be able to stretch further and incapacitate stronger enemies.
-Improved illusions. The Shadow Trap will now be harder to spot.
-Increased size. The Shadow Trap can now catch larger prey.
-May be set to cause damage instead of weakening.]

The Shadow Trap was still creepy, but it looked impressive... and if I'd had a bunch of them inside the fortress back when the Dworgen invaded, things might have been a lot easier. Immune to mundane damage? That was insane. I'd decided to install a couple of them in the hallways of the fortress, on the way to the throne room and the Blessing respectively, just as a precaution. I just hoped that my minions would be able to handle them like they could the Shadow Doors, or it could be a huge hassle.

[Construction improved: Animal Boost
This construction enables a field of energy that boosts the growth of animals within. All animals will gain in size and strength at increased speeds.
Size of field: 60 x 60 feet.
- Field size augmented to 90 x 90 feet.]

The increase to the Animal Boost was lovely, too, especially since we were trying to breed animals for the entire crater. Even so, the real winner was the new construction. Well, there were two, but the first one, I was kind of ambivalent about.

[Construction unlocked: Feedback Tower
This tower comes unmanned and unarmed. It has rudimentary defenses to keep its inhabitants slightly safer than outside the tower. Its real power lies in the feedback effect. Any damage inflicted upon minions inside the tower will be repaid in kind as a feedback wave striking any enemies nearby, disrupting and stunning.
Feedback Towers are not the sturdiest. Their defenses are built to be destroyed. When broached, the tower will emit a powerful weakening pulse centered upon the tower.
Mana Cost: 1250
Construction time: 48 hours]

The effects were not too shabby at all. If you put up a series of these towers close to each other, you could probably create some sort of feedback loop effect to completely ruin an invading army's day. Hrm. Feedback loop. I liked the sound of that. Nice and futuristic. You'd be able to sell anything with a name like that.

Anyway, what I disliked was how the entire structure seemed to be built around the defenders getting hurt and overrun. It fit quite well with the "dispensable minions" part of things, which wasn't really my brand of beer. Still, it could really help put the hurt on anybody stupid enough to try and invade. There was a certain karma to the idea of taking some of the asshole Dworgen and stuffing them in there, too. Hrm. I'd have to think about it. The second new construction, however? That was a godsend.

[Construction unlocked: Scout Tower.
This tall tower enhances the eyesight of any minions placed on top. It has an alarm bell on top, which requires activation from a minion to use.
Mana cost: 1000
Construction time: 24 hours]

I'd created my first Scout Tower the day after we sent the humans packing, right up on the very edge of the crater, looking to the west. Fortunately, the range of my domain had increased enough for that to be possible. Otherwise, I would have had to think up some other system. However, with this tower and a duo of scouts up there at all times, we weren't getting surprised by anything this time around.

There were no details as to the maximum range or anything, but since it worked based on the eyesight of the minion, it probably wasn't reduced to some system-based range. The scouts reported that they could see miles and miles, far enough that it would take an invading army well over a week to traverse the distance on foot. I might have to ask Firth and Tim to stick their heads together and figure out the actual range. I couldn't be arsed myself. I was already picturing Tim raving on about calculating the curvature of an unknown globe and... yeah. Delegation was good for the soul.

I'd created one of each construction by now, to have it done. The lone Feedback Tower looked silly standing alone out in the center of the crater. Even so, it looked like creating one of each construction was a stable requirement for increasing the hoard for any size from here on. I didn't want to be caught having to wait three days because I failed to create them up front. On top of that, I really was swimming in mana these days. I'd taken to creating at least one mana crystal daily. Even if the additional mana regeneration wasn't really useful, they could always be used as healing reserves. Or as gifts.

I was musing whether I should get started on a second Scout Tower, or maybe several, to ensure we had the entire circumference of the mountain covered, when I almost stumbled over Dimodeus. He had halted in front of an opening to... "The Blessing? I was here a couple of days ago?"

"Three days, actually, Onyx. Your boost from the Blessing must be running out soon."

I blinked and checked. Damn. He was right. "That's impressive. But... I'm guessing you didn't bring me here simply to remind me of that?"

His smile mirrored his own personality. Relaxed and resting in himself. He held out an arm and activated the mechanism that opened the door. "It's easier if you see for yourself."

With a curious glance at him, I slowly looked from him to the door then shrugged and slowly nudged it open.

The colors were the first thing that hit me, the rainbow-colored, undulating waves of the wonderful feeling that was the Blessing of Deyra. The sensation came next. A quick burst of heat, almost overwhelming, then blessed, wonderful ease, like settling into a bathtub that's been poured *just* right. Then I spotted the surprise and laughed out loud. "I was right? I was right!" I turned back to Dimodeus and beamed at his smiling face.

"You were indeed. We had a water mage join our builders,

and with her and one of your Talpi shamans, they were able to clear the walls within half a day."

I shook my head at him in amazement. "That's incredible. Honestly, I'd forgotten I even mentioned it to you! Thank you so much!" I couldn't wait any longer and ducked into the room and took a look at my surroundings. Hah. I'd been right. It *had* felt completely off, having the room painted with completely white walls. Sure, the effect of the colors playing on the clean, white surfaces had a therapeutic effect, like one of those lava lamps hippies loved, but it looked plain wrong considering the elegant architecture of the place.

It *had* been wrong. I marveled to see the sight of four walls entirely covered in elaborate, colored mosaics. At first, I simply stood there, marveling at the sight. They were *beyond* elaborate, pulling me closer to take in the details. It was astounding. The pieces of the mosaics were tiny, most of them less than a quarter of an inch in size.

They were covered in some sort of lacquer, and I'd bet good money their colors were still as vibrant as when they'd been created. The time and effort involved in covering the entire room was mind-blowing. Following that, Selys had covered it all with whitewash? That was like making a dub-trance-whatever cover of a Stones album. Sacrilege! The mosaics had clearly been created with the Blessing in mind. The effect of the colors on the tiles made the scenes stand out and seem alive.

I shuffled into the center of the room and tried to get an overview of the detailed scenes. I quickly surmised that the four walls were divided into two elaborate scenes. One painted the scene of life inside the mountain, and the other showed the world outside. Yet, so much was different from the world I knew of today.

The mountain portrayed here was... organized. Straight tunnels went directly from one end of the mountain to the other, as humanoids created elaborate, wonderful constructions in all ends of the mountain. Here was an elaborate, pillared temple fit to rival the glory of the Parthenon in Greece. There, a glorious garden in the crater, vibrant, green, and lush. Everything looking entirely unburnt from Selys' burning, scouring crusade. Yet, suspiciously absent in the entire setting... "Dimodeus?" I inquired. "What, if anything, do we know about the Corren?"

He entered behind me, pondering. "Not much, Onyx. Selys seemed to hold a grudge against them and their creations, but for what reason, I cannot say. She did not speak with those of my status. But, from comments over the years, I can assume that they had already left the mountain when she took over."

I nodded thoughtfully. "That would make sense. If they were able to create constructions like these on the wall here, they should really have been able to fight her off. It's weird, though. There are no defenses here on the walls. No armies, no forces—yet Selys claimed that they were the ones who'd created the Fire Towers." I hummed under my breath, moving closer to the images portraying the inside of the mountain.

"It's really insanely detailed. I... think we can almost use it as a map. See, this part, the one that looks like an art gallery, might actually be part of a series of old ruined rooms I passed through when we left Creive the first time." I clicked the floor ponderously with a claw. "Listen, Wreil is back from visiting Creive, right? Could you get him and a couple of the other top scouts in here?

"There are really a number of buildings portrayed here I would *love* to find, if they haven't been buried by avalanches and collapses. This one looks like a library. Tim would cream his nonexistent pants at that. But especially, I want *this* room." I tapped on a wall, indicating a number of central hubs of sorts right beneath Fire Peak, where all the tunnels from each layer seemed to converge.

"I think it might be somewhere right beneath us, where the staircase following the Blessing down into the earth embarks. If we can find that, we might be able to fast-track traveling anywhere inside the mountain."

Dimodeus nodded. "Should I go now?"

"Mmmmh... no. Not yet. If my suspicions about these mosaics are right, and they've actually made them accurate, like a map, then it might mean..." My gaze swiveled to the other side of the room. "That this could *also* be a map." The scenery on the other side was less detailed but still breathtaking. It was a major panoramic view of a mountainous wasteland, with little greenery and life and few man-made creations to break the wilderness. Yet, right there, in the center of things, was what looked like the Scoured Mountain. If that held true... "Check this out and tell me if I'm wrong. Here and here. Compare those to our mountain."

The officious Ethium moved closer to the walls then looked closer. His gaze swiveled back and forth between the spots I'd pointed out and our home. One was an elaborate city looking like something out of ancient Rome, and the other, a ziggurat of sorts, an imposing building rising into the sky. While they didn't look anything like our mountain... "There is a glow, Onyx. The light, shining from within the center of this city and the other building. It looks to be the same as in the Scoured Mountain. Do you believe that it means—"

"That they could be the other Blessings Selys believed she'd found?" I interrupted. "Yup. In fact, I'm damn near sure that it is. Why else would Selys go to the trouble of covering these walls up? She obviously didn't want anybody else to see. I mean, I could still be entirely wrong, but it *feels* like what she would do. So, if you could get Wreil and Firth and her people up here and confirm whether I'm right? They should know enough about the surroundings to be able to tell us whether these images look anything like the real landscape surrounding us."

Dimodeus nodded and got to work.

I did so as well, but not before I'd taken a deep draught of the liquid in the Blessing. I'd never thought I would find a drink to rival coffee, but here it was.

[You have partaken of the Blessing of Deyra
The Blessing expands your connection with Deyra, allowing

you to approach the utilization of the maximal capabilities of your species for learning. Your body is similarly boosted, increasing your natural attributes, regeneration rates, and learning capabilities.
- Your attributes are boosted by +50%
- Mana regeneration rate doubled
- Health regeneration rate doubled
- Experience gain doubled
Time remaining: 71 hours, 59 minutes]

Yeah. Not even espresso could match that. I said it.

CHAPTER FOUR

The rest of the day flew by. I created a few extra Growth Boosts and a single Animal Boost. Then I went to oversee the beginning of the first defensive wall Creziel wanted to construct to protect our crops from thieves and monsters. Finally, I held a public gathering to spread information about the possibilities and limitations of the training and sorcery areas in the city.

That last one was actually really educational, and not only for the citizens. Some of the new trainees had come up with methods of training that outperformed the ones we'd taught ourselves, like holding a leaf (or leaves, when you grew stronger) aloft with gentle touches of air magic. It sucked for Mental Power, but the Mental Control needed to keep it even in the air was impressive—and so were the gains in training.

I was also able to mollify the disappointed citizens who wanted to become minions and start training by informing them that it was all a matter of reaching the next two levels for me. I had a hard limit on the number of minions that wouldn't grow until the next hoard increase, and Level 45 was the only requirement I had yet to hit.

The experience involved for new levels was starting to

become somewhat of a hindrance, since it increased with each new level. I knew that. Everybody knew that. Even so, the crowd seemed to take my rapid experience gain as a given, a tiny bump on the road. Truth be told, considering the speed at which I'd leveled to date, they probably were in the right.

When I returned to the fortress, I found chaos. Not the bad kind of chaos, though. In fact, once Dimodeus had guided me through the hallways down to the bottom level of the fortress, which seemed to be the central gathering place, it felt entirely like coming home, like returning to a workplace after having an unnaturally long vacation.

This was my kind of chaos. The chaos of dozens of builders and scouts shouting and discussing while some were hard at work. It was all there—the construction sounds, the grunts of effort, the slackers standing in the corner trying to avoid work.

"What's going on here?" I asked one of the slackers. Wreil. He was a dozen steps behind Firth, who was pointing at a builder and shouting. The short-tempered Culdren scout seemed uncommonly animated, pointing and gesturing.

Wreil grinned in welcome. The tall Talpus was looking *good*. His new life as a diplomat seemed to agree with him. He indicated Selys' old scout and shrugged. "Well, we had a little gathering of scouts up at the Blessing and... well, we think you're right. So, we thought, why wait, right? If we can locate the place leading down to where those central tunnel openings congregate *and* those tunnels haven't collapsed, we'll have safe, fast, and direct passage to anywhere in the mountain."

He shrugged. "Turns out, once Firth gets an idea into her head, there's no telling her no."

I moved on over to the massive Culdren. Sometimes, I found it hard to believe that the rough-looking, muscled, winged female was the highest-leveled scout in the mountain. But whoever you asked, the answer was clear-cut. She was the one in the know. Heh. Her levels backed it up, too. In front of us, a trio of heavy builders were busy removing the tile floor to get at the soil underneath. "Hey Firth. Ruining my fortress, are you?"

She turned to see me, then snorted. She was also really, really unflappable. "You wanted to find those tunnels. We're about to locate them. Now stand back. You're distracting the diggers."

I shook my head in amazement. "You know, I need to ask. How the hell did you survive scouting under Selys? She didn't exactly seem the type to take well to anything but complete obedience."

She rolled her shoulders and snorted. "Oh, I obeyed. I obeyed her every order, delivered all the results she wanted... and stayed as far away from Fire Peak as possible. Still almost got myself killed. You and I won't have the same problem, will we?"

I smirked. "Not at all. As long as you do your job and don't lie to me, we won't have any problems. In fact, I find it liberating that you're not bowing and scraping."

Her upper lip rose, displaying some truly intimidating incisors. "In that case, I'll make sure to be extra liberating."

"Heh. Do me a favor then, and tell me. Are we on the right path? Is the image showing the outside of the mountain also accurate?"

"You are asking if you, by sheer luck, have located two other Blessings, which would otherwise have taken years or decades to hunt down, if it would even be possible?" She nodded to the diggers in front of her. "We'll see in a while. But I'm guessing yes. The images match what's out there, and they also match up with a lot of the landmarks inside the mountain."

We didn't have to wait long. The workers soon removed the last tiles and went to work with mining picks and shovels, making the dirt disappear. A bored shaman had learned about our project and joined in, removing rocks and boulders from the soil and facilitating the job for our workers.

Twenty minutes later, the hole was about fifteen feet deep when one of the diggers shouted in amazement.

We all hurried over to see, and I craned my neck to look over the crowd. Heh. Yet another perk of being a dragon.

We'd been right! Right there beneath our feet, brickwork appeared, showing a set of wide stone stairs leading downwards, packed full with soil and boulders. The shaman, a tiny Talpus, young and fresh-faced, imperiously shooed the workers away as she jumped right down into the center of the hole. Everybody was holding their breath as she knelt down on the surface and closed her eyes. Then she stood back up with a huge smile on her tiny face. "Thirty feet or more, then it clears up!"

The cheers all around were infectious. From the looks of it, not everybody got exactly how huge a thing this was, though— but Firth did. She stared into the hole with a calculating look on her face.

I addressed her. "Firth. I want you to take a group of scouts, some fighters, a shaman, and some builders and check out those tunnels. Some tunnels may be weakened or collapsed, and there will be blockades along the way near the Blessing, and probably where each tunnel exits. But, if they're all structurally sound, we'll want to get some of them opened straight away."

She nodded. "Judging from the map, there should be sixteen tunnels. That, plus the work included, would take one group, in a best-case scenario, a week per tunnel. We need to split up into several groups. Bring more people."

I considered her words then came to a swift decision. "Yes. But only enough for two groups, to begin with. Have you considered why Selys decided to close off the tunnels? In part, I'm sure it was to hide the existence of the Blessing, but it was likely also to avoid the risk of having somebody bring forces up to ambush her fortress from beneath."

Her frown made her look angry. "You are likely right. Selys was always wary of attackers. But why only two groups?"

"Because, while Selys might have been somewhat paranoid, I think she is right here. The mountain is still untamed enough that we can expect monsters to make it into the tunnels. So, to begin with, we'll only want to open up the connections we really need: the ones near Creive's domain and near the Soul Carver's old domain, where Ahzel is right now. Later on, we can expand when we control more of the mountain."

She hesitated, then nodded. "I will get the people ready. They will leave within a couple of hours. Make sure that your vassals know so they can clear the area down there and don't attack us by accident." She turned on her heels and started walking away.

I called after her. "Wait. They? You're not going yourself?"

She stopped, looking incredulously at me. "It will be a waste of my talents. Interesting as this discovery may be, the scouting work will be mundane. I will move around outside the mountain for the next while, or in that Scout Tower. It is useful, but I don't trust others to stay vigilant for long periods of time. We need people on the move to spot scouts and others who know how to stay hidden."

She turned to continue, then hesitated and showed her teeth at me. "Having you here has not been boring. I believe you will be killed soon, because you are clueless, but... I hope you survive."

I glared at her back as she walked away. Was that her idea of a compliment? That scout was *weird!* But she was true to her word. A couple hours later, the first two groups, fully equipped with food and weapons, dipped into the tunnel and started the descent. I shrugged and got on with life. So much to do, so little time. Within minutes, the idiosyncrasies of my main scout were buried beneath a mountain of other issues. We got back to administering a society that was learning and growing in all the right ways.

Two days later, Firth returned, striding into my throne room with her scouts at the back. The humans were coming. And they weren't alone.

There were plenty of disparaging remarks that could be ladled onto my followers. They were unprofessional, often uncouth, violent, and didn't always work well together. Also, the fact that they came from extremely different walks of life and upbringings caused an immense number of conflicts. But they were effective, especially when it counted.

Ten minutes after Firth had first come crashing into the room, disrupting everything, my entire council was gathered in the throne room, except for Wreil, who was down in the tunnels, and Creziel, who was racing to return from the fields. Creive and Ahzel were both listening in by means of the Communications Field, and Slither stood among the others.

I cut through the bickering noises surrounding me, smacking one paw down on the tile floor with a resounding clap. The scent of fear lay heavy in the air. "Concentrate. Everybody. We knew this was coming, even if we had less time than anticipated. Now, I need your full attention. We have to plan what to do. What we decide now will decide the future of the Scoured Mountain. Now. Please. Firth, would you be so kind as to tell us the details of the encroaching army?"

The Culdren spread her wings and folded them behind her again. It seemed to be a comfort thing, like cracking your neck. "The human armies are indeed arriving. There are a lot of humans and a few other races, too. This time, however, it looks like they don't have a lot of aerial forces. A few scores of Parvu beasts, mostly. But that might be the only positive piece of news I can tell you.

They have fully armed riding forces, and the Parvu beasts are weighed down with provisions and what may be siege equipment. They carry enough that they are in no fear of running out of food and are likely outfitted for any eventuality. They also have an entire following of non-humans, what looks like non-combat forces. I estimate their numbers to be around twenty thousand."

A shocked hush filled the room.

Firth spoke on, cold and uncaring. "This includes only the humans. The non-humans add another twelve to fifteen thousand."

Fuck. Nobody said anything for a while, but you could see the stunned looks on their faces and the mental calculations that

41

were taking place. Fire Peak alone used to boast over ten thousand inhabitants. However, those numbers covered *all* the inhabitants, and with the recent numerous battles, who knew where we are at now?

If we included everybody in Fire Peak and all the minions under my vassals, we were perhaps up to around thirteen thousand people total, at most. Of those? Perhaps two and a half to three thousand who were used to fighting in some aspect, at most, with a lot of those were divided throughout the mountain. The numbers of fighters throughout the *entire* mountain were sure to be a lot larger, with smaller groups and tribes out there constantly fighting for their survival—but there was no way we were going to win them to our side in time.

I'd been into war stories at a certain point in my life. Who hadn't, right? Well, there was a British general, can't remember which one, who once said something like, "There are countless factors to winning a battle. Willpower. Training. Positioning. Having the better weapons. But you will find that he who argues the hardest that numbers rarely matter is always the one with the fewest soldiers."

That was very much the case here. We didn't know if we outleveled the enemy in general, though our forces were fairly untrained. We did know that our position should allow us to take advantage of the terrain, and our weapons and armor were of a pretty good quality. But counting on that to make up for our fighting forces being maybe one to eight of theirs? That was a losing proposition.

The Culdren scout didn't care about softening the blow. She continued. "They are still at a distance where it is hard to make out their exact composition, and it will be longer still before those of us with skills are able to tell their general levels. However, we estimate that around fifty to sixty percent of their army are regulars, humans trained for close combat, and the remainder are divided between ranged fighters and riders. The riders are the fewest in number. There will also be spellcasters, but we have spotted no full companies of their kind."

I exhaled noisily. "Any good news?"

"Yes. I noticed them very early on. This means we have time to react. I believe it will take them at least three weeks to travel to the foot of the mountain, though parts of their forces will be able to range out and strike at us as early as two weeks from now."

I nodded appreciatively to Firth and turned to face everybody. Regardless how abrasive she could be, when it came to precision and attention to details, she had not let us down. "There we have it. Within two weeks, the mountain might be under attack. We need to figure out what to do and plan for it. For now, I'd like to hear all your thoughts."

Grex was the first to react. He buzzed through the air, yipping with excitement. "Thoughts? Boredom is gone! We can fight!"

I sighed. This was going to be a long day.

CHAPTER FIVE

"In preparing for battle, I have always found that plans are useless, but planning is indispensable. -Dwight D. Eisenhower

For a while, we did not plan, just listened to the thoughts and reactions of all the members of the council and my vassals. Their reactions were as varied as they were, though some surprised me.

A rare few were ready to go out there and take them on, odds be damned. Grex, unsurprisingly, and Roth were also in that camp. At least, Roth was ready to wait for nightfall, so we could "ambush them properly." Most of the others were in favor of letting the army approach the mountain and defend from them on our terms, with ambushes, traps and, if need be, collapsing the tunnels on them.

There was one piece of consensus. Nobody believed they would be stupid enough to climb the mountain. With how few fliers they had and the steepness of the slopes, it would be suicide, unless they let their Parvu beasts carry their troops up in steps. If that happened, we should still have the aerial superiority to take out their fliers. That left an uneasy alliance of

Ahzel, the Aberrants, and Dimodeus advocating ambushes and traps. Meanwhile, Creziel returned and was catching up on the news, leaving Arthor to speak.

"To my surprise, I agree with Roth and Grex." That caught my attention. The shaman continued wryly. "Not that we should attack simply to alleviate boredom or because we are good at ambushing. But that we shouldn't just let them march on the mountain. We should make their approach as difficult as possible, ruin the terrain, ambush them at night, and make them fear for their lives. Slow them down.

"Not because we hope to stop them from reaching the mountain, because that's not likely. For one simple reason: we're growing extremely fast these days. If we make their arrival to the mountain take six weeks instead of three? We will have hundreds of additional fighters outfitted in Dworgen-crafted enchanted arms and armor, and we will have a lot of fighters and mages who are certain to train unceasingly because they'll know their survival depends on it."

That got a lot of support from the others. Ahzel liked the idea of doubling down on the enchanting, and Slither appreciated the thought of training his people's ambushing techniques on an entire army. Dimodeus, meanwhile, clearly approved of the improved odds of having stronger and better-equipped fighters and mages for an inevitable fight.

Timothy and I were sharing glances. It turned out that we were the only ones who had really dissenting opinions.

Tim was the first one to speak up. "I believe we should parley with the humans."

"Par-what now? There's no time for parties. We must fight!"

I snorted. You could always count on Grex. "He means that we should meet with the enemy, try to find some common grounds for peace. And I agree."

Roth scratched his neck. "But we tried that? Why would we attempt to do that again?"

Arthor's scorn was as clear as day. "*We* did not try to talk with them. Mordiel did. *Then he blew up their entire command.*" He snorted. "I doubt it would actually bring any useful results, but Onyx has been known to talk others into things they did not expect to agree to."

I nodded gratefully to him, wide-eyed. That cantankerous shaman was full of surprises these days.

He narrowed his eyes and pointed at me. "Besides, he rarely does anything without an ulterior motive. Also, if you notice, he hasn't really said anything. Onyx is *never* quiet. Not unless he knows what he wants and expects to overwhelm us with cleverness."

I frowned at him, half-affronted. "That's not at all true... is it?"

A series of shrugs and nods were the only response I got.

I shook my head with a smile on my face. "Backstabbers, all of you. Okay, here's what I think: yes, I believe you are right. We'll have the best advantage in a fight inside the mountain. It's what we're used to. The enemy will be half-blind half the time, even if they bring torches, magical lights, and whatnot, and we'll have our Shamans who can turn the mountain against them. On top of that, we'll have Deyra's boosts and constructions to aid us. That's a combination that's hard to beat. I *also* believe that Arthor is right when he says that we should try to delay them and build our strength, ensuring that we are at peak efficiency when they make it here." I held up a claw and saw that I had their full attention.

"There is one flaw with simply combining those approaches. It discounts the enemy. With twenty thousand soldiers..." I emphasized the numbers, watching them pale in reaction. "They're bound to have a lot of special fighters or talents among them. Remember Tellor's final magic trick? Or the tentacled flying beast? Selys' ring of fire? Their powers will be able to counter a lot of our powers, I am sure, or they'll have magic items to do the same.

"So, in my opinion, the best way to handle the conflict would be to avoid it entirely." I nodded at Arthor. "It is like Arthor says, though. Traveling to meet them, betting on the fact that they will agree to peace? That would be folly. I prefer peace... but we should be ready for war. So, we bring a large group with us, hidden behind shadow and illusions. If they're not interested in peace? We take war to them."

Suddenly, everybody was all smiles. Even Grex was satisfied with the idea, probably because he didn't think it was very likely that the humans would refrain from attacking. Heh. I couldn't fault him for thinking that, if that human commander from their aerial forces was anything to judge by. Unfortunately, I had to smash those smiles straight away. "There is one other thing, however. And I doubt you are going to like it."

They all became wide awake at that.

I continued. "We have tons of sayings where Timmy and I come from. You can pretty much find somebody who's made a point of saying exactly what you want to say, only a lot more fancy. You guys know me. I don't care about fancy. I care about doing the job and doing it right. Sometimes, doing the job means looking at the materials you've got in front of you and realizing it might not be enough to build the house you want."

Creziel blinked cautiously. "What are you saying, Onyx?"

"I'm saying that we need to prepare for the eventuality that we might lose this fight." I swept out a claw. "Every one of you here, and all of our people? I know you. I trust you and can count on you to account well for yourself in battle." I shrugged. "So the odds are eight to one? No problem, *if it were only us.*

"However, those odds also account for the people of Fire Peak. Ahzel's minions. Creive's people. The Aberrants. Can you all face me and honestly say that each of those, including those who were slaves a few months ago, will be able to take down eight to ten seasoned soldiers a piece? Even one? Most of these aren't fighters." I looked at each of them in turn. Nobody gainsaid me. Arthor just rolled his eyes. I continued. "I'm not saying we should plan to lose. I'm saying we need a backup plan. Somewhere to run to if all else fails."

Firth narrowed her eyes, then nodded to herself. "You are going after the Blessings."

I smiled. "You're damn right, I am." I grinned. "Well, *you* are, if you agree. Unless somebody else comes up with a better plan, that's what I've got. We try to talk some sense into those human bastards. If it works, perfect. If not, we show them a fancy illusion that we're retreating to the mountain or something... when, in reality, we're setting them up to be ambushed. Then you and a few other high-level scouts take off to find the Blessings. Then we know that we have a fallback position in case they turn out to be stronger than us."

Arthor glared at me. "Which leaves the ambushers in the middle of a huge enemy force, at the mercy of any surprises on the attackers' side?"

I grimaced. "You know we can move fast when need be, but we can improve on the plan. In fact, we will need to. I want all your input, because these details aren't going to iron themselves out."

Roth sat down on his haunches. "We need iron for what now?"

"Solve themselves, Roth. These details aren't going to solve themselves." Timothy came to my rescue. "And he's entirely right. In fact, we'll need lists. First thing we need to do is have everybody agree to the overall plan, and then we are going to get busy."

Dimodeus nodded appreciatively. When it came to administration, he and Timothy got along swimmingly. "I will send for some of the staff who handle the stores in the mountain. I should also ask them for some food. This might be a while."

It took for-frigging-ever. Coming to an agreement on our approach in the first place was hell. But the real trouble started afterward, when we had to delegate, figure out who would handle what. The major issues were that the groupings of the city had very different foundations and interests.

Ahzel's fighters were generally heavy fighters, very unsubtle but high-leveled. A good deal of them were above Level 20. They would make for great close-rank fighters for when the fighting got heated inside the mountain. He was arguing that he'd need all of them to ensure that he was safe inside his domain, so he could keep up a constant delivery of enchanted items.

Honestly, I believed it was rather a question of him having found the way to increase his own strength subtly, and I asked Dimodeus to keep a very good eye on the number of items coming and going to Ahzel's hoard. Still, I had no issues with them staying back. They'd be little good for a fast-moving ambush force.

Creive was looking forward to the idea of going outside the mountain to fight and harrying their forces while they were still marching toward us. While his fliers were not generally the type for silent ambushes, they were fast-moving and hard-hitting and would likely prove invaluable if it came to directed, lighting-strike attacks on their forces.

Heh. Lightning-strike from a blue dragon. I didn't even do that on purpose. However, when I asked him his ideas for fighting inside the mountain, he just said to send them all the way to his domain, and he'd take care of them.

I didn't push him. Creive had earned a rather special place on our team with the way he'd saved my butt several times over. Still, he was rather convinced that his might was such that he'd be able to face down anybody and anything. Ah, well. At least we knew that he was ready to fight—and I'd take a discussion with him to make proper plans for a battle if and when it became necessary. I had him solidly on my side this time. He still was the only one who got to decide the rules for him and his minions. But he loved his bloody upside-down fortress, and the humans threatening that would be enough to know he'd give it his all.

Slither and the Aberrants would be perfect for our plan. They were born guerilla fighters, completely used to working with traps, confusing strategies, distraction, and ambushes. While Slither liked the idea of a huge ambush, he very much did not like the idea of going out into the open. As he stated, it went against everything the Aberrants believed in, staying hidden, avoiding direct struggles and... well, not going out into the open air. To be entirely honest, I figured he was mostly trying to protect his underlings. With the size of the enemy we would be going up against, I couldn't fault him for that at all.

However, as I pointed out to him, part of the issue here was the fact that his people remained weak. If they didn't take the chance to go out and face the enemy on their own terms, they were still going to have to face them later on, but on the enemy's terms. We did not exactly come to a final agreement, but he promised that he would be returning to his people later that day, and we would talk the day after in the morning.

The citizens of Fire Peak were mostly far from perfect for the ambush. We'd killed a *lot* of Selys' scouts in our initial clashes with them and had, with the assistance of the Aberrants, pretty much wiped out the Dragonlings in the mountain, who would have been amazing for this kind of task. Firth seemed to find a special delight in reminding us of this constantly.

This left us with two groups. On one hand, we had the newer fighters who were eager to learn, fight, and train, but sorely underleveled and under-experienced. On the other, we had the survivors among the older, more experienced fighters in the city, who tended to be of Selys' "the bigger, the better" policy. Not exactly ambusher material.

As for my own people, it was mostly a question of keeping them all from wanting to join up for the ambush. With the history we had, and what we'd been through, they feared no one. Honestly, at this point, I was a bit afraid at how overconfident they were getting. Most of it was earned, though, at least inside the mountain. Our regular fighters were somewhere between good and scary good.

Late in the evening, I was sitting on the roof of the fortress alongside Timothy and Dimodeus, as the sun swept past the crater edge above us. The council had gone to their separate responsibilities, and I'd asked the pair to sit with me while we talked over the details.

"Been a while since we last got to sit down and chill, right Tim?"

He snorted and waved at his see-through lower body. "I'm not much for sitting these days, but... I get what you're saying, old man. And yeah. I have to admit, I haven't been the best company lately. Lore's death... I'm not over it. Not at all. So, all of this? I feel horrible saying it, but... I don't mind it. It keeps me from thinking too hard about it. I never wanted kids or anything, but damn. He was... fuck."

"I'm so sorry, Tim."

He waved me off. "I'll get there. I guess. What I wanted to say is, I'm going with you, out there, of course. I have some serious shit I should be working through, and some aggression that isn't just disappearing by itself. So, if those humans aren't planning to turn around? It'll cost them!"

I looked him in the eye and nodded gravely. Then snorted in amusement.

"What?" he asked, half-affronted.

"Seriously. This is horrible. Everything inside me was screaming at me. I needed to pat you awkwardly on the shoulder right now, except I'd be waving a claw through your body."

He barked a laugh. "Yeah, that would have ruined the bromance of the moment." One side of his mouth quirked up. "So, apart from looking at the pretty sky and being all maudlin, what did you want?"

"Numbers. Numbers and lists." I pointed at him and Dimodeus. "Arthor and a few of the others might be good at tactics, planning and such, and tomorrow morning, we'll know who's ready to go. But you two can be trusted to crunch the numbers and make it realistic. So, tell me. If we want to *fly* to the enemy so we can make it there as fast as possible, and we want to be off yesterday, how many people will we feasibly be able to take?"

We had a short discussion on weight, distances, and races.

51

Timothy was slowly coming to a conclusion, and it wasn't looking too promising.

Suddenly, Dimodeus interrupted. He wore an inscrutable smile. "I was saving this for a surprise, Onyx. I believe this qualifies. Could you bring up that map of yours and focus on the western part of Fire Peak?"

Puzzled and quite curious, I did what he said. The overview of the city bloomed into being on the ground in front of us. "Yes?"

"We need to move a street further out toward the wall. Yes, like that. Stop. Please follow that building to the south. Yes."

Our bird's-eye view meandered over the street, watching the evening activity of Fire Peak. We passed by a training area in the poorer western district of the city. Even at this late hour, it was entirely packed with minions working to grow stronger. I half expected him to ask me to stop there, but he didn't.

A couple hundred feet farther north, he finally exclaimed, "Stop. That building on the left has an enclosure behind the building. Please zoom in on the enclosure."

I did what he asked. Then I started chuckling. Soon, the chuckle built up into full-blown rasping laughter. A surprise? You could say that again. When I finally stopped laughing, I looked at the smiling Ethium in front of me, impressed. "Parvu beasts. How the hell? Just... how?"

Dimodeus bowed, then he indicated the map in front of us. The five massive beasts were all lazing about or asleep. "The battle against the human fliers was... not particularly enjoyable inside the city. Those beasts were bombarding everything, and we had no way of defending. Buildings were collapsing everywhere around us, and the mood was rather grim. But suddenly, there were other things slowly wafting toward the ground, both inside the walls and outside."

I smiled. "Downed enemy fliers."

"Just so. Some crashed to the ground out of control, dying on impact. A good deal, however, made it down safely."

I nodded in understanding. My Weakening Fog hadn't killed

anybody outright and mostly didn't knock the stronger fliers out, only sapped their strength enough that they couldn't stay afloat. Timothy's attacks had also only been distracting and momentarily stunning, not killing blows.

The officious Ethium grimaced. "The people of the city didn't take kindly to the attackers finally coming within claw's reach. The first ones to make it down were torn apart. Outside the walls, the Aberrants were doing the same, taking down any enemies for easy experience. However, as the fight above us continued, I had an idea. I quickly gathered some of our people around me—close combat fighters, mostly, those who could not make any difference in the fight above us—and we went to work."

"You? You subdued the fliers and saved their lives?"

"Not personally, no." He waved the idea off with a hand. "And we didn't get to as many as I would like. The distances in the city were too large, and our people generally took to the arrival of easy experience and vengeance with quite a bit of glee. However, we did manage to subdue a few, here and there, and talk some of the citizens into helping. We overwhelmed them, killed their riders, and trussed them up."

I tried to remember the fight. It was a bit of a blur, admittedly, but... "I don't recall attacking any Parvu riders in the beginning."

"Oh no. This is one of eight enclosures. Over the course of the battle, we managed to save a total of thirty-one flying creatures. Later on in the battle, they tended to drop fast with holes in their wings or fully on fire. We saved less of those."

I blinked and looked at the huge beast lying docile on the ground, then back to him, incredulously. "Are you telling me you also managed to save some of the close combat beasts? How about those poison spitters?"

"Both. Admittedly, we are having some issues with the fighters. Your Clencher trainer—Eamus, I believe—has taken to the task with enthusiasm. He has also been healed quite a few times already, trying to subdue those. He remains hopeful that they will submit to him soon. However, the Parvu beasts have proven to be easy to train and even fly. Unfortunate that we didn't manage to save more of their kind."

"You... I." I stopped myself, then shook my head at him in amazement. "When all of this is over with, I may have to put *you* on the throne here. You might have saved us all. You're seriously telling us that those five beasts are all ready to be loaded and can take off whenever we feel like it?"

He nodded. "I believe that should solve most of our transport issues. And some of the others should be ready, if the human army makes it to the mountain."

I glanced over to Timothy. He raised two translucent arms wardingly. "I had no clue. Still, that changes everything. With this, we might be enough to make a serious difference." Then he chuckled and pointed a finger at Dimodeus. "I was going to save this until it was done, but if we're leaving, I want you to see it."

"What?"

He smirked. "Well, I have a surprise, too. I'm not letting myself be outdone by Dimodeus. Though, he helped have it made, so it's not a real competition."

The officious Ethium lit up in understanding and went inside the fortress.

I snorted. "Really? Is it my birthday or something? I friggin' love presents!"

"Sure. Let's go with that. But this one isn't a gift for you alone... but for the entire city."

I scratched the hard ridge of bone above one eye. "That almost sounds like that one time my least favorite aunt decided to skip a Christmas present and donate the amount to charity in my name."

The blue vision raised an eyebrow. "I bet that went over well."

"Yeah, no. I was seven." I snorted. "I look forward to seeing what you guys have come up with, though."

"You won't have to wait long. Dimodeus is a speedy one." Indeed, the tall humanoid was already marching toward us.

In his hands, he held a… "A sign?" I frowned at Timothy. "I'm not getting it."

He smirked. "I knew you wouldn't. And it's not a sign, but a tile. To be glazed and placed on the ground, free for everybody to see." Then he went somber. "Thing is, it's something I did to honor the little runt. Lore. He was always obsessed with knowledge and how to spread it. That's why he chose that name to begin with. We had plans, you know. Still have. But this one is where we were going to start."

I took in the sign. It was twenty by twenty inches and almost empty. There were two large images on it and a number of smaller ones underneath. Two simple things: a furred nose with lines indicating smelling and a green arrow up right next to it. With the way Tim was staring at me, I had to hazard a guess. "Is that supposed to mean… improved stench or something?"

The ghost and the Ethium shared a laugh. Timothy spoke first. "I knew you weren't as thick as you look. Improved Smell. Yup."

"Oooh." Now I *did* get it. "It's a feat! Those tiny figures underneath? Talpi. Stick Kin. Urten. Dragonling."

"You've got it. This is a racial feat. Crawls, for instance, can't get it. Those are the races who can. Try the next one."

Dimodeus held up another tile. It looked almost like a children's drawing, simplistic in the extreme, but well-drawn. The image depicted two humanoid figures, one in color and the other in black and white. The one in black and white was striking at the colored figure, who was… dodging the strike. The movement was central to the image and also had a green up arrow next to it. "Improved… dodge? You intend to spread knowledge through cartoons?"

"Pictograms, oh unlearned one. There is an entire language and history to pictograms." Hurriedly, he continued. "One which you don't have the patience to hear about. And yes. Teaching reading is next… but this is something that doesn't

55

require teachers, that can be taught by one person to the next... and once we're done? We can expand upon it, add writing to the tiles." He pointed to the Improved Dodge tile. "If you see up here at the top, we've included the prerequisites."

"A picture of somebody running... and ten lines. You need ten Agility for Improved Dodge?"

Dimodeus clapped. Timothy beamed. "Exactly. If other feats were needed, we'd add a smaller image of the prerequisite along with the attributes above."

I looked at the tileset and back at Tim. "I have no clue how you come up with this stuff... but I'm amazed. Keep it coming!"

"Oh, we will. I've told you before: knowledge is power. The tiles are being made as we speak. Soon, this knowledge will be right in Victory Plaza for all to see. The know-how of choosing your feat, right under your feet."

"Heh."

He rolled his eyes. "Not a pun, you old fart. Still, for now, we'd better focus on how to beat our enemies with the old-fashioned kind of power."

CHAPTER SIX

"The Aberrants will join you." Slither's mental voice came in clearly through the connection. I was zooming in on the map at the same time, so I could observe him as we talked. He was in a small cave, with Koa'tem next to him and a bunch of higher-leveled Aberrants nodding in the background. "We had a longer discussion yesterday. Turns out there are enough of us who are willing to ignore the risks for the possible rewards." His puppet-like face changed into a rictus of a smile. "Knowing that those who survived in the fights against the Dworgen and the old guard gained five levels or more has helped."

"Hah. I can see how that could be an added incentive. How many want to be part of it?"

"Too many, really. We have hundreds aiming to join up. But it would take at least a week for us to march out there. How—"

"Way ahead of you, mate. It's not going to take a week, and we're not going to march. Okay, hundreds might be a bit too much. We'll want to pare those numbers down a bit and be realistic about it. For instance, we'll have to move *fast* out there. And we'll probably be moving constantly. Meaning, we should only bring those who're able to keep it up and aren't too slow.

"Hrm. Probably only those who are Level 10 and above, at least. Level 15 would be best. We want people who are ready for battle. You decide, of course. But rest assured, we should be able to take at least... fifty of your people with us. Including Koa'tem, if he wants. I know, he's not sneaky, but..."

The spindly Stick Kin burst into high-pitched laughter. "He would not accept staying back. If I fight, he fights."

"Well, that's bloody great, then. In that case, let me tell you the news. You are leaving today!"

We spent a while hashing out the details, then I turned back to the council, plus Firth. "Okay. The Aberrants will be moving out within the hour, carrying enough provisions for a week. I know, that's not enough, but we plan to travel light and forage as we go." The foraging in question would probably be on fallen enemy bodies, but... well, in this crowd, there was no need to make a big deal out of that.

Heh. My old mom would be proud. She always was dead set against food waste. "Creive has already left his domain, bringing almost all of his fliers with him. He has left only the weakest behind, and the few non-fliers he has, to protect his place, along with a few stronger fliers to watch over our shamans as they keep up extracting ores."

My strongest shaman was looking as happy as ever, which meant not very.

I asked him, "Arthor. Have you arranged everything and figured out who's going? We need to leave soon."

"Yes. Most Talpi, except for the majority of the builders and a few of the Crawls. Gert is staying to train the remaining Crawls." He scratched his snout. "Should we send the Clencher Riders? I know. It will take them a while to reach us, but they might be able to make a difference when they arrive."

"No." I grimaced. "I'm not underestimating the Clenchers— they've proved themselves several times over. Still, once the secret's out, and the humans know we're out there, our major advantage is going to be the ability to fly and move our entire force quickly. I simply can't carry several Clenchers."

58

I didn't mention my other reason. We'd lost some Clenchers lately and were down to seven. Two of the female Clenchers were pregnant right now, but if we didn't give them the chance to rest and procreate, there was a risk we'd lose the last of them. I moved on. "Firth? You have your scouts?"

She nodded. "Yes. For whatever it's worth. I have almost no surviving winged scouts left, so I have had to recruit from the people in the city. They are levels 10 to 15, mostly, and most probably will die, but that is quite fine. They will do their jobs."

Such a heartwarming person. "I want you to take steps to ensure that you make it. Get a few magic items from the hoard to protect you. Grex? Your fliers?"

"Ready! So ready! We have all who survived the battle with the humans. Almost all Imps in the city! All have trained hard. We will destroy!"

My mood was lifting as each of them checked off in turn. The shamans were ready. Excepting the ones at Creive's domain, one here in the fortress, and those who were down in the tunnels right now, trying to open direct travel routes to Creive and Ahzel, every Shaman would be leaving with us.

One final detail really put a smile on my lips. The month of peace hadn't gone by without progress. The rest, plenty of food, lack of stress, except for the harshness of the training regimens imposed by Roth, Arthor, and Grex had resulted in... exactly what one would expect. The fortress was teeming with pups and newborn.

And those pups! At this point, every third adorable fur-face coming into this world was an Evolved Talpus. As for the ugly, squealing abominations of nature that were the Crawl? About the same. This single month had seen five Evolved Talpi born and nine normal ones, on top of two Evolved Crawls and three normal ones.

On top of that, I'd seen my very first newborn Evolved Imp. It had the cutest little horns. That was just the development among our own ranks. I had no clue about the rest of the city, but the fact that so many were training and we were no longer letting people starve? It would mean an explosion in the average strength of our people.

That wasn't the best part of it, though. No, it was this: the single shaman who was staying behind here in Fire Peak? It wasn't because he was going to keep up the work on the crops. No, we'd delegated all that to people from Fire Peak and postponed expanding until we knew what was going down.

That single, young shaman, our very firstborn Evolved Talpus who was only just evolving past being a pup himself? He was going to stay in Fire Peak to ensure the next group of shamans-in-training didn't fall behind in their training.

That's right. We already had another crop of prospective shamans in the works, and they were showing so much promise, even the dour Arthor had to admit that they blew past the accomplishments of any past shaman in his tribe. Or any tribe he'd heard of. That was even before considering the effect that Arthor's new feat and the improved Sorcery Chamber would have on their improvement.

Honestly, the layered effects of feats on top of the procreation boosts of the mountain and my Habitats was getting to be pretty insane. Oh, not that the shamans-in-training were just Talpi, now. There were three Crawl pups in the group, too, and even a bloody Imp who was driving the poor shaman teacher insane. Still, the future was looking good for our shaman collective.

Two things to do, then. "Okay, everybody. This is it. We don't know what's going to happen out there. We might be preparing for nothing and come back with a lasting peace... but I wouldn't hold my breath. So, we are going to prepare in any way possible and boost our attributes as much as possible."

Roth's long, furry eyebrows rose impossibly high on his face, and his eyes twitched to the side.

"That's right, Roth. We'll be digging into the hoard. We're going into this with our eyes wide open, and our attributes fully buffed!"

As for my own Blessing, it would likely run out way before our battles finished, but I was still going in fully buffed.

Chaos ensued.

It took a while, but eventually every single one of my minions climbed back out of the piles of magic items, manic grins on their faces with necks, arms, and bodies decked out with items. I feared that they might knock the hoard back to a lower limit, but in the end, there were only so many of my council, and the hoard was massive. Also, since you could only have one modifier to each attribute, that limited the number of magic items you could conceivably use.

We did take a number of Toughness and Strength-boosting items with us, for all the fliers who would need it to keep up with the rest of us when airborne. In the end, Arthor, surprisingly, was the one who exclaimed what I was thinking. "I believe we're ready."

I grinned at him and nodded. "Oh yes, we are. We are going to go out there, we'll dominate the skies, and, if they don't agree to peace, we'll chase those fucking humans back to their homes! Now, it's time to tell the world. Let's go up."

We were back on the roof of the fortress. Sometimes, I needed the intimacy of going into the city, looking into the eyes of my people as I talked to them. At other times, there was a need for a show, for me to be seen by everybody all at once, to seem big, tough and fucking invincible. Heh. I probably didn't do that good a job of that, following in the footsteps of Selys, the walking goddamn mountain.

Reds really had a leg up on that part, since they grew in size a lot more often than shadow dragons. Still, I gave it my very best. Surrounded by my council, those who had been with me right from the start, survived situations we had no right to actually make it through... I did feel quite optimistic about things.

"People of Fire Peak," I began, sending my message to all corners of the city. "We knew that war was coming. That it was inevitable. We beat the humans so resoundingly that their flying army is a thing of the past. This time around, they are mostly a ground army with a few scouts and heavy fliers to carry their equipment. But they are still coming back, like we knew they would."

I tried to layer my news with all of my honesty, make them see that I believed this with all my heart. "You know what Selys would do, if she saw enemies on the horizon. She would take every single one of you, if she believed it was necessary, force you into battle, face the enemy head-on, and keep on fighting until there was but one army left standing. That is not who I am. I will not force anybody to fight who does not want to go down that path.

"Right now, we are going out to face the human army and try to earn peace between our peoples. If we do not succeed in this, we will fight them, ambush them, and make life unbearable for them out there in the Wastes. However, their numbers are such that I do not believe we will be able to crush them."

I paused, letting it sink in. "Those of us who go out to face them now would have to kill fifty of them or more, for each of us, for that to happen. The enemy may reach the Scoured Mountain, regardless of the best of our efforts. I do not tell you this to bring you down. Simply to encourage all of you to work, train, and prepare as well as you can. We will earn you the time to grow strong. This way, if we come back with a weakened enemy at our backs, the mountain will be ready to face them down and crush them! *They can't hold us down*."

At first, I couldn't really see a reaction. Then a sound arrived, like a popping of the ears, and it came on a wave of sound. Cheering. Cheering, roars, and cries mixed into one loud amalgamation of noise. Fire Peak was unified–and they backed us. With everything we'd gone through to get here, that was the best possible start we could wish for.

We took off within the hour. The first leg of the journey would be the easiest, since we didn't have the Aberrants with us yet. As such, I had only Arthor, Roth, and Creziel strapped in on my back, mostly because I liked the company. Behind me followed the five docile Parvu Beasts, each of them loaded with my minions, food, and drink, obeying the orders of a rider on their necks without issues. On either side of me, I had Firth and her scouts and Grex and his uncontrollable horde of fliers. Grex's group flew around a glowing blue center—Timothy, stretched into an unrecognizable blob in order to apply his boosts to as many as possible while airborne.

Our departure was neither quiet nor professional. There was a lot of yelling, swearing, and laughing, from Grex's chaotic bunch, mostly, but my other minions definitely didn't hold back. The crowd responded in turn, reacting well to the exuberant mood with shouts of encouragement and bloodthirsty yells.

But we did take off to rise past the crater and fly down the outside of the mountain to where we'd meet up with Creive and the Aberrants. From the moment we crossed the edge of the crater, I kept up an illusion, stretched far and wide to envelop all of our people and hide our presence in the skies.

An easy job, so far, but it would only grow more difficult, the farther we got.

Firth spent a short while on the Scout Tower with a few of her scouts, while the rest of us flew on. She left one especially fast flier behind in the tower to focus on their progress and catch up to us, if anything unexpected were to happen. Catching up to us would not be an issue. The Parvu beasts were tough, strong, and dependable, but they were anything but fast, for fliers. That was a weak spot. We'd have to stay alert and watch out for any remaining enemy fliers in the days to come— because, if left undefended, the huge beasts would be an inviting target.

Firth didn't see that as a realistic threat, however. We debated as we followed the steep mountainside down past craters, towering drops, and a single, breathtaking waterfall that must have dropped for at least three miles. "They've gotten a bit closer now. It's easier to tell what we're facing. Our numbers were mostly right. Their fliers are few in number. They have five combat groups of fliers like the ones we faced in the crater, but apart from that, we're facing mostly the Parvu beasts."

"That's great news. Means we should be able to tear them apart in the air. We just need to ensure that we always protect our Parvu beasts, or the enemy's scouts might take them down in turn."

Firth assented. "I agree. Not all the news is good, though. The non-humans. We thought them to be camp followers, simply due to how chaotic and staggered their forces were. However, we can now see that they are all armed. Poorly armed, but armed. They are fighters. Auxiliary troops and scouts, most likely."

I grimaced and flew in silence for a while. "That *is* bad news. It means their numbers are much larger than expected. It also makes it that much harder to sneak up on them. Ah, well. We know they'll have surprises ready for us, mages, really high-level enemies, and such. Our best approach seems to be what we were planning all the time, regardless. Hitting hard in ambushes, using my illusions to the utmost, keeping them reacting and keeping them guessing."

"That would seem like the best plan. For now, though, you had best focus on keeping your minions under control. Those dimwits are already struggling to keep up."

I looked back and cursed. She was right. A good bunch of Grex's fliers had strayed outside the radius of Timothy's outstretched tendrils and were now having a hard time catching up. It took a barked command from me, and some high-pitched, heartfelt cursing from Grex until they were back and flying in something approaching an actual formation.

CHAPTER SEVEN

" I wanted to meet interesting and stimulating people of an ancient culture... and kill them." Private Joker, Full Metal Jacket

Everything went as smoothly as could be expected. Creive's minions and the Aberrants were already standing right outside the mountain, and we landed briefly, allowing for the chaotic sensation of people greeting others they hadn't seen for a while. At this point, both Creive's and Slither's people had been through several battles, with or against us, and there were a lot of friendly jabs being shot back and forth. Then came the cries of amazement and greed, as our council unpacked the load of magical items from our hoard for Creive and Slither to divide.

Still, they managed to keep the disputes to a minimum, and once they had everybody line up to receive their items, calm descended on the groups again. I considered speaking to everybody then and there, but decided to wait. These people knew exactly what we were about and had no doubt as to how dangerous it was. Within the hour, the Aberrants had been divided onto the separate Parvu beasts as well as onto my back, and we took off again.

Soon after takeoff, we stumbled upon the first problem. The Imps had no issues keeping up with the Parvu beasts, given how slow they were. But they complained about the strain. Flight was draining on the small creatures, sustained flight even more.

We had allowed for this, slightly, as I'd taken less burdens on me compared to the Parvu beasts. This allowed the ugly critters to put down on my back and hold on mid-air, giving them ten minutes of rest before they went flapping off to rejoin Timothy's boosting presence again. However, if this was after an hour? We could expect serious issues for the rest of the flight. After a brief discussion about distances and possibilities with Firth, we slowed down slightly and introduced a planned half-hour rest after the first half-day's flight.

The next issue? Formations. Creive's people, as well as the scouts, were used to flying how they fancied, doing as they wished if they spotted an inviting-looking target or something that captured their curiosity. However, the illusion I was maintaining was already huge, and there was a limit to how much I'd be able to stretch it without it reaching the limits of my capabilities. It was good training, admitted, but not exactly viable in the long run, especially since being spotted early on could ruin our plans entirely. Fortunately, both Firth and Creive commanded absolute obedience, and soon we had them all almost looking like a real flying formation.

Then, blessed order for a handful of hours, where we simply got closer to the enemy. Before we left, Tim had gone on about how far we'd be able to fly, the average speed of an albatross, and other enthusiastic rantings. I hadn't paid attention after catching the point—namely, that we'd be able to cover several hundred miles in a day, even with our slightly reduced pace. We followed this with a break a bit past midday, allowing people to eat and relax until we started in on the second, more grueling part of the flight.

Impressively, people actually maintained the pace we'd set. However, even with all the items from my hoard, Imps weren't built for long-distance flying. My own Imps were keeping up rather well, but the newly joined Imps from Fire Peak (and a few of the flying Aberrants) simply didn't have the attributes. Hence, I found more and more of them hanging off of me as I flew, like a particularly ugly batch of combat jets refueling mid-air. Hour after hour, more and more Imps joined their number, until I was starting to lag myself.

Oh, and we didn't move forward without a fight. As Selys had promised, the Wastes outside the mountain were a savage place, and that was swiftly confirmed by a series of confrontations. Ambush predators sniffed around on the ground, while the skies held any number of threats, small and large.

Most of them were intelligent enough to realize that our forces were too large to handle, but some either overestimated their own abilities or simply thought they could get away with attacking and retreating with a nice meal. We disabused them of that notion. Severely. Most of our people might be outside for the first time in their lives, but they had still been raised in an environment with a constant threat of ambush. Our combination of powers was enough to handle anything the Wastes had to throw at us.

At least for the first day.

When we finally touched down that evening, in a depression Firth proclaimed suitable for not being seen from the distance, I let them arrange for food. Heh. With the fliers who'd attacked us, we would barely have to dip into our own stores. Then I called Firth over and had a long discussion with her. Following that, I asked Tim to join us, and we went back and forth between the three of us. After a moment to settle my head, I called the entirety of my council over, along with Slither and Creive.

Once they'd sat down, I delved straight into it. "Firth. How far have we gotten?"

"We're almost halfway to the enemy. With our pace, we'll be set to reach them in the evening tomorrow, with ample time to adjust to their progress."

"Appreciate it. For the sake of expediency, would you repeat what you said back there about the way they are dividing their forces?"

Firth held her back ramrod straight as she addressed the others with a serious mien. That flying force of nature could have made for an excellent principal. Heh. Or a professional dominatrix. She had the disapproving stare and strict personality down pat. "If their approach and organization are a measure of their combat prowess, we are in more trouble than we feared.

"There is nothing surprising in their progress as such, but they do not leave a lot of openings. While they travel, they have the Parvu beasts handle most of their loads while they have the ground-based and the flying scouts range out on all sides of the main army, covering any approach. Their irregulars might be the only exception; they travel, surrounding the humans, in a larger, less organized mob."

"Irregulars?" Arthor frowned.

"Non-human allies. They would make for a good target for an ambush, except it seems like they hold mostly ranged weapons." She scowled with disdain. "I believe they do not have the discipline to be truly counted as part of the army. At the very least, once they camp at night, they remain the one exception to a tight security web. Their forces mostly sprawl in an unorganized heap surrounding the main army. Inside the main army, the humans are being very organized, with the different companies keeping to their own, with open pathways between each camp for easy movement and guards both inside and outside of the camp."

I allowed this to sink in for a moment. "This is a big part of the reason I wanted to speak with all of you, and why I believe we should change our approach."

Roth gave a satisfied growl. "We're attacking outright then, aren't we?"

"No."

Arthor crossed his furry arms, while the others looked on in confusion. "Explain."

"All right. So, I'm going to go straight to their army and reveal myself, have a nice little chat with them, right?"

"At a distance," Tim added.

"Right. Address them from a distance, because I don't have a death wish." I winked. "Then I'll either have a friendly conversation with them, or they'll start firing arrows and whatnot at me, and I'll have to take off at speed."

"Yup. And judging from our last interaction with the humans, we have a pretty good bet which choice they'll be going with," Tim added, helpfully.

I grimaced. "Again, yeah, you're probably right. But that's where I think we'll have to change our plans. We talked about two alternatives. We approach them at night then either ambush them in the chaos when they're bound to be chasing me off, or jump them later in the night when they think we've left?"

Nods from both of them.

"We can do better. Whatever little we know about these humans of Nefren, they're not idiots. They have plans and backup plans. Not only that, they adapt to new circumstances. Like the leader suddenly sent their scouts into combat against the Imps, or had that tentacled monstrosity try to take me down with it when they couldn't catch me."

Arthor narrowed his eyes. "You're saying they'll have plans for ambushes."

"In part. I'm also saying that my presence will have them at high alert, so the timing would be bad."

Timothy and Arthor exchanged a look, then the surly shaman grunted. "I can see that. With them all fired up, they would be ready to react. Bu,t if you two insist that we are not to ambush them without warning, I am not sure what we can do about that?"

"See, that's the change I was proposing. So, here's the idea. We plan to delay clashing with them until the day after. We find the most defensible place within half a day's marching distance from where the humans will be camping and entrench ourselves there, build walls, and ready ourselves for an attack."

They all looked around at each other. Grex was the first to speak up. "That's stupid. What's the real plan?"

I grinned and told them. Within the hour, we got to work.

The army was huge. I'd tried to picture inside my mind how much space thirty-odd thousand people, pack animals, and assorted weirdos would take up in the landscape... and I'd come short by a lot. Now, after sundown on the second day since leaving the mountain, we'd gotten close enough to where I could see everything for myself. Sure, even with my incredible Dragon eyesight, I was unable to spot the different types of beasts and humanoids from this distance. But the overall details were impressive enough.

At the moment, their camps took up a diameter of several miles. They were being annoyingly orderly about the whole thing, too. Firth had been keeping an eye on their progress, construction, and choices during the entire time, and had come to the conclusion that they were apparently very well-organized and operated after a very specific set of rules.

Camp was organized in the same manner. Trenches were always created around the full circumference of the human camps. Bonfires were lit at specific places only, allowing guard posts and the like to keep their night sight. All around the main camp, bonfires lit the night in a chaotic, sprawling mess from where the irregulars were camped out.

I turned toward Firth. "Are you sure?"

She gave me a grim smile. For the first time, I noticed that one of her incisors was missing. Not broken, but fully missing. "Entirely. They keep the same divisions. And. They keep the same placements."

"Are our people in place?"

Her smile grew decidedly bloodthirsty. "Yes they are. They are busy preparing for battle."

"Excellent. In that case, you'd better join the fliers. I have to go say hello to some humans."

She leapt, powerful legs bunching together to propel her into the air, where her wings worked hard. Soon, she was hovering high above, circling along with Creive's people and all our Imps. Every single flier was up there right now. They'd insisted. If I got to take what they called a stupid risk, in trying to sue for peace, they wanted to be there, just in case.

They were all hidden behind my illusion, of course. I was taking a bit of a chance here that nobody would be able to spot or see through the illusion, as close as we were... but then again, they'd have to really focus on that specific stretch of sky and be really talented or powerful to boot. I grimaced, looking at the huge number of people on the plain below me. Okay, maybe I'd better hurry this along. I sprang into the air and flew closer to their forces. Time to roll the dice.

"I come in peace. Do not attack. I call for a parley." I repeated the mental message as loud as my capacities allowed. Not the most antagonistic words, right? Well, you'd think my message was a bunch of slurs and insults for the way they reacted. It was like putting a vacuum cleaner in reverse and putting the vacuum head down into a bag of glitter.

Their camp *exploded* into action as light and movement came into being all over the place. Heh. Of course, a large Dragon appearing out of nowhere, when they thought they'd patrolled their surroundings? Yeah, might be an understandable cause for concern. Still, I remained hovering five hundred feet in front of their camp, waiting for their move.

The chaos rapidly turned into controlled action. A bit too quickly for my liking, to be honest. Within about two minutes, I found myself faced by the concentrated front of what felt like their entire collection of archers and spellcasters. I wanted to back off even further, but didn't want to appear too afraid, so I simply stayed there and repeated my request. "This is not an attack. I want to talk about peace."

Five minutes later, their leaders arrived. I'd expected horses. Of course, I had. I mean, every damn fantasy movie I'd ever seen had horses. Horses and dragons. That was a universal truth, right? Not here, though. The twenty-man large group of cavalry that emerged in formation to face me was seated upon a kind of animal I'd never seen before. They looked like if you took leopards and added longer legs and about a couple hundred pounds of extra muscles. I felt pretty confident I could take one down in a straight-up combat, but I wasn't feeling my odds for facing more than one at once.

They came within about two hundred feet of me, when a trio of riders continued alone from the formation. Behind them, the formation closed effortlessly, like they were training on a parade ground. Fifty feet farther ahead, the three riders reined in. Two of them were fully armed in gleaming mail, adorned with gold and shimmering with magic. They bristled with weapons, too. Embarrassing, really. They were afraid to even talk to a tiny Dragon without being fully armed? Heh.

The final rider dismounted. She wore the same armor but held a large, two-handed staff. The moment she was on the ground, she started chanting and gesturing with the staff.

I froze, ready for action. If they were going to act against me, it would probably...

Nothing. Except for a large, glittering circle that sprang into being around the foremost riders. It was golden, too. Showoffs.

I gave a low growl. "I come in peace, I said... but that doesn't mean I won't react. A Dragon gets tetchy when you start casting unknown spells near them, understood?" My words were not hostile, but I made no secret of the threat contained within.

With their defenses in place, they finally felt safe enough to address me. As one, they faced me. Two women and a man. If I'd faced them in any kind of game, I'd have put good money on them being paladins, and probably employing inquisitors to ferret out unbelievers on top of that.

The woman in the center took off her helmet, mirrored by the others, and I got my first really good look at some of the humans of Nefren from up close. Suddenly, they didn't look as pretty and gleaming as their armor implied. In fact, she looked like she'd spent half her life in that saddle - with short, grey hair and a face you could light a match on.

"Greetings, dragon. I am Cartiga, Fourth Shield of the Empire of Nefren. My companions are Lord Gamon and Lady Eveny. What is your purpose?"

A bit uptight, but not outright hostile. That was better than what I'd expected. Heh. But then, my expectations weren't that high to begin with. "I am Onyx, the leader of the Scoured Mountain. My goal here is peace. But. Let me be entirely clear here. I am not here to surrender. Your forces attacked mine already, without provocation. They tried to lay waste to my capital, and we fought them off. I am here to see if that was a mistake, a misunderstanding, or if you are here to attack, without sense, like barbarians."

That took them aback. The guy on the left exploded into bursts of aggression, gesticulating toward me. I could feel his eagerness to attack. The Fourth Shield, whatever the hell that meant, held up a hand, silencing him. The emotions stemming from her were less clear. Guardedness, definitely, apprehension, and... curiosity, perhaps?

She asked. "Without provocation, you say? The information we have gotten says your forces are the ones who struck first. Did you not make your spellcaster eradicate our command?"

I slowly let myself glide down to the earth. It would seem that we were beyond the part where people just started flinging spells. "I did not, though your people might have reported it like that. I have spent a while talking to the one who led the assault, Lord Verneth. He was captured in your attack. Our *human*—" I stressed the word to see if it would make a difference. "—sorcerer volunteered to talk to your command, sue for peace.

"When he realized that your fliers intended to attack us regardless of what he said, our sorcerer friend sacrificed his life to halt your forces. Then, your glorious leader decided he'd attack anyway. Besides that, I find it rather suspicious that you have been so fast in assembling and bringing an army down upon us. It's almost as if you had been gathering the forces even before you knew what your fliers would bring."

That wasn't all we'd learned. It was close, though. The annoying leader of the flying attackers had been severely closed-mouthed and heaped abuse on anybody trying to interact with him in any way. Still, amidst the abuse, he had given up a few pieces of information about the Nefren Empire.

They had a strong military presence and dozens of smaller armies. They had plenty of allies. They were centered around a huge city several hundred thousand strong, which clearly, from his descriptions bragging about their constructions, held a Blessing of Deyra. Also, the flying command we'd taken out was one of only two flying commands in their army. There would be no easy replacement for them.

"I don't believe you, creature! Abomination! You killed the Third Shield, then you killed Lord Verneth, and now you are trying to avoid your rightfully earned fate!" The guy on the left looked like he was about to blow up. His full, wild beard hid half his face, but the rest of it was red with fury.

The leader stopped him with a gesture again. "Lord Gamon. Maintain your peace." She didn't look at him, though, keeping her eyes firmly fixed on me.

I met her gaze straight on. I saw no bloodthirst there. Only intense focus. "I could have killed Lord Verneth, easily. I wanted to, to be fair. He and his attackers killed a lot of my citizens, and he is less than perfect company. But he is perfectly hale and mostly whole, and we are treating him better than his attitude has earned." My eyes didn't veer from those of their leader. Watching. Judging. Estimating. I could feel as the side of my mouth crept up in realization. "But then, you don't really care about him, do you?"

The dull sensations of shock from Cartiga and Lord Gamon were almost confirmation enough, but the rightmost woman helped me. What came from her was nothing less than pure, unfiltered guilt.

Nobody spoke.

I nodded to myself. "Of course, you don't. So, even if I promised to deliver that lord of yours back to you, good as new, except for the arm he lost along the way, that wouldn't change a thing. Would it, Cartiga?"

The leader accepted the accusation without reaction either way. "If you returned Lord Verneth to us, that would allow us to judge the veracity of your claims."

The smile I beamed at her was closer to a smirk. "Aha. And are you going to wait right here until we bring him to you?"

She gave a curt shake of her head. "As much as I would want to perform a proper investigation, our orders are clear. We need to advance until ordered otherwise. Unless we had Lord Verneth with us, in a position where he could speak freely, there would be no reason to deviate from those orders. As for your former insinuation, it is not based in fact. The Fourth is a standing army. We did not have to prepare; we merely changed our course."

Now I did smirk at her. "I might believe your word on that, except that the part about Lord Verneth is, at best, a half-truth. It's clear that, even if I deliver him back to you, nothing's going to change. Meaning, you already know what the result is going to be, and this is all playacting. So, let's cut the shit and talk about what really matters."

Lord Beardface couldn't take it anymore. "Please allow me to punish this monster. Talking to the Fourth Shield like that? It does not bear-"

I interrupted him. "The Blessing. That's what you're after, right Cartiga?"

She hesitated, then nodded, business-like.

"All right. Now we're getting somewhere. I'm betting you're not going to deviate from those orders of yours, unless they result in you taking charge of the Blessing?"

Another nod. "You seem to understand. We are not against the possibility of peace. In fact, I would prefer it. But I cannot defy my orders, or I will label myself as a traitor. That, I cannot do."

"Appreciate the candor. The Fourth Shield has to take orders from the First, Second, and Third Shield, right? It's only natural. Now, there's only one real question left. Are you left with room to think and act for yourself?"

That was too much for the bearded warrior. He drew a glowing spiked mace and slapped the flat of his other hand down on his mount, which sprang into motion.

Cartiga acted immediately. Her loud yell reined in the guy, like he'd reached the end of his tether.

He glowered at me, breathing like he had just performed a hundred-yard sprint in that heavy armor of his.

The Fourth Shield castigated him loudly. "Lord Gamon. You claim to be better than these monsters? *Then show it!* Is this what the order of the Radiant Knights has come to?" Turning to me, she set her teeth, but continued. "We are under orders, that is true. But do not take us for mindless slaves. If you have anything noteworthy to discuss, I am ready to talk. If not... we will meet you on the field of battle. Again, I would prefer if you would give up the Blessing and avoid this unpleasantness."

I observed her, then started humming under my breath. "Well... that is something. All right. In the spirit of sharing, I'll put this out there: I don't give a crap about the Blessing."

That took them aback, all right. Sensations of shock, and from that Gamon dude, outright suspicion came in waves. Cartiga hazarded. "You do not *care* about the Blessing?"

I shook my head vehemently. "Nah. It's a means to an end. It helps my people grow stronger and helps them survive. That's what I care about. Survival. So, obviously, there's no sense in me giving over the Blessing just like that. That would be throwing away an advantage with no guarantee that you wouldn't turn on us right away."

The Fourth Shield interjected, "I disagree. If you were ready to grant us the Blessing, I would be able to negotiate a guaranteed safe passage away from your mountain and a peace treaty that would secure your existence and that of your people for the years to come."

"Pull the other one; it's got bells on."

"What?" The confused look on Cartiga's face almost made her look nice.

"I mean, come on now. Guarantees? Peace treaties? *Words.* You do realize that you're the ones who have already tried to ambush me. What reason would I have in trusting the words of your people? You already have as much as admitted that you're perfectly fine with attacking, even though you *know* that you're the aggressor here."

"I can assure you the word of a Fourth Shield is not wind." She actually looked insulted.

Finally, I'd actually gotten through to her. Maybe not in the perfect way, but still. She was equally outraged and... actually agreeing with me. "Well, that might be right. But if the Second Shield were to act, then where does that leave me? Out in the wastes, without food and support systems, with no Blessing to aid my people." My snort made the bearded guy's temper flare yet again, but I ignored it.

"No. What I suggest is this: I'm fairly new to my position in charge of the mountain. Hence, my people have not had the time to enjoy the effects of the Blessing in full for a long time yet. They would struggle a lot in the wastes. I want to be sure that we all have a chance of making it out there. So, I suggest that we negotiate a fair period for my people to grow. When that period—let's say ten years, for instance—has gone, we will withdraw from the mountain and leave the Blessing for the humans of Nefren to take over." My mental message was offhanded, careless, but I had my full focus on Cartiga. If only she'd grasp the chance for peace here, for—

"No." The word was like a bullet to the brain, like the blade of a guillotine slamming down. It carried finality with it. A single emotion emanated from Cartiga, in waves so strong I could almost feel them. Regret. "My superiors would never accept it."

I produced a regretful "Hrrrm" in the back of my throat. "Oh, come now, Fourth Shield. You would take us to war, just like that? You said that you had the authority to negotiate. I might be able to accept a shorter period of time."

She lowered her head. "That is not the issue. My superiors will never accept the word of a dragon, of a monster, as proof. We need something more substantial in order to be able to come to an agreement."

"Now we come full-circle, do we not? I cannot accept your word, and you will not accept mine, even if you are the ones who came to my lands, weapons in hand and ready for war." I searched her eyes and saw no give in them. With a crooked grin, I added. "I'll even throw in the safe return of that annoyance of a Lord. I won't be sorry to see him go."

She huffed a laugh under her breath. Still she shook her head sadly. "No. It will not be enough. Unless we are permitted a degree of control over the Blessing, I will not be able to talk my superiors into peace."

"Which would mean living under the threat of your swords," I hissed sadly. "War, then?"

"War." Her response was filled with regret, but entirely steelset.

CHAPTER EIGHT

They allowed me to fly off in safety. That was gracious of them. In return, I told my flying minions to remain peaceful, hovering further up in the air under an illusion, instead of descending to attack the enemy in an ambush for the history books. That was gracious of *me*. Heh.

We flew away from their camp and back toward our goal. I spent the time contemplating our discussion. In all honesty, I hadn't really expected them to cave. Selys had been right in that. The Blessings were simply too powerful, able to support the rise and fall of empires and powerhouses.

They could change the power balance of the entire frigging world. As such, they weren't going to accept any scenario that would possibly let us keep the damn thing. I'd hoped that at least I'd be able to take them into discussing the matters, though, win ourselves a few weeks or months as messengers flew back and forth between them and their command.

Heh. No dice. That Cartiga woman knew exactly what she had to work with and what her superiors would or would not accept. Competent leaders. What a pain. If only that bearded asshole had been in charge, we could have them charging into our every trap!

The sky grew entirely dark, and night fell as we flew. Contemplating what they'd said, I couldn't see anything I'd missed, no opening where we'd have been allowed to live in autonomy and grow until we'd be able to move to one of the other Blessings in relative safety. I couldn't help but feel a sting of disappointment. Not at the failure of the peace talks, though. More at one surprising fact.

I'd liked her. Cartiga seemed like a fair person and decent judge of personality, and I had no doubt that if it were up to her alone, we would've been able to find some sort of compromise. And now... now, we would be forced to meet her on the battlefield and try to kill her. Dammit.

Our return was almost peaceful. Almost, because a huge flying rodent tried to make lunch out of a handful of our Imps. Unfortunately for it, one of the scouts spotted the pitch-black body of the nocturnal hunter way before it dove to the attack. The night vision of our people really was a godsend out here. The Imps met the attacker with an orchestrated barrage of fire bolts that brought the beast tumbling, burning past us all, dead before it even hit the ground.

I felt the pressure on my illusion... but was surprised to see that holding it wasn't really tough. My ability with the skill was truly growing.

A couple of hours later, I met with the majority of my forces... and flew right past them. Then, a short while later, we found our destination. A fortress—or, more accurately, what looked like one. Two young Talpus shamans looked like rats that had been through the wringer. They were drenched with sweat, lying bonelessly on the ground. Around them, large walls of rock and soil rose into the air at least twenty feet tall and two hundred feet wide.

It was an impressive accomplishment, creating that from scratch in less than half a day, without the aid of any of the stronger, higher-leveled shamans. It was also a sorry excuse for a fortress. To be entirely honest, I was afraid a strong wind would make it keel over, but the young ones maintained that it would do its job. Probably. Possibly.

The following day took forever to move past. I knew exactly what my problem was. Inactivity. I'd never done well without having something to do, and now I was forced to stay inside the "fortress" and do nothing but maintain my illusion. Heh. The illusion. I had no doubt that the scouts in the oncoming army were shitting bricks right now.

Whoever was watching us right now wouldn't be seeing a spindly fortress with fifty flying menaces lounging about the place and a Dragon right in front of the walls. Well, they would. But, for them, the walls would look even taller and packed with soldiers and the corner towers of the edifice (which didn't exist) would be bristling with armaments and sorcery.

In short, it'd look like the perfect outpost, created to make an encroaching enemy pay for his audacity. If they somehow saw past the illusion and saw that we were a lot less than we wanted to show them, and the fortress was a lot weaker than it should look? Great. Hopefully, that would make them underestimate us further.

Still, the hours stretched into years, like a Friday workday that refused to end. In front of us, on the ragged wastelands, the progress of the enemy army was slow but inevitable. They moved forward as a whole, an unstoppable horde, with their forces drawn in closer than the last day.

The lone exception to the rule were their few flying scouts who were all over the place, constantly roaming and alert. As the foot troops moved, they covered the earth, swarming over the soil like locusts, intent on consuming everything that we were. Okay, this inactivity was really making me more dramatic than usual.

On they came, and I felt my mood sink with every passing minute. Seeing the army in the daylight, stretched out on the march, made them look even more impressive. We were going to face *that?* As they marched, I had to ask myself if we were really fooling ourselves trying to imagine that we could take them on. At this moment, their forces marched between two tall ridges, dark shapes filling every available space inside the canyon. For every hour, I came up with more details or qualities that their forces held which we lacked.

Cohesion and proper training. Not the sword training kind, either. The discipline kind of training. Those were two of our main issues. Some of our close-combat fighters were getting there, but as for the rest? When battle started for our forces, it was typically a mess of singular fighters, encroached in their own tiny universe as they tried to kill the enemy before they managed to end them. No cohesion, no teamwork, no formations.

Not so for these soldiers. They marched in lockstep, ground shaking under them as they came closer to us. Their archers, too. I bet they were the kind who'd be able to line up and send six volleys at our forces within a minute. Heh. Well, we'd just have to make sure that we weren't going to stand there all dressed up and take their shots like those idiots in the movies. The only exception to the discipline were their nonhuman allies, who swarmed ahead of their organized forces in small groups like bands of animals.

Proper equipment, too. Oh yeah. That was a big one. The closer they came, the easier it was to see. Each company had their own custom-made equipment, adapted entirely to the function of their type. The cavalry was a mix of gleaming plate armor, dull leather armor, and bright magic shining from the tips of their tall lances. I had no doubt it had been thoroughly tested for the optimal split between flexibility and being able to take a hit in a head-on charge. I, for one, had no intention of being on the receiving end of one of their charges.

It was like that everywhere, though. Close-combat fighters were arranged according to specialization and equipped accordingly. Infantry had the same kind of armor and carried large backpacks that were likely to hold standardized field equipment, too. Bloody archers didn't have to make their own bows with whatever material was available. Nah, they'd have their own forges and woodworkers to make everything up to specs. Sure, we'd get there... eventually. Yet, at this moment, I felt like we were severely under-equipped for the task.

The thing that had my big boy panties in a real twist, however, was the presence of the spellcasters among the infantry. Firth was the one who pointed that one out. As they marched, they were divided into platoons of thirty to fifty. Each one of these platoons had at least a single soldier in the platoon who eschewed their regular weapons for staves or wands glowing with magic. Damn.

The only saving grace was that they didn't have these spell-casters among the archers, from what we could tell. Still, doing the math, it would mean that they had hundreds of spellcasters in their force, and each of them would likely have trained working in lockstep and adding their gifts to that particular platoon. Meanwhile, we had six shamans in the entire force and a handful of minor spellcasters among the Aberrants. That didn't really feel fair.

At this point, I would really have loved to have my Inspect ability to figure out the powers of the approaching forces. However, that one was, annoyingly, restricted to working within the mountain. The good news was that some of my scouts had lesser versions of the skill and were able to provide me with *some* information on our enemies. The news was truly welcome. At first.

"They're squishy, Onyx."

"Squishy?" I glared at the scout before me. It wasn't a scout I knew, one of the few surviving Dragonlings. I tried not to let my prejudice be obvious. Just because all of his kind had pretty much tried to backstab me, kill, or eat me... I shook my head. I was spiraling a bit. "What do you mean?"

"I mean that they're weak. My skill's [Compare]. Helps me know if I should flee from a target or not. I can compare my attributes to theirs at will. The archers there? Their Toughness is lower than mine. Checked a few. Decent Strength and Agility, though."

Oh. That was actually... "Useful to know. Thank you. Did you check out any of the others?"

The Dragonling pointed. "The ones out front. Furred ones. More agile than me. Also squishy and weak."

So less Strength and Toughness, but more Agility. Good skirmishers, probably.

He continued. "Others with scales are both more agile and tough. Plenty of different races. Haven't compared all of 'em."

"Keep it up. Knowledge is important."

He grimaced in response. "I will. And the leaders." He bared his teeth in a grimace. "Dangerous. Very dangerous."

"Dangerous." Oof. So, stronger than him on all counts.

"Also those cavalry riders. Dangerous."

"Noted. Thank you for-"

"And the ones on the fliers. Dangerous. Also, the fliers themselves-"

"Okay. I get it. Thank you." Geez. Rub my face in it, will ya? Good thing our initial plan involved avoiding every single one of those he mentioned, bar the fliers, and they were few in number.

For half an hour, it looked like they might decide to continue toward us, keep up their march for the final five or six hours at their pace, to face us the same day. I paced nervously, wondering if we'd misjudged them. Were they going to call our bluff? Had they seen through the illusion and seen how weak we really were? Eventually, horns blew, and the massive horde ground to a slow stop.

At long last, the day came to an end. Their force spread out far and wide, and camp fires sprang up from within their newly erected camp. Their defenses were in place. Their guards were marching. Their non-human skirmishers were arrayed all around their main force, keeping any ground-based approach from being realistic.

As the shadows lengthened over the grounds, and the sun

dipped beyond the horizon, I had one final discussion with Firth.

I was hesitant to ask. The entire plan revolved around our having estimated things right. "I... can't tell entirely. It looks to me like we made it?"

She didn't even look at the twilight scenario before us. Just nodded, once. She'd clearly spent plenty of time judging that exact thing already. "It is not perfect. But they are near to where we judged they would be. Not in the center. They are near the edge of the western side, but... it should suffice."

Darkness fell fully, and several hours passed, as I maintained the illusion of the fortress. It was easy to tell that the enemy had moved closer, that more people were focusing on the illusion or both.

My head felt foggy and weirdly pressurized, like the sensation when you have a cold and your ears are clogged. Then the stars came out, and I forgot all about the tiny distracting inconsequentialities for a moment. It was the first time I'd taken the time to really take in the fullness of the night sky, and I marveled at the spectacle.

The look of stars in a world that hadn't been touched by pollution was... incredible. Everything blinked and twinkled like in a Hallmark movie, shining in a wider color spectrum than the pale lights we were used to. Not to mention, the moons! There was one moon up there, closer or larger than our moon back on earth, and it had at least two smaller moons surrounding it as well. From what little I remembered of my childhood physics, that must mean the tides on this world would be... interesting.

For an undefinable moment, I felt at peace. Surrounded by my own people. Taking in a scenery that only a single earthling had observed before me. It was awe-inspiring. Then, I returned to the present, taking in the look of Grex fidgeting with his claws at the far end of our fake fortress, tiny fire bolts springing into being and dying out in a manic progression inside his claws.

I took a deep breath. Then I sent a quick message to everybody present. "It's time."

We took to the skies silently. Or, as silently as possible when your force included more than a dozen Imps, two Dragons, five huge, lumbering Parvu beasts, and a bunch of other bloodthirsty flying races. I beat my wings hard as we climbed high, going far higher into the frosty night air than we usually would.

I covered us all in a wide swath of shadow as we flew, groaning with the effort of it. Multitasking... it was *not* my favorite thing. It did, however, come easier to me now after two days of uninterrupted practice, and knowing that the strain would be over soon helped. The stress didn't.

This was a critical moment. If they had already broken my illusion or managed to spot the unnatural blob of darkness traveling through the night skies, we'd ruin the surprise. However, below us was nothing but silence. Or, at least, the comparative silence of more than thirty thousand people at rest or preparing for the following day.

Then we were there. Resting more or less comfortably inside a circle of shadow hundreds of feet above the western part of their camp. Ready and waiting for action. As agreed, I sent a tiny, focused beam of a message straight at their position. A simple message. "Now." Then we waited.

At first, there was no reaction. Silence continued to reign, only interrupted by the occasional sound of iron against iron and one incredibly loud snore. Then, new sounds appeared, inconsistent with the ones we'd heard before. Shuffling or moving of earth.

Then the screams started.

CHAPTER NINE

"Attack him where he is unprepared, appear where you are not expected." -
Sun Tzu, The Art of War

At the moment, below us, every single one of our close combat fighters was running amok inside the human camp. Roth led one group, Slither and Koa'tem the other. It sounded like they were in a foul mood. Heh. I probably would be, too, if I'd spent the entire day buried underground, not knowing if I would be spotted, where I was going to dig myself up, or whether it would all be wasted effort.

I blamed the humans and their focus on organization and consistent behavior, really. That was what made it possible for us. They stopped marching around the same time each day. They camped in the exact same manner. They placed their forces in the exact same places inside the camp.

Also, they didn't change up their construction or protective measures. Heh. They might, after today. Since we already knew approximately how far they'd travel, we only had to apply a bit of effort on the shamans' part to make sure there was only one appropriate camping ground for the horde, unless they wanted to keep on traveling for several additional hours. According to Arthor, it was almost too easy, making sure the terrain ahead of them was covered in deep mud and inhospitable as hell.

Inside that appropriate camping ground, we'd buried our people. That had been the most nerve-wracking part of the entire scheme. We needed to be able to hide more than a hundred people underground, strengthen the hiding place enough that it wouldn't collapse from having a horde march over it, and ensure they didn't suffocate.

There'd really been no reason for me to worry, though. After the constant work we'd put them through back near Fire Peak over the past few months, our shamans were able to move awe-inspiring masses of earth within a ridiculous period of time. Once they were done constructing the rooms—two separate, large underground rooms which made me think of my grandpa's old root cellar—Creziel went over them both, hardening the substance to the point where he pronounced them sufficient to withstand a rockfall.

I didn't know about that, but I did walk on the ceiling of both dwellings, and all it did was rain down a bit of dust below. Just like that, with a couple of small holes for ventilation, we had all our close-combat fighters hidden near the heart of the enemy.

Now, the plan was coming into fruition, as our forces poured out into their camp. With a sigh of relief, I dropped the illusion of the fortress, while still maintaining my cloak of shadows over the fliers. Let 'em see that it was a fake now - it could only add to the confusion.

I sent a message to my people below. "Roth. They're right north of you. A few hundred feet, no more. Slither. North-east for you, same distance. You know the plan. Hit the targets, then run for your lives. No lingering. No fighting." At this point, there was little doubt somebody with enough Mental Power could hear my message, but as long as I kept it vague... I didn't care.

The first attackers hit their targets. I hissed at the fliers surrounding me. "Any moment now. Stay ready. Nobody moves until I say so. At my mark, the Parvu beasts move to where we agreed."

They all stayed put, hovering nearby, even if it cost some of the Imps. Grex was giving off a high-pitched whine as he buzzed to and fro, longing to close with the enemy. Suddenly, the camp below exploded.

If I'd thought that the initial cries had meant that the battles had started, I'd been entirely wrong. Now, cries of pain, roars, screams, and sounds of battle erupted below us, and the first of the fliers inside the camp took to the skies.

A bloodthirsty smile spread on my face and I growled in satisfaction. "Now. Make them pay!" Then I released the shadow hiding us all and plunged.

We met the climbing fliers midair and hit them like an avalanche, unstoppable and deadly. Fire bolts blossomed into being and impacted the rising enemy fliers, hitting like falling meteors. I focused my sight on one of the few close-combat fliers—a poison spitter, this one—and crashed straight onto its neck, claws-first. The momentary glare of panic in its eyes faded instantly as my impact and bulk hit the neck with a massive crack. I unleashed a Weakening Fog at another flier, pushed off from the poison spitter's falling form, and hovered mid-air, taking in my surroundings.

All around me, our fliers swooped and dipped, attacking any fliers attempting to take off to avoid the chaos of what was happening on the ground. Anybody mighty or agile enough to avoid the plentiful fire bolts from the Imps soon found themselves beset by a whirlwind of surrounding claws and teeth. The fliers from Fire Peak and the few flying Aberrants took this chance to obtain vengeance on those who had tried to take over the mountain.

The hawk-like scouts had no chance of standing up against the fire bolts and soon fell like giant torches throughout the camp below, adding to the chaos and confusion. A single one of the Wyvern-like beasts managed to struggle to the air, despite its face looking half-charred from fiery impacts.

I hit it with a Weakening Fog dead-on and grinned to see the Dragonling scout swoop past its glazed remaining eye and carve open the membrane of its wing. On the far side of the camp, Creive and his minions were doing the same thing, protecting the skies in a show of mayhem that was equal parts monstrous and gory. He bit the head clean off a winged scout and roared with bloodlust.

Below us, there was little fighting. Not in the way you would expect, when you unleashed a hundred persons into the midst of a force tens of thousands strong. Violence, oh yes. There was plenty of that. But our people on the ground did not stand to fight. They flowed around the flying beasts, engaging and moving on without halting, only rarely striking or even defending.

It had been Laive's parting gift. A large jar filled with a dark, caustic substance. "Gurn worm venom," she'd told me. "It's incredibly potent. I spent some time going through the stores in the fortress when I found this. Smear it on a weapon, stab, twist, and move on. Whichever enemy you faced is going to suffer excruciating pain for the next several weeks. Most won't survive. Even if it does survive, it will be horribly weak, unable to move. Just be warned. Whatever you are up against won't feel it right away. Any strike after the first one will be a lot less efficient. Still, I believe it might come in handy."

Understatement of the century. Below, our people were flowing through the enemy camp in two waves. One was led by Roth and the other by Koa'tem, as they sprinted through the flier encampment. For each flier, Parvu beast, scout, or which-ever it was, a single attacker would peel off from the group and launch in to perform a strike against the confused enemy beasts before disengaging and moving on. Sometimes, my Talpi used their atlatls to launch the poisoned spears at a distance without even stopping.

It wasn't flawless. It definitely wasn't pretty. Like Laive had warned, the poison didn't take hold right away, and the enemy fliers, as well as their rudely awakened riders, were deadly. I saw one, then several attackers fail to disengage and fall to the ground, savaged by the defenders.

However, we'd judged the placement well. The defenders in the camp had their eyes fixed outside the camp. On top of that, their fliers and riders were diurnal beasts. They were *not* prepared for a night battle in their own camp and definitely not on the ground. Any bloody flier who tried to take off was vulnerable while attempting to gain altitude.

Finally, with the way they divided their camp, there were no close combat fighters near the flier camp. Nothing to stand against the might of Koa'tem and his whirling staff of death or Roth and his spinning, massive weapon. Especially with Timothy right among them, stunning people left and right.

A stray thought struck me—a late, strange realization. My Talpi really weren't that small. Not compared to the humans. On average, they reached the neck of any human, meaning that all the rest of our fighters generally dwarfed the humans in size. We were what went bump in the night. Literally.

Within two minutes, three at the outside, our fighters reached the far side of the fliers encampment, and our twin streams of forces flowed together to join up. It had been a few minutes since the engagement started, but the enemy was starting to wake up. Horns sounded throughout the camp, and yells of pain and surprise were being replaced by shouts of command and fury. On top of that, arrows were starting to reach into the air to strike at our fliers.

Oh yeah. We were definitely overstaying our welcome.

I dove and sprayed a Weakening Fog as wide and far as I could, right from the trenches on the western side of the encampment and almost all the way to where our fighters were milling about, fighting to defend themselves from the enemies starting to press in on all sides. To my joy, the enemies fell like wheat under a scythe. My breath attack was doing its job!

Half their soldiers remained standing, but a lot of them were wavering. Just like that, our fighters had an open avenue all the way to the edge of the camp. "Come ooon!" I roared and rose into the air again. "We're moving out. Extraction *now!*" The message rang out across the camp, and let any bastard try to stop us who dared.

As it turned out, quite a few of them dared. By now, the companies inside the encampment were organizing and striking out in force. Every one of them wanted a piece of their attackers. Except, we didn't stand still to let them engage us, and we were already gone. Our close-combat fighters sprinted for the edge of the camp. At this point, their camp guards were realizing what was going on, organizing to prepare to defend an attack from within.

They were not ready for our fighters. Koa'tem was an unstoppable force of nature, crushing bone and armor alike with his whirling staff. Roth was like lightning, moving fast enough to confuse entire squads, striking at lighter-armored fighters and weak joints with his massive sword. Timothy ran amok, stunning anybody who dared stand and hold against our forces. Any ranged fighters were met with the constantly moving, almost tower-shield sized tiles of rock Arthor kept moving with the speed of thought.

Our forces made their way to the deep trench on the north side of the encampment – and for a moment, I feared for them. Then I realized that the trench was moving, burgeoning from below. It filled in within seconds, allowing them safe passage across the deep obstruction. Right after they had passed, the soil flowed like water to open up the trench to its former limb-breaking obstacle depth again. God, I loved my shamans!

An archer company suddenly halted near the trench, struggling to reform properly in the heat of battle. We were still very much in arrow range. But, it had been a while since I'd seen Grex and his people. Where were they? In the thirteenth hour, our Imps rejoined us, coming from the *center* of the camp, for some reason.

They cackled, laying a nasty barrage of fire damage into the backs of the archer company on the way. I added another Weakening Fog on top of the damage as an added bonus, then we were gone. A single mage strode forward and sent a wave of frost at our retreating backs, but failed to reach anything but our hindmost ranks. They were able to stumble forward with help from their comrades. We left the main army behind and moved toward our evacuation route.

Now, we were looking into a sea of enemies. It might be hyperbole, since the majority of the enemies were definitely behind us now, but with the skirmishers milling about in confusion as they tried to understand what was going on, I couldn't phrase it any other way. It looked like an ocean of constant movement, of unfathomable forces pulling them every which way.

At the far end of their forces, where the bonfires of the non-humans faded out into darkness, the ground rose incrementally. Beyond that lay the edge of the ridge, where our Parvu beasts were waiting to pick up our people and carry them to safety.

Good thing we didn't need to fight them all. I knew from the start we'd only get one chance at this kind of ambush. After tonight, they'd be on the lookout for strategies like this one. Hurt them badly, then leave. That was the plan.

Part one was complete. Now for part two.

I soared over my people, roaring as I went, then I reached deep down into myself and found that native place where I could access the shadow that was an important part of my namesake. I stretched it as far as it could go. Within seconds, every single soldier below me, including a twenty-foot stretch on either side of our people, was covered in magical shadow.

It did exactly what it was supposed to do: kept the skirmishers from trying to close with us. Our fliers were retreating, too, frantically flying to escape the now-organized archers and mages of the encampment. The close-combat fliers opted to retreat higher into the air, where the enemies would be unable to follow. As for the Imps, one-by-one, they dove and dipped into the relative safety of the magical shadow. From within, the Imps spewed fire in all directions.

I had to hand it to the irregulars. They were not just a

couple of different races, like I had figured to begin with, but a force composed of perhaps a dozen different humanoid races. I saw fur, scales, and differently colored skin in equal measure. The humans might use them as humanoid shields, as less important fighters who didn't even deserve to be brought into the safety of the main camp.

While the non-humans fought, they didn't just throw themselves at us suicidally. No, they kept their distance, unleashing ranged damage on us. Fortunately, my breath attack kept them weakened while my shadows kept them from actually aiming. Few managed to hit anything.

On the left side of our formation, Arthor kept his stone shields constantly moving to deflect any missiles that came too close. On the right, Creziel shot his own missiles at any ranged enemies moving too close. Timothy ranged out by himself outside the shadow, assisting in singling out and stunning anybody who looked like they might pose a serious threat, while detracting the attributes of those around him. A wild laughter followed him.

Those who tried to stand in the way of the front of our retreat did not fare well. Roth and Koa'tem carved them down as if they were not even real enemies. High above, Creive and his fliers kept the air clear of any pursuit.

For a brief moment, our way out seemed clear, as the humanoids were starting to shy away from our forward path, but then a series of stinging impacts hit me, and I watched my health drop by twenty percent. Around me, others fell with cries of pain. I looked around, anxious to see what was going on, and then I spotted him... or her.

A large reptilian form, as tall as a human, but with two sets of arms. The reptile was slithering alongside our retreating soldiers, shouting and pointing... right at me. No, not at me. It was simply telling all the archers and spear-throwers surrounding it to follow along and shoot straight at the center of the shadow. The gathered forces around it were obeying its orders in numbers large enough for it to make a difference.

I tried changing the center of the shadows but quickly reached the limit of my capabilities. That would mean revealing some of the fighters on the outer edges of my shadows. Not a good idea, when we were still among their forces, especially since they were able to follow alongside us and could potentially keep up the bombardment right until we reached our aerial Ubers. Goddammit.

"Everybody! Throw light bombs on my command! All sides. Koa'tem, focus on those archers." A second later, I commanded "Now!" and a smaller set of missiles rained outward on every side of our forces. I didn't wait to see the result, though. I took to the air and closed my eyes firmly, beating my wings blindly. Cries arose as light tried to burn its way through my closed eyelids. When I opened my eyes again, the scenery had changed. Behind me, my people were moving on, shifting outside of the protective shape of my shadows, but momentarily safe. Skirmishers on all sides lay downed or cried in agony with their vision ruined.

I blinked, colored spots floating everywhere in my vision, then I swerved to avoid hitting a tall, troll-like beast. Suddenly, the naga creature was right there in front of me. I spewed a Weakening Fog all over his group of ranged fighters then dove... and grabbed onto the naga with both front claws. The living form in my claws tensed up and then bucked, trying to fight its way out of my grasp.

My return to our column wasn't pretty. The naga thing fought, squirmed, bit, and tore to escape my death grip, and I almost let it drop from the heights. But I was too busy to take the time to reach a height that might kill the damned thing. And... I had an idea. Of sorts. If only the damn thing would stop. Fucking. Fighting!

I returned to the edge of my moving fighters, held up the naga in front of me, and, as soon as the cooldown was available again, I poured a Weakening Fog straight into the face of the stubborn beast. That did the trick. It collapsed into a limbless shamble, only moving slightly. I was able to spread the shadows, which had lapsed somewhere in the middle of my detour. I couldn't run with the creature in my claws and decided to hover above them instead.

The ridge was looking closer and closer. Our Imps were still firing away on all cylinders and, seeing the disappearance of the naga, the enemies were reluctant to come too close, lest they suddenly look like a target, too. I called out for the riders to bring down the Parvu beasts. Of course, that's when the roars started erupting from behind us.

Crap. Okay, the skirmishers weren't shying away from *our* forces alone. They were also backing off from the incoming wave of human soldiers that streamed from the encampment, like army ants who'd been told there was a nice, crunchy bird corpse ripe for the taking.

They were still a ways away, though, except for the damn cavalry. The feline creatures were racing across the uneven ground, and they were *fast*. Whew. Angry, too. I spotted Beard-face at the front of their lines. He had really not taken well to our little surprise. If only he wasn't followed by so many damn fighters with shiny lances.

I glanced behind me. Double damn. There was no way we'd get everybody out of here before the first riders got here. The infantry had no chance of catching up, but we'd have to do something about the damn cat riders. Grinding my teeth, I glanced left, then right, locating the people I needed and issuing commands as fast as I could.

"Slither. Roth. Get everybody without a working set of wings out of here. Grex, keep up the fire, keep all the ranged attackers at a distance. Koa'tem, take this snake person - I want it to survive. Arthor and Creziel?"

The two shamans were right there, ready for anything. I nodded at them. "Get on my back. I'll tell you what we need." I called up. "Creive. I need you, too. Timothy... where the fuck is Timothy?" No time.

Ten seconds later, I was off, running, leaping to get airborne. The shadows followed me, slowly retracting their protection from my people. Suddenly, it was entirely obvious to the enemy that we were getting away, as they were able to see the Talpi and Aberrants clambering onto the Parvu in the distance. I killed off the shadows entirely for a moment.

A huge roar went up among their troops, and, if possible, they increased their speed even further. Only now, they could clearly spot the large Dragon flying toward them.

I had to hand it to them. Those humans were anything but quitters. They faced a Dragon with unknown powers. One who had erupted from nothing in the midst of their forces and was hurtling through the air toward them at high speed. But they didn't slow down, didn't veer. The riders directly in my path lowered their lances. Others farther out in the formation grabbed at their saddles, retrieving throwing spears and readying them for a volley, while waves of magic barreled toward me, not from one, but from *both* far sides of the column. Beardface had a manic rictus of a grin on his face.

"Now!" My mental yell erupted, and I placed a Shadow Whorl right in front of the bearded bastard. Then I followed it up with a Weakening Fog... and turned my direct charge into a climb, beating my wings to gain altitude like my life depended on it. Which, of course, it did. The front cavalry line disappeared from my vision, but not before I'd reengaged my shadows, flinging them forward and into the charging cavalry for as far as I possibly could.

Pain engulfed my hind legs and lower body. Alternating currents of hot and cold struck me, the cold threatening to freeze me and force me back to the ground. Forty percent of my health evaporated in an instant. Thank you *so much* for that frost weakness by the way, Deyra.

But then I escaped the range of the mages' spells and kept climbing. The confused cries of the cavalry riders were drowned out by cries of shock and pained roars from their mounts as they literally stumbled upon the second part of my hastily contrived plan.

Reaching a height I deemed sufficiently safe, I leveled out

and veered back toward my people. I risked a single glance behind me, though, and chuckled grimly to see the chaotic pile of downed riders and hurting mounts. The stone obstacles Arthor and Creziel had forced out of the ground at a moment's notice were not especially tall–probably a foot and a half, in Arthor's case, and less for Creziel's.

But suffering from sudden blindness mixed with the chaotic images and illusions from my Shadow Whorl, they'd done the trick. The charging cavalry had had no realistic chance of clearing two unexpected jumps in a row while blinded. The minority of mounts who'd actually managed the jumps, or somehow smashed through unhurt, were met by the stunning, deafening damage of Creive's lightning breath.

Only a rare few emerged untouched on the other side. They were now milling about, unwilling to charge the rest of our people by themselves. We were going to make it. There was nobody left behind, only the chaos left by our rampage. That, and… Timothy? "Timmy! Get your blue ass back here right now! We're leaving!" My message tore through the night sky.

Our Parvu beasts were starting to take off, now, one-by-one rising into the air as our people crawled on board. It was neither majestic, nor fast, but there was nobody near to stop us. Finally, Tim moved back from his rampage among the fortunately unmagical skirmishers.

I breathed a sigh. We'd made it. The furious roars behind us sounded like sweet, sweet triumph.

CHAPTER TEN

Firth didn't return with us. Neither did most of our scouts. Midair, she caught up to me, claws covered in blood. As usual, she didn't waste her time. "We are leaving."

"What? Now? We've just fought a battle." I knew we'd planned for them to leave, but Jesus. Talk about work ethic.

"Does that reduce our haste? This play fighting of yours will be worth nothing, if we do not locate the Blessings in due time. We will try to send information back to you when we know more. However, their placement is far away and far apart. Do not expect any knowledge for at least two weeks." Like that, she was off.

I was reduced to sending a mental yell at her back. "Good luck. And well done in the battle!" You foul-mooded, antagonistic critter. That last part, I kept to myself. Barely. Even though I had to hold myself back from kicking her from time to time, she got things done. That counted for a lot in my book.

Back in the mock fortress, we took stock of our situation. That, of course, was an oversimplification. First, we took care of the worst wounds, which, without the Ergul here, pretty much meant bandages, poultices, or, for the unlucky Imp, the edge of an axe to create a nice, even stump. It wasn't pretty.

Then, as the adrenaline of the battle started oozing away, tempers flared, and a handful of fights and arguments broke out over things our fighters had done or should have done during the battle. Also, a third of my minions slunk off to have a bit of privacy with one or several others. This, as well, was perfectly normal and a regular part of any battle, as we came down from the adrenaline high and realized we'd survived.

Finally came the well-known parts of the aftermath. Some celebrated results in the battle, newly gained levels, stolen equipment, or simple survival, while others were bemoaning wounds and sorry results. Everything, however, was like a ritual - a set of steps everybody had to go through. The message was pretty simple. "We made it. Oh my god, we actually survived. Well done."

Then, we could get down to business.

"How are they reacting?" Creziel's mental message held a great deal of anticipation. Not only fear, though. A desire for battle. Huh. That was new.

A female Talpus scout I'd talked with a few times smiled broadly. "They're not. Not moving out, at least. They're too busy staying in their camp and licking their wounds. We'll keep an eye on them for the rest of the night."

By we, she meant the few remaining scouts. That was probably our most pressing issue. The last few months had been hard on scouts in the mountain - and sending away Firth and some of our best scouts hurt, though it had to be done. "Thank you... Menea, right? One final thing before you're off. The next few weeks, we'll have a hard need of your gifts and those of the other scouts, but you'll need help. We'll send some people out among the fighters and ask for volunteers to share the burden. Make sure they take the easier tasks, all right?"

She nodded professionally and stalked off.

Turning back to the council and my vassals, I asked the one

question that had been burning on my mind ever since the worst shock of survival had dissipated. "How did we do?"

Creive growled. "We did great. That was so much fun. Nobody saw us coming, and we taught them the value of strength."

"And the value of subterfuge I'd say, right?" I smirked at the huge, blue dragon.

He'd grown. This battle had made him hit some sort of capstone, and he'd actually increased his bulk yet again. I felt dwarfed by his immense form, which was rippling with muscles. He rumbled in satisfaction. "I believe we will have to repeat our test of mettle some day, Onyx. You will be forced to admit that I am the stronger of us... but yes. Your little trick worked well."

Lightning played over his skin, and he bared his teeth in joy at seeing the others edging away from him. "Anybody who tried to make it into the air, we tore apart. A few may have survived, wounded, but we did not leave anybody in the sky."

That was what I longed to hear. "How about your own forces? How are your losses?"

He snorted. "Negligible. A few weaklings didn't make it. We will be able to go again right away, should you want to." A moment of hesitation went by, then he finished. "As long as you pick a good target. There were some strong foes among their ground forces."

Words of caution from Creive? That meant he'd really been fazed by the enemy. Damn. "That will not be necessary, but count me impressed by the strength of you and your people. You did well."

Satisfaction stemmed from him, both with himself and the praise.

Regardless of his words of challenge, I didn't really fear him wanting to go up against me. Heh. If it happened, he'd kick my scaly ass. Especially now, as the effect from the Blessing had run out. Damn, but I felt *weak!* I'd really gotten used to that boost! Anyway, it didn't feel like Creive actually wanted to challenge me. At this point, it seemed more like a habit, like he was acting this way because that was how he was used to the world functioning.

I turned to the others. "How did the rest of you fare? Slither?"

He grimaced. "We have a fair few wounded and lost five of our people, mostly due to their ranged attacks. In a couple of days, all will be ready to fight again. But we managed. Bar a couple, every one of our poisoned weapons found flesh."

"Hah. Well done! Well done indeed, you scrawny twig." Roth laughed at the Stick Kin and slapped his back. "I saw you during the fight. Leaping about between them, disappearing and reappearing where you wanted. You are good! I want to test my strength against you."

The muscular Talpus noticed my glare and laughed even louder. "Some other day. Don't be so touchy, Onyx. We did well out there, of course. Timothy kept the fliers stunned while we took our poison to them, and for the rest, we roamed like we wanted. We lost only a single Talpus."

I fixed my gaze on Timothy. "You did do good, Tim. Only… what happened out there? Don't do it again. Please. We need you."

He didn't react, just looked down. A silence spread over the gathering. It was broken as Slither disappeared into thin air, reappearing next to Roth. He moved slowly around the buff little furball, looking him over, taking in his form and the single wound on the Talpus's arm from the battle.

Roth's clenched muscles and disturbed glance told how well he liked the scrutiny.

Slither didn't care, though. He finished his circle. "I believe... Yes, I believe that my decision to come here was correct. I can see the difference between your forces and mine, how big a difference the levels will make in our survival. Now, we have only to wait and see if the poison works as we hoped."

I nodded. "Does anybody have an estimate on that? When will we know? Laive wasn't too specific on that part."

"No. But we did as you ordered. Made sure that we all used

ranged weapons or threw rocks, so we would get as much experience as possible when they die." The Stick Kin's face split in a nasty smile. "If this Laive of yours delivers, and the poison works as ordered, we should have a fun night."

We did. We definitely did. Anybody who had expected to get some sleep was either terribly disappointed–or Koa'tem, who seemed to be able to fall and remain asleep mid-fight, if he wanted to. After a few hours' rest, the night started to be broken by cries of victory and joy, as the first notifications of experience gain began to tick in. They did not stop. Once the deluge began, all hopes of rest were torn from us, as our people celebrated and leveled.

We met in the morning again. Bleary-eyed, but happy, the council and my Vassals stood, celebrating their gains. It seemed like everybody had gained a level or more overnight.

"My Aberrants have done well. Three levels. That is what most of us have managed. At this rate, we will catch up to your Talpi soon. I even leveled myself. A rare treat." Slither's wide, disturbing smile didn't break.

Roth snorted. "Good luck with that, twig boy. This night was *good* for the Talpi. Most gained two levels, and there are some *fun* new feats."

"New feats?" Timothy was *right* there.

I snorted. "Later, Timmy-boy. Plenty of time for that later. How did you do yourself?"

The answer was, "Not too goddamn shabby." Timothy got a single level, bringing him to 38. Same went for Creziel, who hit 34, and Arthor, who made it to an impressive 39. I made it to Level 44 myself, needing just another thirty thousand experience for 45, the next defining feat, if my theory was right, and a hoard level up.

Roth was the only one who got a feat, as he made it to Level 35. This one was a Defining Feat, too, making it all the more juicy. I was starting to see a pattern, too. His choices were between [Improved Physical Training], letting those he taught improve their physical attributes faster, [Improved Physical

Attributes], giving a fifty-percent boost to his own physical attributes, or [Improved Growth], increasing his future experience gain by fifty percent.

He surprised me, though, choosing the physical attributes. When I pressed him on it, I had a hard time disputing his point. "Sure. It might be better for the tribe in the long run, if I chose the training one. But that won't help anybody if we die first. And I'm going to be one of those standing between them and our enemies. In order to do that? I need the strength." Then he laughed. "With this feat? I'll have plenty of strength."

He told me what his attributes would rise to, and I started laughing myself. Yeah, no discussion there. He'd be able to match any human at an equal level with those gains. If anybody had earned the right to call themselves a defender, it'd be him.

Personal Info:
Name: Roth
Race: Talpus, Level 35 – experience toward next level: 23400/35000
Size: Very small

Stats and Attributes:
Health: 480/480
Mana: 100/100
Strength: 48
Toughness: 40
Agility: 60
Mental Power: 10
Mental Control: 10

Creive was looking satisfied with himself as well. "This fight was not bad for my minions, either. Or me. What we started, the ground often finished as we tossed them down, bleeding. I want more."

Grex looked weird, though. Even for him. Like he was

holding in a fart and wanting to tell a horrible joke at the same time. Enough so that I had to ask. "Grex. What is wrong?"

Then he started laughing. Sheer, maniacal, hysterical laughter. This was B-movie, villain cliche-level laughter. I, and everybody else, couldn't do anything but stare at the look of deranged mirth on the ugly, claw-sized critter.

After the laughter stretched on uninterrupted for way too long, Timothy asked, "Dude. Are you all right?"

Grex finally managed to get his breakdown under control and volunteered, "All right? Yes. We are all right. We Imps were naughty. So naughty."

I frowned. Naughty. "What do you mean?"

"We attacked all fliers in the air, like Creive. Then made a quick trip before fleeing. One of our people died, but..." He started laughing again.

I tried to think back to the fight. They *had* been late in returning to the fight. "Wait a minute. You went to attack all the fliers on the ground, too?"

He nodded, tears in his eyes. He tried to send a mental message, but burst into laughter again.

"So, you and the other Imps received experience from *every single flier* that died?"

Hands over his mouth, he hovered in the air. Then nodded.

I tried to be stern and call him out for risking his life unnecessarily... but looking at him, I couldn't. In the end, I settled for something different. "I understand why you did it. But think about this, Grex. Your returning late meant that the skirmishers had some extra time to attack us. Risking your own lives? That, I can live with. Risking the lives of everybody else? That is unacceptable."

He tried to look bereaved, and completely and utterly failed.

I sighed, gave up. This was bound to become a problem in the future... but for now, I was taking the easy way out. "How many levels?"

"I gained four levels! And a funny feat. All the other Imps

gained even more. Some of the new ones from Fire Peak gained more than ten. No longer will we be dismissed! Overnight, we have become a force to fear!"

I hid my smile, and on the inside, I had to marvel at his audacity. Ten fucking levels in one battle. That *was* going to make a difference. "About that funny feat?"

He savored the taste of it. "[Fire Control] No more will I be limited to regular spells for boring Imps. I can make exploding fireballs. Long, thin streams. Go whoosh. Do what I want."

I shuddered. For a moment, I felt sorry for the humans who'd end up in his path. "All right. Everybody. Let's gather up and listen to Menea. I asked her and the other scouts as soon as the sun came up to keep an eye on the enemy, how many survived, and their reactions. If ever they're going to abandon their approach, it'll be now."

The lithe Talpus scout jumped down from the wall of the fortress and nodded to all of us. "You failed. You did not manage to defeat their fliers."

What the hell? I gawked at the Talpus, then stretched my neck to look at the far encampment. No fliers buzzing about. But the experience... I narrowed my eyes, looked at Menea again, then at the tiny quiver near her lip. "Menea." I asked, with menace in my tone. "Are you seriously messing around with us on something as serious as this?"

Her face erupted into a brilliant smile. "Oh, yes I am." She pointed at the enemy. "I'm not lying, though. You didn't defeat *all* of them. There's maybe a dozen fliers that survived, all told. Of those, I believe some have already suffered permanently from the poison. Regardless of whether their healers are trying to save them, the damage has been done." She held up a single claw-tipped digit. "All the Parvu beasts are dead."

A chorus of growls, yells, and roars celebrated our triumph. I breathed out in relief. What had I done to be surrounded by people who lived only to test my nerves? "How about their reaction? What are they doing?"

"Rearranging, it would seem. With every Parvu beast

downed, they are busy moving all their cargo and heavy equipment on to the only remaining animals that can take the weight."

I blinked. What did she- "No! Not the cavalry?"

She nodded, eyes twinkling.

I released a deep belly laugh. "I bet Beardface just *loves* that his force is being degraded to pack animals. Still, you all know what that means." I faced my people. "They aren't turning back. They are going to keep on marching. Despite tonight, we are still outnumbered and way under strength, compared to them. But we are in an excellent position to lay the hurt on them. So, now I want ideas. How do we make sure that they regret their decision and flee back to the human empire?"

The next few hours were fun and filled with ideas. My people were definitely not all deep thinkers, but when it came to ideas for messing with the enemy? They sure delivered. Hours later, we took off, relocating under my illusion to arrive at the next point of attack.

It was not going to be a short flight. The others had argued that we should trust in my illusion, but now that the enemy knew about me and about my illusion and shadow gifts, I wanted to approach with caution. This meant retreating to the point where they couldn't conceivably see us anymore, move perpendicular to their force behind the cover of an unnaturally large forest, then circle around to camp out at their side. It would be a handful of hours, since we were going slow to spare those wounded who would recover enough to fight again soon. I aimed to make the most of things, and as such, I had an addition made to my cargo.

I made sure to spray it with a Weakening Fog again. Then, I inspected it, to see what we were up against... and cursed when I realized, again, that my Inspect skill didn't work out here.

Fortunately, that annoying Dragonling was nearby, and he could regale me with his profound explanation. "Strong. Agile. A bit tougher than me."

Fair enough. Definitely a fighter, then. As if the strength in its lashing tail had ever made any doubt of that.

Only then, when its arms and long, wide snake body was lolling around weakly, did I have my people tie it tightly on my back. Oh, and Roth tied himself in place right behind it, in case it decided to become problematic mid-flight. Soon, it was waking up, as we were ready for take-off.

I couldn't help myself. "Ladies and gentlesnakes, Onyx Airlines welcomes you to this non-service flight, destined for the city of human ass-kicking. We ask that you keep your arms near you at all times, cause I'm ticklish. Please turn off all magical spells and contraptions."

A bright light emerged beside me. "You call me a nerd? That was horrible."

"I know, Tim. I still couldn't... not." Turning my attention to the long, motionless form on my back, I volunteered. "So. Welcome. My name is Onyx, and this here see-through menace is Timothy. Move to the other side, Tim, so you can be seen. Their neck's kind of tied down at the moment. What's your name?"

A few seconds of silence ensued. A slight hint of suspicion combined with defeat told me without doubt that my new passenger was coherent. Nothing was forthcoming, though.

I took the initiative. "Okay. I'll be up front with you. Regardless of what happens, you're not getting tortured or anything. At best, we'll trade you back to your people, and at worst... Well, at worst, you get to stay with us until this whole mess is over and done with. You might as well get comfortable. At least tell me your name."

"Sigyle."

The word appeared in my mind without the lisp I'd expected. The voice was clearly feminine. A she, then.

"Well, nice to meet you Sigyle, though I wish the circumstances were different. You know, with the whole 'you're invading my lands, trying to kill everyone I know and love' thing."

She didn't respond. For a moment, I wondered if this was going to be another one of those situations like back when I was trying to reason with Erk. Then, she said, "It was not my choice."

"Yeah. I hear you. We don't always have the choices we want in life. Military life is like that, with strict orders and such. Still, when it comes to exterminating a whole mountain of people, that feels a bit weak, you know? Heh. I'm aware, I'm looking at this from the receiving end, but still. It looks quite prejudiced, ya know?"

Frustration. Annoyance. Definitely annoyance with me, but also something else. "No. We do not have a choice. Viperkin in the human lands. We either join the military or become slaves. No middle ground."

I was starting to get a hold of her way of speaking. She definitely wasn't dumb, that was for sure. It felt like she wasn't that used to speaking. Or maybe mental speech didn't come naturally to her. As for her words... I grimaced and let myself float for a moment on an upward draft of wind. "Ah. The old catch-twenty-two. Either you accept a crappy life or suffer something even worse, at the chance of eventually earning a better life."

She didn't respond to that.

We flew for a while in silence, while I let the reality of that hit me. So, if all the Viperkin in the army were indentured servants or thereabouts, fighting to earn their freedom and right to a better life as veterans on the other side... "How long do you have to serve in the army? And does that count for every non-human?"

She hesitated before answering. Mistrust rose to the surface again. I could almost hear her thoughts. "Why is he asking that? Why am I responding? Why shouldn't I?" After almost a minute, she responded. Her mental message was imbued with so many emotions, tangled up in a hate-filled web. Envy. Greed. Desire. Murderlust. "Not every non-human. No. Just... the lesser ones. We must serve for ten years to earn our gold stars."

The... lesser ones? Oh, damn. Hi there, good, old-fashioned

discrimination. I imbued my message with scorn, finding that it came easily to me. "Ah. I see. I'm guessing that would mean that all the species who look like humans get a pass. Elves and dwarves and whatnot?"

"I don't know what elves are. But yes, dwarves. Also tannerites. Any race too powerful for the humans to meddle with. Like-" Suddenly, she stopped answering me, instead asking. "Why do you want to know this?"

I smiled, knowing full well she couldn't see me. Sometimes, it was really nice to meet races with horrible mental attributes. She might as well be shouting her suspicion that I was somehow tricking her. "To be completely honest, because the way that the human army was progressing wasn't making any sense to me. Why have the skirmishers open to the attack like you were?

"But now I understand. So, non-humans in the army are basically treated like a lesser class? First into the fray, there to take the brunt of any clash, spread out around the *real* army at night to soften the blow of any charging enemies or monster attacks. Is that what we're talking about?"

She didn't respond. Didn't need to. The loathing in her mind was answer enough.

"Okay. I'll hazard a few other guesses. Stop me any time I'm wrong." I saw an opening here. The possibility of something huge. "Life expectancy among your forces is horrible. I'm guessing few even make it to ten years. Those who do are probably paraded around as 'good examples of their kind' and whatnot."

No reaction. None. Except for the fresh wave of loathing and shame.

Heh. I'd take that as confirmation. "On top of that, I'm guessing that those of you who do not sign up are all treated the worst. Like slaves. Sent to live in hovels or the like."

"No. They let us live by ourselves, when we do not toil. In zones. Do not interfere. Though, sometimes, humans come visiting. Destroy or cause violence."

Oof. So making non-humans second-class citizens wasn't

good enough. They had to ensure every part of their life was crap. "Okay. For what little it's worth, I'm sorry. Sorry your kind are treated like this. Sorry you had to be forced to be part of this war. And sorry you've been put in this situation."

Suspicion. There it was again. "Why do you care?"

"Well. Several reasons. First off, because I know a tiny bit about how it is to be treated like crap by humans simply due to who you are."

Not a hint of humor. Not a one. Tough audience.

"Second, because we have encountered that exact problem inside the mountain. And defeated it. The former ruler of the mountain also discriminated against the inhabitants inside. Not due to their races, though, mostly, but based on their strength. Anybody who was born of a weaker race, due to no fault of their own, was destined to a life of servitude and slavery."

Focus. She was completely focused on me.

"I took down that despot and instituted a new system, one where everybody is equal, regardless who you are and where you come from. As you might be able to tell from all the species surrounding us."

"You are leading up to something here. Tell it clearly."

"Hah. Yes. I am. The final reason why I care? I see a possibility here. All you non-humans are treated horribly in the human kingdom. Odds are you will die or are horribly mangled before you earn your freedom. So, why don't you come live in a place where we don't care about species? There are rules - of course there always are, but they boil down to 'Don't own slaves and don't cause violence.'

"Apart from that, inside the Scoured Mountain, any species may thrive. And, from what it sounds like, you and your fellow soldiers are desperately due for a change of scenery."

She lay entirely still for a while. Her mind was a confused mess, a turmoil of emotions that I couldn't possibly sort through. At long last, her answer came. "You are asking me to betray the humans. Defect."

"Yep. Sure am. It doesn't exactly sound like they've earned

your loyalty, though. Once you're safe in the mountain, do you really think they'll be able to find you and force you back? Their army will have to go back without you. As it stands, we might have trouble matching the human army. With you on our side, and the mountain at our backs, we'd be able to go toe-to-toe with them and win."

"I... No. They would not be able to find us. But you would not be able to win. The humans are stronger than the Secondary. Also, they would be able to get more soldiers. Ask for help with their allies. Bring a coalition army. It has happened before. Not often, but they might."

Good point there. A nasty thought for the future. "That is a concern. I won't argue that. But be honest with me, here. Would you rather have a life of freedom and equality out here, where you earn your own worth where there might be a risk of death? Or, would you prefer a life in slavery and drudgery among the humans, where you're treated like shit... and you *still* risk death and dismemberment all the damn time?"

She sighed, hissed a word under her breath I couldn't quite hear, then admitted, "Even *if* I believed I could trust you—a shadow dragon, a species famed in the legends for being shady, deceptive creatures—and joined your forces, I would not be able to convince the Secondary.

If I had proof, they might believe my words due to my position, some of them. Even then, there would still be no chance of me convincing them all. Some have offspring, family, or friends back in Nefren lands. If word was to emerge that we had defected... they would pay the price."

Well, damn. That was an ugly thought. Also, a point I couldn't refute. "Hrm. That is a good point. However, my own point still remains. I have no interest in killing off your comrades or any of the non-humans. The humans are the ones pushing this agenda. So, you had better think about how the hell we get past this.

"Unless we come up with some solution, you are all going to be entering the Scoured Mountain to be introduced to the traps and ambushes of our combined forces, in a place where we know all the shortcuts and can see you at all times. Even if the humans might have the power to press on despite that, you *know* who's going to pay that cost in blood."

She didn't gainsay me. Just lay still, not reacting. "It's always been like that. Why should it stop now?"

She sounded resigned. That was too easy, though. "Because we *make* it stop, damnit. We've actually managed it within the mountain. So we are going to find a solution for you, as well. Use your head and wrap it around the fact that you'll be better off with us, and we'll figure out a plan that works. I promise you that!"

I could feel her retreating, closing off against my arguments. "I don't believe you. You promise and you claim a lot of things. But you don't know my people and our plight. Leave me be."

Dammit. I overdid it. Pushed too hard. Now I'd scared her off from the idea. How the hell could I right this boat again?

CHAPTER ELEVEN

"We must free ourselves of the hope that the sea will ever rest. We must learn to sail in high seas." -Aristotle Onassis

"We're not supposed to harm the skirmishers? Have you lost it entirely, dragon? Where's the sense in that? They're *everywhere!*" Arthor's mental voice was equal parts astonishment and scorn.

"That is one way to put it, if you want to be pessimistic about it. Another way to put it is that I just told you that the force we will have to beat is suddenly reduced from thirty-five thousand to twenty thousand. Doesn't that sound better?"

The dead stare he leveled at me made no secret of exactly how stupid he found that. "No. No, it doesn't. You already said yourself that the snake thing isn't on our side, and even if she were, she might not be able to convince them. So, all you're doing is heaping another problem onto our already overflowing stack of problems."

I deflated, collapsing to the ground. We had arrived and were now looking down from a plateau onto the hind right flank of the bulk of the enemies' forces moving slowly below us. I'd asked the Talpi and Timothy to chat, seeing if perhaps they might help me see a way through the problem.

Except, I was getting nothing, and I couldn't blame them. "You're right. Damn you, but you're right, Arthor. It's only... Can't you see it? We would be able to convince thousands of battle-trained soldiers to our side, weakening the humans' side at the same time as they're bolstering ours. On top of that... it's the right damn thing to do, dammit! The poor bastards don't want to be there. They just want to live. And we could make that happen. If only I could see the path."

Arthor huffed but relented ever so slightly. "I see your point. You have a soft heart for aiding weak, helpless critters. It's one of your more... tolerable qualities. But it cannot be done. Our targets are right in the center of all of those skirmishers. How could we ever hurt our enemies if we had to make our way through them each time both going in and out? We have already ambushed them from below. They will not fall for that again."

"I know. I know. But... this is who we are. How can we show them we're on their side if we kill them by the hundreds?"

He walked over close to me. His usual haughtiness mellowed for a moment, and he patted my flank. "You will have to come to terms with reality. Sometimes, life is not like you want it to be. And remember: even if this is a horrible choice for the non-humans, it was nevertheless a choice. They knew the risks when they decided to join the human army, and the fault lies with the humans."

"So, they should have already come to terms with being slaughtered by other non-humans to defend some assholish human slave-drivers?" I snapped. Immediately, I knew I'd overstepped. "Sorry. That was not okay. Let's get to it. We'll have to find out how best to lay the hurt on them. Obviously, our shamans are going to be key here. The benefits of rearranging the terrain in our favor cannot be underestimated."

Creziel had been quiet until now. But suddenly, his gaze traveled from me and onto the enemies below. Wide-eyed, he looked back at me. "Onyx. I... think I might have an idea. It's risky and it will be hard to do well, but... we might be able to make this happen."

Moments later, Creziel was sprawled in the dust, outlining the nearby area of the Wastes... badly. Brilliant mind he might be, but his drawing skills left something to be desired. He got the point across, though, as he outlined the vast plains reaching from here to a depiction of a mountain several feet away.

With his claw, he drew a circle with tons of tiny dots inside, clearly made to show the humans. Then he created seventeen more or less equidistant lines in the ground between the enemies and the mountain. "This is how many days Firth initially believed it would take them to reach the mountain, right?"

Timothy corrected, "Sixteen left. We spent one day planning and getting ready, three traveling, and then what's passed since yesterday. She said some would be able to attack nine days from now. Though, you may argue–"

"Yes, okay. Sixteen." Creziel interrupted. On all fours, he leapt across the ground, erasing the lines. then drawing sixteen new ones. "Firth is already gone, and we've delayed them a bit already, so we may be off by a number of days here. Also, with their flying troops as good as gone and only ground-based scouts remaining... they're bound to slow down, right?"

I counted twenty-five new lines, nodding my approval. "Sure. We'll have to ask the scouts to estimate how fast they're traveling now, but... yeah, of course. That was the entire point."

Dust-covered and kneeling on the ground, his grin beamed maniacally up at me. "Well, in that case, aren't we posing the wrong questions here? I mean, the whole reason we came out at all was to slow them down and give our people in the mountain a chance to prepare and improve."

"*And* to whittle down their numbers, making the inevitable clash tip in our favor." Arthor corrected.

"Right. Right. But what if... we didn't need that? What if we slowed them down enough that they won't realistically be able to make it to the mountain? Or, it'll be costly enough that they'll *have* to turn around?"

I glanced at the others. Skepticism seemed to be the prominent theme here. "Sure. I'd say that I was intrigued by the *what*, but I wanted to hear the *how* now."

"Well, if you look at their columns down there, you will notice one thing about their cavalry. They may have loaded all those big ugly creatures down with cargo, but they haven't changed the way they move. Those nice, tight formations. Very pretty. Also predictable."

Slowly, ever so slowly, a grin spread on my face as I watched Creziel explain his plan. Within minutes, I found myself nodding along with the others, as we started embellishing on Creziel's ideas. I ended up calling the rest of the council over to explain the plan and to hear who had anything to add. Two hours later, we were off to set it into motion.

"I can't believe we're stuck back here and have to work while they get to have all the fun. This feels like we're being punished." Roth was standing on top of a hillock, peeking over the edge and complaining. Multitasking.

To me, it felt like it was more a complaint against not going to battle again right away than against the actual work. "Don't worry. There's no doubt you'll see action at some point here. It's simply a question of when and how. Maybe we can cook up some insane ambush again."

He snorted. "I'm not Grex, you know. I can survive for a couple of days without risking my life. I'm just saying this feels like an unfair division of the work. Okay, I *may* be a little bit envious of Creive and Grex right now."

"I get it. I really do. But honestly, I believe you should be happy you're right here. The humans still haven't had a chance to show their power, and I'm afraid Creive's underestimating them quite a bit. Grex also, but he doesn't care."

"Sure. Creive always did seem—ooh, I think they're attacking!"

We had traveled back the way we'd come, covered behind

my illusion... only we had edged farther toward the mountain than before, in order to take us to a safe distance in front of the encroaching army. Enough to give us a bit of the afternoon and all of the night to work in.

We might have been exposed, as it were, flying right back across the line of sight of the entire army, a couple of hours' flight out. Instead, we'd flown at a larger distance then doubled back to edge down right on the other side of a low hill that the human army would have to cross. Then we'd parted, and the ones who stayed behind got to work. Heh. Okay, this very moment, not a whole lot of work was being done.

Gawking, however... yeah, there was no discussion that our attention was well and truly drawn to the center of the human formations. We knew where to look. When Creive attacked, he made no effort to hide it.

A blazing lightning bolt darkened the sky for a split second. Roth jumped up and down at the edge of the hill. "Go Creive! Go!"

Indeed, it looked like lightning had indeed struck, in the form of a huge Dragon shape landing in the center of one of their archer divisions. Everywhere around him, smaller shapes flitted. Even from a distance of several miles away, we could hear the cries rising from their ranks.

Letting Creive and his tough, winged minions loose smack dab in the middle of a lightly armored division seemed like cheating, but... well, it was effective. Okay, that was an understatement. It was a massacre.

At the same time, on the other end of the human cargo train, bright missiles formed into being. I wasn't entirely sure, but it felt like I could hear whoops of joy. "Grex and the Imps have arrived, too." Their attacks looked different than they used to, though. Instead of the usual singular firebolts blossoming into being in a chaotic, unpredictable mess of bright death dealing, now the bursts were fewer, but a lot brighter.

"Looks like they are keeping to the plan, so far. The Imps are attacking in bursts to try to take down the sorcerers in the ranks of the close combat fighters. Try to remove them from the equation, while Creive lays the hurt on the archers." A single, brighter light erupted, echoed by screams. "Except for Grex. Looks like he's experimenting with that new feat of his."

Roth laughed. "That is a good Talpus strategy. Take out those who would be able to hurt you, then you can collapse the tunnel on the rest at your leisure."

"I agree. I'm... not sure if we've bitten off more than we can chew, though." It looked like my worries were unjustified, as no unforeseen traps were sprung on our fighters. We flew on, struggling to make the most of the distraction so we could arrive at our goal unheeded. Meanwhile, the bursts of firebolts and the cries continued unabated as the Imps and Creive's forces ran amok.

Roth whistled in amazement. "I really hope we will never have to face Creive. Look at him *go!*"

I had to silently agree with him. The archer regiment he'd attacked was a thing of the past. Age-old history. Pottery shards at the bottom of a crater. A boy band hitting puberty. Not a single form stood against him for long, and he'd leapt to the next company to continue the carnage.

Then, suddenly, a muffled explosion rang forth from below, and new cries of pain arose. These were different, though, monstrous. I couldn't see what was going on but breathed a sigh of relief when a blue shape rose into the air again, beating its wings hard as it escaped into the sky.

Behind Creive, his minions followed, fleeing whatever had just happened. Seconds later, the bursts of fire bolts died down as the Imps also decided to leave the scene of battle. I gasped to see more than one flying shape fall out of the sky as they strove to gain height.

This wasn't good. But was it bad or catastrophic? Too early to tell. We would know when they returned to us. But we were nowhere near done yet. "Time for round two." I grinned. Around me, all eyes were fixed on the battlefield, waiting for what was coming.

At first, there was cheering. The human army stood tall, weapons raised into the air as they launched derision and threats at the retreating monsters. They'd done it. They'd actually managed to fend off those bestial, erm... beasts. Those dastardly dastards.

I huffed a laugh. They had *no* bloody clue what was about to transpire. Every single worker and shaman watched now, transfixed at the scene as they waited for what they knew would happen.

The first attack couldn't have been more perfect. The human forces stood gathered in victory, all those who had, moments ago, been involved in a bloody struggle celebrating their survival, right out in the open. Then the rocks fell.

The cavalry had drawn into a defensive formation, seeing the airborne attack. Heavily laden as they were, they'd likely not be as effective in battle, but they were still prepared. Even so, they'd arranged into pretty formations, ready to react when they had a target. Tight and close. The first salvo of rocks hit three mounts simultaneously.

The effect was... horrible. Even at this distance, I winced at the sight of one of the feline mounts that was hit squarely on a shoulder, and collapsed downward, mewling loudly. Another mount right next to it was struck on the leg, and its piteous cries could be heard where we stood.

The enemy army froze for a moment, then exploded into movement. The waves of movement and sheer large-scale chaos reminded me of tossing sticks and stones into an ant colony as a kid. Massive confusion, followed by a lot of activity, but little guidance.

The bombardments didn't cease, though. Every few seconds, another rock fell with a massive impact. In general, they stayed above the cavalry section of their army. Sometimes, they hit. A cavalry soldier on foot completely disappeared under a heavy rock. He did *not* get back up. Only rarely did the rocks slam down into the soil to no effect.

Two of the few remaining fliers from the army took to the

skies., one spitter and one millipede thing who had somehow made it unscathed through our night ambush. They beat their wings heavily, working hard to rise up and do something about the attackers. Heroic. Stupid. Hadn't they *seen* the impact of Creive and the Imps?

The millipede wyvern thing—I'd have to have somebody tell me their real name—was faster than the spitter. It had a larger wingspan and greater strength. That only meant that it was the one to be faced with the bone-breaking impact of Creive diving at it, claws-first. At this distance, I couldn't tell if it died on impact, or if the blue Dragon had to bite or claw at it first. Regardless, its lifeless form was tumbling through the air seconds later. When it hit the ground, it buried several infantry soldiers beneath it.

Meanwhile, Creive's minions were hot on Creive's heels in their attempt to get to the spitter, but they were beaten to the point by a concentrated stream of fire. Moments later, the spitter tumbled through the air as a blazing fireball evaporated a wing. They were too far away, but still, I could almost picture Grex's cackling laughter.

The entire time, the bombardment continued. I was torn between pity and grim satisfaction. Turnabout might not always be fair play, but I'd be damned if they didn't deserve this. Fire Peak sends its regards, you smooth-skinned bastards! This had been Arthor's idea, and I approved wholeheartedly.

Right this moment, our Parvu beasts were circling far above, riders unleashing their heavy load of rocks and debris. They'd be far enough up they were ostensibly beyond the range of any mages, protected by Creive and the others to boot.

An eternity passed, broken only by cries of pain and the sounds of impacts. Then, the humans finally found a measure against the bombardment. First one, then a second translucent shield shimmered into being above the cavalry. The next time a rock hit, it bounced off the shield, sliding down the side of it.

The sliding rock almost hit an infantry unit right outside the shield.

For a moment, there was silence, then weak cheers arose again... right until the following rocks crashed down outside of the circumference of the two shields, hitting the center of an infantry group.

The next minutes brought a deadly game, with the human mages slowly rising to the threat and restoring order, with magical shields coming into play everywhere inside the encroachment of the human companies. Finally, it seemed like the entire human force was covered, and the bombardment slowed. But it did. Not. Stop.

I cursed, then spoke to my army. "All right. Everybody back to work. The excitement is over. We knew they weren't defenseless, and we've hurt them again. Now, we prepare the next surprise for the bastards. This one is going to be even more costly—at least, if we do it right."

People grudgingly got back to work. This part had been a bit more difficult, mostly because we'd brought few of our actual builders with us. We hadn't exactly expected that our outing would require a lot of building or digging. But, that was the name of the game, and we were in a hurry. We had a large area to prepare. On the other side of the rise, the human forces slowly got back to marching again, now with shimmering shields in place all over their forces.

A grim smile split my face. "It'll be like that, eh?" I thought. We'd just see who could keep this going the longest. It would be interesting to see their reaction when they realized that we kept the bombardments on continuously, circling the Parvu beasts out one at the time to rest or to refill their load of rocks. It meant, of course, a less effective bombardment, but it also meant that the human army would have to keep their shields active all the damn time. Heh. Not to speak of the effect it would have on their morale.

The effect of the attack itself wasn't to be ignored, either. Everywhere, I could see unmoving forms, cavalry or soldiers that weren't getting back up. With the Parvu riders concentrating their attacks on the cavalry at first, the effect was, as expected, worst on their forces. At least thirty mounts lay dead or hurt on the ground. Every single one of those mounts had been carrying massive weights that would now have to be moved to other mounts or added to the burden of the common soldiers.

For every downed giant cat and every delay, we made them walk that bit slower, stretched the time our people back in the mountain would have to train, gain attributes in peace, and prepare equipment and weaponry. On top of that, their provisions couldn't last forever. If they ever got to the point where they realized they'd have to forage in order to make it back, we would have won. Unless they planned to eat our dead. That was a disturbing thought, somehow, hypocritic though it may be.

Roth hadn't gone back to work yet, the lazy sod. He grinned. "You know what? There are so many of those non-humans down there, if they divided all the cargo onto them, they probably didn't even need the cavalry. But, I bet they're so afraid of everybody who doesn't have smooth skin that they don't even stop to consider it."

Heh. He could be an insightful little critter at times. "It was like that back on Earth, too. Only, we feared other humans, people from other countries and races. It isn't only fear, though. Also a mix of distrust, knowing deep down that you're probably in the wrong... yeah, it's a whole thing. But you're right. And that's exactly what we're betting on."

He looked at me sideways. "Do you think they've realized by now that we're only targeting the humans?"

"Heh. If they haven't already, they will soon. Bastards didn't even think to expand their shields to the non-humans. It'll be fun to see how they react when they realize we're only going against them."

"Fun." Roth wrinkled his nose. "I just hope they don't act against them. They haven't done anything."

"I agree. Hey, let's go see how the work progresses."

We walked down the hill together, looking at the shamans hard at work. They had also been observing the battle, which was probably a good thing. They looked pretty bedraggled. Drenched in sweat, the furballs smelled like dogs who'd rolled in something then decided to go bathe in a puddle on a hot day. I didn't say anything, though. They were doing amazing work. I walked up to Creziel, who was ordering a handful of diggers around. "Do you think this will work?"

He looked at me sideways. "The theory is sound. I can only guess at the hardness we need, and as for the weight they can hold... we shall see, I guess."

CHAPTER TWELVE

The enemy army continued marching closer throughout the rest of the afternoon. In the late evening, they camped, and Timothy joined me, looking down upon them. He smiled at me. "They have marched for longer today than they did earlier, haven't they?"

"Yeah. I believe so. They might be catching on."

He snorted. "Doesn't take that much brain power, really, when we mostly attack those who carry their cargo. I think even you might figure it out, were the roles reversed."

"Hardy har. So, tell me this, if you're so clever, you bloody light show. How are we going to keep this up? I mean, they have shown themselves to be relatively quick in adjusting to whatever we throw at them, and there's so goddamn *many* of them."

He looked at me sideways. "You didn't seem like you were doubting the approach earlier?"

"Yeah. That was in front of everybody. You know, playing the role of a leader. With you, I can afford a bit more. So, thoughts?"

He faded out of focus for a second, then responded thoughtfully and less flippantly. "Okay, this is what I think. They *are* reacting and are able to tackle whatever we fling at them. *But*–and this is the big but–"

"Heh. You said big butt."

He glared at me. "Every time I think you're actually showing yourself as a real adult, you go and prove me wrong."

I bowed my neck graciously. "I do try. You were saying?"

"Right." He held up a translucent hand then glared off into space. "Now I can't remember what the hell I was talking about. *Why are you like this?*"

"Only to mess with you, my friend. Only to mess with you. I think it was something about how they're able to tackle everything, but..."

He brightened. Not the light, but his expression. Heh. "Oh yeah. What I mean is, we're actually succeeding in what we want, so far. We're taking down those who carry the cargo, we ruin their morale, and we make them move slower. On top of that, they're pulling extra hours now, so the soldiers have to work harder, and the spellcasters even harder?

"That isn't really a good thing for them. Especially if we keep it up and keep them guessing. Like with this surprise Creziel's made. Also..." He paused, pointing with a bright finger behind him, back at our troops. "We've got dozens of people with plenty of experience when it comes to ambushes, traps, and nasty surprises. Especially Slither and the Aberrants. I bet you every single thing I own, they'll be running out of provisions or soldiers before we'll be running out of ideas to fling at them!" He beamed at me.

I nodded in time with his words. "That's actually a load off my chest, man. I have to say, I was having some doubts here. So, this is what we'll do. We'll pass on the challenge to all our people, ask them to come up with nasty surprises, then the council will take on the best ideas on a daily basis and... wait a minute. You'll bet everything you own? You're a ghost! You don't own a fucking thing."

He grinned at me. "Yup. Looks like I win, no matter what, eh?"

We worked through the night. I even joined in, now and again. It was mostly for show. Even though I could make the dirt fly to make a golden retriever proud, I wasn't nearly as efficient as the Talpi, who had added some impressive attributes to their instinctive feeling for earth.

Creive and Grex joined us at some point during the night. Grex was grinning like a cat who'd gotten into the wet food and knew the gastrointestinal results were inbound. Creive was... less enthusiastic. Uncharacteristically so.

Grex performed a flawless pirouette in the air, coming to a hover in front of me. "That was fun! So easy! You should have seen the infantry. *Do something! But they're all the way up there, and my arms are so short.* And the spellcasters? Pfoom! Kablow! Goodbye! Firing together like this? Effective! Even mages with shields had trouble."

I nodded, trying hard not to grin like a child at the antics of the enthusiastic Imp. "So there were no issues?"

"Meriz died." He shrugged and bobbed in the air, as if it was a matter of no consequence. "He was too slow. We said get out. He didn't get out in time. Those mages. So slow, but... powerful! And many." The grin returned, dialed up to eleven. "Less now."

Creive grumbled. "I agree with your little nuisance there. Not the part where he said this was easy."

"The spellcasters were powerful?"

He growled. "Yes. One in particular. I did not get a chance to see them. A few damaged me slightly, but one of them... almost hurt me badly. An air mage... but something more. It wasn't only wind. Tried to wrench my wing out of its socket. They came close to succeeding, too. I dislike that. If somebody is able to challenge me outside the mountain, they are... impressive."

"Good call on leaving, then. You did the right thing. How about your people?"

His growl had a different tone, now. Deeper, more... animalistic. "They had fun. We lost a few. Nothing special. Half came back with me. The other half are back with some of the Imps to protect those slow, flying cargo beasts while I rest."

I almost facepalmed at that. "Good that you focus on recuperating. It's important. I'd appreciate it if Grex and you took turns in resting, though. I'd like to have somebody in charge all the time. One other thing. I... know you don't much care about the lives of your minions. But think about this. You ruined two of their archer regiments. That still leaves more than two thousand archers.

"Now, they know what to expect. They'll adapt, be prepared for new attacks from the air. There are many of them. What I'm trying to say here is: *They can keep this up longer than you can.* Do you really care little enough about your minions that you don't mind returning to the mountain without a single one to stand beside you?"

The blue Dragon huffed and turned, sneering. "Don't stick your snout in my business. How I treat my minions is for me to decide." He started walking away with a departing message. "I will ensure that the ones who earn it are kept alive. If ever my forces are close to becoming weak, I will find some new minions."

That was not what I'd wanted to hear... but it was probably the best I'd get from Creive. At least he seemed to understand the issue with the overwhelming numbers in the human army. I was more concerned about Grex on that topic. That... might take more than one discussion.

Right before sundown, we stopped and started withdrawing under our illusion, on foot this time. The Parvu beasts were kept busy. At any time, there'd be at least two of them in the air, while another was reloading the large boxes strapped to its back and the rest were off a ways, sleeping, resting, or eating. It meant that we kept the mages engaged all the time, spending their mana to protect their people, keeping them stressed and, hopefully, getting tired and sloppy.

It was a bunch of tired, cranky critters that walked the wasteland. Still, we made decent time, ensuring that we'd stay well ahead of the army. As for myself, I played pack mule to the exhausted diggers, letting them rest instead of having to walk. Creziel surprised me by insisting that we stop a couple of times to add some extra surprises for the enemy.

The builders and Arthor didn't look happy about it, but they didn't complain, either. Damn. If this had been my crew back on Earth, I'd have to draft up some sort of special contract, ensuring that they stay with me forever. "Nobody wants to work anymore?" Not happening in this company!

We were maybe an hour behind the rest of our people when Creziel stopped working, panting heavily, and limped toward me. He looked... drained. I'd have to insist that we take a break soon, and give them a chance to sleep. Proper sleep, too, not just a couple hours.

Behind the filthy, matted fur and the tired lines of his face, however, the Talpus had a manic gleam. "They're almost there, I believe."

An understanding grin spread on my face. "You want to see it?"

He nodded weakly, and I assented. I looked at the people hard at work around me. The hardest workers, all the shamans, and Timothy, who was stretching out ultra-thin tendrils toward all the workers, boosting them as they labored. He'd come a long way from the diffuse, out-of-control blob of light he'd been right at the start. Or the "See-through hentai nightmare wannabe" as he framed it... whatever that meant.

I shook my head and started counting. Twenty-five total. That was doable. I sent a message to everybody. "Gather around, everybody. We're taking the scenic route."

In minutes, I had everybody latched on to my harness and slowly rose into the air. Not far, this time. I didn't need to go high in order to ensure that we had a good view. The enemy army was a handful of miles behind us.

Again, I was taken aback by the size of their army. Looking at their legions darkening the lands, it was hard to see that anything we'd done had had any impact at all. Heh. Except for the skies. They were entirely free of anything. At least, I had my view of the horizon back, entirely unobstructed... except for the occasional rock hurtling through the air to tumble off their shields.

I scanned the horizon, looking for the place. "The traps are to the right of those two large boulder arrangements, right?"

"Exactly." Creziel's response held not a single doubt. Well, he was the one who'd toiled on them.

The non-human skirmishers were already flowing past the boulders on all sides. To my amazement, it looked like we'd been dead on with our estimations. "They're going straight for the traps. Remind me that we'll need to reward our scouts. Estimating their route from miles away... that can't be easy."

"Right. It helps that they're still mostly sticking to their old formations... though some things look to have changed, maybe? I can't really see it. Do the infantry formations look different to you?"

My eyesight might not be as sharp as that of the scouts, but it would serve here. "Indeed. They've mixed their infantry up with the archers, it looks like. It's a counter to Creive and Grex. Creive won't have such an easy time with the armored infantry, and Grex and those... really shouldn't try to take on a group with a dozen archers among them. Damn."

"True..." Creziel mentioned, not sounding concerned at all. "Have you noticed that my calculations are holding up?"

"You're not hearing a single word I'm saying, are you?" I laughed and focused. Indeed, not a single trap went off among the lightly armored skirmishers who spread forward across the ground with little apparent organization. Our target was farther behind, in the center of the enemy army.

Maybe five hundred feet behind the skirmishers, following a few columns of infantry, the regal feline cavalry, led by our illustrious Lord Beardface, was barely to be seen beneath all the crates, timber, and bags that were tied to their broad backs. They trudged ahead, heads down and panting, weighed down by their burdens. So damn close. Not only that, they were going the exact way we wanted them to.

Creziel laughed softly as the last of the skirmishers went past, and the human infantry formations started marching onto the terrain. "Yes. I am a genius. Just another minute. You will see. You-"

At that exact moment, his laughter stopped, as the soil collapsed, and the entire front ranks of the infantry simply... disappeared.

"Fuuuuuck!" My outburst came instantly, unstoppable as I watched, crestfallen. So. Damn. Close! A few more fell in as the ranks failed to stop in time, but then they stopped, and their ranks descended into chaos. From above, a handful of forms swooped down, and fire broke through the shields at several places, hitting a few of the feline mounts.

Then the Imps fled away into the heights. I could almost hear their insane cackle, even through the cries of pain and confusion. I failed to halt a chortle from emerging, then sighed. "Okay. It's not all bad, Creziel. This *is* going to cost them. At least a hundred infantry went into those pit traps... and with the surprises at the bottom, not many are going to crawl out again. Still... what went wrong?"

Creziel didn't respond. "It should have worked. We had everybody jumping up and down on the traps to sense how the earth reacted. And those beasts weigh at least five times as much as the infantry apiece."

Timothy floated to hover in front of me and joined the conversation. "It could be any number of things. We may have underestimated the weight of their armor and equipment. It may be because they are so much closer together than the cavalry. It could also be the resonance effect from the infantry walking in lockstep and-"

"Resonance effect?"

"Yes." His eager smile beamed toward me. "It's known from many studies, where companies or whole armies march in formation, across bridges and such. It's the effect where the resonance—"

"You misunderstand me, man." I cut him off. "I mean, resonance effect? Don't make shit up to sound clever!" In fact, I might have heard about the resonance effect at some point, but I did so enjoy annoying him. "Anyway, regardless of what the cause was, the solution is the same, right? Make the upper layer of earth harder."

Tim glared at me, then raised a finger at me. "Yes." I deigned not to notice the bunch of curses that followed after.

CHAPTER THIRTEEN

"It's nice when you meet up with an old friend and see how much you've both grown." -Unknown

"Cartiga. Lady Eveny. Beardface. *So* good to see you all today."

The consensus on the people facing me was clear. The feeling was not reciprocated. Especially not by Lord Gamon. Last time, it took him a while for his face to grow beet red. This time, that was the starting point, and it only got darker from there. This was bound to be a *nice* chat.

It had taken a bit of yelling into the aether in front of the army before they'd showed up, to be honest. It was almost like they were expecting me to stab them in the back or something. Heh. Eventually, the leaders of the human forces did arrive, however. Nothing like last time, though, with them parading out in front, all fancy and trusting. No, this time they halted their approach a mere hundred feet in front of several mixed companies of infantry and archers. The cavalry had unloaded their cargo and were looking eager to charge.

Cartiga didn't waste her time. "Do you want anything, Onyx? The others did not want to meet with you at all, but I wanted to hear what you had to say, hear your excuses for your cowardly ambushes."

It didn't look like her heart was in it. Honestly, it felt like she was trying to prod me and get a reaction. Might as well oblige her. I huffed a low belly laugh. "Cowardly? Remember how we parted? Your last word. *War.* If I choose not to face you on a field of battle that favors you, you call that cowardice.

"Come now, Cartiga. Don't be ridiculous. I doubt you even believe that yourself. Oh, and if you are afraid for yourself, I'll give you this guarantee: I swear in the name of Deyra, I will not attack while we're talking or right after. I even called off the air bombardments for now. As a gesture."

She squinted at me, calculating. "Okay. Say I believe you... what do we have to talk about? Our goals have not changed, and neither have our orders."

I shrugged. "I just wanted to exchange pleasantries. Hear how you've been. Catch up with Beardface. Oh, sorry. Lord Beardface."

He growled. Actually growled. Not a bad one, either.

Cartiga held up a hand to him. "If you intend to waste our time with childishness, this meeting is over. I will call for my people to attack in two minutes."

"That's what's wrong with youngsters these days. No patience. But okay. Let me come straight to the point. I wanted to offer you an out."

She didn't get it. "An out?"

"Yes. A way out of this unfortunate situation." I shrugged. "Listen, it's not like you wanted this. That's clear to everyone. Some of the more... war-hungry leaders in your army probably did." I very pointedly did not look at the boisterous cavalry leader. "But you didn't. This is all about following orders, not wanting to lose your place in the hierarchy and whatnot. Oh, and a little bit about honor and nonsense like that, I expect."

I waved a claw nonchalantly back and forth. "But mostly, you want to do your job and go home. So that's what I'm here to tell you right now: *From here on out, I'm pulling out all stops.* We've played nice so far. Been humane, not used the really dirty tricks. So, this is *the* chance you get. Go back home. Tell your leaders you think you would have been unable to make it all the way to the mountain, let alone face the forces we have waiting for you there.

"Take whatever punishment they're bound to feist on you. And live. Don't come back here, just stay and live a long, satisfying life. Or better yet, return as a friend. I wouldn't mind meeting you if it weren't for the situation, I think. Probably not your friends there. They look like they wouldn't exactly feel welcome in my company."

I inclined my head. "I don't need an answer right now. But know that, right now, you get the chance to stop it and leave in peace. The next time, I will either be asking for your surrender or standing over your corpse."

Gamon and Eveny were quick to speak up about the inevitability of our defeat, the training of their troops, their higher levels. Even as they boasted, their emotions ran clear and hot. Hate. Fear. Disdain. Heh. I didn't care about their opinion, though. Only hers. Not that-

"We do not need time to deliberate." Her thoughts came quickly, with an undertone of regret. "Nothing has changed. Also, I believe that you are trying to scare us into an unwise decision. Our forces are strong, well-trained, and many. They are used to harsh battles and harsher losses, and your traps and ambushes will not wear them down.

"Besides, I believe that you are already throwing your strongest at us. So go now, and do your worst. We will settle this on the battlefield. There is, however, one thing I do not understand."

I tilted my head in question. "Ask."

"Why are you not attacking the Secondary?"

I grinned at her. You didn't get handed an introduction like this often, if ever. I looked at all the non-humans spread out in every direction of the compass, leaving only my retreat free. "So you noticed that. You *are* clever. Well, far be it from me to keep secrets. Let me enlighten everybody at the same time." I raised my neck as high as I could, started expanding my mental message to include everybody, as far as I could reach. "People of the Secondary. We have kept you out of this conflict so far. We have not attacked you, except for when we needed to escape."

"What are you doing?" Cartiga's suspicion was written clearly on her face.

"Explaining. Like you asked." I continued, spreading my message to everybody. "There is a reason for this, and it is this: *you are not our enemy.* Inside the Scoured Mountain, we have plenty of races like yours. They are not secondary. They are not treated less. They are equal to anybody else."

Beardface wasn't stupid. I had to give it to him. A look of realization suddenly appeared on his red-mossed face, and he barked an order. Then, he charged at me. The cavalry followed.

I leapt and beat my wings, rising into the sky. The charging leader grabbed a throwing spear from a quiver next to his saddle and flung it at me with all his might. Still rising, I was unable to turn swiftly, but I did manage to present my scaled behind to his throw, instead of my softer underside.

The pain was still ugly, and it took around fifteen percent of my health, but then I was up in the air and rising fast. As I flew away, I finished my message. "Your glorious leaders attacked me moments ago, even while we were talking peacefully. Why? Because they *know* what I want to say. That you don't have to fight and die in an empire that treats you like slaves.

"You don't have to wade through blood and gore in conflicts that have nothing to do with you, for the unlikely chance that you'll actually earn a decent life afterward. You, all of you, are welcome in the Scoured Mountain. As equals. Join us, and be free."

They were getting closer now, and I had to withdraw. Not without spitting a few insults back at Beardface, though. Attacking somebody at a parley? That was just rude.

A few minutes later, I was back with my council, who'd

insisted on waiting nearby. Roth undertook the painful task of pulling the spear out from my butt, with way too much mirth.

"Did it work?" Creziel sounded hopeful.

I shook my head. "Too early to tell. Way too early. But, it's bound to have an effect. At the very least, it's going to deepen the schism between the human army and the Secondary. Depending on how the humans react, it's only going to get worse from here on out."

Timothy floated over to me. "I have to admit. I didn't see it at first. Now, I have to apologize for arguing against you going to talk to them again. I didn't think it was worth the risk. But this..." He gestured at the spear in my ass. "On top of the actual results, definitely was. It's brilliant. Now that the Secondary has been presented with an opportunity for freedom, they will have to ask themselves some hard questions. Like '*what has the Nefren Empire ever done for me?*'"

"That's one thing." I agreed. "But honestly, I don't think that's going to bring a lot of people over to our side. The important part is, really, what the humans are going to do now."

Arthor sighed. "Speak plainly, lizard! In Deyra's name, you exhaust me."

"I'm sure you'll see it, Arthor. It's a leader thing. When you're confronted by someone and you, as a leader, are in the wrong, the way you react has consequences. And it all depends. Are they going to ignore it? Deny it? Come up with empty platitudes on how they're going to change things in the future?" I smiled. "We can't guess... but the answer is going to influence how the non-humans are going to react, for sure. Right now, I'm just spouting empty promises, but if the humans were to suddenly put out guards on the non-humans or something, to ensure that nobody wants to defect? That would skew things."

Arthor nodded. "I can see that. So, what do we do in the meantime?"

"Same thing we do every day, Arthor. Try to stall an enemy army." I grinned at my people. "You were going to gather suggestions on how to slow our enemies down, right? So tell me. What have you got? This is going to be *fun!*"

Okay, it wasn't *that* fun. Turns out, a lot of our people weren't exactly strategic geniuses. That, or their idea of simplicity or the level of violence involved was off by an order of magnitudes. One of them suggested that we could perform surprise attacks and then "have our fliers drop and pick up our attackers mid-flight and be away a lot quicker."

Another insisted that our shamans should be able to create custom rocks for the bombardments of their forces. I actually agreed on that one, though it would probably be way too time-consuming compared to the effect. And, as long as the shields were still up, it would be a waste of time.

The next week was... not exactly fun. But it was definitely more fun for us than it was for the human army. We kept up our bombardment 24/7, kept moving ahead of their army on foot, and kept laying traps for them. Weird to say, but warfare, after a while, turns into work. You wake up, you get to work, you estimate how far you've gotten compared to what you wanted to achieve and adjust your goals accordingly. But Slither and his people? They came through. When it came to traps, they were downright scary.

Damn, but we tried a lot of things. With some of the ideas, I had to be impressed with the theoretical insight of my minions and their mindset. First, the bombardments. Our rocks weren't making it through their shields? We took bigger rocks, combined the assaults. Turned out, three larger rocks, one of them a massive boulder tossed by Koa'tem, had no problem making it through some of the weaker shields they were using.

That made for a couple of fun hours, until the humans adjusted, adding another layer of shields. Heh. Also, our pit traps. Oh my lord, they had fun with the traps. The first few days, we created a few traps here and there, to keep them on their toes and keep them guessing. Heh. Also, because our people needed some rest, to be fair.

But next to our own traps, we had the Aberrants letting

loose. Damn, but they were creative. There were tripwires, cleverly disguised. Tiny caltrop-like objects carved of bone or wood that would pierce the foot of anybody stepping on it. Ankle-deep holes covered with leaves and a thin layer of dust, ready to break the leg of any cavalry stepping in. It felt like the Aberrants were working off decades of pent-up nastiness.

Timothy threw himself fully into the task as well. It might have been the mental distraction or it might have been the possibility of helping the Secondary. Whatever it was, he spent every waking moment trying to use his knowledge to improve our traps and other nasty surprises. I encouraged him however I could.

Not one to be outdone, Creziel was constantly attempting different thicknesses of the layers of hardened soil, promising me he'd be sure to manage to hit that magical point where the cavalry would crash in, but not the infantry. Well, he didn't deliver at first. But my other minions? They had fun.

The first time Grex decided to build a tiny cairn on top of each of the three traps we'd made that day, I scolded him. But he just grinned at me and told me I was going to love this. The following day, when we started the march for the day, he and the other Imps left behind a landscape littered with cairns... I couldn't help but be impressed by the deviousness of his mind. When their army arrived, they'd be sure to spend ages trying to locate which ones were real and which weren't.

Of course, we varied the actual traps, too. Sometimes, we'd make a tiny trench, just enough for a single person to fall in and break their progress. Periodically, we'd make them extra deep or lethal, litter them with filth-encrusted rock spikes at the bottom. The Talpi and the shamans made a sport out of it, and our other people started joining in with suggestions, too.

Sometimes, just for fun, our shamans would start altering the terrain to make it less approachable for the enemy forces, making potholes, turning tiny streams into waist-deep mud, raising barriers of earth and such.

I had my fun, too. Now and again, I'd surprise them, swoop

down silently out of nowhere in the center of a cloud of shadow and lay a single Weakening Fog on a large group of enemies. While their magical shields did stop my beautiful body from entering, not all of them stopped my breath attack, and I abused that.

When I hit it right, my breath weapon had anywhere between twenty to fifty of their numbers out of commission for hours on end. At best, that meant a massive additional burden on their cavalry. At worst—that one time I managed to hit fifteen of the feline mounts—they had to stop for half a day, or they'd be forced to leave the beasts behind.

After a while, they got better at keeping shields active to stop magic attacks, too. More burdens for their spellcasters. The only real annoyance was that we couldn't use our Talpi too often for ranged hit-and-run attacks, because they were so damn consistent at keeping the Secondary out in front.

My very favorite pastime, however? Didn't have anything at all to do with traps, attacks, or hurting anybody. No, winning hearts and minds turned out to be the most fun I'd ever imagined. See, the thing was, we were marching relatively close to the skirmishers. In fact, we were usually only a few hours out. More than enough time to fly to fetch the Parvu beasts and escape safely, in case the cavalry decided they'd had enough and wanted to try to take us down once and for all. What that meant, though, was that we spent a lot of time staring at the non-humans as they marched across the wastes ahead of the human army.

I don't know who started it. But it was a handful of days after my latest chat with the human leaders that I came upon Menea on the edge of where we were currently digging a batch of pit traps. The scout wasn't digging, wasn't creating cairns, but she was hunched over, fiddling about with something, and I got curious. Idling closer, she heard me way before I reached her, reacting only with a glance before returning to what she was doing.

What lay before her was a flat rock holding a couple of slabs of meat. We weren't hurting for food these days. Not in the least. The human army didn't waste time burying their dead soldiers, mostly removing their armor and arms before moving on. Sometimes, if the pit traps were particularly nasty, they didn't even bother with that. A number of Creive's strongest soldiers were hard at work traveling behind the human lines, carving the good slabs of meat from the bodies and returning with it. It was a grisly sight, but the arrival of the steak express never failed to elicit cheers.

Each evening, we would spend time together, feasting on the meat. Some had even taken in the lessons from Povel, the Talpus builder who so enjoyed experimenting with cooking. They added what little herbs and seasoning elements we could find nearby and cooked the meat over bonfires. Creive complained that it took all the joy from the food when you couldn't tear it from the body, but even he couldn't claim that the flavor wasn't improved from the experience.

That was what Menea was busy arranging. Four thick slabs of meat, slightly charred from the inexpert barbecue and drizzled with tiny sprigs of... whatever flavored herbs they had found. They looked like twigs, to be honest.

"Preparing a feast?" I asked.

She nodded, continuing to arrange it *just so*. "Yes. For the skirmishers." She pointed a hand vaguely in the direction of the enemy army.

"You're... Really?" I couldn't even come up with a comment.

She stood up, brushing her hands. "Sure. They're not our enemy. You said it yourself. We want to make friends with them, right?"

"Sure, but... you realize that we're trying to starve their army, right? We're trying to make them run out of food, water and energy, so they can't continue. Giving them food..." I trailed off.

"You're wrong." She didn't hold back. "We're trying to starve the *humans*. Not the others. Who do you think is going to go without food first? The humans or those the humans think are monsters?"

"That's... actually a great point. And, if they're working on low rations, odds are they're going to look a lot more favorably on us, if we try to help them."

She shrugged. "I didn't think about that. I thought back to when the tribe was starving half the time. Wasn't funny. Besides, some of the others already started doing it a few days ago, and I've been watching. The skirmishers eat it. So they don't think we're trying to poison them or anything."

I nodded, but already, my mind was elsewhere. It was brilliant. Obviously, a few meals here and there weren't going to change a lot concerning whether or not their army would make it. But it *might* change the skirmishers' view on us entirely. Saying something was one thing, but actually delivering proof was something else entirely. I blinked, returning to the present. "Listen... sometimes Creive's fliers bring back some items along with the food."

"Sure. A few spears, some armor. It doesn't always fit, but it's good quality. Better than what we make in the mountain outside Fire Peak, at least."

I nodded. "All right. I know there's way more in their packs than armor and weapons, too. This is what we'll do. We're stepping this up."

"You mean give them more food?"

"Ayup. And equipment. Also clothes, where they're able to carry all of it back. We've all seen them. Half of the Secondary isn't even outfitted properly. So, what you're doing here? It's an excellent idea, and we need to do more of it."

So, that's what we did. We stepped up our looting efforts, pilfering anything of use from the corpses. Uniforms, cloth, flint, and steel, whatever they had that an under-equipped army would be able to use, we took it and left as offerings for them to pick up. They took it all; not a single thing went back for the human army to recoup. We were watching.

Our approach was working. Every day, the enemy forces

were slowing down by tiny increments, being forced to carry more and more baggage, while their mages had to keep up a consistent output to maintain the shields they needed to defend themselves from our bombardments. Every day they were moving slower was a day we could use to show their skirmishers that we were the good guys here, and they should absolutely jump ship. Except the human leaders were persistent fuckers, and being annoyingly competent about things.

They changed things up constantly to adjust to our attacks. In the days after we first introduced the traps, they tried several approaches. First, they made their forces deviate in course over the day. However, since they were such a huge force, and we were able to build quite a few traps, that ended up costing them time, and they *still* hit the occasional trap.

Then, they made the skirmishers go out in front and poke the ground with spears at intervals to check for traps. That worked, sporadically, until Creziel started pouring a slightly thicker layer of soil on the traps. Then, they started sending the non-humans out in formation to trigger the traps.

That was efficient. Horribly so. The first time they did that, at least a dozen skirmishers disappeared as one into a single pit trap. However, either somebody in the human ranks had a little compassion for the non-humans, or they knew that using them as mobile minesweepers might hit a breaking point for the Secondary. The next day, they had a new development: six humans walking slowly among the foremost skirmisher ranks.

I was away from the ranks when that happened, but Arthor was quick to move back to me to tell the unfortunate development. "They're using earth mages."

Indeed they were. The bloody humans had enough mages they could use them as living trap detectors. Like Arthor said, they'd be able to do the exact same thing with little effort. Behind the earth mages, a solid mass of archers marched, keeping a constant eye on the sky. There were so many, a head-on approach looked dangerous enough that even Creive didn't like the odds.

So, we had to wait for a day and a half until the weather was on our side and we got a dose of heavy rain–heavy enough to cover Creive's and my approach behind an illusion. It took half an hour of waiting within a heavy rain cloud to ensure they were in a good position and weren't ready for us, then it was all over and done within ten seconds.

I dove low and hit as many as the archers as I could with a Weakening Fog, then followed up with a Deafening Roar to stun everybody nearby. Meanwhile Creive swooped close to the earth, dipping down to take out all the earth mages he could hit. Finally, a bunch of Talpi with atlatls leapt out of their trenches to fling spears at thm. There were shields. Sure there were. But none that could withstand the bulk of Creive for more than a split second, especially when there were also spears flung at them.

When we returned to our people, we looked like giant, flying hedgehogs. Both of us were riddled with arrows, and I was particularly low on health. That wasn't something I wanted to chance repeating. But we succeeded. The humans stopped putting their mages in between the skirmishers, letting them investigate from within their own ranks instead.

Annoying, since there was no way we could take them on directly. The good news was that they failed to reliably catch most traps in time from within the safety of the army, and therefore, they were still slowed down.

When it came to the Secondary, the humans didn't half-ass their approach. No, they decided right away to mess up horribly and show the non-humans they were not to be trusted. After I started addressing them directly on the regular, they sent human guards out among the non-humans to make sure there wasn't going to be any deserting. Heh.

I wasn't entirely sure what they thought that was going to do, and obviously we couldn't ask. But from my experience, there was no more surefire method to ensure that you'd lose a worker than proving that you didn't trust him. Here, they went and did that all by themselves! Suckers!

We made a habit out of trying on a daily basis to estimate the distance remaining to reach the mountain. It involved a lot of guesswork on the parts of the scouts, but over the days, we were able to see the effect of what we did. For the first while, the number of estimated remaining days stayed relatively constant because the humans covered a lower and lower distance.

When they started using the earth mages, however, their speed started increasing. Creziel insisted that the shamans would be able to outlast any remaining human earth mages and make it a duel of stamina. I was hesitant whether that would actually be true, what with the sheer number of humans, but gave him the chance.

It paid off! There was no way to tell if it was the constant work on the few remaining earth mages, if their attention spread too wide or... something else, but they slowed right the hell down again, as the pit traps started to take more and more human casualties again.

Slither... Was being an unholy horror. During the day, he'd let himself get transported and sleep most of the day away. Every night, he would fade away into the darkness, slip through the enemy lines, and spread terror in the human camp. His death toll wasn't that high. His skills were costly, and the number of enemy mages, along with their constant vigil, minimized what he was able to do. However, every day, the Stick Kin returned, grinning, as the horrified tales of his exploits must be spreading through the human ranks.

Everything was looking our way. Finally, we were starting to see results. Real, constant results. Until now, the humans had soaked up the casualties and marched onward without flagging or deviating and without us being able to spot any real holes in their formations. But now, things were happening left and right.

One morning, we had our first group of cavalry falling into a pit trap. Eight or nine feline beasts fell in and did *not* emerge back out. Most of the riders were dragged out unscathed, but the poor mounts were done for. Creziel wasn't sure exactly why it had finally happened, but he said he had some excellent ideas on how to repeat the success.

Then, later in the day, shields started failing for their army. Not once, but twice. The initial shields held, but either due to exhaustion or sloppy work on the mages' part, there was no secondary shield, meaning part of the salvo from our Parvu beasts hit the army with deadly effect. Finally, at night, the most groundbreaking reaction came, as an entire group of deserters from the Secondary slew a human guard and jumped ship to join our side.

CHAPTER FOURTEEN

Right on the verge of our triumph, the humans finally revealed their secret weapon. Somehow, they'd managed to figure out when Creive would be absent from the skies. Either that, or they got lucky. Because the only fliers present above them were about a third of Creive's minions and a handful of Imps, including Grex. Nobody was prepared for a counterattack, not when everything was finally going our way.

Fire was the first sign that something was going wrong. The singular, brief illumination of the Imps' fire bolts in the dark made our scouts cry out and wake the camps. I didn't need as much sleep, so I was already up, chatting with Timothy about the only right kind of coffee. The moment I heard the cries and saw the fires, I knew something was wrong, and I was airborne in seconds. I saw Creive's form slowly rising below me.

At this point, I cursed my build and the lack of aerial speed. I activated Aerial Burst of Speed, and the wind beat against me as I soared through the night sky, already too late. The colors turning the moonlight into a kaleidoscope ahead of me were enough answer to that. Those weren't Imps creating those colors. There were blue, white, and green explosions, and between those flashes, I saw something even worse.

My people were falling.

A Parvu beast dropped out of the sky, engulfed in a blue, burning fire, with one wing almost obliterated. The other wing was also riddled with holes. I beat my wings faster. A mile more, then I'd be there. Even as I had the thought, I knew I wouldn't make it. Another Parvu beast fell, this one burning with bright, white fire.

It was too covered in whichever attack it was under to be able to see it fully. My Imps were circling in the air around the enemy, yet their firebolts were being absorbed or... ignored. I couldn't quite tell. As the third Parvu beast fell with an inhuman cry of suffering, I finally got a good look at the assailant.

It was a single attacker. A scout. A weak, unarmored flier, one of maybe a handful of fliers left in their army. Maybe the single one not trailing along, suffering under the poison. Unassuming, easy pickings for our Imps. Unimportant.

Or so we'd thought. There would be no reason to keep a particularly good outlook after the remaining fliers, given how few were left. However, we'd forgotten two details, one from our battles with their flying battalion and the other from the ongoing conflict. One: the scouts were incredibly fast. Two: the humans adapted really well.

In this case, they had taken a page from our own damn playbook. There, strapped to the back of the hawk-like scout were not one, but four figures. Each of them was a damn mage. Bursts of color spread outward from wherever the scout flew. Where the colors hit, our people died.

My mental shout rang out. "Flee! Come back to camp! Now!"

It was too late, though. The Parvu beasts were slow and unwieldy. The Imps less so, but they weren't the focus of this attack. No. I was less than half a mile away when the final Parvu beast fell, attack after attack pounding away at its flank.

The moment it fell, the giant hawk veered to face me... then dropped downward, back to the safety of the welcoming army. I cursed and cursed, but I was too late.

There was no rest for the remainder of the night. Just one grim realization after the other. The first was the worst one. We'd been winning every single battle so far, but in one fell swoop, we'd lost the chance to stop them before the mountain. It might not seem like much, one attack out of many, really. But with the Parvu beasts gone, we'd lost the only chance we had to quickly relocate all of our people out of the reach of their army. And they bloody knew it. We'd been kind enough to show them exactly what we relied on the damn beasts for.

So now we were down to fighting them on the run, pitting our movement speed and endurance against theirs. From here on out, they'd have full mage accompaniment again, given that they didn't have to keep up the aerial shields all the time. Their morale would improve, too. We could probably forget about drawing the non-humans to our side, too, when they could see that their side was back to winning. Gods-fucking-dammit!

It wasn't all bad news. At first, I'd feared that our entire contingency of aerial fighters had been annihilated. They hadn't. We lost two Imps and three of Creive's fighters. The moment they realized that their attacks weren't having any effect on the humans, they'd pulled back and only attacked from a distance, and the humans focused exclusively on the Parvu beasts.

So, even if that meant we were well and truly screwed on the bombardment side, we at least still had the rest of our forces mostly unharmed. If they dared try to range out and annihilate us? Well, they'd pay, that was what! If they tried that trick with the flier again, we'd overpower them and smack them out of the sky.

With that in mind, we started the next day prepared for a marathon. A marathon was what we got, too. The shamans and diggers earned themselves a steady spot on my back, given that they worked themselves to the bone preparing traps even as we moved. Meanwhile, our fliers circled the enemy, looking for openings or possibilities to make the humans pay.

Except, the humans weren't being considerate at all. They were back in formation, infantry and archers mixed to counteract any flying strafing, with their mages near the front to locate our traps. With the threat from above mostly removed, they did a lot better at that. Bloody hell!

The following days soon blurred into one long, infuriating struggle as we kept retreating and trying to delay their forces, to reduced effect. We sent a flier to the mountain to let them know what was going on, give them a deadline and tell them to send any fliers that were trained enough to join us in battle. Then, we dug deep down and did what we could to hold them back. Quite often, it didn't feel like much, and we revisited the plan of going against the Secondary. That would enable us to hit 'em harder, engage in more hit-and-run tactics, and go all-in on the guerilla attacks.

What kept us from it were the few defectors who'd fled from the Secondary and, surprisingly, Grex. The defectors were able to corroborate everything that Sigyle had said. Non-humans were definitely on the B-team. Some of them bought into the whole shtick about the superiority of the humans and their ilk, but there were so many who just wanted to earn the rights to live their lives in peace without being seen as slaves or less. The mood in their camp was definitely close to bursting. There was talk everywhere about defecting and uprising. The ones who'd split were those without families back in the empire, those who were ready to risk it all.

Somehow, Grex became completely enamored with them.

"They are small! Weak! Like we were. But ready to fight! Like us! We will help them. Help them learn and grow, level up. Free their own people. As we have." It was probably the least bloodthirsty declaration I'd ever heard from Grex, but once he'd laid it out there, nobody could find it in their hearts to disagree with him. The parallel to how all of them had started from nowhere and slowly earned the liberties they had today was simply too clear. So, we used it instead.

On a daily basis, we'd ask them for input, names, details we could use against the encroaching human forces, then I'd spend at least an hour circling the Secondary and extolling the possibilities they'd have with us, at the same time expounding on the injustices committed by the humans, both in the army and back in their empire. For the sake of fairness, there was a lot of injustice to start with.

Oh, they tried to stop me. Of course they did. Mages hidden among the Secondary. Archers along the outer edges. Once, they even went so far as to divide their companies out to march among the non-humans. But when they did, we made them pay. Whenever they overextended, left formation or spread out too far, I was right there to punish them, as were Creive's troops and my own fliers.

After a while, they fell back to their original plan, ignoring my words and taunts, even as it cost them in terms of people jumping ship. They still kept their guards inside the non-human camp, but seemed to use them only as a safeguard against the non-humans attacking them directly, not interfering with the Secondary and adding suspicion everywhere. Unfortunate.

That, it would seem, was the right choice for them. For every non-human that fled from their ranks, they got rid of the most outspoken and adversarial. On top of that, we weren't exactly equipped to handle the pressure of having a ton of additional people to care for and feed. As such, the retreat slowly turned into a muddied affair, where, every other day, we'd gather a group of soldiers from the Secondary and a few of ours to have them march back to the relative safety of the mountain ahead of ourselves. It cost us. It cost us in time, manpower, and food, and the numbers that defected from their army was probably negligible in the long run... but I honestly couldn't say that I regretted it in the least.

Two weeks dragged by, and the mountain grew slowly larger behind us. As we got closer, we started receiving messengers from the mountain, informing us about the developments that had taken place in our absence. We sent them back with orders, plans and an ugly truth: we weren't going to fend off the humans. The Scoured Mountain was going to see battle.

At this point, our failure was inevitable. We were less than a week away from home, and the losses the humans were taking were, at this point, like a drop in the ocean. Oh, we still hurt them. Anywhere between a few scores and a hundred humans fell to our pit traps and surprise attacks on a daily basis, and we'd receive between ten and twenty deserters daily. We'd caused terrible harm to the human forces. Their fliers were gone, the number of their mages had to be dramatically reduced at this point, and their archers had been decimated.

We'd probably taken out three or four thousand of the human soldiers by now—nearly twenty percent. That made the odds look a bit better. If we managed to sway the skirmishers away, we'd be at maybe sixteen thousand humans to our two and a half to three thousand defenders. How magic and tunnels would change those odds, we had no clue.

As for the attackers, Beardface must not have been lying about their training or indoctrination or whatever. They marched on nonetheless, and if they hadn't broken by now, there was no way they'd do it when they had the goal right in sight.

We made the inevitable decision and called for a council of war. We warned our people, then, at night, I flew all the way to Fire Peak, spent a few hours talking to Ahzel and various minions who needed to know that; yes, I was still alive. Yes, they still had to continue with the orders we'd given until told otherwise. Also, yes, shit was about to go *down*.

The morning after saw a large circle of our people gathered on one of the foremost rises on the Western flank of the Scoured Mountain. We looked down on our processions as they marched over the wastelands. In front of the human army following them, our forces looked tiny and insignificant, like a testament to our failure.

Everybody looked grim. Especially Dimodeus and Wreil. Understandable, since it was the first time they'd seen the enemy forces. Wreil gawked. "You have fought this?"

Grex cackled. He really sucked at reading the room. ""Fought *and* won. For... a while, at least."

I cleared my throat with a rumble, attracting their attention. "Listen. I won't beat around the bush."

"Earth-ism, dude." Timothy interrupted.

I sighed. "I won't waste your time, I mean. We failed. There's no way that we are going to stop them before they reach the mountain. So, now we need to plan for the next steps. What do we have to work with, both in the terms of soldiers and equipment? How do we handle the defense of the mountain? How do we best divide our people? Where do we plan to defend and how?"

Dimodeus nodded officiously. "I should probably start... but first, I believe that somebody has arrived who has something she would like to say. I told her where she could find us, if she made a decision."

I blinked, surprised at the sight of Sigyle arriving, sliding off the back of one of Creive's larger flying minions. The snake-woman slithered closer, eyes unwavering as they focused on me. For the briefest of moments, it looked like she was going for the throat. "Sigyle?"

She stared, unmoving. Then she bowed. "I have seen your mountain. You did not lie. I will join your forces. On one condition."

I gave her a soft smile. "Ask it. But it is a bit late for this. We could really have used your help a couple of weeks ago. Now..." I pointed a claw to indicate the enemy army right out there.

She slithered a bit closer. "I believe you are in the wrong here. You will come to understand why. Since I learned that you are actually letting our people join yours, I have pondered how best to aid you. And that is where my condition lies."

She told me... and I just looked at her, mouth wide open in astonishment. Then I burst into laughter. "Granted. Granted and a hundred times granted. But... you are aware of the risk you're taking?"

"I am. But it is acceptable to me. This could work to the advantage of all of us."

I laughed again. "Oh, I agree. Does anybody here have anything to say against Sigyle's plan?"

Arthor was the only one to respond. "I believe I have told you before, dragon, about the dangers in trusting those you do not know well... but I have to admit that I am willing to risk this as well."

I smirked. "That's the closest you'll get to a wholehearted endorsement in these parts, Sigyle. I'd say he gets easier the longer you've known him... but that would be a horrible lie. We'll do it." With a rumble, I sat down and observed the people around me. "Well, that improved my mood quite a bit. So, hit me with the other news. How are we doing, Dimodeus? How's Ahzel handling the enchantments?"

The day made its way closer to noon as we discussed the developments and shared the information about situations, troop composition, and losses. Inside the mountain, they had been doing extremely well. The first, impressive piece of news was that the Corren tunnels from underneath the Blessing did indeed go straight to the far corners of the mountain, that they had not been breached in any places and was sound of construction today as the day they'd been created.

The staircases went straight down, then tunnels moved out from the staircases on each layer. It was a testament to Selys' efficiency that they'd managed to hide the tunnel exits all those years.

"As you requested, we have only cleared the two tunnels so far. The one emerging near Creive's domain and the one half a day's travel from the Soul Carver's old home. It means that we are able to transport ore straight from Creive's domain to our forges in Fire Peak. Once it has been forged, it goes straight to

Ahzel for enchanting." With a self-satisfied smile, he continued. "We have caravans moving every other day, fetching ore, delivering equipment for enchantment, and retrieving completed weapons and armor. At this point we are perfecting the whole rotation. I believe you will be very pleased to see the stores at Ahzel's."

"Harh. I'm sure you're right. Well done on leaving everything with Ahzel. His domain is the closest one to the nearest entrance to the mountain, right? In that case, the first thing we'll do after mobilizing our people is to have them pay him a visit and get outfitted."

Training progress was impressive, too. After hearing about the attribute increases that people were experiencing from their continued training sessions in the capital, even Roth couldn't find something to complain about. "Eight attribute increases in a month on average? That *is* good. No. It's *great!* Because some are always slackers. That means that some have worked hard enough to counter that. I will need to hear about their training programs."

I snorted. "Of course you will. In due time. Let's maybe focus on survival first? How about levels?"

Dimodeus shook his head. "That part is less impressive. We have been ambitious in sending out scout groups in larger numbers, with warrior and spellcaster groups ready to move in. Except, the upper layers are only now starting to really see the resurfacing of some of the tougher monsters. We do use the techniques you told about to subdue monsters and have everyone share in the experience, but... it remains slow going. Our forces have maybe gained three to four levels on average since joining us, with acceptable casualties."

"Three to four! Dimodeus, that's—"

He held up a hand, stopping me. "Not very impressive, I am afraid. As you may recall, an overwhelmingly large number of volunteers were former slaves with few or no levels. Gaining the first handful of levels is easy." A tight smile made its way past his officiousness. "They do learn fast,

155

though. And their enthusiasm is beyond reproach. They wish to thrive."

"Great. That leaves us with an excellent position. We have new, enchanted equipment, we have ways to move fast through the mountain, and we have a lot of ambitious fighters who want the chance to earn their levels. Heh. And we have a surprise, courtesy of Sigyle. So, ideas. How do we capitalize on this?"

CHAPTER FIFTEEN

"Consider the source. Don't be a fool by listening to a fool." – Sylvester Stallone

"There we go, Lord Verneth. Company from your own ranks."

Lord Verneth's eyes widened as he took in the sight of Sigyle. The very unlike pair looked at each other, then back at me. Then the expected outrage exploded from the human. "What is this?"

I glared at him and sighed. He looked exactly like the moment we'd pulled him off his ugly, wyvern-like mount and dragged him all the way back to the mountain to languish in one of the prison cells. Which... used to not be a prison, but Selys' old larders, but details, details.

Tall, regal, a veritable poster child for army recruitment. If ever they were to invent the cinema on this world, this guy was sure to become a media darling. Well. If it weren't for his voice, which was nasal, wheedling, and just plain grating. Oh, and the fact that he was missing an arm. Oops. I checked out his details.

Personal Info:

Name: Eufrenius Verneth
Race: Human, Level 38 – experience toward next level: 29205/38000
Size: Medium

Stats and Attributes:
Health: 560/560
Mana: 220/220
Strength: 50
Toughness: 56
Agility: 38
Mental Power: 20
Mental Control: 15

Eufrenius. *Snort.* Yeah. A decently tough and strong bastard, but without his magical items, I'd be running rings around him. Doing the math, I was pretty sure he had a feat giving him extra Toughness... but nothing else to aid him, apart from the three attribute points per level, which was normal for humans. Also, it looked like the Nefren Empire didn't believe in Training Chambers, or he'd have additional points. Interesting.

I engaged him, trying to keep my temper in check. "Lord Verneth. You are a prisoner of war. As you've so tediously explained, that means we would be in our rights to interrogate you, starve you, and torture you to get any useful information we believe you might hold on the empire of Nefren. Am I right?"

He sneered. No. That wasn't an apt description for the contempt he didn't even try to hide. He *radiated* scorn at me. Despite physical circumstances, he managed to give the whole "looking down on me" vibe a pretty damn good go.

"And not even that you manage to do right. Beast. Behind those wide eyes of yours, there must be a tiny brain, or you would not be capable of summoning mental speech. So, get on with it and tell me why you have dragged me here to meet with this *soldier*." He somehow managed to make that word sound filthy.

"I might as well warn you now, if you are going to threaten its health or torture it or something like that, it will not work on me. So, go ahead and eat it already. I will not cave before your bestial tricks. I have explained what happened with your sorcerer already. The treacherous bastard deserved to die for siding with animals. If you are too dimwitted to understand, I will not repeat myself further."

I shared a glance with Sigyle. Even after having tried to talk with him several times over, he got to me. This... wasn't an act. He actually was like this. "No. I have no plans of killing either of you. That wouldn't grant me anything. As a matter of fact, I plan to lead you back to your comrades in arms."

He blinked then roared with laughter. "So, the army has arrived, has it? I expect you will be throwing yourself on their mercy? Oh, I look forward to forwarding *that* message." The sensation of smugness was so strong from him, I swore I could smell it. A moment later, it was replaced by confusion. "But what do you need this beast for, then? What even is it doing here? A..." he squinted at her smudged armor, then continued offhandedly, "Captain of the Secondary? It should be with the army."

"She." I stressed the word. "Is a prisoner of war. As are you. And I will be returning her, the same as you. I expect the good-will to be the same as for you."

Given the sensation of mirth oozing off of him, I had no doubt how far from the truth that was.

I ignored it, though, pressing on with the task. "There is but one message I would ask you to forward to the leadership.

It is this: I deliver these two powerful leaders back to you safely as a gesture, to show you that their power will make no difference, and to prove to you that what I said about Lord Verneth's treatment on our first encounter was true. Turn back now. You know how much your progress has cost you. I promise you, if you press on now, it will only become worse. The chance for peace is gone. But you still have a chance to survive."

Lord Verneth blinked. Then he bent in the middle and dissolved into hysterical laughter. It took a while for him to come up for air. Long enough that I was starting to have serious doubts about his sanity. But when he finally managed to regain control of his faculties, he wiped tears from his eyes and addressed me.

"Ah. That was the best thing I have heard in this dreary place. I am going to love forwarding that message to our leadership. Now, let us be off. I cannot wait to be allowed the chance for a clean uniform and actual food."

I was impressed beyond myself. It took more than a little effort to be as much of a dickhead as this dude. But his arrogance actually helped. Within a couple of minutes, we were off, and soon I dropped off the pair a couple hours ahead of their armies before flying back to the mountain by myself. Now, it was all on Sigyle.

We'd debated it for a while, and this was actually her idea. She argued that her sneaking back into the camp was an unlikely prospect with the additional guards they posted in and around the Secondary's camp. But being sent back as a token gesture should bring her a brief interrogation before being reintroduced back to her forces as an insider.

When I returned to the mountain, everything dissolved into work. *So much work!* There were so many decisions to be made, so much to prepare in order to be ready for the human army and have our forces and equipment in place. Even Timothy complained at all the organization that needed to be handled.

"See, I'd read about this, that most conflicts are decided way before the actual battles. That the organization needed to ensure that the soldiers arrive to the place where they need to be, fully equipped, outfitted, and well fed is often more important than the actual fighting prowess of the fighters.

"Oh, and making sure that they have new ammunition, reserves, and replacements at hand and ready to switch in at a moment's notice. That messengers are ready to relay orders. In a protracted battle, proper preparation is key, and a tiny failure can cost you everything."

Huh. That was new. "Uh huh. I thought you weren't exactly a fighter. Where does this military wisdom come from, Napoleon?" He didn't respond right away. In fact... heh. I didn't know a see-through projection was able to squirm. "Timothy?"

"You don't need to know."

"Uh huh. We're planning a war here. Of course I need to know. If I should bring in Arthor to help us with the planning, I would rather be aware now."

"You're bluffing." He rose into the air to stare straight into my eyes with a deadpan look.

"Am not. You know the deal. We want people who are actually good for the job here, not those who struggle on regardless."

"Fantasy series."

"What?" I'd been teasing him, but... "You're basing actual life and death decisions on goddamn Lord of the--"

"No, I'm not!" For once, it actually seemed like Timothy's temper was boiling. "These aren't old goddamn *we'll just call for the eagles* fantasy books we're talking about. I know you probably won't believe me, but a lot of fantasy series are very realistic and do an excellent job at lining out some of the issues that can happen.

"Food or water goes bad. A shipment of arrows doesn't reach its destination. A messenger is slain and there is no backup. There are so many things that can go wrong. Sun Tzu or whatever may harp on about the theories behind warfare, but if you want to know what happens to a unit in a desert when their water goes bad? I'd trust a fantasy writer who's done his research."

I blinked. "This was *not* the road I expected this conversation to take. At all." I tapped the ground with a claw, thinking. "Okay. I won't make fun of you for drawing... shall we say, unconventional inspiration for these very real issues. Still, I think it might be a good idea to have someone like Dimodeus double check the numbers on some of the logistic issues and have Roth give a once-over on the decisions we make on equipment. You disagree?"

He shook his head briskly. "I'm not a fool. I already do. Inspiration is one thing. It gives you a good basis to make your decisions. You still need to apply it to the present situation."

I exhaled noisily. "Glad we're agreed. So. We're taking all the shamans with us? Even those who are currently finding us ore?"

He grimaced. "No. I believe we should keep up the production of equipment for as long as we can. If the conflict draws out, a couple of weeks' worth of enchanted weapons might actually make a difference."

"All right. If you say so, dude." I tilted my head. "Hmm. I think maybe we'd better bring a spell caster in, hear their opinion. Who should we ask? Arthor? Or... Raistlin?"

He looked at me with disgust. "I can't believe nobody's eaten you yet."

All told, though, the preparations were going well. Creive was keeping an eye on the human army along with all of his fliers, ready to move in case they tried something. We still placed traps to ensure they stayed slowed down. I spent most of my time out in the wastelands as well, accompanying my people and being seen. At this point, however, we didn't expect them to do anything too rash and unexpected before they hit the mountain, and we reciprocated in kind.

They tried ranging out twice, once with the human forces and once with the Secondary. The first one was the cavalry forces charging out in the early morning, bereft of their cargo. It was an obvious attempt to catch us unprepared and do some damage. We slapped them down *hard*. I was there, but hidden behind a veil of shadow like I often was these days, aiming to keep up the practice and improve my skills.

When we noticed them, they were still quite a bit out. It would take the cavalry about ten minutes to reach us at the breakneck pace they were keeping up. It took Creive, me, and our fliers less than five minutes to hit them from above in a devastating counter ambush. Before they even noticed our presence, we swooped in hidden in the darkness, crashing into the center of their flanks and causing widespread mayhem.

Claws and teeth tore, Imps and other ranged fliers unleashed damage at the weakly defended rears of the feline mounts, and my Weakening Fog made the beasts dip and slow. I was glad I'd taken the time to dip into Deyra's Blessing again, when I was back in the capital. To be honest, I wasn't sure if I could ever get used to living without it again. The boost in attributes—a fifty percent increase to my attributes and doubling of all regeneration rates and experience gain—was a godsend. Heh. Literally.

We might have been able to take their cavalry out entirely on that day. Unfortunately, they did come prepared. Within seconds of our attacks, magical shields and counterattacks sprang up from a handful of mage riders in the center. Quite a few of them struggled to cast their magic and control their mounts at the same time. Still, they mostly managed, and we were forced to pull back and attack through the plentiful holes in their magical defenses.

We harassed them all the way back to their forces and cost them at least a third of their cavalry. That might teach them to believe I was gone simply because they couldn't see me.

Their second foray was harder to adjust to. During one evening, they simply decided to send out the Secondary en masse. In small, unorganized groups, they loped forward, shouting and hollering. It was the first time they'd really involved the non-humans in a larger move and, to be honest, I couldn't believe it had taken them this long.

Possibly, they just didn't trust them. Or, they were starting to become too unruly in their ranks, for obvious reasons. But that decision ended up costing the humans even worse. We wavered between options for a few precious minutes as the noisy horde grew closer, before we reached a decision. We for sure weren't going to face them at this point, not after all the trouble we'd gone to in order to avoid killing them.

Once the decision was made, the path was simple. We sent most of our people loping back toward the mountain. We loaded as many ranged fighters onto Creive's back and mine as we could carry. Then we hid behind an illusion.

We spent a brief moment observing our forces to ensure that the non-humans weren't catching up to our running forces. A few of their races were long-limbed and athletic-looking, but to be honest, it didn't look like they were really pressing hard. My forces had the attributes to keep up their pace for a good, long while. Long enough for us to put the hurt on the humans, at least.

It was quite simple. Every winged and flying unit we had went after them, along with all the highest-leveled ranged attackers on my back. We moved as close to the human forces as possible, hidden behind my illusion. The moment the first shout emerged, we unleashed every single ranged weapon we had at close range, right into their flanks.

Without the Secondary to spot us, we managed to get damn close. Their shields and the infantry company we hit practically imploded under the combined force of my Weakening Fog, Creive's lightning breath attack, our Imps, and about thirty ranged attackers flinging spears and whatever from our backs. We left them bleeding, reeling, and exhausted, struggling to rearrange their forces so they could strike back at us.

Then we retreated and did it again, only from another flank.

A few hours later, the Secondary had been withdrawn to their regular circle around the forces, and we were back with the remaining infantry, who were taking a well-earned break. We were admiring the experience gains from the battle and laughing at their mistake. They weren't going to do that again any time soon, especially because we'd returned to see one final surprise: a large number of non-humans took the chance away from the control of the human guards to defect to our side. So, beside the battle losses, they also lost hundreds of allies, with not a single strike struck on their side.

Somewhere during the struggle, I hit Level 45. Finally! That would mean that... yes! My minion count had more than doubled again. Now, I could have 5000 minions. At this point, I might be hitting the limits on how many citizens of Fire Peak actually *wanted* to join our forces. Also, we were definitely way past the number of minions who were ready for battle. The actual numbers weren't that important to me. The vital part was that now, they'd all be able to join me and use our constructions to grow at speed.

Even if that was monumental, it was not the part that had me the most excited. I hurried up to put my attribute points into what I wanted (Mental Power and Toughness again. With the number of enemies, I needed to be able to take and give punches.) and gave a cursory glance over my personal info.

Personal Info:
Name: Onyx
Race: Young Shadow Dragon. Level 45 – experience toward next level: 13370/45000
Size: Very large

Stats and Attributes:
Health: 1410/1410
Mana: 1880/1880
Strength: 66
Toughness: 141
Agility: 183
Mental Power: 188
Mental Control: 242
Mana regeneration rate: 15456/day
Health regeneration rate: 188/hour
*Attributes increased by +50% and regeneration rates by +100% due to the Blessing of Deyra.

Looking good, especially the way my Mental Power had outgrown my Agility. I would probably try to keep Toughness, Agility, and Mental Power relatively balanced in the future. Avoiding hits, the ability to take a punch, and my Mental Power had all done their part in ensuring my survival. Not only did Mental Power increase the effectiveness of my breath weapon, it also improved my illusions and shadow powers.

Now, however, came the really amazing part: the feat. Another Defining Feat. By God, did it not disappoint!

I was starting to see a pattern. My first Defining Feat had given me a choice between improving myself, my minions, or my constructions. A choice of path or personality, as it were. I'd happily gone with Codex of the Trainer, giving my minions a constant +50% experience boost.

The second feat had expanded on that, asking me to choose which of my construction types should be buffed. Knowing that I wasn't going to avoid conflict in the future, I'd gone with the battle-oriented choice there, Gift of Battle, boosting my war-oriented constructions by +50%. And now... now, it seemed like I was getting a similar choice, only it revolved around my vassals. I'd bet good money on the next Defining Feat giving me a choice on how to boost my minions.

[Congratulations. By reaching level 45, you have unlocked access to your third Defining Feat. Choose one of the following: [Stronger Vassals. Every vassal of yours has their Strength and physical damage increased by +25% for as long as you are alive.]
[Tougher Vassals. Every vassal of yours has their Toughness and armor boosted by +25% for as long as you are alive.]
[Arcane Vassals. Every vassal of yours has their Mental Control and Mental Power increased by +25% for as long as you are alive.]

It wasn't the toughest choice, this time. Obviously, I wanted all of them... and both Ahzel and Creive would probably go straight for the Strength… but I cared about the one thing that had been on my mind right from the start. Survival. As long as my vassals were able to survive a fight, they could be back another day. With that in mind, I chose Tougher Vassals.

Arthor hit Level 40 and chose a, to me, surprising feat: Faster Mental Recuperation. It increased his mana regeneration rate by 50%. Usually, he was all about his mental power. But then, with him having toiled for weeks alongside the other shamans, I guessed that he had gained a new perspective on his shortcomings. Damn, it would make a difference when it came to large constructions in the future.

Creziel finally hit 35 and got his first Defining Feat. Improved Earth Construction. Given his aptitude for construction, this was not a huge surprise. It did feel like a cheap feat, knowing that Arthor had gained Earth Mastery at an earlier level, improving his mastery handling *any* kind of earth manipulation.

Right up until Creziel showed me the difference. The tiny Talpus was a lower level than Arthor. His Mental Power was also quite a bit lower than the lead shaman's. But when they each tried to raise their barricade, right next to each other, Creziel's rose faster, higher, and was more durable. According to him, it was like a mental blockade had simply disappeared, and now the soil did what he had always wanted… as long as he was trying to construct something.

The enemies were getting close to the mountain now. The ground was already starting to rise slightly. I, for one, couldn't help but feel a tiny bit of awe at the vision of the majestic peak high above. It was hard to imagine, looking at the barren sight of the mountain from the outside, that the inside was teeming with life in a constant struggle for growth and supremacy. However, soon we'd be able to show them just what they were up against.

In the meantime, a scout returned with regards from Firth. His message was short and to the point. "We found the first Blessing. It was a huge ruined city, exactly where we expected.

Much larger than Fire Peak, but almost entirely reduced to rubble. Not a single building is still standing. It must have been destroyed decades ago. Centuries, even. We had to move on, though. It was teeming with monsters. Not your regular monsters, either. A large family of behemoths I've never seen before. Dozens of them. I doubt we would ever be able to come close to touching them. And... they were above Level 30, every single one."

I took that in. It was a disappointment and the best thing that could've happened, all at the same time. Sure, Level 30 monsters were nothing to scoff at, but the scout told me they looked like they were entirely ground-based, meaning we'd be able to take them out from above. Heh. In theory, at least.

But I was honestly hoping there'd be a chance to learn more, find a library or something, and find all the bloody secrets of those enigmatic Corren. Who were they? How'd they manage to hold then lose several bloody Blessings? Especially when they clearly were damn progressive, both when it came to knowledge and the workings of the earth?

I put it out of my mind for the time being, though. What was most important was the fact that now we had a fallback position, somewhere to run if everything went south. It wasn't perfect, and being out in the open would be damn unfortunate, but the promise of having a place that would probably hold us and allow us to grow in safety until we were strong enough to face down any enemies? Yeah, I'd take that.

That was still in the future, though, and would hopefully never become relevant. For now, we were celebrating that the humans were doing exactly what we wanted. So far, they were marching straight for the tunnel entrance we had expected and planned for. We were ready in case they decided to move elsewhere, but for now, they played along with what he had hoped.

Our shamans had the terrain fully prepared. Once again, I was resigned to the fact that, not unlike large parts of my job back on Earth, a lot of warfare seemed to boil down to sitting on our asses and waiting for things to fall into place.

CHAPTER SIXTEEN

The human army was invading the Scoured Mountain. It felt like this moment needed an announcement, some loudspeaker coming up with an intro song or a ridiculous "Let's fight!" I was tempted to do it myself but forced the childish part of me way back inside where it belonged.

I had missed really spending time inside the mountain. Missed being able to inspect anything at my leisure, go everywhere with my domain map, as long as it was within my own eyesight or that of my minions or vassals. Now, I finally got the chance to observe the invaders in detail as they poured through the tunnels toward our positions. I was a mile away from the action, but I could see everything, Inspect anybody. It was amazing!

They sent the Secondary in first. Of course they did. No way were the precious humans going to go first and take the losses from traps and whatnot when they had all these handy non-humans ready to carve the way. In the tunnels, we wouldn't be able to double back and hit the humans following after. At least a full third of the soldiers from the Secondary were racing through the tunnel right this moment. I observed them as they ran toward our lines, weapons in hand. It was a long, shallow tunnel without any side tunnels, less than twenty feet wide. No chance of any distractions here.

I was not impressed. Not at all. They did not look maltreated, not as such. They clearly could use a bit of extra meat on their bones after the long, hard trek, but there were no wounds or anything to suggest outright abuse. Their levels, though... I had to hurry to get a general idea, but it had me frowning.

I'd gotten the same gist from the deserters who'd joined us along the way, but if these were the ones who were representative of the state of the Secondary? We could handle them. They ranged between Level 5 and 15 in general, with only the occasional outlier being higher. Those were definitely the veterans. They were also typically the ones carrying torches in preparation for the darkness of the tunnels.

My scouts were ready. They spotted the first attackers in front of them in the tunnel and started retreating, yelling as they went. The enemy followed. This time, they went all-out, however, and sprinted for all they were worth. My people were chosen for their speed, however. This was a sprint, not a marathon. They kept a comfortable lead, letting the hunters catch up a tiny bit.

Now the numbers were really starting to tell. When they were spread out on the plains, it was easy to discount how many attackers there really were, but here, in the shallow confines of the tunnels? The attackers looked like a veritable avalanche of flesh, scales, and fur, not like an actual army that could be defended against. As for the humans, they hadn't even started arriving yet. The numbers looked endless.

I could see everything. On top of the scouts, I had two of my shamans hidden behind a thin, fake wall, just a few hundred feet beyond the entrance to the main tunnel. Lurking inside their tight confines, they held back the fog of war, gave me an unobstructed view of what was coming, and formed the crux of our plan.

Yet another key player arrived now. I spotted the tall form of Sigyle, slithering along in the center of a small group of Viper Kin, shouting orders. Behind her... they arrived. With less than twenty feet of distance between their forces and the Secondary, the human infantry came marching in. Where their tight formations, marching in unison, and practiced movements hadn't availed them much out in the open where we'd been able to attack them from all sides, in here, it was looking decidedly intimidating.

I did *not* want to put my people up against those controlled formations. Not even somebody like Koa'tem. In moments, he'd be surrounded and overwhelmed—at least, if they were able to maintain their grit in the sight of his fury. Judging from their levels? They would be able to. It was *not* pretty.

Their levels started right about where the Secondary's ended, with an average going from between Level 15 and Level 20, and a good deal of soldiers hitting higher numbers. Frigging twenty! Only my forces and the Dworgens, now sadly reduced in numbers, were able to match that average.

I grinned to myself. Good thing we weren't planning to meet them head-on. Sigyle's group passed by my shamans now, and I judged the distances, counting the seconds. Then, my mental shout rang out. "Now! Slam it shut!" Before the message was even fully out, I started running.

I cleared a corner in the tunnel, covered in a veil of the thickest shadows I could summon, and I found the non-human forces spread out ahead of me. They milled about, confused and shouting, looking in fear at where the tunnel opening behind them had suddenly disappeared entirely, along with the remaining light of day. They were shut inside the mountain. Trapped with the monsters.

It was all Creziel's invention. Well, it was a bastardization of the sliding pit trap we'd created back in the Soul Carver's old domain, only standing upright. The shamans had spent a good while creating a slot that could guide the door to where it needed to go, working on the material of the ground in order to reduce any kind of friction, and finally create the door—a custom-built slab of rock, relatively thin, but hardened to the best of Creziel's abilities—until they were able to move the damn thing faster than an Ikea sliding door. On top of that, this thing came with a weight of several thousand pounds and was one-way.

The door slammed into the opposite side of the tunnel with a resounding boom, and the shamans locked it into place with a pre-prepared slab of rock. That was not sliding back any time soon!

The skirmishers quickly realized that, too. At first, they tried to make the blasted thing move, then started pounding on it with maces, or in some cases, fists. To no effect whatsoever. Creziel had done his job well. When they realized this, panic started to set in. Some glanced in the direction our scouts had gone, but the forward progress soon ground to a halt. Those in front started smashing away at the wall where the door had arrived from, guessing that it hadn't moved by itself.

Nobody moved forward. Nobody wanted to charge into the unknown without an open way out behind them. Instead, the foremost ranks were slowly pulling back to the others, weapons fixed on the darkness. Behind them, and from the other side of the door, orders and panicked shouts rang out in a cacophony of noise.

But one person shouted louder than anybody else. Sigyle. Her orders rang out loud and clear, drowning out any other voice. When she shouted, people died.

It was so abrupt and unexpected that few even managed to defend properly. People were standing around, peering nervously into the darkness or arguing among themselves, when soldiers next to them would grab weapons and ram them through. A huge, bipedal, were-bear-like person was standing head and shoulders over the crowd one second. The next, he was on the ground, pierced through the neck and both armpits.

Within the span of ten shock-filled seconds, the length of the tunnel was turned from half-orderly masses of soldiers into a blood-drenched abattoir. Now, it was my turn to react. Closing the mini-map, I faced the non-human ranks, let the shadows drop—and roared!

The wave of fear that spawned in return was almost tangible. For a moment, I had to struggle to keep the animalistic part of my brain from taking over, diving into the masses to rip, tear, and slay. But, even as I pushed that part deep down, Sigyle handled what needed to be done. A few loud orders rang out from her and were repeated within seconds from hundreds of people farther along the line. Split seconds later, the front ranks lowered their weapons.

I took my cue, let my gaze roam over their ranks, inclined my head slightly, and sent them a simple message. "Welcome to the mountain. Follow me."

Just like that, more than a third of the nonhumans of the Nefren army defected to our side, with not a single attack made by our forces.

The basis of it had all been Sigyle's idea. She insisted that she would be able to talk a large number of the more influential soldiers of the Secondary into deserting to our side, when they made it into the mountain.

If we made it look like there'd been an actual struggle, and the human army wouldn't be able to confirm whether they had been killed or deserted, she believed they would not be able to punish the families and other non-humans back in the empire.

We then ran with that idea and expanded it because... well, why the hell not? There was clearly no love lost between the humans and the non-humans, and since Sigyle already knew those who would never submit peacefully, she would be able to single them out and... well, dispatch them.

It was a nasty business, but it beat the alternative. In the end, Sigyle agreed to join us. She clearly saw more of a future for her people inside the mountain than back in human lands, and if she had to get her fangs dirty to bring her people with her? Well, the evidence was bleeding on the cavern floor behind me.

We retreated through the tunnel system for a while, switching tunnels every so often to confuse any followers, then we had most of the non-humans disarm. Sigyle and her chosen soldiers were very obviously allowed to keep theirs. I spent a moment explaining that their weapons would be returned to them as soon as they had proved themselves trustworthy and that they would spend a couple of days being led to their new home in Fire Peak.

I also told them that they would not be required to fight against their own forces, unless they volunteered. That seemed to reduce the stress among their numbers. They did not start the march right away, though. There was still no telling what was going to happen, and we might have more of the Secondary join them before the day was over.

I did not envy them the trip. The huge group of around four thousand nonhumans were nowhere as fit as our people on the whole, and the climb would be grueling for most, since they had already been marching for ages on limited rations. A bunch of my builders and a good number of Aberrants who were not ready for all-out war would lead them through the Corren tunnels toward Fire Peak.

It would be a hungry couple of days. We didn't have enough to spare for these numbers down here with us. When they *did* make it to Fire Peak, they would have to somehow divide the people safely inside the capital and manage to feed them with a growth system that was already pressed as it was. Still, in the days and weeks to come, I might end up envious of their fate. Even with a third of the non-humans suddenly on our side? We were vastly outnumbered.

I rushed through the tunnels, checking in on the mini-map and updating my forces on what was happening as I ran. Sigyle and some of her closest soldiers followed behind me. The human infantry had sent for a couple of spellcasters and finally brute forced their way through Creziel's hardened door. Now, the humans were stalled in the tunnel beyond, looking in horror at the empty space that, moments before, had been filled with their forces. Now, there were only corpses and uncertainty. From the far end of the tunnel, a couple of my scouts lurked from behind my camouflage spell, keeping tabs on their progress (and keeping the fog of war away from my mini-map).

We were ready for them, though. The next mile of tunnel held several additional sliding doors like the one we'd activated. A few of them were adorned with pit traps in front, just in case they thought their mages would be able to break through our barriers in peace. Let them send more of the skirmishers first.

Sigyle and her people would be ready to welcome them and explain the new situation, at the point of the sword, if need be. We also had a nice surprise with two tunnels, one being a trap tunnel and the other an exit tunnel we'd be able to funnel the Secondary into then seal off. We'd empty their ranks before they even managed to pick a fight with our forces.

Heh. We were ready for a fight, too, though. We'd blocked off a couple of tunnel mouths to make sure they'd get to where we wanted them. It was a well-known cavern. I'd watched it several times over and visited it twice as well. Creive's home. He'd insisted. If the invaders had to break their backs on a place, he said his hoard was the perfect place for it. We were as ready as we were ever going to get.

The enemy remained there for a while, sharp-looking ranks in front, mages right behind, ready for anything, while nothing happened. Then shouts went out... and they started backing up?

They were retreating? They were retreating! One company after the other were backtracking now, leaving the tunnels entirely. My scouts followed tentatively, nervousness becoming increasingly replaced by elation. I had to see this for myself. I ran through the tunnels, spreading the news as I passed. We might actually win this one without further conflict.

The humans *were* taking the logical approach here. They

had no way of knowing what happened. They only knew that thousands of their soldiers had disappeared into thin air, leaving only corpses behind. That, coupled with my threat from when I sent Sigyle and Lord Vernethback to them? If I were in their shoes, I'd be reevaluating my life choices right now.

CHAPTER SEVENTEEN

"If you're going to tear down a hero, you should never forget that you're tearing down someone else's hero. You're tearing down somebody else's son. You might have to face her one day." - Kevin Costner

The humans retreated, non-human skirmishers among them. The mountain echoed with emptiness, like it was holding its breath. My scouts slowly followed the skirmishers on their way out, making sure that it was real. For a while, there was nothing but retreating forces to see, and my vision through the mini-map abruptly cut off at the edge of the mountain. My scouts followed the enemies almost to the end of the tunnel, sharing looks of relief, even as they kept gazing at the retreating enemies. Smiles erupted, and a few cheers rang out among them.

They celebrated too soon.

Ten minutes later, it started. Moving in lockstep, the reverberations were the first thing that hit my scouts. I saw one Talpus put his head down to the ground, then leap up in alarm. Moments later, they heard something. One of them started running back from where they were. The other stayed... and soon, I had confirmation. The humans were coming back. They had only retreated to re-organize and rethink their approach. This time, they didn't throw full companies of Secondary soldiers ahead like cannon fodder.

Still, they didn't let their precious human soldiers go first and face the brunt of our ambushes. Of course not. A smaller smattering of non-humans, lightly armed and armored, had spread out right in front of the human army. Damn. The humans had apparently become suspicious enough of the skirmishers that they didn't trust them to act by themselves. Clever, but... frustrating.

That did neutralize the point of the next couple of sliding doors we'd prepared. I doubted that we'd be able to steal away the few hundred non-humans that preceded the shining human formations, close as they were to the rest of the enemies. No. We would have to move straight to the real battle. Heh. Somebody was going to enjoy this. Creive had been looking forward to testing his mettle against theirs.

I sent the message for our shamans to shut the doors before retreating. We could do with the extra time to make sure that we were ready. But... yeah, we were. We'd planned this, we'd prepped the area as best we could, and we were prepared to lay the hurt on the enemy. The only detail I really hated was that we weren't going to avoid hurting the skirmishers. Because... Creive's domain was *ready*.

The soldiers poured into the cavern. In tight formations, they moved in unison, terse commands and shouts penetrating the silence among the defenders. As they pushed away from the tunnel opening leading to the cave itself, they divided into companies, forming up on the far side of the huge place. We let them. It was all according to plan.

I dispensed with the mini-map this time. They were right there in front of me. As their numbers grew, so did their tension. There was fear there and a *lot* of trepidation. The amazing part was that the fear was mostly on their side. I couldn't completely blame them. I knew for myself how impressive the sight of Creive's domain had been the first time I saw it. We'd added a *lot* since then.

I still didn't quite know what to call it. His... fortress. Or bat tower. War-prepped stalactite. Ceiling castle. Whatever. The construction hanging from the ceiling was looking deadlier than ever. Every single corner of the deadly-looking upside-down tower created by the Corren had been gone over by my shamans.

They had removed any non-essential constructions, added protective formations to any defenses, and closed off any openings. What remained now was oppressive, threatening, and more than a little scary, just like Creive himself. Every visible part of the place brimmed with defensive constructions, armaments, or Creive's minions.

As for Creive, he was standing next to me on an open platform on the lower layer of his castle, overlooking the incoming army. It was a new addition, created after *somebody* brought the lower part of his castle crashing to the ground. And it allowed us to oversee the entire cave below through four openings facing the cardinal directions.

All the while, we remained protected from harm. That's right. A glimmering sheen surrounded the entire room—a blue dragon construction, apparently: Protective Cage—anybody who wanted to face off with Creive and me directly, would have to punch through a massive, protective shield first. It felt nice being able to flip the bitch on those bastards.

"They do look impressive as they stand there all lined up, don't you think?"

My query made Creive snort. He responded arrogantly. "Like it matters. I look forward to seeing what they can do. Like I told you, this is where they will break. Look, they haven't even brought all of their forces. They underestimate me. Us."

He was right. If I did the math right, and that had never been my strongest side, they had only brought about three to four thousand soldiers into the cave so far, and it looked like the influx of new soldiers was slowing down. To be honest, I'd probably have done the same. They were, rightfully, nervous. But this looked like something we could use to our advantage. "Agreed. Well. How about we make them pay for it?"

Creive nodded, eyes fixed on the enemy companies. A loud shout had them slowly moving forward. "A bit more, and we can get this started."

"Yeah. And we've got our other fighters ready to move in, if need be." I eyed the far end of the cavern, where our forces were hidden behind a layer of illusion. A couple of hundred fighters waited, mostly Aberrants, led by Koa'tem, bolstered by Roth and a dozen of our most talented fighters.

I doubted that the illusion would be able to keep them hidden from thousands of soldiers and dozens of spellcasters throughout an entire battle. If it did, great. Then we could ambush the hell out of them later on. I wasn't betting on it, though. They were mostly there in case. If we were hard pressed, they could move in quickly to aid Creive's minions. If the human forces spotted them and went for them, they could lead them farther into the mountain, to introduce them to the Aberrant and Talpi way of warfare: traps and ambushes.

I eyed the foremost enemy companies that were slowly shuffling across the uneven flooring of the cavern. "Looks like they're getting there, aren't they? Want to do something about it?"

It was true. The lead non-human skirmishers were ambling closer over the uneven ground, readying throwing weapons and, in a few cases, bows and arrows. Behind them, a row of four companies of heavy warriors were marching forward, followed by another four archer companies.

"The non-humans are too few and too weak. They cannot hurt us. I will ignore them, save the surprise for their main formations."

Fair enough. As the non-humans drew closer, missiles started flying through the air toward us, and I had to agree with Creive's assessment. They couldn't touch him. Honestly, they probably wouldn't be able to cause any damage, even if they'd been left untouched. Most of the missiles would just bounce off the shield surrounding Creive and myself.

Whatever few shots might range higher, toward the minions waiting on the higher levels, would be met with a different kind of protection. Namely, the fact that my shamans had carved stone shields, crenellations, and other types of protection for the minions to hide behind. But even so, Creive had activated his Air Control and thrown a strong headwind against the enemies. Enemy missiles were simply flung wildly off course.

I grunted in approval. "Good call. The non-humans won't be able to do much damage, and their archers will pretty much be useless now. Those human companies might have some tricks up their sleeve, though."

Creive snorted. "Sure. We have already ensured their archers will be useless. They believe those swords will hurt us? And the shields? Are they blind? They must reach us first."

I joined him in a low laugh. The bottom part of his fortress was at least fifty feet off the ground. They'd have to build a really impressive human tower to reach our position. Still, there was no doubt they'd have some strategy planned, some weapon hidden to unleash... oh.

I nodded in appreciation of the scenario unfolding below us. "So, that's why they brought shield carriers." In front of us, the foremost human infantry formations were seamlessly blending in with the archer companies... and suddenly, every archer had a fighter accompanying him, ready to protect him with his large shield. "That looks efficient. No easy way to hit the archers, if they're protected. Smooth move, too. It looked really well-practiced."

Creive rumbled in agreement. "That would have been really annoying, if their archers were any good. Besides, they're getting in range."

I nodded and closed my eyes to slits. I knew what was coming. Poor damn soldiers.

Below me, the ground of the cavern lit up. One second, it was dark, lifeless soil. The next, it held a slowly growing grid of blue light. Light that seemed to be growing, covering the entire area within several hundred feet of the fortress.

Soldiers cried out in shock and surprise, drawing back. Too late. Way too late. The foremost companies were well within the squarish area of the grid and too far away from the edges. Plus, the brightness of the light was growing.

The pitch of the cries was changing now, from surprise to outright pain. As they grew, so did the brilliance of the light, until I had trouble seeing anything below from the blinding light.

Creive called the construction a Lightning Web. It stretched from four poles placed at each corner of the construction—poles which, I might add, had been cleverly disguised by soil and stone by my shamans. The result was a nasty, deadly surprise.

Now, the lightning was reaching its maximal power. I tried not to look too close, not to see the details, as the enemy soldiers beneath me were cooked in their armor. But it was inescapable. Here and there, what I deemed to be high-level soldiers struggled against the elemental assault, trying to flee the area and failing, falling. The torrents running through them were simply too strong.

Creive said he'd tested it and found it "effective." I did not ask... didn't want to know more! The only thing I could say for certain was that he was entirely right. The soldiers below us were being cooked alive.

A few patches erupted inside their forces, with paler light shooting out in circles to enclose groups of soldiers. Shields. Those must be the mages inside their formations, trying to protect themselves and their comrades. Except... within seconds, the shields started fading away again. Two, no, three shields remained active, though, standing against the test of the lightning, while the rest of them disappeared and the people within died horrible, messy deaths.

Then the luminescence disappeared, leaving spots in my vision. It was so sudden that I was left blinking and wondering what the hell just happened. I was drawn to the sight of

Creive, as he slowly lumbered toward the edge of the chamber.

He shot me a parting glance. "Now I get to have fun too." Then he roared and leapt into the open air.

I joined him within seconds, leaping from the edge of the shielded chamber and veering straight at one of the shields that still held strong on the ground below. A glance at the edges of the cavern beyond showed me that no other forces were incoming. Not yet, even though Creive was already homing in on one of the few shields still standing.

The shield I went for was at the far end from Creive. The humans inside were standing stock still, bright shields enclosing every edge of their forces. Shocked into submission, then.

The soldiers below weren't. They were clearly rattled by what had happened. Dead soldiers lay in piles on all sides, and only about a dozen huddled inside the shield of one spellcaster. But, the moment they spotted me, they raised weapons in my direction, and the first arrows flew.

I didn't mess about. It was a question of time before the larger part of the human army reacted, and I didn't want to be caught up in that. I dove at them and sent a Weakening Fog their way, growling as it faded away the second it hit the glowing shield. *How strong is this shield?* I landed hard fifty feet from them, picked up a corpse, and flung it at their group. It passed straight through the outline of the shield and hit one of the archers. *Ah. It only works against magic.* That made sense. So, some spellcasters only had shields against physical attack. They were among the piles of corpses now. A lucky few also had shields against magical attacks. I bounded across the ground and flung myself at the humans, even as an arrow affixed itself in my wing, like a nagging pain.

I had to admire their courage. They stood tall and faced me, swords and spears reaching toward me behind their shields. But I wasn't playing around. Not today. As soon as I breached the shield, which let me pass without any sensation whatsoever, I unleashed a Deafening Roar, and that was enough to seal their fate. Whether it was due to low levels or my massively increased Mental Power, the shockwave of my skill dropped almost all of them insensate to the ground. Just two of the fighters remained standing, trembling legs indicating that they were not unaffected. A minute later, they were all dead.

Creive was already back inside his chamber when I made it up there. He licked blood from off a claw as he glanced at me before looking into the distance. "That was a test. Now. Now, we will see their true strength."

Time proved him right. A while later, a blue haze appeared among the remaining forces. Another magic sphere, but this one was different. For one, it was larger than the others. On top of that, it was obscure, swirling mists hiding the figures within. Slowly, the shield started moving toward us.

Creive grunted. "This is it. This will be their strongest. See. They hold the weak ones back. They know that their participation will be inconsequential for this test of strength."

I squinted, trying to make out what was inside the damn sphere and failing. There were definitely more figures within... but how many? Five? Fifty? I couldn't tell. "You don't plan to face them head on, do you?"

He growled with bemusement. "They do not face me one-on-one, do they? Why should I give them that honor? No. They try to take me down in my hoard... meaning, that is what they'll taste!"

The shield was coming closer now. We still hadn't seen anything ranging out from within the shield. In fact, there was nothing at all to be learned from it, no sign of what we'd be facing... no sound, even. The human army was arrayed in formation, waiting, silently observing the colored shield progressing through the cavern. I zoomed in on the minimap to watch their expressions.

Hatred, hope... and nerves. One grown-ass man was visibly chewing his nails. So, they weren't sure whatever they were up to was going to work, either. Interesting.

Now, the blue-white shape was starting to navigate among

the corpses. It undulated slightly and moved a bit sideways occasionally. "The shield has got to be focused on a single person. It moves like it follows somebody, at least."

Creive grunted. "Let's start testing their strength, then." With his frown, the Lightning Web ignited below us again.

I squinted, then tried to focus beyond the glaring light. The shield below was still going strong and... not dimming at all. It was still moving forward, too. "That didn't do much. What's next?"

The blue dragon looked straight at me and bared his teeth. In the bright light, the huge form looked demonic, almost feverish. "Now? Now, I show them our real strength." He unleashed a massive roar into the cavern, and his mental voice slammed out for everybody to hear. "You would challenge me in my home? Creive? You may believe that you are strong, but until now, you have only experienced the fake strength of a shadow dragon. Now? Now, you will feel the real strength of somebody who knows and values Deyra's words. Now, you will *suffer!*"

Fake strength? How bloody rude! I saved that discussion for later as a mental command rang out from Creive, reverberating into the fortress above. It was tinged with bloodlust and eagerness. Seconds later, the fortress responded.

For a couple of seconds, I was completely blinded. From below, the shimmering of the magical shield fought with the blinding luminescence of the Lightning Web as it sparked and spattered back and forth in dazzling movement. Now, it was also joined by numerous streams of light that rained down from above to impact the sphere of magic from above. Darker streaks also rained down alongside the other attacks. Those had to be non-magical attacks from Creive's minions. Those others, though. "What *is* that, Creive? I mean, not the arrows or the fire attacks from your Imps. I recognize those."

"Lightning towers. They work differently from your Shadow towers. These add lightning damage to anything shot from within their protection," he said proudly.

I nodded appreciatively. That would deal extra damage and...

probably some stunning effects or worse on top of the regular missiles. Nasty. I remembered my experiences with getting shocked from electricity at work. Yes, that was plural. Apparently, I'm a slow learner. But I definitely didn't relish the thought of going up against that in combat, having to fight through the experience of getting shocked. Heh. In addition to the "minor" inconvenience of getting hit with an arrow or other missile, of course.

The magical shield below didn't waver, though. It *was* dulling somewhat, perhaps, but the forward progress continued, as it moved even closer. Creive hissed under his breath, "A bit closer. Yes."

The sphere was a few hundred feet from the bottom of the tower now.

I glanced at Creive. "Listen. I don't think that the magic is getting through that shield. Do you think we should stop the Lightning Web and have the Aberrants attack? We ought to hit them before the rest of their forces attack."

He looked like he was about to lunge at me. Instead, he growled right in my face. "No. I will beat them. You will see. In moments, they will enter the range of... now. Watch!"

I watched, and I saw. Now, the blinding lights were followed by other missiles. Heavier ones, impacting the surface of the sphere below with dull booms. Large missiles, too. I frowned. "What are those? They're moving too fast to be rocks."

He grinned maniacally, crouching at the edge to peer down upon the shield. "They *are* just rocks. But we have made massive slings for my largest Culdren. They can fling the rocks hard enough to break the shell of a Vouren. I would like to watch them take that!"

I... very much would not. I couldn't help but feel a knot of nervousness building in the pit of my stomach. "They're still moving, Creive. We need to do something else!"

"No! Look. The shield is failing."

It was dimming. It was true. The brilliance was slowly fading, and within, a bunch of figures were slowly growing visible. A circle of people holding staffs. Was that a circle of mages holding the shield in unison, surrounding a smaller figure? Did it even matter, though? What mattered was that they were growing close to us. They stopped advancing. "I... think they've gotten in range to where they wanted to be, Creive. Be prepared."

"Oh, I am prepared. We are protected. We are shielded. What would they even be able to do to me?"

I had no clue. I just knew that the fact that they'd moved this far without showing their hand gave me bad nerves.

Then the swaying started.

At first, it was more of a gentle push. A slight sideways movement that I almost ignored as a figment of the imagination. Then came another. This time, it was enough that I felt it, as a shudder moving through the entire fortress. Like that, I knew what they were going to do. Because it was exactly what I'd planned to do to Creive himself, ages ago, when I'd first faced off against him.

"They're bringing down the fortress. We need to move on them *now!*"

"No! We will keep up the attack. The shamans have hardened the structure."

I sprang for one of the openings, even as another, larger, shudder went through the fortress. I was fairly certain I heard a loud cracking noise somewhere. "Does it *feel* like it's holding? Do it already!"

Then I leapt out into the air.

Bad timing. I hissed as a missile from above impacted on my back. The pain and lightning short-circuited my brain for a second, before I managed to focus again and get my wings cooperating. Then I zoomed in on the magical shield and started circling to approach them from behind, where the risk of being shot from the fortress wasn't as huge. I sent a message to the Aberrants. "We need all ranged fighters out to hit the shield now!" Then, I concentrated on speed.

Behind and above me, the sound of beating wings alerted me to Creive's arrival.

His mental voice sounded anything but satisfied, though, as he complained. "This is not necessary. We will-"

I never found out what he was about to say. A massive rumbling sound drowned out all other noises in the cavern. Then it was joined by screams. I looked behind and up... and saw Creive's fortress tearing itself apart as a widening crack traveled through the top of the huge construction.

Panicking, I sent a message to the Aberrants again. "Move! Move back! Now!" Then I glanced at the huge stalactite, only to see that Creive's minions had gone beyond waiting for his instructions. They were taking the matter in their own hands, flinging themselves from the fortress and into the open air.

Below, I could see the almost see-through facade of the magical shield moving again, as the humans were rushing back toward the protection of their army. Torn between possibilities, I looked back and forth between the two major exits of the vast cave. Finally, I swore and halted my dive, beating my wings hard to return to our forces.

I made it into the safety of the open tunnel amidst a rush of Creive's minions, who were fleeing for their lives. There were... a lot fewer than I recalled seeing earlier. Hopefully, they were right on our heels. Creive did not follow us. He was beating his wings hard, following the humans, seemingly caught up in the mindless need to attack them.

Then the fortress fell.

In my time as a construction worker, I'd been exposed to a lot of noise. I'd seen mansions torn down, huge silos brought down by explosives, and even one very unintentional collapse of a three-story building, as a planned demolition went all kinds of wrong. I'd never heard anything as loud as this. My people and the Aberrants had retreated into the relative safety of the tunnel, and I hit the ground running, rushing in behind them. Then, an explosion of dust removed any semblance of vision, even as the noise deafened me completely, and the tremor of the impact sent a wave through the ground hard enough to throw people around inside the tunnel.

I still sent constant mental shouts toward Creive, trying to find him, tell him where we were, which way he'd be able to escape, anything. But there was no response at all. Then, I retreated into the mini-map to try to see if I could spot something. Anything. There was nothing. I don't know why I would have figured otherwise. The map showed everything as it was in real life, and since real life was covered with dust everywhere, so was the map. Then, I brought up my personal info and saw my experience slowly climbing up. The stupid idiot. He was still attacking the humans, all by himself!

There was nothing I could do right now, except have my people attack blindly. We were so badly outnumbered that it wasn't even funny. But even so, I tried different things. I knew the tower was nowhere near wide enough to have covered the entire cave, but with the lack of any vision at all, at least the humans wouldn't be going for us any time soon. I would be able to watch the layout from the room above, while the dust was still settling further down, giving me a chance to react before the humans were ready. Maybe we could ambush the fuckers and turn it around on them. Except... even at the very top of the tall cave, the dust wasn't settling. And the vibrations weren't stopping.

I heard a mental voice from behind me calling my name. It sounded uncertain and panic-filled—and I recognized it instantly. "What, Creziel?"

His mental voice was unnerved, panic shooting through his every thought. "Onyx. Onyx. Pull back. We need to. Need to flee! Now!"

"*What?* Creziel, make sense, dammit. I need you to focus. What's going on?"

"It's coming down! Right now!"

"What's coming down? The rest of the fortress?"

"No! The entire cave! *It's all coming down!*"

We fled then. Ran for all we were worth back into the

tunnels to get as much distance between us and the collapsing area. I sent message after message after Creive, trying to reach him, to no avail.

After a while, we found a place which Creziel deemed safe, and we all collapsed.

At that point, I finally allowed myself to despair. The humans weren't coming after us any time soon. According to Creziel, he had felt large enough vibrations to believe that the entire cavern might be filled, at this point. The human forces might even have been crushed as well. That was the good news. The bad news was that we'd tested our strength against theirs and failed. Horribly. Creive was gone, along with his fortress and half of his minions.

At a certain point, the hoard had faded away as well, leaving me blind in the area, as well. I had no way of knowing what was going on out there now, except for here in the tunnel where my people were.

Creive's minions, those who had made it, weren't looking hurt. Covered with dust, sporting blank, shell-shocked expressions, sure, but those who'd escaped had mostly been entirely unhurt.

I couldn't believe it. The power it would have taken for that mage to bring down the fortress by himself, even though it had been strengthened by my shamans. Now, it was all gone, all rubble and—

My introspection was interrupted by a sound. A scoffing, something from further down the tunnel moving toward us. I hauled myself up, started growling. They had already gotten through to us? If so, they were going to regret it. I peered into the distance, bracing myself for a conflict. Then Creive crossed the corner and limped toward us.

Saying that Creive didn't look good would be an understatement. In fact, it looked like he'd taken a nice, long shower under a waterfall made out of boulders and swords. Every part of his body looked battered. One eye was entirely closed. He favored his left foreleg, and his wings looked raw and chafed like they'd taken a sandblasting. Still, it was nothing compared to the look in his eye. The fire had gone out. The fight was non-existent. He barely spared me a glance as he limped past me and lay down next to some of his minions. Within the minute, he was asleep.

CHAPTER EIGHTEEN

It took us half a day to find the tunnel where the humans entered the mountain. Half of that was taken up by simple rest and discussion. We left Creive to his own devices to begin with, but the remainder of us, fortunately, were up for it. Most hadn't even struck a single blow. I'd managed better than most, and even I had just received 8300 experience for defeating that single group of soldiers.

I did earn another 4200 experience, my bonus from Creive as my Vassal… which showed exactly how much he had gone berserk inside the cave. Since I was awarded only five percent of the experience Creive gained, for him to grant me half as much as I'd earned myself, he must have torn the human forces *apart*. It still hadn't been enough. Far from it.

We had to reopen one of the tunnels we closed in the first place to lure them toward Creive's domain. We had scouts going in first, tiptoeing cautiously under my Camouflage, armed with the knowledge that the humans could be anywhere, up to anything. Had they opened any of the other tunnel openings we'd collapsed? Were they questing up through the mountain even as we searched for them? I had scouts spreading out to try and find answers.

It took us about half a day, a lot of backtracking and choosing alternate tunnels for us to actually find a way back that didn't involve passing through Creive's now-collapsed cavern. Now, we were on the very edge of the mountain, standing right outside the tunnel mouth from which, only half a day earlier, the human armies had poured in. We weren't acting right now, simply waiting for our questions to find answers.

My trusty shamans and Timothy were with me, as was Roth, staring down upon the human army camped down below us. They were unmoving, as they had been for more than an hour now. Everybody else was back inside the mountain, resting, waiting for orders.

Timothy seemed jittery, his form wavering like I'd struck the antenna of his television. "Why aren't they fleeing already? Or *are* they even fleeing? Are they going to find another entrance to the tunnel system? Man. I wish I still had nails, so I could be biting them. This is so damn nerve wracking!"

Roth seemed less anxious, twirling his huge sword in an elaborate rhythm around him, humming off-key under his breath. "What? Why? We're ready. They come back, we kick their asses in another place."

I glared at him, and Timothy looked aghast. "Roth! What the hell are you talking about? We lost this battle!"

He snorted. "That's not what it looks like from down here. Sure, big blue lost his house—so what? We can just build a new one. Can even make it the wrong way up, if he insists. Did you *see* how many people they lost? Heh. And we stole a ton of their skirmishers. As for me, I'm happy I'm not the one who'll have to grow plants to feed all those new faces." He stopped, then chuckled. "A couple of them looked like they would be fun training partners, though. That Sigyle. How would you go about dodging those attacks of hers, when she isn't stepping but sliding?"

Creziel groaned. "The farming. Oh, for the love of Deyra. The farming. We were just getting it under control, too."

Arthor cut them off. "You are both wrong. Roth. This was not a simple win. Did you *see* Creive? I am not sure that we will be able to rely on him from here on. As for you, Onyx, it was not a loss, either. They proved the strength of their spellcasters, sure. But they also gave away exactly how strong they were. They did still lose a lot of people, even though they managed to struggle back out."

That was the one detail we managed to get from Creive. He'd fought them, right up until the ceiling started collapsing, and their army was already retreating by then. He confirmed that most of the remaining human forces made it back out.

Arthor nodded at Creziel. "As for the future? Forget about it. The future doesn't matter. Not if we can't control what's happening now." He pointed down to the army, where it looked like a ripple of motion was running through the assembled forces as they started setting out again. Back toward the mountain!

I summarized the situation as succinctly and eloquently as I knew how. "Well, fuck!"

Within seconds, we were scrambling back toward the tunnel opening. We never got there, though. First off, it was premature. Second, they weren't aiming for the tunnel.

I mulled aloud as I opened the mini-map. "Where the hell are they going?"

Scanning over the dreary terrain, I found nothing. It was all gray, hidden by fog of war, but I had flown over the nearby terrain enough times by now that I knew there should be no surprises here they could use to their advantage. No openings into the mountain. No hidden doorways that led them straight to the Blessing. I wasn't letting anybody shut the damn thing off again, that was for sure! It was just boulders, cracks in the ground, and the steep flanks of the Scoured Mountain rising into the sky above, like a giant monument to the inadequacies of man and monsterkind.

"Arthor? Creziel? This is still the lower level. You know the surroundings. Any nearby openings?"

Arthor answered unequivocally. "No. Not a one. The nearest one is half a turn around the mountain, and that would mean at least two days' walk in this terrain." He narrowed his eyes then mused, "They're not going to... climb the outside, are they?"

They were. Half an hour later, we confirmed the fact, as the army kept marching straight at the mountain. The insane humans were actually planning to climb the outside of the mountain. That, or they were harboring some secret plan that I really couldn't understand.

They'd left part of their forces behind, too. All of their feline cavalry was currently camped out at the foot of the mountain, along with around a mixed force of a thousand humans and non-humans to care for them. They'd spent some time digging, and it looked like they were entrenching themselves, building fortifications in case we were going to attack them. They'd also left a huge part of their equipment behind.

Packs lay in orderly rows alongside neatly stacked items of all sorts. Spare weapons, carts bulging with crates, piles of long-worked wood and iron of what looked like siege equipment—there were mountains inside their barricades as they dug in.

Obviously, we'd be able to tear their fortifications apart, if we bothered to dedicate a good deal of time and effort to it. This wasn't them trying to start a siege. It was more along the lines of keeping us from attacking their cavalry and leftover people while we focused on the remaining forces.

Which we would. Because they were on the move. The rest of the army was approaching the western flank of the mountain, marching in the lee of two larger ridges that stretched out on either side of them for miles and miles. Soon, they would either have to do something about whatever their plan was, or they would have to start ascending the side of the mountain... and I didn't give them great odds for success on that.

Sure, the humans looked like they were in peak form, and

they clearly didn't give a rat's ass whether the non-humans were going to make it... but this wasn't climbing Mount Olympus in Utah. This was fucking Mount Olympus, Mars! The height of it made Everest back on earth look like a tiny little afternoon climb. Some of the cliff faces were near vertical for hundreds of feet at a time. The last mile or so reaching for the pinnacle was entirely unscalable, looming *outward* at times. They were planning to take an army up that?

No, they'd have to have a secret plan. Perhaps they were going to drill right into the mountain soon and create their own opening? Even now, they were getting closer to where the ridges met, and the hillside was turning into mountainside, steepening, as the soil was replaced by boulders and scree. Yeah. That was probably it. Aaany moment now.

They didn't stop. Their forces spread out across the inhospitable terrain and kept up the climb, only slowing marginally as the terrain steepened. I watched in confusion.

Arthor cursed. Loud, long and emphatically. "It's the damn earth mages!"

I looked at him in confusion for a while. Then, I got it and started cursing as well. Straight from the heart. I rose into the air to confirm our fears.

The non-humans were clearly ordered out in front, to ensure that nobody sneaked up on the front of their army, same as always. That held true. It might be a little paranoid here where the hillside was slowly turning into mountainside, except... okay, maybe it wasn't. We'd totally take advantage of it, if we could attack straight at the humans.

However, it looked like the Secondary was having a pretty easy time of it so far. Apparently, they had switched up forces somewhat, only letting those non-humans range forward who had a physiology that would be able to handle the more challenging terrain. Rat-like soldiers were scurrying up the incline alongside several of the werewolf-like soldiers I'd seen earlier. Strong or agile soldiers capable of moving on terrain that would make regular humans pause. As for the regular humans...

There they were. The bloody mages. Not too far from the front of the human forces, well-hidden inside a group of infantry and archers and surrounded by... yes, of course. Surrounded by the leaders of the damn army themselves. Cartiga was *right* there. Meaning, if we tried to ambush them, we'd have to contend with the strongest enemies of their entire army. Lovely.

Where the mages approached, the terrain slowly, subtly changed. It was still steep, sure, but the army pressed on assuredly, looking as if the footing underneath them was solid asphalt, not scree and gravel. Finally, masses of soldiers from the Secondary who were less suited for climbing formed the rear guard, following the human soldiers and ensuring we couldn't simply hit 'em from behind.

I sat down next to my shamans again. "You were right, Arthor. The mages are right there in front. How are they doing it?" I mused. "Creziel. Arthor. Would you guys be able to improve the footing for as large an area as they are?"

Arthor scoffed. "No. But they are humans. They are stronger than Talpi. They receive three attribute points per level, where we receive one. And not only that... I do not know how it works for humans. But we have a natural affinity for earth. These human mages seem to master more elements."

"What... so they combine elements?"

Creziel nodded. "It would make sense. Combine fire with earth to force the soil to stay in place. Or air and earth to make the loose gravel move like you want it to? I do not know how it would work, but..." he waved a skinny, furred arm at the army in the distance. "It works. Clearly."

I closed my eyes, deep in thought. Then I opened them again and followed the path in front of the army. "They can't mean to climb the damn mountain, though, can they? I mean, even if they won't just fall to their deaths without any prodding, they're wearing fucking *armor*. That's not proper climbing gear! Also, won't they, like, fall over from the thin air? This is all kinds of wrong!"

Timothy stared thoughtfully at the enemies in the distance. "Your brain is stuck on Earth, old-timer."

"What? No. You can't just ignore physics, man. I'd think you'd be the first to accept that, being a big dork and all."

"Impressive how you can be entirely right and one hundred percent wrong at the same time. Nobody's ignoring physics here. But you're still stuck in Earth mode. Thin air? Have you ever had any trouble breathing in Fire Peak?"

"No, but I'm a bloody dragon. That would be-"

"Have any of your minions, even though they've grown up in the lower layers of the mountain?" He interrupted. "Of course they haven't. So, pressure, air, and the atmosphere isn't the exact same as on Earth. And proper climbing gear? What does that even mean, if you have thirty Strength and twenty-five Toughness? If we say that peak human physiology is like fifteen in each attribute? Who's to say that this isn't perfectly navigable terrain for a high-leveled army?"

"Dammit. You're right." I grimaced.

"I know." He frowned into the distance. "Honestly, I blame myself. I should have considered the possibility. Just because our people would have trouble scaling the mountain, doesn't mean they will, especially with mages to alter the terrain. There are no entrance tunnels nearby, but that doesn't mean they won't be able to circle the mountain and find one."

I exhaled noisily. "You know, I blame you, too. How could you?"

He flipped two see-through fingers at me. "Carl. Nobody is doubting why dragons are going extinct! Nobody!"

Half an hour later, we were meeting with the entire frigging council and Creive inside the tunnels. Arthor had laid out the development with little fanfare, making no secret of how we'd messed up.

He rounded off, stating, "That leaves us with all of our forces in the wrong place and a need to figure out how to stop them from climbing the mountain. And, whatever we come up with, we are going to have to move fast. Because the enemy does not look like they're slowing down."

They exploded into chatter and shock. I had to enter the conversation. "Stop. I am sorry, but Arthor is right. We messed up, and now we need to react. So, our plan B needs to be discussed, agreed upon, and arranged quickly. We are already behind schedule as is, and all the preparations we've made included the humans trying to enter the mountain. On top of that, we'll need to tell everybody about this recent development, and fast, so we can adjust our plans. I know I'm usually the first to waste the time on banter and chatter, but we're a lot of people here, and right now we're only taking actual suggestions and questions." The worst of the chatter died down, and I noticed Roth raising his arm. "Yes, Roth?"

"The Secondary. They're still surrounding the enemy. Do we still avoid attacking them? We can't hurt the humans on foot, if we can't get to them."

I cursed and grimaced. "Good question. The answer will have to remain the same as before. They are not the real enemy. And, as you have seen, they would love to get away from the humans. However, if we are unable to find a way to deal with the army without hurting them... then we *will* have to hurt them."

Grex was as indomitable as usual. "We have all the fliers right here. Should we go attack right away? Climbers are good targets!"

"They would be, I guess. Except, I'll bet you my old Mustang they're still maintaining their shields while they climb, to protect them from above. We'd have to hit 'em hard to smash through that. It's an option though, and not a bad one. Especially once they start climbing the steeper parts."

Grex again. "Harass them?"

"We should... except we're almost in the same position as out in the Wastelands. Shields protect them, and their archers and mages are ready to punish anybody to get close. I'll listen to any suggestions to get past that, though."

Creziel suddenly blinked. "We should drop rocks on them."

I shared a look with some of the others. "Erm. You remember we lost our Parvu beasts, right? We're out of strong carriers. Or..."

I realized what he was getting at at the same time as he grinned, nodding as the penny dropped for me. "Exactly. We don't need as strong carriers as we used to. There's no need to travel miles to drop the rocks. And there's ammunition everywhere." His grin widened. "Our fliers can pick up a rock and drop it half a minute later. One more thing. We don't *just* drop the rocks on top of their shields. We drop them on their shields *and* right in front of their forces."

Most of the others stared at him, confused. Arthor was nodding, though, as were Timothy and myself. "Great idea, Creziel. This way, the rocks will crash downhill and circumvent their shields. That should create total confusion and make life a lot harder for them. Worsen the conditions for climbing, too. If we're really lucky, we can even start an avalanche on their asses."

"Avalanche?" Roth appeared really confused by the idea, until Timothy explained the concept. "Ooh. Like a tunnel collapse where it starts spreading."

"Close enough, I guess." I shrugged. "That should hurt them. Other ideas?"

We shot down a few ideas that were either impractical, farfetched, or impossible to pull off.

Timothy turned away from where he'd been talking with Arthor. Then he introduced himself into the argument. "Okay, bear with me on this one. I know you're in a hurry to get back up to Fire Peak and get started on... whatever we can do to prepare up there, really. But would it hurt us to be half a day late?"

"I... don't know. Hard to tell, right? I mean, nobody knows what the consequences could be for that. But it'd have to be for a really good reason."

The ghost grinned. It was not a pleasant grin at all. It held an inherent promise of pain. "Oh, I think I can deliver on that. You might not like the process, though."

I had to agree with him on that, as I started on my sixth taxi flight of the day. This was *not* an enjoyable task. Oh, but Creive was enjoying things even less. He spent at least five minutes outright refusing the task, talking about his dignity as a dragon and whatnot, until I talked him over. Then the work started... transporting our entire frigging army up above the human army.

I could take more than twenty people into the air on average. Creive could handle quite a lot more weight than me, but he didn't have my efficient and not at all demeaning leather harness that allowed my minions to hang on tight. So, he'd carry less people than me... but then, he would get there a lot faster.

That was all logistics, though. The end goal, however, was pretty simple. We took every single person who was willing to go, whether they be close combat fighters, spellcasters, builders, or... anything, really, and transported them up above where the humans were currently doggedly making their way up an easy climb, slowly closing in on a steeper cliff face ahead.

That's where we left them. Right out there in the open, far above the humans, with Creive's minions and our Imps to keep them company on a wild, wind-blown mountainside, with gusts of winds that were dangerously strong, sometimes enough that I'd fear to be blown right off the cliff face, if I weighed the same as a Talpus.

The key part? They were at least five hundred feet above the human army at this point. Soon, the army would be within range of a thrown rock. Heh. That was pretty much the point of the entire thing. Timmy had harped on about kinetic energy, "basic school knowledge," and stuff, but it was pretty simple, really. Even smaller rocks, thrown from high enough, could kill. So, why limit ourselves to letting our fliers dump rocks on the enemies? Why don't we take everybody we can up high and, y'know, keep them tossing stuff down on the humans as they climb? Sure, our people would be extremely exposed out there, but the humans would be even worse off.

It took a couple of hours, but then we had them all gathered on the cliffside. My people ran about, gathering ammunition while the humans were coming into range below. Then, I finally got a better idea at what the army was planning to do in order to master the mountain. I took to the air and took in their progression.

The non-humans were already scaling the forty-degree incline like they'd been born to it. Behind them, the human infantry was slowly starting to move up the mountain face as well. On. Frigging. Steps! The goddamn earth mages were actually using their magic to carve out rough steps for the army underneath. Like this, they would be able to master all but some of the entirely vertical passages. Hrm. The bloody cheaters would probably have some way of managing that, too.

Heh. We weren't going to make it easy for them, though. Timothy nodded and I gave the order, and suddenly, rocks flew from every single one of our soldiers.

Tim had spouted something like "Rocks fall, everybody dies," like it was supposed to mean something to me. It definitely wasn't what was happening down below, though. We'd been timing things to have our flying creatures start dumping rocks and fire bolts everywhere on the shields first at the same time, overwhelm them as much as possible and spread their attention, then let the rest of our people join it.

I could hear the shouts from below. Roth's shrill voice rose in rhythmic cadence, counting down, then they started their bombardment. With a grunt, I released the heavy boulder I'd been carrying as well, watching it plummet end over end through the air, to hit with a momentous impact. Not on their shields, though. That was the entire point. Right now, they'd be spread thin, trying to strengthen shields over the heads of their entire force. So we hit the ground right in *front* of the human forces and let gravity handle the rest.

The boulder I'd dumped hit the steep mountainside below

the non-humans, bounced, actually looked like it picked *up* speed, then slammed into the climbing ranks of the humans. It wasn't alone, either. Everywhere, bouncing, skidding and falling rocks were tumbling down the mountainside, dislodging other rocks to crash into the human army as a literal rockfall. The humans were *not* prepared.

They were professional, sure. Shouts went up, and shields clicked into position from the front ranks almost immediately, locking them into a pretty, defensible formation. The rocks didn't much care. Gravity was a mean old biddy. Sure, my people might not be the strongest in general, and a lot of the rocks tumbling down the hill at them *were* stopped by the shields.

But the number and unpredictability of the missiles made it impossible for them to protect themselves efficiently. One shield wrenched its carrier backward as a rock hit it right on the corner, and the three rocks tumbling right behind it were followed by screams. Those were just the rocks that didn't jump the ranks entirely, impacting formations dozens or even hundreds of feet farther behind among the army.

The effect on their forces was insane. Within seconds, pained cries and screams were everywhere, and entire companies were crumbling, fleeing, or lying prone on the ground in an attempt to hide from the worst of the bombardment. For once, their leadership was flummoxed. Suddenly, the attacks they'd gotten used to for weeks now were actually getting through their defenses, even though their shields were still intact.

The main group of leaders did react. I spotted them through the dust here and there. They were on the move but clearly didn't know what to do. Cartiga yelled orders left and right, and my good cavalry friend took to the front line to protect people behind his clearly magical shield. Where they went, soldiers organized and tried to rally against the attack. But they still had nothing to throw up that could handle the force with which the rocks and boulders impacted.

We poured everything into it that we had, which, given that

we'd spent hours collecting ammunition beforehand, was no small feat. Even as our fliers kept flying back and forth, bombarding them from above, forcing them to maintain their shields over their entire force, we kept up a constant assault.

There was no finesse to it, no carefully organized barrage. This was several hundred people tossing rocks over a cliff edge as fast and hard as they possibly could, without even spending a moment to look below and see whether our attacks hit or not.

I helped as I could, flickering back and forth alongside Creive, carrying large boulders in my claws to add my part to the attack and maintaining readiness to deter any possible counterattacks. Creive, close to me, was looking bad. His wounds were all closed by now, but heavy scars adorned his sides and his wings. His demeanor was dark, too, and he hissed every time he tossed a rock down on the humans, sometimes punctuating it with a burst of lightning. With occasional glances between my frenzied movements, I did find the time to observe the effect of our bombardment.

It was brutal. Soldiers were crushed by rocks, panicking at the lack of options to do something. Entire companies disappeared from view behind billowing clouds of dust. On their right flank, our missiles started a small landslide that buried an entire archer company. Here and there, some forces were managing an effective defense, single mages erecting magical shields to protect their sides or earth mages growing barricades that the forces could huddle behind.

But the chaos and unpredictability of our attacks made concerted efforts a nightmare, and we didn't stop. We had plenty of ammunition stocked up. First one, then several of the magical shields above their heads faded into nothingness, as the mages on the ground were hit and distracted, and suddenly our Imps and other fliers were free to dump rocks and attack with impunity. Things were looking bleak for the humans.

Their salvation arrived without fanfare in the form of a single humanoid. I didn't even see him at first amidst the chaos, dust, and general mayhem. But, from one second to the next, the dust clouds started settling, starting at the front of their ranks and moving outward. We kept up our attacks, obviously, rocks continuing to plummet down the mountainside at lethal speeds, racing at their forces in order to hit... A wall. A wall of force. Another damn magical shield, except this one stretched for the entire range ahead of their forces and held back every single rock and boulder tumbling down, despite the force behind them. Behind the shield, a single figure stood, holding up a staff horizontally in front of himself.

It was a damn dwarf! That low, wide figure; wild, unkempt beard; and ferocious, battle-ready look? It could be nothing else. The bastard single-handedly spread out a forcefield that stopped every single one of our rocks, allowing the forces behind him to regroup, reassess, and reform.

Five minutes of grinding my teeth, even as my people kept up the bombardment, and rocks started piling up against the shield. Then the dwarf lowered his staff and retreated toward where Cartiga stood. Where his shield shimmered and dissipated, a handful of fresh shields sprang into place, replacing their defenses. We'd been held off, and now the human spellcasters were adjusting.

It wasn't without cost for them, though. At an estimate, a full quarter of the remaining human forces were either killed or hurt right now. Our missiles had caused a lot of injuries, but the worst enemy had been the smaller landslides which had buried entire companies. The non-humans on the lower levels had been hit bad as well, but their looser formations and lighter armor had allowed more of them to escape the attacks.

Their medics and healers, spread out over the mountainside, were surrounded by an influx of soldiers carrying fresh wounded to be treated, fighting against the ruination of the terrain and the steep drops below. Surely, they would have to realize the cost and stop now. Or, their morale would break. There was no way they'd be insane enough to keep up their progress with how many people were out of commission now. It would be insanity.

CHAPTER NINETEEN

"It's not the strongest or the most intelligent who will survive but those who can best manage change."- Charles Darwin

"They're insane, Tim. They really are. What'll it take to stop them? I've started using my illusions and shadows from a distance to complicate their ascent. Do you know what they're doing? They're frigging *ignoring* me! Every so often, somebody is hurt or killed, and they just soldier on? What's wrong with them?"

Timothy was flying alongside me, nodding along to my complaints.

They had spent hours recuperating after our attack, then they'd continued as if nothing had happened. They left behind a mountainside littered with corpses, and ten to fifteen percent of their forces in total. Not the full quarter I'd first hoped. Their healers had worked miracles, and living soldiers kept appearing from where they'd been hiding, partially buried and worse. A large group of living humans was left behind as well, along with a sizable number of the Secondary, those who had clearly been wounded too badly to continue. Crushed arms, legs, and worse. The first row of humanoids was slowly starting the trek down to the interim camp at the foot of the hill to join up with where their cavalry had holed up. Looked like they were counting on our not bothering to take down those who abandoned the fight, when we had a real threat in front of us.

Tim mused. "I... think they're making the right choice here."

I glared at him.

He shrugged as he floated midair. "I mean, for them. Not for us, obviously. Let's be real here. Sure, we hurt them, again, but they keep adjusting to our attacks, and as long as they make it to the top of the mountain and have enough soldiers left over? Fire Peak won't stand against them. If it were only the humans, sure, but we still haven't managed to get the Secondary on our side."

"That's what pisses me off. We keep hurting them, and they just take it and keep on coming. That kind of mentality? It's insane! Can we... I don't know, man. I don't know what we should do. Can we really make it to the point where they give up?"

"Maybe not. I read somewhere that medieval battles rarely saw more than ten percent of armies killed before the victor was decided. They obviously haven't gotten that memo. Or they have some spells to keep them going. Or insane brainwashing techniques. Maybe we *will* have to crush them entirely. From what you said, Cartiga sounded like she wasn't completely out of touch, though. And we *are* doing good. If we keep this up, there will come a point where we've whittled down their numbers to the point where we will be able to defend against them, even if they make it to the top."

The peak was coming into sight now as we rose alongside the windswept rocky sides of the mountain. I grunted from the exertion as gale-force winds tried to force me sideways. I had to work for it to keep to my path and rise toward the edge. The final mile of the mountain's peak was... well, you couldn't really look at it without flowery descriptions like "barren nobility" or "fortress of primal grace" ambling their way into the mind.

It was completely and entirely unscalable. Not even the most agile beasts among the Secondary would be able to climb this. "Well, the surprise has passed now, and we're back to regular business with us trying to wear their mages down. I'll call it and say they've got enough mages that we won't manage it in time."

Timothy rose in the air like the winds didn't affect him at all, because that was exactly what was happening. "I don't disagree, dude. They're stubborn as hell. And that bloody dwarf? He must have been the one who brought Creive's fortress crashing down, too, shielded by the other mages. I'd say we've done good work so far, but it's not enough. On top of that, the way they're approaching, they've cut us off from bringing our greatest strength to bear.

"No traps, no bringing down the tunnels on their heads, no constructions that can help us in our fights, and worst, no system help. No constructions from your hoard, no minimap. So... what do we do?"

I hit an updraft, relaxing as the wind carried me upward. "We need two things, I'd say. First one's obvious. We need more to fling at them, like we just did, more firepower. We hurt them badly, and they *are* in a shitty situation, exposed on the mountainside like they are. Even if their mages can protect them from way too much, and the Secondary keeps us from sneaking in unseen from the sides."

"Do the same, but do it harder. Check. How brilliant, boss. That's going to work for sure."

"You know, sarcasm really doesn't look good on you."

"I'm a frigging sentient rain cloud with the ability to adapt how I look. *Anything* looks good on me, if I want it to." He blurred for a moment and reformed, now with a floral bonnet adorning his head. Large letters stood out on the purple surface of the headpiece. "You were saying?"

I glared at the letters. S-A-R-C... "Yeah yeah yeah. You're so bloody funny. Ignoring you now! The second thing we need to do is figure out how the hell they plan to scale the crater in order to counter it. Because that's when they're really going to be vulnerable, climbing on a vertical cliff face."

We were going over the crater now, and I stopped to hover for a while, looking down upon the capital far below. It looked so small at this distance. At least the crater was wide enough that they wouldn't be able to throw our own tricks back at us and just toss boulders and rocks down from the crater edge. Or... at least so I believed. "Hey, Tim. They won't be able to use our own tricks against us, will they? I mean, they can't dump rocks from the crater edge here and hit all the way within Fire Peak?"

He frowned, then shook his head. "Rocks? No. The laws of conservation of-"

"Dude. It's me. Plain speech, please."

He rolled his eyes. "Okay then. Fire Peak is far enough from the edges of the crater that gravity won't allow them to dump rocks off the edge and hit that far. Arrows and spears might, possibly. I'm not too sure about spells. They'd need siege equipment or something if they wanted to fling rocks, and you saw that they left all of that at the bottom of the mountain. If they try to go back for it, we can crush them. Hmm. Maybe, if the person in question had enough Strength to make the speed extremely fast. I'd have to calculate..." He trailed off, pondering.

"I'll take that as a no, and you get back to me if whatever sidetrack leads you to a different conclusion, right?" I was about to descend, then changed my mind and landed on the crater edge.

He followed me down, even as he raised a hand in an obscene gesture. His brows remained drawn together in thought. Clearly, he was elsewhere.

I spent a moment lost in my own considerations right there on the edge. Of course, edge was a bit of an understatement. It was at least a hundred feet wide, and there was no real danger of falling. The occasional remnant of tilework underfoot provided for solid footing. Pacing back and forth, I just didn't get it. The rise of the outer cliff face would test any mountain climber back in our world beyond their capabilities, even if height sickness wasn't a thing. There was no way they would be able to make that climb, even with mages ready to carve steps into the wall.

Even if they did, somehow, they'd have to descend the inside of the crater, which was even worse. But they would have to know that. The fliers who'd escaped and that bloody Lord Verneth I'd released would have explained that already. They would have to be planning for the climb, and have a way to beat it. Or–my gaze trailed downward–circumvent it entirely. "Eureka, bitches!"

"A what now?"

"I know what they're going to do. I have an idea what we should do to defend against it. *And* I know how to prepare against the bastards."

The throne room was packed. There were tons of people I didn't recognize. People of all sorts of species and ages, gathered here with a common purpose. All thanks to Dimodeus. I'd asked him to put things into motion, and he had delivered. Within an hour, we had every single builder, earth, and water mage within Fire Peak standing around us, while Dimodeus and Tim were arranged on either side of us. I told Dimodeus, "Thank you for setting this up, mate. We'll be relying on you when we need to arrange the defenders as well."

Then I addressed the crowd. "I've said this to my own people often, but it's not common for me to get the chance to talk to the people of Fire Peak face-to-face."

Timothy interrupted. "Yeah, you keep haring off to fight off invading armies. So damn distractible, aren't you?"

I laughed and sensed a tangible lightening of the mood. "Like Timothy says, sometimes it feels like there's always something keeping me from just being around in the city. I aim for that to change in the future." I let my mental message grow more serious. "But for that to happen, we will have to get rid of the invaders on our doorstep."

Gravely, I pointed a claw in a western direction. "You all know what's happening. Right now, a large human army is climbing the mountain. We will try to delay and deter them, but odds are that they will reach us in a matter of days. A week at most. So we need to be prepared for them." I frowned.

"At first, I couldn't see how they were planning to climb to the crater edge and make it back down safely with an army in the tens of thousands. I'm a bit embarrassed to admit how long it took me to come to the inevitable conclusion. They're not planning that at all. They have a number of strong earth mages, including one extremely strong dwarf spellcaster. Once they reach a height where they can sense the crater within, they will be able to create a tunnel to reach us. And, once they make it within the mountain? We'll be hard-pressed to beat them. Their numbers, levels, and military training are, to be entirely honest, beyond us."

There was a lot of nervous shuffling at that. A large Urten moved forward, looking up at me with a challenging glare. "We've trained. Hard. Cause you said we'd need to. Now you're saying we're not good enough?"

"No. I'm damn proud of you all. Even Roth says you have performed better than could be expected, and Roth is a damn strict trainer. But I'm saying the numbers are against us. At this moment, we have maybe eleven to twelve thousand humans still climbing as well as around six thousand non-human skirmishers.

"If we manage to convince the non-humans to our side, our perhaps two and a half thousand will still be too few to stand up to their numbers. I'm *also* saying that you haven't yet had the chance to level enough to be able to face off with them on even terms. These humans have spent years fighting, leveling, and training in formations. We've never had that chance."

"So... what? You just throw us at them? You were supposed to be better than Selys!"

"I damn well intend to be better than her!" I grinned at him. "Like I said, we'll be outclassed *if we meet them on even terms*. So let's not! We'll preempt their plan to tunnel through to the crater and use it against them; turn the situation on its head and arrange for them to finally be able to get a taste of the real power of Deyra inside Fire Peak."

The next hour, we spent dividing the tasks. I'd have to go get Creziel, Arthor, and... well, every single shaman except for the one working for Ahzel. We were going to need their powers more than ever, both for the construction and the battle itself.

Turned out that the Urten who spoke up, Matzca, was a member of one of the crews who was usually assigned to the hardest, dirtiest work possible. Carrying offal, handling excrement, digging in the roughest, most dangerous places. He'd managed to insult one of the prestigious City Guards early on in his life, and that essentially locked him away from any chance of real advancement for the rest of his life... until now.

Now, he was ready to prove himself, and it showed. He was only Level 6, but his attributes showed that he must have been living in the training areas since they were erected. His physical attributes were impressive at his level.

Personal Info:
Name: Matzca
Race: Urten, Level 6 – experience toward next level: 2810/6000
Size: Large

Stats and Attributes:
Health: 250/250
Mana: 110/110
Strength: 23
Toughness: 20
Agility: 21
Mental Power: 11
Mental Control: 10

Urten received three attribute points per level. Pretty good inside the mountain. Once I did the math and included the feat that gave him a point to Strength every two levels, I learned that he'd gained a full eighteen points from training. Even Roth agreed that was insane. At Level 6, he'd be able to wrestle a newborn dragon to the ground. At the rate he was improving? There was so much potential here.

His temper was also something I could work with. He was direct and confrontational, and he didn't waste time. "Okay, dragon. You get the shamans up here to handle the mountain-side, make sure it doesn't fall down on our heads, and we take care of the heavy work, dig a tunnel straight through to the outside. Then we start building. What do you want, exactly?"

"Fortifications. I'm not entirely sure what's best to create. We'll have the shamans to harden the soil and rock to ensure the enemy mages can't just bring it crashing down... at least, so I hope. Then, once we've got the bare bones of our defenses in place where they're climbing toward, we start adding all the fun stuff.

"I can place Shadow Towers and traps all around, Outposts, move the Illusion Defense–in short, create all sorts of nasty defenses that will help level the playing field, make sure that their levels and training won't count for much." I grinned. "And having them face an enchanted set of fortifications filled with defenders and Deyra's constructions, while Creive, Ahzel, and I attack them from the sky? I think that would do it."

"That, we can do. Hmmm. It won't be a wall, I think. Just needs to be steep on their side. Then, we can circle in people on our side as we please. Don't know much about all the rest, but if you make sure we have the time, I'll create a solid place for us to set our feet and throw those damn smoothskins off the face of the mountain."

Timothy added his say. "You know, everything I've read over the years says that one defender in a siege will be the equivalent of ten attackers below."

I added all the scorn to my mental voice. "Aha. And what

does Gandalf have to say about those odds when the enemy has an archmage or three hidden up the wazoo?" Ignoring Tim's furious stumbling, I turned back to Matzca, nodding appreciatively. "That'll do the trick. I'll make sure Creziel makes it up here to discuss construction –I bet he has some solid ideas, too. We will get people to handle everything else. If you provide the bones of it, we will handle the rest."

The massive Urten looked into space, frowning. "Will you be here to protect us while we work?"

I shook my head. "No." I smiled at the suspicion arising from him. "I will be out on the mountainside, buying you the time you need to finish your defenses."

Turned out, that wasn't happening. Not the way I was imagining, at least. Once I returned to the council, I was, quite simply, voted down. To my surprise, Creziel was the one to lay it out for me.

"Onyx, we believe the issue here is rather simple. Where you come from, there are no levels. You're used to, what did Timothy say, numbers and armaments deciding who wins and loses. Here, numbers may help, but levels are the true factor. You saw it for yourself, when Selys was killed and the rest of Fire Peak simply surrendered."

"Fair enough. I get your point. If we take down their collective leadership, we'll win. Is that it?"

Creziel nodded.

"I am definitely in support of that plan. But... well, we've been wracking our collective brains for weeks and haven't managed anything like that. So... what can we do now that we couldn't do before?"

Arthor smirked. "I can help you there, dragon. Seems to me we have a new set of shortcuts through the mountain?"

"Suuure. What's that got to do with anything, though?" We'd just *come* from down there. Going through the tunnels again seemed... counterproductive.

"Well, what if I were to tell you that the magical shields of the humans don't reach into the ground?"

It didn't take long to find the Blessing. We just had to follow the noise. When Tim and I got there, we found Roth and Koa'tem trying to kill each other. Around them, Aberrants as well as my minions were spread around the edges of the room, watching the engagement with interest. My ears rang with the strikes from Roth's two-handed sword being flung back from Koa'tem's huge iron staff.

The match-up seemed completely lopsided at first. The large Crawl was about two times wider than the Talpus and half again as tall. Even with Roth carrying the absurdly long sword, his reach was far beyond that of the squat little Talpus.

Roth flung himself straight at the strong, armored fighter, and I expected to see him flying back... except I'd forgotten how fast he was. When the Crawl struck at him, he slid right under the swing, reaching, stretching... then his strike was forced wide by a quick slap with the other end of Koa'tem's staff.

I blinked. The parry had been hurried but completely under control. I'd seen the evolved Crawl fight before, but never had the chance to really take in his combat prowess. Keeping up with Roth's speed? That was impressive! Shaking my head, I moved onward. "Okay, what's going on here?"

Roth was rolling back from a quick jab and jumped to his feet. "I got bored. I wanted to see what the big lummox could do with that huge stick he's carrying." He shrugged, grinning. "Turns out he's not half bad. You mind coming back in half an hour? I need to show him who's better."

A rumble from the large Crawl was apparently laughter. He didn't say anything, though.

"Sorry, but no. We have serious business right now."

Roth flung up his paws in frustration, and a few disappointed expressions dotted the room.

I grinned. "Besides, this is the kind of fight we will want everybody to be able to see. Once we've beaten the humans, we'll put it up in one of the large plazas of the city, give everybody a chance to watch you beat the hell out of each other. We'll make snacks!"

That got a round of cheers. Suddenly, a shape emerged from behind my front leg. "Serious business, you said?"

"Jesus *balls!*" My heart jumped into my throat. I knew instantly who it was, but it still took the adrenaline a bit to die down. "Slither, would you stop living up to your namesake?"

"I doubt it. Sneaking up on a dragon is good practice." The emotion coming from him was pure enjoyment.

"Heh. Well, it's your funeral if I accidentally step on you."

"Wouldn't be good practice if it was easy." His eyes gleamed with humor.

"In that case, you are going to love what we're about to do." I motioned for everybody to come closer and looked them over. Suddenly, the room seemed crowded. About eighty people total. Forty of those were my minions, and the rest were Aberrants and a few quickly chosen from the volunteers in Fire Peak. Inspecting a select few, I nodded in satisfaction. No underfed, underleveled creatures forced to stay in weakness throughout their entire lives. Not these.

These were the crack troops, the best of the best. Not a single one among us here was below Level 15, and most had reached Level 20 or higher. "I asked for the best we have. The toughest, strongest, and fastest, most tenacious bastards. I asked only for those who were ready to volunteer, prepared to risk their lives. And you all answered. We have even had to turn down a large number of volunteers because their level was too low or their attributes not high enough for what we're about to do."

I enhanced my mini-map onto the floor in front of me, zoomed slowly in on the inside of the crater surrounding Fire Peak. "In mere days, this will likely be the center of the battle that will decide the fate of the Scoured Mountain. The humans keep climbing, keep throwing back our attempts to hurt them and stop them. We shave numbers off their forces, but they shrug it off, even going so far as to leave behind their wounded to fend for themselves while they keep climbing to face us.

"They mean to eradicate us, no matter the cost. That's the deal. We

have just sent all our best builders and shamans out there to prepare defensive structures to toss them off the mountain and kick them back to the human kingdom with their tails behind their legs. If they make it up here before we're done with the defenses, though? We'll be screwed. With them loose in the crater, we'll be facing superior numbers and superior levels. Despite how you all know I don't care about races, facts are that humans get more attributes per level than most races here."

Roth snorted. "So, you're saying we'll lose?"

"Like hell I am! I'm saying we don't want a fair fight with those bastards. We can't let 'em take Fire Peak, either. If they get hold of the Blessing, they'll settle in and go defensive. And we do *not* want to try to dig those assholes out from a defensive position." I took a deep breath, looked seriously at the people surrounding me. "What I'm saying is, we *need* those defenses up and running, or we *will* lose. And it's up to us to hit the enemy hard, make sure our builders get the time they need to create everything!"

That lit a fire in their eyes. Roth gripped his sword with a wide grin. Koa'tem rolled his shoulders. Behind us, fighters were boasting and shouting out their intentions.

Slither was the one to actually ask. "What does that mean, though? We've been trying to delay them for a month. We've got hundreds of people on the mountainside *right now*, trying to slow them down with rocks and flying attacks. It's not working. What's different this time?"

"Great question." I showed him my teeth. "The difference? To date, we've been aiming to hurt them, take out specific forces and weak points, shave off their numbers. Now we know they don't care about numbers. We are going to cut off the head. We're taking out their leaders."

We moved through the Corren tunnels, and we moved *fast*. This was part of the reason why we didn't let everybody who wanted join us. We would need to cover a lot of distance, and we'd have to do it as quickly as possible. That meant that we'd need everybody to have the attributes to move fast and keep it up for a long time. Sure, I would still be able to grant some of them a break on my back, but I had my limits.

I'd wanted to bring more heavy hitters, too, but we simply didn't have the time. Creive and his people were needed in the air to protect our people from surprise attacks in case they decided to use that giant hawk to launch a surprise attack outside the mountain again. Even with the tunnel, Ahzel and his minions would take too long to join us. I considered having Ahzel join us for the attack alone, but decided that the enchanted items he was having delivered to us on a semi-daily basis were more important for now.

It had taken hours for me to confirm that my vague plan was actually a possibility. Hours in the throne room with a handful of talented scouts and Arthor in front of the minimap, hotly discussing the geography of the mountain versus the outside. Of course, having inherited the very well-explored minimap from Selys helped a lot. Even though I'd never been this way myself, there were so many tunnels, caves, and offshoots depicted, we eventually concluded that we had what we needed. That it could be done. Probably.

We traveled light. Enough food and water for the trip and the way back, weapons, and tools. Shovels, pickaxes, and the like. They'd probably be needed for when we needed to break through the collapse Selys had created at the tunnel end. Otherwise? We didn't bring anything. Just ourselves. We ran, talked, and plotted as we moved. The mood was great, light, and focused. We knew what we were doing was essential and that it might make a real difference. Hell, if we managed to take them all out, we might win the war here and now.

There were still a few tiny steps between us and that distant goal, though. First off, literal bloody steps. Whoever the Corren had been and how they'd been shaped, they apparently decided that stairs were the perfect way to descend miles and miles of bloody mountain. No consideration for the anatomy of dragons, at all! At least the stairs were wide enough I had no issues fitting, but even so, a single footstep covered two steps at the time, making me tilt precariously as I walked.

The others had an easier time of it, even if they didn't enjoy the trip. Apparently, the descent was pretty hard on the muscles, and I had to admit that it did look like one of the many exercises my ex-wife paid large amounts to be subjected to in her fancy gym. I could feel a stairmaster pun right on the tip of my tongue.

A never-ending descending, quadratic staircase. Walk a hundred feet. Turn left. A hundred feet. Left. Repeat *ad nauseam*. The only distractions I had were my comrades and having to maintain my concentration. I was using the time to practice using my shadows religiously. I needed them to be strong, unbreakable, and coming to me as second nature. Also, I needed it yesterday!

A few times, we hit spaces where the stairs were walled off from the regular tunnel system, clearly demarcated by the well-crafted walls that I still wanted to learn how to make. Again, every so often, a side tunnel would divert from the staircase, moving downward into the darkness. We only had the map up in the room of the Blessing to compare to and choose the right exit, but it turned out to be pretty damn easy. Whatever else you could say about the Corren, they had been accurate in their work, and it was only a matter of counting the exits until we hit the right one.

Once, we had to summon a bit of additional willpower to push past the place where the access to the Blessing had been broken open. Creziel had repaired the hole, shoving dirt into the opening until the pressure from the brightness shining out from the Blessing wasn't physical anymore. The sensation was still tangible, emanating from the layers of soil, luring you to stay for a while, maybe take a moment to investigate the place, contemplate the wonder of it.

It was a lot weaker, though, more like a memory of how it had been. This time around, though, it wasn't working for me. Instead, I got into a dark mood as we kept going, thinking back to how I'd been distracted by the sensation and backstabbed by the Dworgen. Watching my people getting killed in front of me, while I could only watch from the other side of the magical force field... yeah, that was a low point.

It put a fire under us, though, and a few hours later, we hit our exit. I quickly checked the direction with my minimap, then we were off, marching at a quick pace through the side tunnel.

Whatever the Corren had thought about construction in general, they were all about functionality. Everything in its place and a place for everything. The staircase and subsequent exit tunnels? They were obviously one hundred percent functional. Not a single painting or mural to distract from the trip, just one neverending trip with plain, boring walls to look at. The tunnels still moved at a slight descent, but at least the terrain had leveled out, and now we were walking across a level brick surface. Satisfied sighs around me told me how our soldiers enjoyed the change, right up until I took the easier surface as a chance to increase the pace.

Finally, after an uncertain number of hours, we finally stared into the sight of a collapsed tunnel, leading out to the western exit on the third layer from the bottom of the mountain. Almost there.

CHAPTER TWENTY

"To hear, one must be silent." -Ursula K. Le Guin

We were ambushed right outside the damn tunnel. It was so bloody stupid. We were all in such a hurry to get moving that we barely waited for Arthor and the shovel-and-pick-wielding fighters to clear the piles of dirt before we started pushing through. Fortunately, Roth was one of the first ones through the opening, and his surprised shout woke us all up swiftly.

It was a colony of Pinheads. Those low-leveled annoying ambush critters. I'd completely forgotten about their existence. One moment, Roth was walking through the piles of rock and soil, the next he was dodging and diving, swinging his sword around him as the needle-looking bastards plummeted at him from the ceiling.

As shocking an experience it was, the Pinheads were both low-level and completely unsuited for any combat that wasn't based on ambushes. Within a minute, the last few of them skittered into a tiny crack in the wall where we couldn't reach them. We moved on, slightly more conscious of our surroundings. Sure, we might have gotten to the place where we were the predators inside the mountain, but that definitely didn't mean that the place was bereft of dangers.

Twisting tunnels, dark corridors, beautiful scenery, and ugliness. Not for the first time, I marveled at the differences in the underground. You could spend hours marching through dull, dirt-colored tunnels to break into an underground series of lakes, water dripping from stalactites into pools below, creating beautiful music from the lingering echoes. Heh. Or, at least, so I imagined. We marched so fast through the mountain, I only had the chance to catch the smallest glimpse at what the mountain had hidden for us. Some day. Some day, I'd get the chance to really go explore. Not today, though. Today, we had a goal and a plan, and we were *right* there.

Arthor didn't hesitate. He leaped off my back and moved straight for the end wall of the small cave. Then he nodded and turned around. "This should be it. I can feel the end of the wall on the other side. Move back. You need to figure out when and how we move. In the meantime, I will be busy, and I will want silence to ensure that I can catch any movement, once I get closer."

I didn't comment, just moved back to the others. For most of us, this would be the chance to get a brief lie down before everything kicked off—and it would definitely kick off! The only real question was if we were walking into an ambush or not.

If we'd calculated everything right, the human army would be *right* there, on the far side of the wall, camped out for the night on the mountainside and surrounded by alert guards and mages. *If* being the key word here. But they *were* aiming straight for a particularly difficult passage, and, according to the scouts, odds were good that they wouldn't try wrangling the passage after a full day of climbing under the bombardment of our troops. On top of that, they'd also been very consistent in the layout of their camp, keeping their leadership, which was our ultimate target, at the protected center.

Three hours later, we were lined up behind Arthor in as orderly a fashion as was possible among our people. We were fully armed and ready. In fact, my people looked outright blood-thirsty. There was a dangerous gleam in their eyes, and their bared weapons glimmered with magic and a promise of violence.

Arthor, on the other hand, looked like crap. I'd seen him work hard before, but the fifty-foot tunnel surrounding us all spoke measures about what he'd had to handle.

His mental message was still clear as day, even though he looked like a worker who'd just finished a twelve-hour shift working the jackhammer. "Somebody's right out there. Who... remains to be seen. But we managed to hit where the army is, at least. There's a thin layer of soil remaining between us and the outside. Feels like it's a pretty steep surface out there. Tell me when you want to get started. Until then, I'll be resting."

I answered him straight away. "Now. If you can. We are in the early hours of the morning, and we won't find a better time to hit them."

His shoulders fell, but he assented. "Okay. Are you ready?"

"Whenever you are." With that comment, I summoned my willpower and called the shadows around me, wrapping my surroundings in as thick a layer of darkness as I could. Then the soil faded away before us, and the bright starlight shone in on everybody as we prepared to sneak into the center of an enemy army that outnumbered us more than a hundred times over.

I've had my share of tense experiences. Hiding behind the bed in a certain young girl's apartment while her parents were berating her for "napping" instead of doing homework? That was a fun one that had definitely grown even more fun with each retelling. Then, there was that time when a SWAT unit hit the administration trailer I was napping in. Heh. That was an interesting way of figuring out that your employers were full-on money launderers with a side business in embezzlement. Fun times, those.

But this... Whatever I'd tried in the past had nothing on our current experience. Walking amidst a throng of sleeping bodies, knowing that every moment, some mage might be able to notice our presence and call an alarm on us. Yeah, I was pretty sure I was leaking a bit as I walked.

We'd emerged out of a nascent tunnel right next to a company of archers on the outer edge of the encampment. We knew we were leaving an open entrance into the mountain behind us. However, if they did manage to find it, I almost welcomed them to try.

I'd rather face them in there, where we could use the mountain against them. The very second the stars started peeping into the tunnel, I established an illusion to maintain the image of the mountainside being unbroken. That part was easy. Finding our way across the human multitudes covering the sheer, rocky inclines of the mountainside, while maintaining that illusion *and* the cover of shadow surrounding us all? Less so.

Again, the discipline in the human army worked to our advantage. While the slanted, rubble-strewn terrain didn't invite well-formed, razor-straight formations or encampments following exact measurements, they still tried their best to retain their discipline. Even though the tents and cooking fires were sprawled out over the rough surfaces, they tried to maintain distances between the different encampments, relatively straight pathways to make it easier to move between camps, communicate, carry provisions, and whatnot. In the early hours of the morning, that left us with a relatively open path to choose, even if the terrain was tricky.

Okay, tricky might be an understatement. For those who have never tried moving along the edge of a mountain without a beaten path, it's not exactly easy at the best of times. There will be loose rocks, scree, outcroppings you need to navigate, and difficult passages. That's a best-case scenario. I wasn't exactly a climber, but I've seen my share of climbing shows. Rough terrain was part and parcel of the package. Having to handle a terrain like that with a hundred people trying to move silently, was not a best-case scenario.

Again, though, the humans helped. They'd cleared the worst obstructions and managed to make passage slightly easier.

Even so, it wasn't silent. Far from it. Most denizens of the mountain were used to traveling silently, silence being a requirement for the success of an ambush, the deciding factor whether they would eat that night... or possibly *be* eaten. But many of them had never been outside the mountain before. Neither had they had to sneak their way across hundreds of feet of forty-degree incline, surrounded by enemy soldiers.

We were *not* moving perfectly silently. Rocks clattered across the ground, and scuffles and grunts were clearly audible for anybody who would listen. I expected to hear somebody cry out at any moment, except... nothing happened. Then I realized why. We were not moving in a cone of silence, either. Everywhere, there was a layer of noise and small sounds. Though the vast majority of the soldiers were asleep, the camp was busy.

Even before sun-up, there were people hard at work, preparing food, repairing items, handling every task known to man. If they had to turn their heads to look at every new noise, their heads would be gyrating like that possessed woman in the movie. To help us out, most people moving around the camps carried their own torches, kindly ruining their own night vision.

Above us, we could see large, translucent domes covering the entire night sky. The magic shields, the ones covering the army from the bombardment of our forces. From this angle, it was actually rather easy to see that it wasn't a single shield. Well, there was one large shield, ostensibly the dwarf's, but underneath it, dozens of smaller shields were spread out to catch anything that made it through. Every other second, a flash of light appeared where another missile was deflected by the shield. God. No wonder that they weren't reacting to weird colors.

We had our scouts ranging ahead to plot the course. I was glad I didn't have to. Not just because I had to focus on my illusion and the shadows, either. Even with the humans' discipline, the mountainside was a broken mess. Adding to the difficulty, finding where we were going wasn't exactly easy. For five minutes, then ten, we found our way across the barren landscape, moving among the sleeping multitudes. We often had to move directions drastically to avoid workers, fires that were placed close to our path, or any number of things. On top of that, we couldn't tell exactly where we needed to go. It was not like they...

I blinked, watching the Talpus scout pointing ahead of us. Okay. My bad. They *were* indeed announcing their position to make it easier for us. About three hundred feet ahead of us, on the far side of an infantry encampment, a row of tents were set up in a wide half-circle, illuminated by a ring of torches... exactly like the original arrangement that Mordiel had blown up.

We were nearly there. Circling around the infantry unit, there were only a couple of minutes left before we had unfiltered access to the camps of their leadership. Sure, there were a handful of well-armored guards stationed around them, but Slither was here. We could take them out quickly and silently.

Then the leather workers appeared. Three young humans, hands filled with armor, chatting softly among themselves, emerged from between two tents and walked straight out into my circle of shadows. They halted abruptly, one of them dropping his goods with a cry of alarm.

Then Slither was among them.

Emerging from right behind two of them, his clawed hands worked lightning-fast, stabbing into the backs of both.. Then he leapt for the third worker, claws first. They stabbed right into her throat, and he rode her to the ground.

For a moment, all was still. Our soldiers stood in shocked silence, holding their breaths as they waited for the shoe to drop. Nothing happened. Koa'tem moved forward, picked up a corpse, and flung it over his shoulders. Seeing that, two other soldiers followed. Quick thinking, there. That way, they wouldn't be discovered until after the fact. Slither started lathering his claws with a dark, caustic substance again.

"Aah. Intruders. I knew you would try something." The mental voice appeared out of nowhere. From the panicked look on the faces of everybody around me, they could all hear it. It was crisp, concise, and laden with condescension. "Evil always acts at night. I will admit that I was starting to think that you worked differently from other monsters. I am glad you did act, though. Perhaps we can finally put a stop to your pestering minions."

Then a shout rang out. Not from within the tents of the leaders... but from the tents *behind* them. With shouts and questions, all around us, soldiers woke up.

I am not afraid to admit my head imploded for a moment. When you're talking worst-case scenarios... this was probably it. But then I remembered. We'd planned for this. They knew what to do. "It's a trap! Looks like their leaders are in the tents behind the central circle! Move! Find them, but be ready to run! Slither!"

We had been discovered. That was not hard to realize. But that didn't mean we were completely screwed. Not yet. Despite everything, there was no way they'd been awake, waiting to spring an ambush for us since the last one. So, they'd planned for this. They had still been awakened in the middle of the night with no preparation and no clue where we were.

On top of that, we were ready. We had plans and contingency plans. On all edges of their encampment, noise and light emerged, as Creive and the Imps started attacking. They weren't seeking to get close or risk anything, merely cause as much noise and distractions as possible. From the screams, they were doing a damn fine job of it.

I sprang forward, started running for where we'd heard the voice from, while I spread my shadows as far and wide as I could. If this was a trap, there would be soldiers everywhere, but we still had a chance to finish what we came for—or go for second best.

Our forces poured past the infantry camp, while, all around, people were waking up, preparing weapons, and trying to figure out what was going on. We wasted no time clashing with them as we ran forward, attempting to find what we were aiming for.

Somebody decided to make it easy for us. In the half-darkness of the night, a translucent light sprang into being fifty feet behind the half-circle of tents we'd originally aimed for. A protective, shimmering globe appeared, covering a large section of ground and giving us a very convenient target.

Within moments, we were right there, looking down on the solitary figure standing at the center of the circle.

It was the dwarven mage. He stood tall (for his kind, meaning not very) in an earth-colored, gold-embroidered robe. Holding his staff aloft in a warding measure, he encased a row of tents with the shimmering white light. From within, familiar figures were emerging. Cartiga. Beardface. Lady Eveny. At least Lord Verneth wasn't with them. I made a split-second decision and pushed back the shadows around us, so they only surrounded us on the outside.

The dwarf blinked at the multitude of bestial soldiers suddenly appearing out of the darkness before him. I had to hand it to him, though, he recovered fast. With a challenging smirk, he acknowledged me, even as the leaders centered on his position, armed and armored. "Come to challenge me, then? Let it be known. You are not the first dragon I have slain. Hargren, the Heart of the North did not come upon his name by accident. I have—"

"Listen." I interrupted. "First off, that's a horrible name. Second, I don't care who you are. Third... monologuing is a horrible survival trait."

It was a risk. A bad one. We'd talked about the possibility of sorcery getting in the way of our attack and agreed we'd have to chance it, if it happened. We *had* to act. There was no way we were just going to wait around while their forces closed in on where we were.

To my extreme relief, there was no protective sorcery keeping Slither from making his move. The Stick Kin appeared out of nowhere... right behind the mage. His claws pumped like pistons, even as they sparkled with lightning. The first two strikes didn't do anything, though. The dwarf's staff moved supernaturally fast, reaching over his own shoulder and knocking away Slither's attacks with more force than the movement portrayed.

And he started frigging monologuing again! "Hah. You think me unprotected against your vile tactics! I will–"

We never learned what he wanted. Seeing that his attacks weren't working, Slither pulled back... then he started stretching. I couldn't name it in any other way. His limbs elongated, moving farther, hitting in ways they shouldn't be able to.

I had to hand it to the dwarf. Hargren was talented. Somehow, the key-guy actually managed to block the next, unpredictable strike with his staff, and the one after that. But on the third strike, Slither managed to slide his claws along the dwarf's staff and slice into his unprotected fingers. The spellcaster cried out in pain, and Slither faded away, into the darkness beyond.

"Now! Attack! Everybody but the dwarf."

I didn't wait for the rest to follow, just sprang into motion, aiming straight for Cartiga. The initial shock from Slither's attack had dissipated, and the humans reacted now, too. Lord Gamon charged toward me with a cry of fury, then veered, as Roth somehow outpaced me and challenged the brawny fighter.

Sprinting along, I shot a Weakening Fog at Cartiga and Lady Eveny, though I was forced to angle it to avoid hitting my own people. Then, I followed up with a Shadow Whorl centered on the damn dwarf, knowing that one only impaired my enemies. Unfortunately, it seemed like the dwarf had earned his grandstanding. Even wounded, he ignored the effect completely, swinging his staff around, gathering arcane energies to him.

I looked at Cartiga, who was pulling back behind the dwarf and Lady Eveny. Then, I took a split-second decision, veered, and leapt... straight at Lady Eveny. We needed to get to their spellcasters. If she or the dwarf decided to shield Cartiga, we might not be able to do what we came to do.

She cried in terror, fired a bright spell straight at my face, and dodged to the side. My night vision disappeared behind spots for a moment as my head was rocked back. Ten percent of my health disappeared along with my vision, but not before I'd swiped out with my claws and felt a moment of resistance, along with a pained cry.

My vision slowly rushed back in. Around us, the human soldiers were becoming aware of what was going on and rushing to the defense of their leaders. Some of them were arriving in formation, too, proof that some leaders simply acted better under pressure than others.

Our forces acted immediately, if chaotically. A large part of our people veered off to face the soldiers, but the rest continued to face off against the human leaders. Roth was a blur of movement against the bearded cavalry leader. Cartiga was facing off against Koa'tem with her sword and shield and, impressively, pushing him back. Meanwhile, I prepared to pounce against the human mage who was huddling on the ground in front of me, wounded.

The world exploded.

Everywhere, our forces were flung back. Not only ours, though. The humans as well. It came from Hargren. That damn dwarf was kneeling, forcing a wall of gale-like wind force outward and forcing our attackers back, along with the human soldiers. The only ones still standing were the leaders in their midst, who stood in the eye of the storm, unaffected. Even Koa'tem had trouble standing against the hurricane-force winds that roamed in a widening circle around the spellcaster.

Lord Gamon used the surprise to lay into Roth, yelling with each strike. He was using his superior strength to force his way onward, even though spots on his arms and legs were covered in blood from Roth's attacks. I gasped to see him grunt and force one of Roth's strikes to the side and slam the tip of his sword right into Roth's upper arm. Blood spouting, the Talpus fell back with a cry.

"Roth!" I forced myself into motion, struggling against the oppressive power from the dwarf's spell... and shambled into a lumbering run. I had to finish this damn mage opposite me, or

I wouldn't be able to help. Lady Eveny's eyes widened massively, even as she slid backward on the ground, but she managed to summon another bright spell at me. This time, though, I closed my eyes, choosing to take the hit straight on... then I was right there. I bit down, and my teeth closed around the struggling human... and I forced them closed. The sensation of her life blood exploding inside my mouth was beyond compare.

With a shudder, I shook it off. No time to indulge my baser instincts. Cartiga screamed something unintelligible at me, while her shield started glowing with a purple, pulsating light. Koa'tem was flung back, blood springing from his chest. He scrambled away. Cartiga followed. The light filled every inch of space at her front and stretched out toward Koa'tem.

I sprinted ahead, fighting against the head winds all of the way, and leaped in the way of the purple light, shielding Koa'tem. Flying in the face of everything a shadow dragon should be, I charged head-on, claws swinging. I was going to tear her apart, regardless of whatever spell or skill she was trying to cast.

My claws impaled her upper arm near the neck, and my world dissolved into pain. I pushed through, even as my health plummeted with every tiny move. I pulled my claws back, feeling completely drunk. Watching her through a haze, I heard her pain-filled laughter.

Her teeth were gritted as she addressed me through the pain. Her arm looked like some bloody carnivore decided to use it as a chopping block, but her eyes were focused. "Mirror of Suffering. Never lost a duel. Never expected to use it on a dragon, though." She wavered a bit on her feet, then found her balance. "So come on, you beast. Strike. Let's stop this charade and *end* this."

I saw a lot of things in that gaze of hers. Resignation. Defiance. A shitload of pain. I nodded and almost fell over. "Agreed. Time to end this." I moved toward her, baring my teeth for an attack.

And, a second before impact, I sent a message. "Slither. My target."

Cartiga's pain-filled concentration was completely focused on me. Her shield was raised to ward off my bite, Mirror of Suffering ready to punish me. The entire front of her body was covered in a dark purple light, making her look almost demonic. Then, there was a moment of confusion... and Slither appeared behind her. His claws impacted her neck from behind, where her light and the skill effect didn't reach.

I barely noticed her drop to the ground, before Slither was yelling at me mentally, telling me we needed to get out. I finally noticed my health, blinking below twenty percent. Without taking the time to look around, I sent a message. "Pulling out. Now." We'd done what we came to do.

Then, I staggered back where I came from. Out of the corner of my eye, I watched as my people fled from the gale-force winds of the swirling hurricane-like circle surrounding the dwarf. He didn't follow it up, though, instead kneeling on the ground, both hands bracing themselves as if he was about to collapse. His head was still raised, though, and the magical forces pulsing from him didn't waver.

The remainder of my soldiers were struggling to extricate themselves from the clashes with the enemy soldiers. The bloody form of Koa'tem backed off, along with Roth, from a bloody, pulped form that I could only partially recognize as Lord Gamon. When he'd fled from Cartiga, the evolved Crawl had apparently helped take him down. Everybody else was retreating as fast as possible, just this side of panic. I helped as I could, unleashing my Weakening Fog, roaring and slashing at the air. I added no finesse to my strikes, merely the desire to scare them off.

It worked, though. Despite their discipline, nobody wanted to be heroes here, especially when the opponent was a punch-drunk, slavering dragon. Wise choice. Behind me, Koa'tem and Roth were doing the same, helping our people move back from the fights and doling out punishment. They were all clambering toward me now, climbing all over me. Soon, they were all there.

I was lost inside my head when Roth slapped me on the flank. "Heal yourself, dragon. You're no use to us like this."

Head buried in a sea of pain and confusion, it took a while for the meaning of his words to get through to me. Oh. Dammit. I touched my necklace, consumed a Mana Crystal, and roared as my flesh started knitting itself back together.

For a moment, I looked right into the weary, hate-filled eyes of the dwarven mage where he knelt in the calm center of the raging storm. He was trembling. I considered going against him. He looked worn. Spent. But then sense came back to me, and I finally realized that they were all here.

All my people. Clinging to my harness. Depending on me.

I flung myself off the mountain.

CHAPTER TWENTY-ONE

"True friends stab you in the front."-Oscar Wilde

Success. Triumph. Vindication, even. We'd taken a huge risk, and it bloody paid off. Even with their leaders ambushing us, we'd managed to eliminate three of their leaders and poison the dwarf mage who, so far, had been the singular enemy who'd given us the most trouble. Let Lord Verneth be the one to lead their armies onward. Pretty please!

Pick your poison, they say. In this case, literally. Unfortunately, our night time ambush out in the Wastes had spent all of the lethal poison we had. In this case, we'd gone with a different approach and opted for the Marretseed poison Laive had concocted. Apparently, she had managed to strengthen the paralyzation effect and turn it into a slow-working poison that dumped the targets into long-lasting comas. We didn't have large quantities of the stuff, but we didn't need it, either.

Roth, Koa'tem, Slither and myself had smeared the stuff on our weapons and claws, making damn sure we didn't get any on ourselves. That was why we didn't push our luck with that damn dwarf. From the moment Slither managed the first couple of scratches, he was going down. Sure, I would have felt a lot more secure if we'd managed to kill him off, but this... was a good alternative.

The experience spoke clearly. They had been high-leveled. Not as much as Selys, sure, but everybody who managed to get a strike in on either of their leaders had gained at least half a level. I hit Level 46 myself. As for the rest of the fight, we hadn't done much damage. We'd fought defensively, focusing only on making it out of the battle alive, once we'd gotten to the leaders.

It had taken us quite a lot of time to transfer all our forces back to the remainder of our people outside the mountain. Mostly because we had not been in the best of shape after the attack. That included myself. The mana crystal I consumed was continuously healing my wounds, even as I plummeted toward the ground far below, with way too many soldiers hanging on to me for dear life.

Hence, my landing held an uncomfortably large degree of "controlled crash" to it. I was fortunate that I managed to avoid smooshing any of my minions on impact. Then we had to handle a *very* fast round of triage before I struggled up to Fire Peak, carrying two dozen badly wounded soldiers who needed to see the Ergul as soon as possible for healing. Finally, I spent a while with Creive transporting our forces back above the invading army.

I took a look at the forces spread out far below us, then at my people, who were continuously moving back and forth all across the mountainside, securing ammunition then dumping it down on the enemies below. A few of us had taken to digging into the mountain with picks because we were running out of easily accessible rocks.

"Are you sure?" I asked Creive.

The huge blue dragon was glaring down on the massing individuals below. He stood right near the edge of our plateau, making no attempt to hide himself. "Yes. Your silly strategy is working. Their shields are failing. I have seen a handful of missiles overwhelm their defenses in the last half hour. They also sent the final flier away a while back to tell the human empire back home they are failing, I expect. When the two of us join in the attack, it will be even worse for them. If any of them want to survive, they should start pulling back shortly. If not, I will feast."

I nodded eagerly. "That is amazing. Thank you for keeping an eye on things. That means all we have to do now is push them, make sure that they know we aren't going to hold back, then, hopefully, that's it. By this time tomorrow, we might see their backs as they start trekking back toward human lands."

I didn't comment on the niggling doubt about the hawk that had fled. They might be vying for reinforcements. However, with their main flying army crushed, I couldn't see them bringing anything in time. They'd have to risk all their flying forces on one enemy. Still, the thought wouldn't go away.

Creive unleashed a bestial roar that reverberated out over the mountainside. His eyes gleamed with undisguised bloodlust as he answered. "Then we slay them, one by one, and take their strength for ourselves."

"Yeaaah. We'll see about that, Creive. All honor due to Deyra, but we're looking to *end* the conflict with the humans, not escalate it and ensure that we continue this war forever."

He snorted. There was a lot of hatred and disdain in that snort. "That is your take on it, not mine. For now, I will pay them back what they did to my home." With that, he took off into the air, heavy wing beats bringing him toward a large stack of boulders.

Somehow, the humans still didn't get it, though. At this point, I couldn't tell if it was a matter of persistence, stupidity, or simply because they didn't like their chances of being able to make it all the way home to the human lands. But the human army stayed right down there, didn't push onward, just... huddled down like a tortoise, waiting within their shell to see if we would go away.

Of course, we weren't going anywhere, either. We were starting to really hurt them. Every now and again, one of our missiles, either by our flying minions or our people on the mountain, made it through a hole in the shields. The cries and heavy impacts below showed that we were finally getting somewhere. Their morale had to be at the breaking point now.

Their desperation finally resulted in an unprecedented move. Following a sudden explosion of shouts and movement, their army started re-arranging. No retreat, however. Amidst a lot of confusion, the rough circle of non-human skirmishers outside the human camp contracted and started pulling inward.

I cursed as I realized what was going on. "Damn. They actually did it." The human leadership's interest in survival finally outgrew their desire to keep the non-humans at a distance and showing them they were worth less than the humans. They were being annoyingly clever about it, too.

They still kept maybe half of the remaining Secondary in a protective circle outside the actual army, but the rest of them were divided liberally among the rest of their forces. I cursed, then I sent out a message to all our forces. "Stop bombardments for now. Return for new orders."

This avenue of attack had been stymied. Still, that opened up for another range of moves. Before, sneak attacks had been completely impossible due to the chaotic disposition of the non-humans. Making our way in and out again without tearing through the skirmishers had been unlikely, at best. Now, with their forces thinned and stretched over a chaotic landscape, with us having the aerial superiority? The gaming board was redefined.

Once we had the chance to re-evaluate the changed landscape, we started our aerial bombardments again. Not as before, however, where our people had thrown missiles indiscriminately down-hill, as long as they ensured they'd make it past the surrounding non-humans and into the human camp.

No, now it was mostly the flying minions and a few of the high-level ranged warriors who were allowed to attack, and only when they were certain they had an all-human target. A lot of people grumbled at the unnecessary complexity of it, but I insisted, and my council backed me up. They could see the end of this conflict as well, and wanted the Secondary on our side, just as I did.

As long as their shields were mostly down, we were free to punish them. They were still stuck, unable to range forward. Even if we couldn't attack indiscriminately, overall, the power balance hadn't changed with their move. They would need to be able to adjust the terrain ahead of them in order to proceed, while still being able to protect themselves from attacks from above, and that wasn't happening. For every hour that passed, more humans fell, while we solidified our defenses higher on the mountain.

A day later, the stalemate finally broke, as the human army started moving again... to return their climb up the mountain.

"What happened? Where did we miscalculate?" I'd gathered as many of the council and my vassals around me as possible. Arthor was still returning to Fire Peak through the Tunnels, Creziel was working all he could to prepare the defenses up above, and Grex was harrying the attackers where he could. The remainder of them were there. Emotions running through my gathered minions were... not happy. That's putting it mildly.

Wreil was the one to answer. "We didn't go wrong. Not really. But the dwarven mage is back. He is being carried on a stretcher and looks like death, but he is still managing to adjust the terrain ahead of them. And they are moving."

"Dammit. Damn it all! They must have some healers or... magical items to weaken the poison. He should have been unable to do anything but drool and pray for death for the next week, possibly month! We're so screwed!" I realized that I was not exactly building confidence and reined in my temper.

"Okay. We will handle this. Like we've handled everything else, we are going to adjust and beat them at their own game. At this point, the average soldier must be ready to do nothing but desert to avoid the stress of our constant attacks. They can't have much left to give." I gave a decisive nod, which only felt a bit contrived, then opened the table for input. "Suggestions. How do we handle this? What is the plan?"

Creive surprised me by being the first one to speak up. He usually waited to hear the plans before joining in with his opinion. This time, however, was different. He cut through the low discussions with a decisive strike. "My plan is simple. I am leaving."

Everybody grew completely silent. Even Roth didn't say anything. The only emotion I felt coming from Creive was one of conviction. Not fear, nor anything hostile. Just decisiveness. I had to gather my thoughts for a moment in order to come up with a response that wasn't a string of expletives. "That really sounds like bad timing for our fight, Creive." There was so much else I wanted to ask. I kept it simple. "Why?"

He sneered. "I have told you before. I want to follow Deyra. Fight and thrive. I do not intend to follow your path toward death and destruction for some obscure idealism. With my domain ruined, I have no real reason to stay. I still would, if we were winning. However, that is clearly not happening. So, as I said the very first time we met, I will simply leave the mountain and build a hoard elsewhere. It might be slower growth outside, but those damn humans will not be able to match me in the skies or even follow me."

Roth finally couldn't hold back his response anymore. "So, you're leaving us to fend off this huge army like a damn coward? Scared to face that mage they have? That's a fine *vassal* you have there, Onyx!"

The huge blue snapped his jaws shut in front of the Talpus. "Call me a coward? I will tear you apart!" He growled, lightning playing across his body. "This is not my fight. Do you want to die for some stupid creatures in Fire Peak who were trying to kill you a few weeks ago? Good luck with that! My concern is for me and my own growth. Onyx here has sworn that he will leave me alone to make my own decisions for me and my minions. Unless that was a lie, hmm?" He fixed his gaze on me, muscles bunched up.

239

I pondered my response for a few moments. This was falling apart too quickly. "No. I promised Creive free reign as my vassal without any intervention, and I stand by that! I will not deny that I am disappointed in you, however. I believed that you were not afraid of a fight. That you were starting to see the point of our approach."

"Afraid of a fight? Never. This is not a fight. Fighting would be tearing down the non-humans below. *They are trying to kill us all.* You impose rules that do not belong. Demands that are not of Deyra nor make sense. No, for as long as you were winning, I was willing to accept your choices. You did not try to make me bow to them, after all. I even recognize that there are times where your sneaky approaches will be better than a direct one. But now you want me to be part of your doomed battle. And that, I will not stand for."

Fuck. I knew he wasn't on board with our politics, but I honestly thought he was slowly coming around. Also, despite what Creive said, this wasn't only a matter of losing his hoard. The look in his eyes when Roth mentioned that human spell-caster was clear. It was fear, plain and simple. No way was I going to get him to admit to that, though. How to salvage this, then? "What can I offer you that will entice you to join the fight?"

"At this point? Nothing. You will remain embroiled in this pointless war until the end. I intend to find a real challenge out there, where I can test my strength and build my own realm *on my terms*." His tone softened somewhat. "I do not mind remaining your vassal. You are a clever leader, and it strengthens both of us. But I will not die without reason."

"In that case... I might have one thing to offer you. How about this? If you stay with us... I will show you the opportunity to win your own Blessing."

The look he gave me was all predator. He looked like he wanted to eat me up, scales and all. "I'm listening."

"Okay. Then let's be realistic. This might go wrong. I agree. There is a very real risk that the humans are going to overwhelm our defenses, make it into the crater, and take over the Blessing. If they manage that? We're screwed. But we know about two other Blessings."

"And you would promise me one?"

I snorted. "Hell, I was going to anyway. From what Selys said, I can't manage more than one Blessing, anyway. I have three vassals, and Ahzel looks to be pretty comfortable where he is. So, yeah. Those were my intentions. Whatever else people might say about me, I've always tried to do right by those who work under me. So what's the plan?"

"You promise to give it to me?"

"Give it to you? No. You'll have to earn it. By all accounts, the place is riddled with monsters. A lot of them are above Level 30, too. But... here's the fun part. From what the scouts said, they're all ground beasts."

"No fliers?"

I shook my head. "Not from what they were able to see. It's a large, ruined city."

"You're telling me that you will hand over the Blessing *and* a ton of experience on legs?" His incredulity was tangible.

"Yes. It won't be easy. In fact, I'm sure there is trouble lurking for you somewhere there. But that's how it works, right? Nothing comes for free in this world; you need to earn it. And I'll hand over the location."

His eyes narrowed. "Right. And all you want in return is...?"

"For you to stay in the battle and protect the skies. Fight any flier. You and your minions are the ones who are the best prepared for that. So, that's my demand. Stay, fight, do your part, and even if everything goes wrong, I will tell you what you need to get there. I will leave one of the scouts with you before the battle, who can guide you."

He thought about it for a while. The hunger in his eyes left no doubt as to how much he wanted it. In the end, however, he bared his teeth and responded with finality. "No. We have already tested our strength against the humans and the dwarf. We are not strong enough, yet."

I cursed inwardly. "Let me be quite frank with you, Creive. That's a load of crap! You want to flee from the mountain because you're afraid and because they ruined your home. We haven't faced them head-on yet with our full might." I looked up and at the large blue. He didn't back down.

Even so, I could sense his emotions. Guilt. Defiance. Underneath that, a roiling layer of fear. I exhaled in disgust. "If you decide to flee, I won't try to stop you. Having to take you down would weaken my forces even further. But you won't be my vassal any more. You and I? We will part ways. Should we meet again, it would be as enemies."

He laughed aloud. It was the first laughter I'd heard from him since his domain was destroyed, and it seemed... wilder. More unhinged. "Like you could stop me, Onyx. If you insist on us being enemies, then so be it. I have one offer for you, though, before I leave."

"I'm listening." I growled.

"Let me remain as your Vassal. Tell me of the Blessing. Let me conquer it on my own. In return, I will promise that I will let your surviving forces retreat to join me, when you are beaten."

It was a crappy alternative. I wanted the blue menace on my side, yes. The alternative did beat what we had right now, and the Blessing wasn't doing us any good as it was. Still. Creive had just proved beyond debate that he couldn't be trusted in a tight spot. Having to rely on him hosting and feeding us if we came running with enemies at our backs? No. It wouldn't do.

I growled. There was no good alternative, so I decided to try, one final time, for a less crappy one. "No. No, I am not rewarding you for leaving us when the going gets tough. I've told you what the options are. Either stay and face the fliers or flee and face the world."

He snarled. "Then I would still be facing the sorcerer! He already took everything from me!"

I nodded. "Yes. You would. And I won't lie. With your own actions, you have already lost all trust you had earned with us.

But it would still leave you to grow with the aid of a Blessing. Also, you are fast. So, you are the one among us who stands to most likely get out of that conflict alive. So, there it is. Fight and earn your own Blessing, or flee with enemies everywhere."

He glared at me. His eyes promised death, and his body tensed as if he were ready to jump me. But I knew his answer. It was right underneath the surface. The fear. His world had been turned upside down.

A brief while later, Creive and his forces had left, and I was busy cursing. We'd just lost our best weapon of attrition. On top of that, I was sad to see him go, out of a purely egotistical sense. I wanted to help Creive, and he'd been getting there. It just hadn't been enough.

I decided to contact Ahzel. There would be no upside to keeping something like this a secret, and we needed to adjust our plans accordingly. However, where Creive had been a nasty surprise, the chat with him was far more pleasant. In short, he believed he'd found the right place for him down there in our old lair, and he wasn't going anywhere.

In fact, he outright *reveled* in the kind of steady, productive growth he was going through right now, slowly expanding his wintry domain while outfitting all his minions (and a lot of mine) with enchanted items. Even better, his eagerness for battle didn't diminish when he heard that Creive split. It would just mean more growth for himself.

I'd worked with people like him before. Ambitious, but as long as you provided them with a clear route to growth and self-improvement, they weren't going to rock the boat. Heh. I sure as hell didn't hope so, at least.

"Good. With that out of the way... this is when we talk about alternate plans." I turned toward the others. "Somehow, the dwarven mage is fighting against the poison, and he's strong enough to guide their way up the mountain, even if he's near comatose. We need to either take him out or delay them for long enough that our defenses are in place when they reach the peak."

We spent a while debating the possibilities. In the end, Creziel was the one to recommend the strategy we went with, even if most of the others hated it.

"It's cowardice. That's what it is. That little weakling just wants to avoid fighting." Roth usually didn't go at Creziel's throat like this, but he was furious. The hair of his fur stood on end as he stood with his fists clenched.

For once, Creziel didn't back down. "You can call it what you will, Roth. But I believe it will *work*. And that is the most important part of the plan. If you come up with a plan that involves fighting that has a chance of success, they would all prefer going with that instead of my plan. So, go ahead!"

My favorite little bodybuilder Talpus opened and closed his mouth like a suffocating fish. "I... liked you better when you were Level 2!" Then he stormed off.

I blinked. "Okay. Weirdest insult I've heard in a while. We need to get to work, though. So, what do you need from us, Creziel?"

"Spellcasters. All the spellcasters you can spare from Fire Peak. That, and protection, of course. If the humans decide to send that dwarf after us, there is no way we will be able to protect against them."

"You'll have it. What else?"

He shrugged. "That's it. Like I said, we're not stopping that dwarf. His powers are too much for us to match." His small eyes glinted with mirth. "But that doesn't mean we cannot make him loathe us."

CHAPTER TWENTY-TWO

Creziel was hard at work. There was nothing to be seen, though. He knelt near the cliff edge with his eyes closed and both paws touching the rocky surface. A tiny smile played on his lips.

I walked closer, glanced in passing at the four other unfamiliar spellcasters who stood next to him. I didn't know them but had helped fly them a while back. Looking over the edge, I saw an almost vertical drop with the human army gathered below. That little dot, right there, *might* just be a stretcher. Fighting down the desire to hock a loogie down the mountain, I squinted at the steps getting slowly carved into the mountainside below.

"Hrm. How are you doing, Creziel? It's a bit hard to tell, but I can't really see if they're slowing down or not."

Holding up a single claw, he continued whatever he was doing for a moment more, then opened his eyes and rose. "Oh, it's not properly working yet, Onyx. My distance for manipulating the earth efficiently is nowhere near enough to reach them down there... yet."

His tight, happy smile made me smile as well.

He grunted, indicating the other spellcasters with a digit. Two of them were kneeling right near the edge, close together.

I saw nothing at all happening, though. If I didn't know better, I'd think they were doing some of those Yogi Bear mental exercises Cait always wanted me to join up for. Pfah. Not happening. I always bloody hated the stench of incense. "What am I looking at?"

"Air mages. They are working together. Deeva on the left is catching and amplifying the local winds. Then Mavo steers them straight down toward their forces."

"Damn. Perpetual hurricane headwind? That's just mean. And the other two?"

"One's a water mage. Usually handles boring tasks in Fire Peak, he says. The other is a frost mage."

"And they are... waving and pointing in the wrong direction?"

Creziel laughed. "They are going to go uphill a bit. Then they will find reservoirs or streams and redirect them to lead straight down at the enemy. After the frost mage has made it as cold as he can without it turning to ice."

"Noo." I marveled in incredulity. "They're going to send a bloody freezing waterfall at the enemy? With those freezing winds on top of that? It's going to be damn uncomfortable climbing the mountain through that!"

The Talpus nodded in satisfaction. "Yes. And I believe we can invent even more ideas, once we get more of the spellcasters up here. The rewards you're promising should do the trick."

It was a pretty simple stratagem, and I loved it. In truth, I was pretty annoyed I hadn't come up with it by myself. I was totally taking credit for it, though. Heh. So, we might not be anywhere strong enough to face off against the enemy spellcasters? Who cares? We didn't need to. We could use what mages we had to turn the terrain against the enemies before they even came into range.

We'd let the various spellcasters of the mountain have their fun, while Creziel used his special gifts to do what *he* did best – manipulating the earth to harden to a formerly impossible degree. We'd make it so hard for that damn dwarf and all his tag-along spellcasters to make any progress that they'd be dying from exhaustion when they hit the peak, earning us the time we'd need to construct our defenses. We'd be one hundred percent ready for them, and the best part was, we wouldn't even have to face them.

I nodded graciously and tapped at the rock in front of me with a claw. "So it's working?"

He grinned. "That's not the rock I'm working on, but yes. Once they hit about two-thirds up the cliff face, where the climb gradually turns even steeper, that's when they'll find that the rock is suddenly harder to work with. Then, while they're stuck there, frozen and chilled to the bone, we can start preparing the next passage."

"Okay. I get it. And we should get some more shamans in to help you as well."

Creziel's lips tightened as he considered. "Yes. But it's a balance. We also want to keep enough shamans up near the Peak so we can prepare the defenses."

"Agreed. We wouldn't want to go to the trouble of keeping them back, only for our defenses to be insufficient." I considered it for a moment, then decided. "I think, for now, we should bring every shaman up here, really make it hard for them. Arthor returned to the Peak a while ago through the Corren tunnels. He's sleeping right now, but once he wakes up, we'll make some changes. I'm thinking his powers are more suited for this kind of warfare, while yours are better suited for preparing our defenses?"

"Agreed. Besides, we don't want Arthor creating any constructions without supervision. They would be strong as anything... and structurally unsound enough that they'd tip over by themselves."

I laughed. "I'll make sure to tell him you said that. Seriously, though, great thinking. I am really, really glad we have you on our side. Now, I'll get to fetching some shamans and other spell-casters and check in with Dimodeus, while you make life difficult for that dwarf asshole."

If it seemed anticlimactic, that was... because it was. After weeks and weeks of struggle, ambushes, and outright battle, we'd basically given up on defeating them in direct battle before they reached the peak. But we still had the chance of learning whether the mountain and the elements could help us defeat them instead.

As the ascent worsened, so would their conditions. At this point, they were more than a third up the mountain, height-wise, probably closer to half than not. But, climbing-wise, they still hadn't faced anything remotely close to what would be the worst challenges.

When Arthor returned and heard what we were planning, he didn't like the idea. No, he *loved* it! According to him, this—avoiding direct battles and letting the mountain handle things for you—were proper Talpus tactics and exactly what Deyra would have wanted us to do. He took over from Creziel and instantly went to work using his impressive Earth Mastery and Faster Mental Recuperation feats to harden the mountain against the humans' coming.

After a long chat with Dimodeus, the word spread about what we were doing, and we soon had about two dozen spell-casters of varying strengths and levels working at any hour, experimenting, changing, and doing anything in their power to make the Scoured Mountain throw these invaders back.

It was working, too. It actually made me feel a bit bad about how we'd done so far. They tried to adjust to our tactics and completely and utterly failed. Watching the mages and workers toiling together hundreds of feet further down the mountain, as gale-force winds blew ice-cold water around them, was a lesson in futility.

From the moment we really started to get our spellcasters working together and experimenting, they were introduced to one facet of misery after the other.

Oh, we didn't stop with our regular bombarding attacks. There was no reason for that. We were a lot more selective in our attacks, though, since we had to aim better to avoid hitting any non-humans. This was easier than you'd imagine, with the Secondary now living cheek by jowl with the humans.

While they'd been invited inside their ranks? They were *not* friends. So, any gathering of people would be either fully human or fully non-human. In practice, that gave us some easy targets. Sure, we couldn't just lob stones over the edge like we did to begin with, but then, we had to roll with the punches. We *were* doing damage.

Finally. Fucking finally, their morale was starting to break, too. For the first time, I was receiving reports of human soldiers, by themselves or in smaller groups, fleeing down the mountain. I honestly just wondered how it took them this long. At this point, there must be enough spellcasters dead, and with the dwarf half indisposed, their shields were anything but solid. And, if they were, they didn't always protect against magic, as well.

We were abusing that for all we could. A few of the less risk-averse (which was saying most) Imps also took to sniping in smaller groups in order for their combined attacks to sometimes push through the shields.

The shields still held, though, in general. At this point, that was no surprise. I actually opened up to the possibility of us starting targeting the non-humans, but, of all people, Roth insisted that we shouldn't. He was backed by Wreil, which was less of a surprise.

"Okay. Wreil, I get. You are the perfect person to help the non-humans become a part of the mountain. In fact, once we get news that they're approaching the top, we will want you in place to welcome them. But Roth? You've wanted me to dispense with the waste and just attack indiscriminately since... well, the entire time we've struggled against them?"

He raised his furred arms in a shrug. It incidentally also showed off his large muscles. "You said it. And I blame Wreil, too. But... there was one thing I didn't think about. I am in favor of attacking... and this is an attack, too. Wreil made me see that."

I *thought* I had an idea of what he meant, but... "Explain?"

Wreil smiled. "I have been observing their forces for some hours. Your attacks are working in more ways than you might have considered to begin with. From what I have deduced, the humans have made no secret of the Secondary being worth less than the humans, right?"

I shrugged. "Sure. Both in action and words."

"Well, now they're forced to be right next to each other, and the hatred on both sides is escalating. And the humans are being attacked by us 'monsters' while they are forced to stay near *other* non-humans. In the past two hours, I've seen three fights between humans and non-humans. I think that some soldiers of the Secondary are using the chance to unleash their tempers on the so-called 'superior' humans."

"Aaah. Of course. They used to not want to share anything with the 'non-human scum,' and now they depend on them for defense. Heh. That would bring tempers to flare." I considered the situation for a while. "Increasing dissatisfaction and tension. Tempers flaring. We should abuse that, shouldn't we? Maybe add that to our speeches?"

The former scout stood tall and smiled. "We most definitely should."

That painted the picture of how the next week progressed. Our spellcasters competed against those below, both in terms of strength and ingenuity. When the humans figured out a way to use air to repel the descending icy water, our mages countered by creating some sort of reaction that shrouded everything down there in a thick, freezing fog. Timothy was rather proud of that one.

Then, they tried shooting arrows into the air to hit our spell-casters, but a simple weave of air made sure they rained back down on the attackers. Just for once, we weren't outmatched. The terrain, position, and, most probably, the weeks of grueling work the enemy human spellcasters had undergone ensured that they didn't have the strength to outmatch us. So far, we could throw back anything they tried.

Personally, I also believed that the *kind* of spellcaster we had made a huge difference. They had war mages. We had spellcasters from all cants of life. People who were used to doing anything from heating apartments to pressure washing paved streets to fighting off lesser monsters—we had a lot of versatility. Now, they were allowed to give their imagination full rein.

And it worked. Watching the dwarven spellcaster on his stretcher, toiling to break down the hardened mountainside, while, on all sides, workers were parading back and forth in freezing wind and fog to carry the removed soil and rocks out of their path? It made me so happy I wasn't them. The soldiers lasted half an hour at most, then they had to take turns and go shiver under blankets to regain their body heat. On the first day, their speed halved. On the third, it was even worse.

On top of that, I addressed the non-humans down below at least twice a day from the cliff's edge. Outside my domain, my telepathic distance was much reduced, but I was still able to reach well into their forces. Heh. Enough for them to understand me. Oh yes, they understood me. The first day I talked to them, dozens of archers tried to shoot me down. Fat chance of that, with the air mages at my back, but I had to give them points for effort.

My message was simple, though. I took every single filthy truth that the humans were trying to downplay and laid it out there. "You know they hate you. That they think you less than they are. Barely real people. Yet, you stay with them because you believe there is no other way to build a life for yourself.

"I am here today to tell you that there is. You can simply leave. Sneak away in the dead of night. We will find you, and we will take care of you. And if you do not leave? Do what you feel you can. Because you know what is going to happen. You are always going to be the first sent into battle, sent to test for traps. When you reach the top of the mountain, you will be sent against me and my minions... and I don't want that. So, here's what you can do."

Every day, I spent half an hour suggesting alternatives to their current course. My minions were only too happy to help with ideas. Some of them were straight to the point and actually helpful, while others were downright bloodthirsty, like taking the chance to stab sleeping humans and quickly fleeing.

The real point wasn't to get them to actually do all those things, though any little bit *would* help, of course. It was the psychological warfare of it. Getting the humans to tighten their security, fuel their paranoia, and increase the current actions against the non-humans. Any way we could make them expose their real feelings toward the Secondary and stoke the fires would be to our advantage.

Up above, our people were working to prepare the peak for our defenses. Creziel was in charge of that, but I'd cleared the wide strokes of it with him. What he was planning was nothing short of diabolical, and I gave him the thumbs up to get to work. Watching that work unfold was going to be incredible... as long as they were able to finish in time.

At this point, they'd managed to tunnel through the crater wall to the outside and were hard at work widening the outside approach. We wanted the humans to have a nice logical path to the peak so they didn't spend too much time debating whether other avenues would make for a better, less contested climb.

Fortunately, the mountain was helpful in this approach. I mean, after hitting age 30, I never again contemplated climbing a single mountain in my first life. Hell, the two sets of stairs to my upstairs bathroom left me winded at times. However, Timothy was, as usual, helpful with a ton of information.

Apparently, you couldn't just climb a tall mountain whichever way you wanted. No, there were routes. These routes were quite often severely limited in number by the natural circumstances—weather, wind, inclines, possibilities for erecting camps, and whatnot. Back on Earth, the only people choosing other routes tended to be loners or people seeking new challenges.

Heh. With the thousands of soldiers camping out below us? That wasn't really a possibility. They needed to have some less angular stretches along the way for camping. There was no real way around that.

Unfortunately, that was one place where the mountain helped the humans more than our side.

Because the rise and fall of the ascent was anything but onerous. Near-vertical climbs were followed by nice camping spots, horrible, scree-filled rises with footing guaranteed to break legs replaced by relaxing climbs of sheer granite or similar that almost looked like they'd been carved to improve the ease of ascending the mountain. In short, though there were ugly stretches, we weren't going to see any marathon passages where the human army might be entirely defeated by the mountain itself.

I finally found the time to have a proper chat with Dimodeus back in the capital. Of all the people back in Fire Peak, he was the one I was the most happy about getting on board. He was worth every reward I could throw at him, and I rarely told him no. He did everything he could to make Fire Peak thrive and was quickly becoming the central bloody linchpin of my entire organization in the capital. His only issue? He was so goddamn proper. If we were back on Earth, I'd bring him with me on a three-day bender, ruining those morals of his.

"So, in short, even with the lack of help from the shamans, we're keeping up with the expansions on the fields and irrigation. The currently working fields are producing as expected, and we have workers doing the manual labor to prepare the initial canals as well as the water reservoirs for the remaining third of the crater. We will need the shamans to harden the material and level the canals off properly afterward, of course. Still, I am quite confident that we can save a lot of work for the shamans this way."

I snorted. "I love how you just assume that we're going to win our battles against the humans."

He inclined his head. "That is your task. I, meanwhile, will focus on making Fire Peak thrive."

"Ah. Delegation. You're a quick learner, dude. How are we doing on the preparations for that, though? I mean, getting everything ready for a battle."

"That... will take some explaining. All told, however, the takeaway should be that we are doing well. Ahzel has been delivering better than expected, and I believe his expertise has grown. The benefits from the weapons and armors have increased. Of course, with Creive's domain closed and no new high-quality ore, the quality of our weapons will be decreasing a lot. What should we do?"

"We cannot do anything right now. We need Ahzel up here soon, anyhow. We will need him and his minions for the battle, and we want to have him training with the others before they all arrive. I will talk to him later today."

"Understood. As for the crafting up here? I have a few surprises." He beamed a tight smile at me and clapped his hands twice at a guard who ducked out of the throne room.

I tilted my head in question, but he just spoke on.

"The Dworgen have delivered beyond expectations. We have had to adjust our expectations and have kept a lot of high quality items here in the capital instead of sending them to Ahzel. He would simply not be able to keep up with the enchanting. The enchanters here in the city are overburdened, as well. In result, your hoard is, once again, overflowing with items. It will take a lot of time for everything to gain any magical effects, but the armor in particular is of high enough quality that they will be able to hold high-end enchantments."

I nodded in satisfaction. "I love it. Once we get closer to the battle, we will open the hoard to everybody."

"Everybody, Onyx?"

"Yes. With reservations, obviously. Anybody who is ready and willing to fight. We will keep the stronger items in the hoard, so the hoard's effects don't diminish, but we want everybody properly outfitted for the battle."

"Understood." Then, a wide smile spread on his face, and he waved at the entrance door. "That was not the real surprise, however. This was."

The large double doors leading to the throne room were flung open, and in wheeled a large contraption. Dragged by three huge Urten, it was a mixture of dark wood and polished metal. It looked like it weighed several hundred pounds, clunky edges combined with the long, sweeping curve of... "Is that a frigging ballista?"

"I believe so. A few of the Dworgen have been near-obsessed with the making of it since they heard about the principles, and I gave them the go-ahead to keep working on it."

I gaped, walking closer to take it in. The ballista was massive, sharing only a slight resemblance with the versions I'd seen in medieval movies. This was more a welder's wet dream, at least fifteen feet long, iron combined with... "What is the bow made of? That doesn't look like wood? How the hell does that handle all that tension?"

Dimodeus chuckled. "Yes, Onyx. As you know, we are woefully short of forests down here. This is... a lovely alternative, in my eye. You might remember the Flesh Abomination that attacked Fire Peak, I believe?"

I slapped the floor in surprise. "Well, slap my ass and call me Tiffany."

"Pardon?"

"Nevermind." I took in the long curve of the material of the bow and chuckled to myself.

"That's...what? A rib? Never mind. With its weird body, who could tell? I love the karma of it. I seem to recall that nasty thing being a tiny bit taller than this, though?"

For one glorious moment, Dimodeus' officious demeanor faded, and he waggled his eyebrows in response. "Well, that is probably because that thing is one of the smaller versions. We have two that used one of the larger bones."

I marveled at the thought of that. The thing had towered above everybody, including myself. "But... will it hold?"

"So they proclaim. Our main enchanter says the theory is sound. He has procured a number of its bones for himself. Something about the beast taking in more magic than the average animal, strengthening the material in the process. I confess, I did not question much beyond the initial confirmation."

I waved it off with a wing. "Good enough for me, as well. If the specialists say it'll work, and they've tested it? That's all we'll need. So. We are adding ballistas. Ballistae? Anyway, that will be a lovely addition to our defenses."

He smiled. "It will. Especially once you take into consideration that we already have crews for all of them. And we have had a large batch of crossbows created as well." Seeing my rapid blinking, he added. "Your Crawls. It was Gert's idea. She insisted that their role as front-line fighters would not be sustainable in the long run. Her reasoning was rather good, with stronger, close-combat fighters being available. And, since they are strong enough to handle the weapons, with the steadiness needed for accuracy... I could not but agree. They are showing great promise."

Amazing. That was just... "That Gert. She's taking my job away from me, being as wise as she is." I chuckled. "What else? How are we doing on the training?"

The stately official grimaced. "That is one area where we are under-delivering. Not the training inside the city. In fact, a good deal of your minions are already reaching the point where their attribute increases are becoming hard to earn. Your minions are *strong*, Onyx... for their level."

I noticed the way he said that. "For their level. That's the issue, then?"

"Exactly. We still have been unable to find an effective way to level our minions. I have instituted a new approach, where we have several higher-level hunters and scouts joined by groups of lower-leveled fighters. They roam the mountain, then, locating proper prey and subduing it, allowing everybody to share the experience from the kill."

"I can see some of the issues. It's hard to find the proper prey, I guess."

"Exactly. It cannot be too strong a group, and they need to be cautious, because a failed approach can leave a full group of low-leveled fighters at the mercy of strong monsters. Add to that, that the Flesh Abomination absorbed a lot of the existing beasts... we are still creating an updated map of current monster growth and expansion. Finally, we have a serious shortage of competent scouts." He looked apologetic.

"Yeah, yeah. We killed all the old ones. I know it. Can't be helped. It's not your fault, mate. You do the best with what you're given. Still, keep considering approaches. We'll find something that works. Until then, we keep this up. What else?"

"Let us see. We are working on what you ordered. The emergency plan. Oh, and the deserting companies from the Secondary have made it up here. There is little tension, and they are being received well. So far, they are fitting in perfectly. I am truly impressed by how little trouble we see from them."

"That's incredible. I'm glad that they got here safely. As for their behavior, it makes sense. They're used to taking orders, and I believe they've been treated so badly in the human army that, as long as we treat them with respect, they'll fit right in. Any luck with getting them to join our forces for the fight?"

He held two fingers apart slightly. "Little. Part of their forces join us every day, both from the desire to strike back at their former masters and for the rewards we offer. But it would seem that their reticence holds true. They are afraid of what the humans may do to their kin if they are ousted. And some are simply afraid." He smiled. "Those who do join us, however, are amazing. They are of lower levels than the humans, but higher than most volunteers from Fire Peak. While they might not be as well trained as the humans, their own kind have made sure to train them decently. The best part, though? Their eagerness. Those who decide to join up are looking for payback."

"I can relate to that. Give them all they need!" Hell. That was one thing I'd learned for sure in my years as a foreman.

One golden rule. Reward those who show up at work, do what they're supposed to do, and go home afterward.

Those who deliver past that, do better than asked for? Give them what they ask for, and then some. These are the people you'll want with you!

Apart from that, the situation in the capitol was about as could be expected. The good thing about an impending invasion was that there were few dissenting voices. With the Dworgen and the former city guard defeated, everybody left in the place accepted the situation as it was.

That didn't mean that they were giving us their full aid unasked, obviously. However, it did mean that most people didn't mind helping, and the rest at least refrained from working against us. That, by itself, was about as good a starting point as we could hope for.

CHAPTER TWENTY-THREE

"Uninvited guests are often most welcome when they leave." -Aesop

The success with our new approach was undeniable. Their army slowed down more and more, and you could *see* the toll our sorcery and surprises took on their workers. After a handful of days, the dwarven mage arose from his stretcher. Wreil insisted he still looked weakened, but after that, their speed improved slightly, along with his strength, one would assume. Even so, their progress was not without its cost. To my chagrin, the spellcasters' experiments were taking a heavier toll than back when we still had the Parvu beasts to bombard them nonstop.

It was too much to expect that the invaders would take that sort of pressure without reacting - and react they did. The first attack came almost without warning, in the middle of the night, as two large groups of camouflaged humans scaled a stretch of the mountain *next* to where we expected them to climb. Fortunately - for us, heh - one of the climbers lost his grip close to the top and went tumbling with a loud yell, giving us a brief heads up.

We got a chance to organize and half a minute to prepare before they hit us. The ensuing attack was as brutal as it was short-lived, though. They fell over us, yelling, charging recklessly, formations and discipline forgotten in sheer bloodlust. Mostly humans, with a few non-humans in the mix.

For a moment, the surprise attack threatened defeat, but then Timothy went on the offensive, floating into their midst, stunning the attackers left and right. We flung them back, then. Even with surprise on their side, they were still out of their element, and the fact that all our people had night vision evened the scales.

That moment marked a change in the dynamics, though. Before, the human army had focused exclusively on pressing onward to reach their goal. But now, they were flinging forces at us at all hours of the day. Sometimes, they climbed in their dozens, sometimes in their hundreds. Sometimes, they were humans only, other times mixed with skirmishers. The methods and approaches were different. Occasionally, they would climb straight up toward us, trying to reach us through speed. Sometimes, they'd try to circle around, reach us from above, or find a point where they could fire down upon us with ranged attacks.

But the important thing was they stopped holding back. I took it as a sign that we were actually getting to them, and they would be in trouble if they didn't act, and I called for assistance from Fire Peak. It didn't take long until we had additional soldiers there to safeguard our spellcasters. Most of them were green as grass, and the clashes were bloody. However, we had all the odds on our side. Better positioning. Air support from Grex and his Imps. Timothy and me, and, again, we had the spellcasters.

That was the single place where the humans held back. They didn't risk their mages in these attacks. It was all infantry, ranged fighters, and the occasional squad from the Secondary. At most, the spellcasters below expanded their shields to protect the attackers on the first part of their climb. They allowed no large-scale attack by the non-humans, though. They clearly didn't trust them to move by themselves. Heh. Probably clever of them. We'd make a huge barbeque and welcome them aboard.

We were receiving everything I'd asked for now. Experience points for our fresh fighters, a chance for them to be part of a fight with reduced risk and gain in levels, along with actual hands-on experience, too. For each of them who flung an attacker to their death with a well-aimed rock or throwing spear, they gained a little experience, a little strength, and a tiny taste of what an actual battle was like.

Our Imps and other flying fighters under Grex were also truly coming into their own. At this point, their movements seemed carefully choreographed. They moved into formation to join for attacks as naturally as they spread out right afterward to avoid any return fire. We practically stopped losing any of the fliers, due to their speed and improved training. Their levels kept climbing, too. Grex went so far as to admit that the new Imps and other fighters joining from Fire Peak were becoming acceptable, too.

We were improving, even as we were forced farther and farther back. Still, it felt like we were failing. Even with them losing scores of fighters each day, the constant clashes kept our spellcasters from focusing as much on preparing the mountain for their approach. We could tell from the speed of their advancement.

After two days with several attacks each day, we had to admit that this wasn't sustainable... for us. While the attacks were deadly to the human army, they only lost a fraction of their full strength every time. Miraculously, some fighters managed to slink away and survive each time. They would be able to keep it up and still arrive with lots of people to spare. I grumbled at the realization, especially since our gains for our new fighters had been incredible. Each of them had gained several levels, and we had only lost a few of them. Our Imps were having a ball, too, enjoying the free target practice. But we would have to find somewhere to dig in and punish the enemy.

We stuck our heads together and came up with two major plots, two locations where we'd be able to really lay the hurt on them and, hopefully, halt them entirely.

At least, so we thought. The first location was a huge failure. Our elemental spellcasters were planning to work together for something big. They told us that they believed they might be able to work with the single water mage and create a blizzard—an actual localized blizzard—and unleash it upon the camp of sleeping humans when they stopped for the day on the plateau below us. It would be very localized, very taxing, and potentially very deadly, engulfing a nice stretch of deep snow and frost to impede their progress and rob them of their strength.

The first part went well. You could *feel* the temperature plummeting, and soon, the first snowflakes were floating through the air. Except, somehow, they knew what we were up to. Perhaps that damn dwarf was able to sense the magic. Perhaps they had other safeguards in place. The only thing I knew for sure was that, this one time, the human army decided to pack up all their shit during the night and perform a night-time climb.

There were a lot of humans lost during that night, not to mention equipment or foodstuffs left behind. However, the following day saw them well beyond the reach of the spell and us with a bunch of tapped-out spellcasters. Quite a bit of leveling for them, though. Oh, and Timmy hit Level 40 and got himself a new feat called Burst of Speed. He could spend mana to double his flying speed for however long he had mana. The cost was extortionate, but the versatility of the skill was insane. He'd been hard to hit before. Now, he was almost as fast as Roth, when he was using his skill.

Regardless of leveling, we were starting to become fatalistic. The prospect of holding them back seemed more and more unrealistic by the day. Our fighters were still gaining in levels, and at the pace they were going, we'd have five days at most before we'd be defending ourselves at the peak. There were still more than ten thousand humans left. Creziel was the one to come up with the perfect place for the final attempt to stop them, and I had to admit that the theory was promising.

We surprised the crap out of them the following day. We pulled our spellcasters back entirely, leaving only our fighters and fliers to defend the current climb. At this point, that was practically a walk in the park for the humans. They ascended rapidly, as one would expect. Well, rapidly in comparison to earlier climbs. We put up token resistance, flinging rocks, Imps firing, and everything. It was all for show, though. While we were going through the motions, the spellcasters were up above, preparing the real counterattack.

The following day, we were ready for them. We'd pulled back during the day before, as we did every single day, matching their progress at a large enough distance that they couldn't quite catch us. It allowed us to keep up the pressure on them as they climbed, attacking them and slowing them down, while staying at a safe distance from any retaliation. Now, however, we were gathered, and we were prepared. This time, if all went well, we wouldn't damage them and pull back. We wouldn't slow them down then retreat to repeat everything all over again the following day. We would stop them *dead*!

I hovered above the Scoured Mountain. The strong winds pushed me insistently, treacherously switching directions every other moment. I let them pass over me, making tiny adjustments to adapt to their insistent nudging and stay where I was. Below me, our trap lay in wait. It was a river bed. That was it. An ordinary river bed, carved twenty feet or more into the rock of the mountain for about a mile before it spilled out over the mountain in what would undoubtedly be a waterfall rivaling the majesty of the Niagara falls.

First off, there were several carved passages of the kind across the mountain, allowing rainwater to spill down the mountain or melting snow from the heights to fade into wild streams with the coming of spring. Nothing to it. The river bed was dried up at the moment, filled with rocks and boulders.

There had been no rain the past couple of days, though the

weather felt oppressive. The river bed looked wholly undramatic—an easy climb for the day. The only special detail about this river bed was that it was longer and wider than most others and made its way between two smaller peaks, ragged spears stabbing into the sky. In short, this was the only way the human army could conceivably choose to march.

The forty-five degree incline looked like a relatively easy ascent. A walk in the park, compared with some of the climbs the human army had weathered over the past days. It would have been a walk in the park, too, except for what we were planning. At first, when Creziel came to me with the idea, I was dubious. But then I shared it with some of the others, asking for input, and they loved it.

Especially Timothy, who went completely batshit. He went on about hydrostatic pressure or something until he went blue in the head. Heh. Bluer. I honestly didn't hear anything after when he said that he thought it was the perfect solution.

Here I was, flying, overseeing everything. I'd made a few swoops over the enemies, threatening an attack, along with the Imps, just to make everything seem "normal" to the humans. However, we were really in a holding position for now, waiting for the attack to happen. I had to admit that I wasn't as enamored with the approach as Timothy, but I could see how efficient it might be.

We needed it to work, even if it meant that we'd be attacking non-humans alongside humans.

They were climbing now. I could see that damn dwarf, too. He wasn't in the lead, not by any measure. No, there were scores of lightly armored soldiers climbing before them, scouting the way and pinpointing any issues.

Shouts and commands broke the silence from time to time as they pointed out traps and potential issues. Here, a stretch of the river bed had been covered with a patch of see-through ice, creating a treacherous footing for anybody trying to climb that way. There, a series of short ascends had footholds and handholds that were virtually crumbling, with a little help from our shamans. They were annoying details, slowing down their ascend slightly, but they were also, all told, nothing they couldn't handle. They'd had worse and overcome it.

Where they pointed out the problems, spellcasters rushed to counteract the issues. Here, a stocky human stretched a swathe of fire ahead of him to melt the ice. There, a handful of workers ran to carve handholds that *would* hold. All the while, the spellcasters' magical shields were still following along with the rest of the army, bringing its protection with it.

Only once did the dwarven mage move to help. A single, massive block of ice stood tall at the center of the passage, between the peaks, blocking the entirety of the twenty-foot-wide riverbed. After a brief discussion between two other mages, they called out. The short, robed spellcaster made his way up, slowly climbing the rocky, winding path carved deep into the mountainside. Mere seconds after he arrived there, the ice block lay shattered, and he stood to the side as others started ranging ahead of him again.

Their ascent continued unperturbed for a couple of minutes. Then, a cover of fog rolled over the landscape. Heavy clouds of fog, moving swiftly down from above. This happened several times on a daily basis, when a cloud passed over us. But this time, the clouds were heavier than usual and dark enough to obscure vision entirely. It was a signal. A signal that our trap was about to spring. Below me, the dwarf tensed. Damn. He must be able to sense the magic conjured within the clouds.

He shouted a command, which rang down the mountain, repeated again and again,and their forces readied themselves for an attack. Shield formations slammed into place, the tinge of magical shields grew even darker, and ranged weapons were readied, pointing in all directions. It was perfect, and it was horrible. I wanted to be able to avoid hurting the non-humans, but... the line had been crossed now. This was about survival.

The sound was almost imperceptible at first. It started as a barely audible whisper, a promise of things to come. Then it grew into a louder rumble, building up within seconds into something that could be heard clearly from up here in the skies. I glanced up and smiled. Grex and his Imps were there on one side, Timothy on the other. Ready. Waiting. Then it came.

I don't know where Creziel got the idea. Snow was something that only rarely came to Fire Peak, and he had to be unfamiliar with the mechanics of it all. However, once he sat down with Timothy and started theorizing about what one might do with such a natural phenomenon, things had taken off. They had taken the idea of the spellcasters collaborating to create a snow storm and then run with that. Timothy started with the notion of avalanches, moved on to combining it with rock falls then abandoned all of it as too uncontrollable, too hard to guide. Finally, they got to... this.

The water streaming down the river bed didn't look impressive at first. Tidal waves, tsunamis, flooding, those were all facts of life. I'd watched all sorts of news reports and movies about them. I was probably expecting something more overwhelming, something bigger than the one-foot wave gushing down the mountain.

Timothy, however, grunted in satisfaction. "Poor bastards."

"What? You think this is enough? That tiny wave?"

He scoffed. "I could lecture you on the pressure again, but... just watch. This is only the start. They haven't even breached the pool properly yet."

No, thank you. No more lecturing. He'd spent enough time on that, talking about the PSI and whatever. I only cared insofar as he was right in his theory, that a high enough water pressure would actually be able to overwhelm and smash the magical shields of the humans. His claim was that it would be able to smash the shields and their forces. Either that, or it'd work sort of like in those books about the huge desert planet and wouldn't register as an attack, actually bypassing the shields altogether. In the latter case, he insisted, the effect would be even more devastating.

So far, I couldn't see it working. Shouts and orders reverberated back and forth inside the river bed, and the human army parted, moving as high as possible to the edges of the hollow. The first wave slid harmlessly between their forces. They did look nervous as all hell, and there was a deal of pushing and prodding as their retreating masses were pushed back to where they couldn't avoid the streaming water anymore.

Still, little happened. One soldier lost his balance and was dragged down the river bed for a while, until somebody caught his arm.

Then, we heard the inhuman roars. They sounded like the noise a heavy downpour gives when it's beating against the roof. It kept increasing in intensity and loudness. Finally, it was arriving. From higher up the mountain, the real wave came streaming.

It had ended up being a lot of work, but Timothy promised me the end result would be worth it. The shamans sealed off a mountain lake at the top end of the river bed, a few miles higher up on the mountain. Then they birthed an abomination of a snowstorm, draining all the moisture from the air for miles. Finally, some of the elemental mages worked all through the night to heat the snow, convert it into water. In the early hours of the morning, they'd finally managed, heating the rest of the frosty mush enough that it was closer to liquid than not.

Half a mile ahead and above, the river bed turned, moving upward at a steeper pace. Now, with the fury of an unleashed god, an avalanche of near-freezing water slammed into the turn. It exploded upward thirty feet or more in a foggy cloud before exploding down the river bed toward the army.

Fuck. Okay. I owed Timothy an apology. Possibly a gift. What do you give a ghost who can't hold on to anything? My mind was taking off in all sorts of directions as I watched the oncoming masses of water, trying to take in the scope and utterly failing. Turns out, if you take large masses of water and add gravity, you get... mayhem. Absolute mayhem. A boulder was flung over the edge of the river bed. A fucking *boulder*. How do the physics on that even work?

I shook my head, trying to focus on our situation and said to the other fliers. "Ready? Once it hits, we take advantage and attack. We only get one shot at this!" I barely noticed their responses as I watched the roaring water churn downward faster than a speeding car.

The first ranks... disappeared. There was no other way to explain it. One moment they were there, the next, they were completely lost within the waves. Next in line stood the dwarven mage.

He stood alone. In knee deep water from the first spill, he faced his oncoming death face-on and didn't flinch. Then, moments before the wave hit, he pushed both arms forward in a warding gesture, a white-blue blast cut through the river bed... and the entire army disappeared in an explosion of water and fog.

We waited impatiently, hovering in the air, ready to dive. There was no attacking right now, or we'd be pulled under ourselves. The force of the oncoming water was undeniable. However, as hard as our spellcasters had worked, they hadn't been able to create unlimited water. Already, the water masses thundering down the mountain were growing less, and it was just a matter of minutes or less before they would die down entirely.

Slowly, the all-covering fog dissipated. The roar was growing less, to the point where you might almost be able to hear somebody yelling... if they stood right next to you. Now, I was starting to be able to see the result for myself, through obscuring clouds and... ice?

It took my mind a while to understand exactly what I was looking at. When I realized it, I started cursing inside my head. Long and hard.

I couldn't see Hargren, the frigging Key of the bloody North. Why was that, you ask? Because he was hidden under ice. That's right. Ice. Not water. A huge block of ice had grown from out of nowhere, covering the entire stretch leading up to where the dwarf had stood, rising in the air above him at an angle. Instead of smashing through the ice, the goddamn water had chosen the path of least resistance, streaming at full speed into the air and falling down again farther down the mountain. Mountains of water created the hugest impromptu waterfall I'd ever seen, exploding up into the air and smashing down farther down with the fury of God.

The human army wasn't saved. Not by any stretch. A lot of the water still slammed down again into the river bed farther downstream, wreaking havoc, and where it hit, it was insanity. However, the blockade did manage to disperse the water at a wider angle, robbing the water of some of its momentum, funneling quite a lot of it outside the river bed. Hence, instead of a scenery with an army that was entirely swept away, we were looking at wounded, confused, and scared groups of soldiers. Some groups were torn along with the remaining water masses, some had been broken... but all told, they were alive, and they were recuperating.

"Change of plans!" I growled. "We need to strike only those who are exposed. Before they recover. Spellcasters and ranged fighters only! Move on if they look like they might defend themselves or strike back. Move *now!*"

I was true to my own word and pulled in my wings, closing my eyes to slits against the wind that redoubled, trying to force tears out of my eyes. I swept down upon a human mage who was doubled over another wounded soldier, bright light expanding over his bleeding forehead.

"No Doctors Without Borders in this world." I growled, gripping the human in a claw and taking off within the second. At the apex of my leap, I tossed him away. With a muffled scream, he hit the closest mountain edge and went over. I pounced on the next one.

It was a gruesome attack. No. Let's call it what it was. Slaughter. The shocked soldiers were in no position to defend themselves against our lightning attack, reeling as they were. We made full use of it, killing spellcasters and archers left and right. I slashed and bit, threw soldiers off the mountain, whatever was the fastest. Fires all around me attested to the Imps joining me, and where we went, cries followed.

One minute. Two. Five. Our attack was overwhelming and fast enough that the enemies didn't know how to react. Even where their squad leaders were waking up and adjusting, we didn't stay for long enough for them to marshal a coherent defense. The few who rallied their soldiers around them, we simply avoided. Timothy was in their midst, stunning soldiers left and right, breaking up attempts to form ranks and move against us.

Finally, however, I slammed headfirst into a shimmering surface and growled. A magical shield. I looked upon the wide, tear-filled eyes of a sodden human spellcaster twenty feet from me. He was kneeling, trembling, but his hands were flung out toward me, and his mouth moved, as if in prayer.

I smashed against the barricade of his shield again, felt it waver, and I carved him down. Dripping with blood, I spotted my next target, a female human spellcaster, but I got only a few feet before I hit another shield. Behind that, I saw another shield go up. Growling in frustration, I sent the command wide. "We're done! Leave. Now!" Then, I leapt into the air. I swear, I heard a sob from the mage before me as she realized that she was going to live.

CHAPTER TWENTY-FOUR

"Conclusions?"

We were gathered right above the basin, watching the last spots of snow slowly melt, water running in a gentle stream toward the river bed. The silence of the gathered people here was underscored by the cries of the enemy downstream.

"We failed." Arthor's tone was harsh as ever. "Their losses were staggering. Everybody in front of the dwarf was hit by the wave and died. Those farther down the mountain were also badly impacted, and their remaining healers will be working throughout the night."

I growled. "And their spellcasters?"

Wreil replied. "That part was a success. They had a good deal of spellcasters out in front. And, in the aftermath, we managed to finish maybe half of who remained with not a single loss among our own. In the days to come, they will have trouble keeping up their defenses, especially while that damn dwarf sleeps."

I nodded. The sour taste in my mouth didn't go away. "Even so. We failed."

"Yes. Hargren is still alive. Their numbers were not impacted too much. They will reach the peak in days. A defensive battle is inevitable."

Goddammit. Weeks of struggle and bloody battles... If only I'd managed to get to Hagren. Or if the fliers formerly of the human army had been ready and could join us. Or... dozens of hypotheticals made themselves known inside my mind. It hadn't been worthless. I knew that, deep inside. Our people had earned a chance to grow stronger and prepare themselves.

Still, right at this moment, it felt like a waste of lives and effort. We might as well have surrendered and pulled back entirely. Then—I growled and shook my head to dislodge that annoying voice. Self-recrimination wouldn't help us any. "All right. We will keep up the aerial attacks and the ranged attacks, until then. We want them weakened for whatever final battle we get into. And if we *do* find any weak spots before then, we'll be ready to punish them. Anything else?"

Arthor nodded. "We need to find a counter to that dwarf. Anything. We have nobody who is able to go up against him. So, unless we find something or somebody who can do that, we might as well not fight. They will push their way right through our defenses and march on Fire Peak, and that will be it."

Timothy stood near the mountain edge, looking downhill. "I disagree."

We waited, but nothing more seemed to be forthcoming. I snorted. "You *might* want to elaborate on that a bit, dude. We're not inside your head, thankfully."

He shook himself and turned. "Sorry. It's pretty gruesome down there. What I mean is, yes, we need to find some action against the dwarf. Still, I believe Arthor is being a bit fatalistic."

"He does tend to do that." I ignored Arthor's infuriated protest. "Is he wrong, though?"

Tim held up a hand to scratch his head, then glared at it as it went right through himself. "It's a matter of scope. I mean, yes, the dwarf is powerful. Is he more powerful than Selys was,

272

though?" He looked at our tiny circle. When nobody responded, he continued. "Exactly. If you noticed his actions down there, he didn't just face the wave head-on or hold it back with his magic. He diverted it, making sure that its force was wasted. It was a clever move. He doesn't have endless powers.

"Yes, we're in a shoddy situation, and yes, the presence of a spellcaster as powerful as him, combined with their numbers and levels are putting us in a bad position. Still, that doesn't mean we're doomed. It just means we'll have to get inventive. And I have ideas."

Arthor scowled at him. "*Just...*"

"No. When Tim's right, he's right." I interrupted. "Selys survived flying *through* the fire shield around Fire Peak. I doubt that tough runt down there would be able to duplicate that. So, that's already *one* option we have, even if getting him to hit the shield in the first place is a bit of a stretch. Still, let's use that to set the tone for the next few days. We are going to plan to take down that little bastard. And once he's down, the rest will be easy pickings. This is still winnable."

I've had my fair share of rush jobs over the years. Lots of cut corners and ugly details hidden behind plaster. I'd argue that it was rarely my own fault, and I generally tried to be upfront about these things with the customers... but that would be both irrelevant to the point and a bit of a horrible lie.

Still, there was no discussion that the work on our defenses over the next few days was among the worst. We were rushing *everything.* From the placement of our weapons and traps to the installation of defensive structures, size of crenellations and... everything. From day to day, our defenses had suddenly gone from this thing that might save our bacon to our sole option.

Suddenly, people had *opinions.*

The number of available fighters, workers, and spellcasters was fluctuating wildly, too. Now that things were heating up, a lot of people were getting cold feet and suddenly hiding in the city or taking their chance with disappearing into the lower layers of the mountain. However, that also went the other way. With the conflict drawing closer, a lot of people in the city were also realizing that they couldn't hide from this. It was going to come, no matter what they did. Hence, suddenly we had more workers on our hands than we knew what to do with.

Unfortunately, the same couldn't be said for spellcasters and soldiers. A lot of the people who had joined our forces to be trained to fight were now opting out. After a few discussions with Dimodeus and Timothy, we decided that we *would* let them leave the forces. The alternative was too police state for us, but that, in so doing, they would lose any chance of any future position in our forces.

Personally, I'd lost any kind of calm mental state a while ago. I was constantly on the move, back and forth between the front lines to the new defenses and back to Fire Peak itself. I was overseeing the work, mediating, resolving differences, threatening people... whatever it took.

There was always a demand on my time, and even Dimodeus was starting to appear frazzled. Therefore, I might not have been in the perfect mindset for when Firth returned.

At first, I just gaped at her. The brawny Culdren looked exactly like she had when she left. Devil-may-care, strong, independent, and totally obnoxious. I roared. "What the fuck, Firth? *Now* you arrive? You said two weeks!"

She didn't react, merely sneered. "I did. For the *first* message. Which I sent. And then circumstances worsened. Do you want to hear why or not?"

I almost tossed her out right then and there. I didn't need the complications. Didn't need her acidic tones, and I definitely didn't need any further distractions. But... fuck me, if we couldn't do with our own fall-back option. Having to rely on the grace of Creive, in case things went south? I didn't like that at all. Still, I didn't even try to hide my temper.

"Tell me. We're in no position to mince words. The crater is getting attacked tomorrow, and a fall-back position would be damn nice."

She didn't back down. "You would not be in a position to complain to me if I were dead, either. If you wanted me to rush here earlier, I would be dead. As would all of my scouts. Few enough made it back here as it was. You received my messenger, then?"

"Regarding the first Blessing? Sure. You said that the ruined city was filled with high-level monsters, and you couldn't get any closer."

"Exactly. After that, we moved straight south. Until then, we had been able to move relatively fast. I believe it's because the monsters in the city fed on anything coming close. However, the farther we got from the city, the more we were beset by other monsters. Flying ones, too, and fast ones, ambush creatures. We had to slow down to a crawl, hide ourselves, and move only when we were sure nobody was around."

"Why didn't you just travel by night? Your eyesight—"

"You think we didn't?" The scorn in her mental message was clear. "I've been scouting for my entire life. *I know what I'm doing.* So, listen to me when I say this. Had we not slowed down, we would have died. All of us. As it was, we were ambushed four times."

I took that in... then I narrowed my eyes. "I hear you. And I respect your problems. But the entire fate of the mountain may rest on what news you have. So, your outbursts aren't helping. If you cannot keep calm, I'll have to find somebody less experienced for the job." I stared straight at her to make sure I got the point across. "Otherwise, please continue."

She glared but nodded. "Two of our number died to a large, frost-based creature that burst from the ground at night. One I had never seen before. Still, after two weeks of constant hiding, creeping around, and living on scraps, we actually made it to the location indicated down in the Blessing."

I held my breath. "And? Was it there?"

"Yes. And, near as I can tell, it's unapproachable. There—"

"What?" The outburst flew from me before I could stop myself.

With narrowed eyes, the muscular Culdren beat her wings then settled them behind her again. "This was not like the first Blessing. No monsters roamed wild here." She interrupted herself. "No. That is wrong. What I mean to say is that the place was home to a varied settlement of dangerous monsters, like everywhere else I have seen outside the mountain.

"They fight and fuck and roam around, struggling for supremacy, procreation, and survival, like anywhere. Except for where the Blessing lay." She started forming a shape with her strong, veined hands in the air before her. A construction, tall and layered. "There was a single construction. A huge place. A tower, but not a tower. More like a number of layers, like the mountain itself, but constructed, reaching into the sky. Entirely defenseless. No mountain around it to protect it from the outside world."

A... ziggurat or something? From her gesticulation, I came to think of the Hanging Gardens. Huge, tiered constructions. "The monsters didn't attack there?"

"They didn't even dare approach. We soon learned why. The construction was abandoned long ago. Plants had taken over the place, taking over entire layers of the place. But one place was still maintained, still protected."

"You're shitting me. Somebody still lived there?"

"One person. A humanoid. You will understand that we didn't just approach blindly. We had a Nailwing catch our scent on that day, but the moment we got within a couple of miles of distance from the place, it retreated."

"...which means?"

I could *see* her offense at my ignorance. "Nailwings don't pull back once they have spotted prey. They're infamous for it. They will follow you for weeks and not attack if they see no openings. They may stay at a distance and keep an eye on you, waiting for you to relax and forget about it. They don't flee. This one hit a certain position, then it turned around and flew, all-out, like it had a dragon breathing down its neck."

I blinked. "That *does* sounds suspicious. What did you do then?"

"What we do. We scouted the place. Working a circle around the huge construction, we searched for any sign of traps, opponents, or harmful magic. We found nothing, except for the topmost floor." She indicated a wide, flat platform. "In this single location, plants were kept back, or didn't grow, and other signs of decay were halted. There was nothing to explain why, no reason why it should not be touched by nature.

"It was a simple platform, all bricks, no decoration. A simple statue stood in the center of the platform, of a humanoid. It was recognizable from afar. Very similar to the ones depicted on the walls here in the mountain." Her eyes met mine. "A Corren."

I nodded. "I guess it was to be expected. They *were* the ones in charge here, as they must have been near the other Blessings. So, they created the place. What happened then?"

"Callem went to investigate. It could have been either of us, really. We tend to take turns investigating risky spots, depending on what needs to be looked into. Callem was one of the best of us at spotting traps, magical or otherwise."

"Was?" I was getting a sinking feeling in my stomach.

"Yes. He performed a circle of the platform from above, looking for anything suspicious. Nothing. But then he crossed the line. He didn't even touch down, just skirted across the area of the platform in the air. Then the statue awoke." Firth sighed, shaking her head. "I don't know if it was a statue or a real Corren, frozen in place. But words hammered from it, right into our minds, like you do. *'You do not serve the Corren. Suffer.'* And that was it. Poor Callem burst into flames, and the rest of us fled as fast as we could."

Damn. That was... nasty. Also unhelpful. "I'm sorry to hear that. Did you learn anything else?"

"Nothing at all. The Corren didn't even register to our gifts. I can scry levels, as long as they are not too far from mine, but this creature or statue... I couldn't even tell if it was alive or not.

Whatever it was, it would have been able to crush us all without even moving from the platform."

Oof. That was a kick in the nuts. There was nothing to be had for us there, then, leaving us only with the other Blessing as a possible fallback position if things went wrong. With tons of non-fighters to protect and humans on all sides? Yeah, I wasn't looking forward to that at all.

CHAPTER TWENTY-FIVE

"Clarity is the preoccupation of the effective leader. If you do nothing else as a leader, be clear." -Marcus Buckingham

The time of the battle would soon be upon us. I stood on the center of the battlements, taking a moment of pleasure in the solid ground beneath my feet. The defensive wall felt enduring... permanent. Watching the enemy army climb closer had been an anxiety-inducing affair, and thus, it was a bit of a surprise that, at this moment, I found myself with a sensation of peace verging on solemnity.

That peace was utterly broken as Arthor stumbled up next to me, looking like a weasel who'd run a marathon and then gone a couple rounds in an heavyweight boxing match. He looked *spent!* Surprisingly, he also looked rather satisfied with himself, as he sank down to a knee.

I squinted at him. "I'm usually not one for genuflection, mate. What the hell happened to you?"

"Genuflection? Pfah. Perish the thought, lizard. I'm here to tell you that they tried what we'd feared."

A shiver ran down my spine. "They tried tunneling through?"

He nodded, breathing heavily. "They did. Not too far down. The outer shell of the mountain isn't that thick in the upper layers." He raised his head to me. Pride blazed in his eyes. "We held them back, though. Collapsed their approaches as quickly as they built them. That dwarf may be strong… but humans do not have other earth mages who can compare to us!"

I smiled fondly at him. "I've never doubted the Talpi. You know that. But today, you've outdone yourselves. When we kick these bastards off the mountain, we'll be shouting from the rooftops how the Talpi beat the Key of the North."

Arthur nodded. "One step at a time."

"I agree." I halted, then asked. "Sorry, mate, but I have to ask. You look like sodden shit. Do you guys have the stamina to do your part?"

He snorted. "Better worry about yourself, lizard." Then he strode off. Slowly.

After a while, my zen slowly reappeared, and I looked down over the mountainside, at nothing at all. I had never been a man of introspection. Action, always. I'd prided myself in the fact that I didn't waste too much time on words or thought, but always created. Even though, deep down, I knew. I knew that one of the main reasons I kept myself busy at all times was to avoid introspection. Avoid looking deeper into myself and taking a closer look at all my flaws, failures, and regrets.

Right this moment, however, with my life possibly coming to a close in the next few hours, my thoughts were invariably drawn inward. The life-threatening part wasn't anything new—but this was it. The final fight. So, I got a bit maudlin. To my astounding surprise, I didn't hate what I was seeing. That was a first. I'd made my share of mistakes. I had many regrets. The way things progressed with my ex-wife and my daughter. Probably should feel worse about the way I let myself and my health go, too.

But this time around? Thinking about the life I'd led in this world? I was surprised to find that I actually felt good about myself and the choices I'd made. Not always the results. Definitely not. There were too many losses, too many shadows left where companions should have stood. I'd made my share of mistakes. More than my share.

Still, this time, I'd made them with my eyes open, conscious about the path I wanted to take. To my surprise, that made a huge difference. While I still beat myself around the head for the mistakes I made, I also found myself dwelling less upon them... because I knew I'd done my best and given it my all.

That knowledge... was liberating. Watching the sun slowly crawl over the horizon, I found myself at peace with myself and the universe as a whole.

Of course, that's when Timmy arrived.

"Looking very zen, there." The blue apparition floated slowly down from above, arms spread wide, with an inscrutable look on his face, and his head strangely tilted to one side. His legs were positioned weirdly, too.

"...Really now? A Christ impression? Starting to think a bit much about yourself, are you?"

"Blessed be, my son." He laughed and shrugged. "I mean, try to think about it. We have quite a few things in common. We both died and got better. Also, Jesus died on the cross, and I have to deal with your presence on a daily basis."

I laughed. Couldn't help it. "You're *such* an ass." We stood in silence for a while. Then I asked. "Any regrets? Something you'd want to change?"

He nodded, smile gone. "Lore. I still miss the little runt. You never really got to know him, but... seeing his mind open up was a miracle in itself. There was such a brilliant mind there, and... suddenly it was gone."

Lowering my head, I suddenly couldn't look at him. "I don't think I ever said this, but I am so sorry. I know that it was my decision that led to his death."

He shook his head. "Not your fault. I mean, I blamed you at first. Of course I did. But you didn't betray anybody. And you were trying to help 'em all. Don't accept responsibility for something that isn't on you."

"Thank you. Really."

Silence stretched. After a while, I glanced at him again. A melancholy smile played on his see-through visage. Then he continued. "To be honest, though. Even with what happened with Lore... What we've done here? I'm feeling good about it. We can always discuss whether we could have done more, or done things differently, but... we gave it our best, and nobody can ask for more. I promise you. I won't try to end things by throwing myself recklessly into combat again. Instead, I'll try to build something good, honor him that way."

I assented, coughing to clear my throat of whatever lump seemed to have stuck in there.

A couple minutes later, Timothy chuckled darkly. "Besides. Even if we wanted to change anything, it's too late. To say it in a way your old ass can understand: the game plan is set. We can just wait for the whistle before it's time to make our play."

I once got my ass into deep trouble. My first dive as a foreman was with my own company, and I was doing all right. Had a couple of nice jobs, enjoyed getting the entirety of the paycheck for myself, even if the hours were insane. Then I messed up. Took a contract with a politician.

I know. Rookie mistake. Still, he seemed on the level. Another red flag. Heh. As I quickly found out, the contract I signed was a quagmire. All sorts of murky shit, which basically made it impossible for me to complete my jobs at a satisfactory level and not get sued to oblivion. Which he would.

That was the big issue. I'd tied up so much money in that company. Basically, I'd lose everything. Arguments were starting, and things were commencing to come to a head between us, when I figured out what to do. Basically, I gathered all my people, explained to them what was going on, and asked them for their help.

They brought horror stories to the politician one by one, enticing him with a bunch of stuff he could use in his lawsuit. I was underpaying my workers, making them work in unsafe conditions, hitting on the secretary—all sorts of fun stuff. He fell for it, spending a lot of time talking to these people, promising them the world when they'd testify. Then I pulled the rug from under him.

Every one of my workers retracted all their accusations, all at once. Then, I declared bankruptcy with my company... after I'd used every trick in the book to empty it of all the money I had tied in it. Heh. It still wasn't pretty. The lawsuit took two years, it was costly, and I lost, obviously... but I will never forget the look on his face when he realized that the only thing he'd be taking with him from this experience was a nasty lawyer's bill, since my company wouldn't be able to pay.

How the hell could this be relevant to my current situation? Well, it taught me that, if you wave desirable things in front of somebody's nose, they often forget to look at what they need, in favor of being enticed by what they *could* have. That was exactly where we were at.

In theory, the human army would, if they so choose, be able to tunnel their way through the rock farther down and then breach the crater at a different point where we hadn't had the chance to spend ages on defenses. We needed them to *not* realize that. Therefore, we'd spent a lot of effort and a lot of time to make our defenses look less formidable than they actually were.

What the human army saw when they finally breached that final rise was this: the entrance to a long tunnel, protected behind a reverse slope defense, broaching a wide span between vertical cliff sides. Yes, we'd made sure that they would be able to spot the tunnel straight away. It beat shouting, "This is what you want, guys. Come on and get it!" I could have built some illusions to create the same, but with how many high-level people they brought, somebody would've seen through it. We needed something real.

Basically, though, that was it. We had a long, several hundred feet wide, twenty-foot tall defensive embankment with a large tower on either end, one huge stone door in the center, and the goal in sight right behind it. Oh, sure, the defenses were brimming with our soldiers and armaments, and a heavy shimmer to the air spoke quite clearly about the fact that we had magic defending us as well.

Still, that was it. No obvious traps, no visible siege machinery—visible being the key word here; they were all hidden behind large boards—no huge unscalable facades towering up way above them. A simple, forty-five degree climb reaching right up to this vertical facade and the goal in plain sight. Hell, we'd even been kind enough to take the steep incline and cover it in tall, tiered steps, about five feet tall apiece, leading toward the defensive construction. Basically, I'd asked them to keep us looking as underwhelming as possible. We definitely didn't want to scare them away.

Heh. Our own presence might be too much, as it was. The defenses were packed with our fighters, ready for anything. We also had reserves waiting right inside the crater, ready to reinforce us. We were looking *good*. I stood on the rightmost side of the wall and Ahzel on the left. In between us was a beautiful mix of ranged fighters and spellcasters, with close-rank fighters standing ready on the wall right behind them. It would take little time for us to switch from ranged combat to close combat.

Where we used to sport homemade equipment, shoddy atlatls carved from bone, and whichever armor we'd been able to scrounge and adapt from fallen foes, now we gleamed. Our ranged fighters were lightly armored, but the close-rank fighters were decked out in mostly metal armor now, depending on their attributes and preferences. Crawls held new-made crossbows, looking lethal and threatening. Almost every single soldier liberally shone with the magic enchanted items, or in some cases, carved in threatening runes upon the items.

The towers on either end looked like crap because... well, because they were. Still, they were both Feedback Towers and manned by Ahzel's toughest fighters. If the enemies spent energy to take down the towers, they'd regret it, and Ahzel's people were likely to survive.

Our winged fighters were there, too, of course, hanging out far above us, ready to intervene at my order.

The weather was horrible, and I loved it. Rain was pouring down on the enemy in swaths, cold enough to numb fingers and ruin bow strings. The wind was blowing hard enough to enforce the sensation of so many lovely school outings in my past. Was the weather intentional? Of course it was. With the elemental spellcasters on our team, we'd be morons not to take advantage of it. On top of that, the approach leading up to our defense was out in the open, while our defenses were covered and mostly out of the rain. The end result was that our enemies would arrive wet and freezing, while we'd be well-rested and ready for them. Heh. In theory, at least.

I looked around me and had to fight down the sinking feeling in my stomach. So many people I knew and loved here. There was Timothy, in the center of a group of ranged fighters, chatting with a Crawl. There stood Roth, twirling his sword in his hands. Wreil. Gert. Grex. People who had been with me for a large part of my new life, who were now, again, throwing themselves into a life and death situation on my side. Farther back would be others, Arthor on his way back to Creziel... people with wildly different personalities, yet all of 'em dear to me.

My mental voice rang out over the defenses. "I will be brief. For all of you who stand next to me today, I am proud. And I'm thankful. That you take it upon yourself to protect the mountain and the lives of everybody else... That means a lot. Today, a lot will be decided. But one thing remains. The fact that you, today, stand before us all as heroes. So, remember your training, don't get cocky, and, most importantly? Don't get killed. You don't want to miss the rewards I'm throwing at you, once we've won!"

Laughter and cheers met that comment, and a lot of them raised their weapons in salute. Nice weapons, those. I could see the magical sheen on a lot of them. I laughed and growled in approval—but on the inside, I couldn't hide my fear. How many of my people would be dead by tomorrow?

The humans wanted to talk. I couldn't believe it. The bloody dwarf actually showed up with just one other person at his side, and they started climbing the incline, moving closer toward the walls.

I almost chuckled at the thought of seeing the tiny bastard having to scale the huge steps we'd put in - except, when he reached the first one, he lightly leapt the full five feet, as if somebody boosted him from below. Showoff. A third of the way toward the battlements, they stopped and waited.

Timothy was adamant I shouldn't go. "It's a trap. I mean, it has to be, right? We have *nothing* to win from you going out there."

"Probably is. Still, if they try to break us, we have our surprises ready on the towers." I smirked. "Besides, he brought a friend... I'll go ahead and do the same."

Ahzel was... confused. That was the only way I could feasibly put it. To be completely honest, I'd expected him to act up when I told him that he'd be joining us in the battle against the human forces. I mean, it didn't exactly seem like he'd wanted to join our team properly, even if crafting on our behalf was okay with him.

But he'd surprised me. Not so much by his joining us for the fight—he had already stated his number one goal was to follow Deyra, fight, and grow—but by being surprisingly chill. In fact, he had exclaimed that he was entirely satisfied with how everything was going. He was building up his forces, making them train hard, both in and outside of the training and sorcery chambers, and was becoming quite proficient with enchanting. But he *was* missing the personal growth from fighting. Hence, the chance to go claw-to-toe with the human armies was just what he was itching for. The current development, however, didn't sit well with him.

"I don't understand. You are taking me within a handful of feet of our biggest threat... and you expect me to *not* attack him?" We were slowly rising in the air, beating a slow circle above where the dwarf was waiting for us. The rain was still pouring down, making it hard for us to spot any surprises, but I'd checked the area extensively from the map and found nothing.

"Very much so. That's an order." I searched for the words to try to explain it to somebody, who definitely did *not* have the word armistice in his vocabulary. "The point is, we might not *need* to fight. I know it's part of Deyra's instructions... but think about it like this. If we fight today, people are going to die. Lots of people."

His face didn't show anything, but his emotions very much did. It was the mental equivalent of a shrug. "Sure. And the rest of us will grow stronger. Besides, your scouts did the count. There are still almost ten thousand humans out there, with impressive levels. We will be so much stronger for it."

"True. But even if we ignore the fact where you and I might be among those who die... think about it. This is going to be a tough battle. There is no doubt that a lot of our people are going to die. Think about your own domain. If you gain five levels, but lose half of your minions, that is going to slow down the growth of your domain, right... are you then really doing Deyra's bidding in the best way possible?"

"What are you implying? Of course I am! Live. Fight. Thrive. It's not complicated."

"Wrong. If you were able to thrive better, grow faster, if you hadn't fought... have you really made the best choice? Are you doing Deyra's work... or are you just taking the most straightforward path, when your domain could be growing faster and stronger if you decided to avoid battle?"

He was silent then, for a while. I didn't press him on it. But once we completed the circle, I addressed him again. "Look, I'm not implying that fighting is bad. I've waded through enough blood to get to where I'm at to know that you can't always avoid fighting. But, I also believe that you should choose your battles. I think our forces are stronger for having you on our side, when I could, most likely, have finished you to gain a few levels."

He scoffed at that. "You think! I would have made you pay!"

I turned my head and smiled as we flew. "Most likely." He didn't deny that we could have managed, though, and I took that as a partial victory. "Still, there you have my answer. I might not be right, and it's always easier to see when the conflict is over and done with. However, I truly believe that the mountain could grow impressively with just a year of peace. So if there's even a chance that we can reach a tentative truce with those damn humans? I'll take it." I squinted downward. "What are you seeing? To me, it looks like all the human forces are too far back to join them."

Ahzel growled. "If they are hiding any ambushers, they are well-hidden. I have had scouts watching them the entire time. They have not placed any traps. If you insist on this folly, we might as well go meet them." We descended in silence for a while, until he continued, thoughtful.

"I don't agree with trying to sue for peace with the humans. At all. But I understand your reasoning at least. And... in some situations, it might apply." He showed me his teeth, eyes filled with cold fire. "But it's a good thing you brought me with you. Because I believe eating that dwarf is going to help me grow immensely."

Before touching down, I Inspected the two humanoids, reveling in the fact that I could finally see what we were up against. The bloody snob, Lord Verneth, was as I remembered. Nothing had changed, from what I could recall—which made sense. It wasn't like I'd seen him on the front lines.

The dwarf was on another level.

Personal Info:
Name: Hargren Levengar
Race: Evolved Dwarf, Level 48 – experience toward next level: 5780/48000
Size: Medium

Stats and Attributes:
Health: 1320/1320
Mana: 1672/1720
Strength: 40
Toughness: 132
Agility: 30
Mental Power: 172
Mental Control: 144

That dwarf! He was a powerhouse. Apart from Selys, and possibly Tellor, he was the single person with the highest attributes I'd met... and that included all the dragons. His Mental Power easily had mine beat, his Toughness was close to mine, and his Mental Control was high enough he could easily handle protracted battles. Of course, attributes were one thing. He also had years and years of fighting and honing his skills, every feat he'd amassed and access to spells on top of that. How was that fair?

We touched down in front of the two humanoids, about fifty feet away. I opted to land on the same tier as them, so as not to stare down upon them from above more than I would otherwise.

Seeing the dwarf from up close made for a difference. His spellcasterness, the Key of the North, looked like absolute sodden shit. Even after standing around for at least five minutes, he was wheezing and panting. His beard looked like a rat that upped and died, plastered against his face. He was pale, and had definitely lost a lot of weight over the days since we last met. The only thing that was unchanged was his demeanor. He stared me straight into the eyes, and there was fire there, and a challenge. This dwarf was not done. Not by a long stretch.

His companion looked better... for a certain degree of "better." Lord frigging Verneth. He was still missing an arm. Not apologizing for that. But the rest of him looked improved. Not that he'd been starved or anything while he was a prisoner with us. But it looked like being back with the humans did him well.

He was looking healthy, standing tall with a gleaming breastplate, carrying that old hammer in his remaining arm. Oh, and he was as smug as ever. Nothing new there, either. That, if anything, warned me that this was likely to be a trap. No way was he going to accept any kind of diplomacy that didn't carry a downside for us.

Ah, well. I'd play nice, right up until things deteriorated. "Hargren. Lord Verneth. So nice to see you." I dipped my head. "This is Ahzel, one of my vassals." Ahzel next to me had no plans of playing nice. He just glared and set his feet, teeth bared. I continued unperturbed. "He's delighted, too."

The dwarf smirked. "Clearly. Well, we are not here to bandy words. Only to demand your surrender."

I snorted. "That's really what you want to go with? Not 'Oh, we've lost half our forces on this misguided mission, maybe we should try to find a peaceful solution,' or something based in the real world?"

Lord Verneth took over, his mental voice dripping with venom and... anticipation? "Please. Like we are going to find a common standpoint? Cartiga insisted you could be reasoned with. Look where that took her. No. We are here to tell you to stand down. If you do that, we will not slaughter your forces. Instead, we will allow them to be inducted into the Secondary."

I looked at Ahzel. His eyes didn't deviate from the pair in front of us. Probably a wise choice. "Yeah. That's not happening. Of course, you already know that. Sure, your Secondary could probably do with a little bolstering, given how many have left you. Oh, and I doubt that they are feeling good about everything, as it stands. Do you even think they are going to fight?"

The one-armed leader gave me a look of sheer derision. "Fight? Oh, they are going to fight, if they know what's good for them. They know the consequences."

"Wow. And here I thought I couldn't think less of you. Thank you for correcting me. Also, how bloody moronic are you? Can't you see, that's going to backfire on you at some point? Those are thinking creatures, yet you continue to treat them as less than you and expendable. They talk. The way you're acting... it's not sustainable."

He laughed. "Oh, that is priceless. If you really believe that I am letting any of them go back home to their bestial brethren and share what has happened here, you are even more naive than I thought. Whoever survives these clashes will have to be spent elsewhere. That's sad... but it's pretty common. Some of them just won't get it into their stupid heads how they should serve the Nefren Empire."

For a moment, I was speechless. He was really talking, quite calmly, about how he was going to get several thousand thinking creatures slaughtered? I'd thought him a tool from the start, but this was beyond that. All playfulness gone, I tensed and asked, "This isn't an attempt to negotiate, then. What is it?"

The dwarf chuckled. His deep-set eyes looked almost black. "Why, a trap, obviously. Cartiga would never have approved, of course. Good thing Lord Verneth is in charge now." He closed his eyes to slits and brought his staff to a horizontal hold, even as magic started spilling from his hands.

"Take off, Ahzel!" I complied with my own command, even as I threw everything I had at the two humans. First, a Weakening Fog enveloped both of them, then a Shadow Whorl fixed itself right in front of the dwarf. At the same time, a layer of frost hit them both from next to me. Beating my wings hard, I only had a split second to be surprised. I really wasn't expecting our attacks to hit home. Why didn't they protect themselves?

I got my answer seconds later, in the form of a cut-off roar, followed by a large white shape falling through the air next to me. There was no time for me to react properly, but the surprise did keep me from beating my wings harder. That, at least, ensured that I wasn't still increasing my speed as my wings, head and back in quick succession impacted with the magical shield that the dwarf had cast... enveloping us all and trapping us within.

Air rushed around me, muddling my mind as I saw the ground rush up toward me at dizzying speed. A loud, pain-filled crash next to me showed where Ahzel crash-landed on the uneven steps.

My body engaged before my brain did, and my wings started beating. A few wing strokes brought me back to the ground with a graceless landing. Suddenly, all I could see around me was the bright blue light of the magical shield created by the dwarf. Not around himself. Around all of us. He'd effectively shut us in with him. I roared. "Betrayers!"

Hargren's eyes were sunken, but filled with fire. His mental voice was clear and promised death. "*We* are the betrayers? When you have done nothing but attack from behind, cheat, and deceive? I never promised you safe haven. But I promise you this. You will die, cut off from your bestial friends, with just that other monster to keep you company."

As he spoke, a dull light shone around him, and the soil moved around him, slowly traveling upward, covering him in earthen armor.

I laughed then. "You think we didn't come prepared for this?" My mental voice rang outward, reaching for my minions on the ramparts. "Attack now! Let 'em fly!" Turning back to the height-challenged bastard, I was about to come with a quip, when something felt... *off*. My mental messages, to me, had always held a certain sensation akin to speaking into a phone.

You released your message, trusting in the technology to carry it to the recipient. When the connection was off, even if you couldn't tell straight away, there was something about the kind of silence you'd get that would prompt you to *know* that your words weren't getting through. Same thing here.

Somehow, I could tell that the magic wasn't carrying my words the way they should be.

Then it clicked. That damn shield. Of course, this little prick was proficient enough that his shield would protect against both magical and physical attacks... effectively cutting my communication off from the outside. Damn. We'd have to survive until my people saw for themselves what was going on.

I unleashed another Weakening Fog at the pair. The one-armed fighter shuddered, but the dwarf didn't look like he registered the attack at all. Damn. That bloody earth armor would probably keep the magic from seeping into his skin. I growled. "Close with them, Ahzel!" Then, I followed my own advice and leapt closer to tear them apart. Magic or not, they wouldn't be able to match up against two dragons.

Within seconds, I was reeling, one leg flayed to the bone. Thirty percent of my health was gone to a single attack. Motherfucker! Ahzel was retreating to a distance, too. At least his frost breath looked like it did have some effect on the dwarf, weighing him down and slowing him. The Lord? Not so much.

I'd underestimated him, horribly so. I figured he wouldn't be a threat with one arm. Except, I'd never really gotten to face off against him in our past clash. I'd just avoided him and weakened him, little by little, until he'd fainted like a dainty lil' thing. But this time, the hammer he was carrying was making things hard for us.

I couldn't tell if it was the weapon itself, a skill of his, or a combination—he *had* managed to make it glow with a menacing light, but I'd never tangled directly with him back then. Unfortunately, now I had to go through him to get to the mage, and he was not making it easy. Somehow, he could make that hammer of his throw out terrible waves of force, enough to hurt us badly.

"Distance attacks on the human. We take him down, then we focus on the dwarf."

Lord Verneth laughed. It sounded absolutely unhinged. Hatred tinged with quite a bit of strapped-to-the-bed insanity. "Oh you will, will you?" He planted the hammer head-first on the soil, drank down a potion, and grabbed it again. A series of jolts went through his body, as if he was strapped on to a low-current electric fence. "Well, let's not speculate. We'll find out shortly if a human will be able to match up against a pair of overgrown lizards."

We sprang into motion. The tall fighter went straight toward us, while Ahzel and I leapt to each side, unleashing our breath attacks on the tall bastard. Only, now he shrugged them off like it was water.

My Weakening Fog attached to him with no effect, while Ahzel's frost breath gave him a blue tinge, but nothing else. Now we were both trapped inside the magical shield with him, our large bodies left with little space to maneuver. Within moments of his charge, however, we confirmed one beautiful detail about the tall, muscled aristocrat.

He was slow as balls. That low Agility of his, and I'm guessing him not being accustomed to fighting on foot? That bit him in the ass. As such, avoiding his attacks was not really an issue, as soon as we learned the reach of those force waves. That relief lasted right up until the dwarf decided to enter the battle.

It started as a glow. An almost imperceptible dark glow near my left leg. On instinct, I veered to avoid the area, which was what saved the leg, as a spike of stone slammed out of the soil, trying to impale my leg. Seconds later, a cry from Ahzel proved that he was under attack, too, and I saw him limping slightly from one leg. Then, the dwarf unleashed a bolt of fire straight at my head, which I only barely avoided.

Soon, Ahzel and I were leaping, dodging, and flying to avoid constant elemental attacks from the dwarf, all the while we had to keep ourselves out of the ranged of the demented lord, who had taken to laughing uproariously, even as he ran untiringly at us, constantly unleashing those waves. My health plummeted further and further, and I could thank my build for giving me the Agility needed to avoid most of the attacks.

Ahzel was seeing the same problems as I was. His lower Agility caused him some trouble, but he must have some additional combat or Toughness-oriented feats, because the dwarf's attacks didn't have as much of an impact on him as they did on me. Still, his lower body was scorched and pockmarked from the many elemental attacks... and the bloody dwarf wasn't even breaking a sweat.

As for our enemies? Nothing. Nothing at all. The bloody human was looking more and more manic by the minute, but apart from that, I couldn't see any visible effect of our breath attacks. There must be a... regenerative effect in the potion he drank. Or maybe something to make him more resistant.

Regardless. It didn't see like we were getting through to him. When we moved to get closer to him, his wave attacks were almost impossible to avoid, and they bloody *hurt*. The dwarf? Well, that stupid earth armor of his limited our magic to a negligible degree, as well as our physical attacks. It also made him weigh five times more, so we couldn't just toss him around, which Ahzel realized, to his detriment.

I reluctantly touched my necklace and activated a Mana Crystal, feeling my wounds close up and scorch marks fade away.

The dwarf laughed a mirthless laughter and lowered his staff for a moment. "Oh. How interesting. There is only one more in that neckband of yours, is there not? Good to know." Then fire built in his hands again, and I sprang to avoid his attacks.

How long had it been? Two minutes? Five? Everything stretched and lost definition as we played a deadly game of tag inside the closed-off magical shield. Ahzel got one lucky strike in on Lord Verneth, giving him a heavy limp, and it looked like our breath attacks were finally starting to have an effect on him, slowing him down even further. But the humanoids both still stood strong, and that bloody Hargren was nigh-untouchable.

"Surrender, beast! We will kill you, and this white menace, but we will promise to spare your minions. Do you not want them to live?" The dwarf sneered at me, even as lightning crackled over his fists, ready to unleash.

I stood, panting. I was down to thirty percent health again. I'd have to bloody use my last mana crystal soon, then it was just a matter of time. Was it really the worst? It was preferable to death, at least, for my people. Urgh. I couldn't believe I was actually considering it. At least, I could try to stall him. "I... might consider that. Except, I don't trust you in the least. How can you make me believe a single word of what you're spewing? Why would you keep your promise?"

The dwarf shrugged. "It costs me nothing. I will take great pleasure in adding another two notches to my dragon kills. And my human friend here will be satisfied to see you flayed for the insults. I can guarantee them all a place in the army back in the empire. I will even swear upon Deyra, to-"

A shadow appeared above us, and I sighed in relief. I interrupted the dwarf. "You know what? Never mind all that. The tables have turned again. Screw you and the cat you rode in on! I look forward to gaining a level or two from taking you down!"

I was expecting a proper boom to punctuate my taunt. The actual impact made little noise. More of a loud 'plick' sound, like a nail hitting glass. But within seconds, it was followed by several more impacts, and some duller noises, like rain hitting a tin roof.

The dwarf looked up, frowning, and I grinned to see the air above us swarming with Imps, with the ballista bolts adding to the attacks. "What?" He snorted. "Those are just mundane attacks. They will not-" He frowned even deeper as another set of ballista bolts hit his shield.

Now it was my turn to sneer. "They will not what? Be able to touch you? Think again, buster."

To be completely honest, I had despaired quite a bit about being able to break through the spellcaster's shield, when they finally attacked, but Timothy had been quite adamant about this.

He insisted that the ballistae were the perfect weapon against the spellcaster's shield. I thought that you couldn't just guesstimate these things, but he disagreed. Since we *had* already seen magical shields overload and sometimes break down entirely, there was a clear limit to how much pressure a shield would be able to handle before breaking down, at least locally. Now, we were attempting to capitalize on that. He also tried to explain to me what that guy who had an apple fall on his head said about gravity and force, and eventually I got the gist of it.

The result came along with the next salvo. This time, when the first ballista bolt impacted with the shield, it actually punched all the way through, and it was immediately followed by a fire bolt from one of the Imps. The next three fire bolts were absorbed as the shield closed again. But that solitary fire bolt actually followed the hole made by the ballista bolt to hit the ground next to our very own Keymaster.

I smirked. "How do you like *them* apples?" I sprang to action.

The next minute saw the duo struggling to both defend and attack, as several more missiles made it through the shield.

I had to keep watch myself, as some of the ballista bolts sometimes came too close to my body, but I had to hand it to them, they had gotten pretty damn good at aiming. The dwarf actually started taking hits, and one of the ballista bolts managed to hit him in the shoulder, flinging him to the ground. When he got back up, his earth armor looked a right mess, and he looked *pissed*.

Finally, the two humanoids had a snarled back-and-forth while fighting and started moving back down the mountainside.

I pushed the attack, seeing the opportunity to finish them off once and for all. Lord Verneth was starting to look downright feverish as well, icicles hanging off his armor from Ahzel's frost attacks. But then I realized our situation. We were only a couple of hundred feet from the foremost fighters in the human army, and the dwarf was moving slowly in their direction, defending as he went. *And the shield went along with him.* If we didn't do anything, we'd be dragged right into the center of the army.

It was probably an ugly sight. Ahzel and I flung ourselves repeatedly at the edge of the shield, struggling to smash through it. We applied claws, teeth, sheer force, and even some desperate blows with our tails to try to break through... and still, the shield held.

On top of that, both humanoids were making the most of our predicament, and we were forced on the back foot again.

Ahzel's wounds closed as he used a mana crystal, and I prepared myself to use my second crystal. We were less than a hundred feet from the leading edge of the human army now. We needed to do something. Add more...

The shield suddenly went opaque, then completely blinding in front of my eyes. I flung myself at it again, feeling a ripple of pain in my hind leg as Lord Verneth hit me yet again... then it burst. I slammed gracelessly through the shield, sending an Imp spinning away with the force, and watched Ahzel follow right behind me.

I made a split second decision, then sent an abrupt message to everybody. "Retreat." Following my own command, I flung myself into the air, beating my wings heavily as I worked my way back toward the wall. Within the first couple of yards, air in front of me tried to solidify again, before promptly breaking apart... then we were gone. Back to the safety of the defenses.

I took in the look of Ahzel as we crashed, more than landed, down on the solid stone of the wall. He looked like crap, and I was sure I was little better. But we'd managed to avoid their trap and figured out a solution to the dwarf's shield in the process. In the lack of better options? I'd call that a draw.

CHAPTER TWENTY-SIX

"This will be the last message I will get the chance to tell you. Brave fighters of the Secondary. Know now that your leaders are going to throw your lives away in the battle to come. Most of you have already come to terms with the idea. What you do *not* know is that none of you will survive. Your own leader, Lord Verneth, made that quite clear to us.

Ask him yourself, though I believe that you already know the truth of it. You have all come too close, have learned too much of what the Nefren Empire thinks of non-humans. That means that you will die. So, before the battle, I want you to consider. Do you really want to die like that? Spent as bait in a struggle that only aids the human empire? Or do you want an alternative? Do you want to avoid this? Because if you do... we will help you find the way."

I turned back toward Timothy. "Man. This always leaves a bad taste in my mouth. It feels like the German propaganda back in the second World War."

He grimaced, turning away from the steps leading from the enemy up to the wall. "Well... you're not wrong there. It *is* kind of reminiscent. The difference, of course, is that you're actually

299

telling the truth. And the poor bastards on the other side probably know that, too. Anyway... you've got your answer now." His translucent arm pointed behind him to the enemy. "The humans know you're right, too. They're bringing in the humans first. No non-humans."

I smiled. "Excellent. The damn dwarf is staying quite far back, too."

Tim grinned. "Yup. Unless my theories are wrong, which they aren't, he's going to have to stretch his shield to make it cover that far. Now, even though I still think it was stupid of you to test our theory like that—only idiots test in production—you must have scared that high-leveled bastard well."

I squinted down at the approaching formations, ignoring the tickling sensation from the Talpus who was climbing my knee to refill my necklace with Mana Crystals. Maybe one in four of the remaining human soldiers were pushing forward. They were starting to climb the steps with effort, boosting each other up in turns, with shield-bearers moving first to keep our people from harming them.

Of course, I might be deluding myself, but I did think I spotted the edge of the shield right in front of the first troops. It was hard to see. "Good. That shield of his would mean trouble, because we don't want them to reach us all the way up here... but I think we've managed, Tim. I don't think they noticed the surprise."

He nodded merrily. "I can't wait to see it in effect."

"Same. But, for now... let's make sure that they don't get the chance to notice it on their way up." I turned to the defenders and sent a mental shout out to everybody. "Ranged fighters and spellcasters? Attack at will."

Within moments of my command, missiles rang out from the ramparts. Most of them fell short, but a good bunch rained down on the shield in a drumming noise. I heard a triumphant shout from Roth. The throwing spear flung from his atlatl had actually punched through the magical shield and flung an attacker down a step.

Their approach was awkward as hell. Their pretty formations were clearly disrupted by the need to climb the tall steps, slowing their speed down to a crawl and leaving tons of openings for our people to fire at them.

We took the openings. All across the ramparts, people slung throwing spears, flung magic, or shot bows at the approaching enemies. The ballistae fired unceasingly, and the effect was undeniable. Magical shields were breached left and right, leaving missiles and magic to tear into the enemies. I did say shields, plural. These were definitely not the work of our dwarven friend. These were individual squad mages—the mages who'd been our targets since day one, who were overworked and understaffed—and it told.

They were taking casualties for each step going forward. But now, they had finally made it to the battlefield, where their discipline could show. Even with the challenging terrain, they moved expertly, protecting their partners, making sure no individual soldier moved too far ahead of the others. Their levels were showing. Only lucky shots were able to take down soldiers with a single shot. The human soldiers were tough enough to buckle down and continue from most hits.

Timothy was looking nervously down the steps in front of us. "Professional bastards, aren't they?"

"They really are. Look." I pointed. "There are two soldiers down right there. Yet, the others just close ranks and keep coming. It's impressive, really." I grunted. "I'd better join in. They're getting into range now." As promised, I let my breath attack sweep over their ranks, watching as Ahzel mimicked me on the far side of the defenses.

That had an effect. The front rank soldiers on my side visibly slowed down, and a few of them slid slowly to the ground. Ahzel's attack was less effective. The shield bearers ducked behind their shields and strode on.

I was starting to feel nervous now. Our defenses were limited, by choice. There was no way we'd have been able to create effective defenses where we could place all our defenders at the same time. As such, we only had about a thousand fighters on the rampart at the time. Looking down was enough to make us feel pretty damn overwhelmed.

Our fighters were doing well, though. They kept up their onslaught, unleashing hell on the attackers. Their lack of proper shielding was really showing. Especially our spellcasters were able to capitalize on the fact that they were running out of mages who could shield from magic. Ahzel unleashed some skill of his, creating a whirling tornado of frost in the center of a formation, while a spellcaster flung waves of fire at the company next to them.

The Shadow Towers were constantly active, too. Hard to spot, the eighteen constructions stood equidistant on the battlement, spewing streams of weakening missiles at the attackers.

Yet still they came on. The first fighters were approaching the battlements now, and their hateful roars drowned out the shouts and commands among our people. Among them, archers were starting to take potshots at our defenders. After all of this time, the humans would have bottled up so many frustrations, I couldn't imagine the slaughter that would transpire if they made it through.

I didn't really care to, either.

I looked at the foremost shield bearers coming closer to the wall, raising their shields to protect themselves and secure their position, readying a position for the soldiers beyond them who carried... poles? Ladders? Didn't matter. I raised my head and roared, flinging my defiance to the heavens. My mental shout rang out for all to hear, friends and enemies alike. "Now! Shamans! Let it rip!"

The human soldiers reacted instinctively, ducking behind their shields, activating skills and feats to prepare against whatever was coming from us. Additional bubbles of magical shields were activated from spellcasters and, probably, magic items alike. Yet, our attack didn't come from above.

Our shamans had worked hard over the past weeks. However, with all the manual labor at their hands, they had managed to finish and harden the battlements early, allowing runecrafters to take over and create the final defenses. That left Arthor, Creziel, and the rest of the shamans with plenty of time to prepare one final trap.

This one was all Arthor. Creziel and I had come up with plenty of ideas for traps and surprises for the area leading up to the battlements. Yet, Arthor overruled us. "We don't want a lot of traps. We want *everything* to be a trap." Just like that, he outlined his plan. Make it look like we'd created a terrain constructed to inconvenience the enemies, when in fact, it hid what it really was.

I'd been afraid that the dwarf would spot what was going on, but Arthor assured me that was unlikely. Because, unless he knew what he was looking for, there would be no magic, no constructions resting inside the soil to give away the surprise. Only if he took heed of the weakness of the rock below his feet, he might notice. Him having just spent his mana in an earth duel against my shamans probably didn't help him any, either. Heh. They were going to find out, right about now, though.

A sensation buzzed through my legs. A deep-seeded vibration, like being reclined in a massage chair, right before it really gets going. Then it increased, working its way up to a loud thrum.

On top of the shields that the human army had up, another shield appeared now, vaster, encompassing the entire force.

I smirked. So, the dwarf could sense something was happening? Well, this wasn't going to help him any. This attack was coming from down below.

The human shield bearers were too professional to be entirely distracted. They were continuing their approach, opening ranks for the first ladder carriers to come forward. All across the stretch, lanes were made ready in the sea of humanity. I watched nervously as a team of lightly armored humans sprinted across the final stretch, a long ladder held between them.

Then the first crack sounded.

It was loud. Louder than any sound should have the right to be. It echoed over the battlefield, making the entire setting pause for a second, as if the world took a breath. Then, the first step started crumbling.

Soldiers across the battlefield stepped forward or jumped down to the step below, trying to avoid falling. However, as the vibrations increased to an audible hum, the step kept crumbling away, pebbles and larger pieces of rock drizzling down on the next step. There, cracks were forming, too... and expanding, outward and downward.

Now, the human army panicked. Training or not, watching the mountainside crumble underneath your feet was something they weren't prepared for. The foremost ranks fought to fling themselves up to the relative safety of the battlements, while those behind were either caught up in their defenses or looking around for a safe spot to stand. Except, the cracks were widening... and the vibrations were spreading.

It happened in seconds. The entire central step broke away, and with it, hundreds of soldiers frantically tried to fling themselves to a safe position, to find somewhere to stand, proper handholds, anything. In that moment, the devilry of Arthor's plan was revealed. Because there *was* no safe haven here. The entire approach leading up to the battlements had been constructed in two rounds.

The first was a simple, forty-five degree climb, evened out, hardened, and smoothed out to provide something akin to an all-covering slide. The large steps had been tacked on afterward, constructed from the soil and rock that was left over after carving out the battlements, and hardened just enough that our shamans would be able to make it crumble away. Shields or not, unless the attackers thought to actually push their shields into the underground (if that was even possible), their magic was useless here.

The effect was widening now, reaching the outer layers of the approach. Humans fought among themselves to reach safety, get to the edges of the mountainside, run back down, anything. But there *was* no safety here. In moments, the crumbling steps turned from an unsafe place into avalanches of stone and people rumbling down the mountain at an ever-increasing pace.

A single archer stood on an island in the center. A solitary rock outcropping had somehow escaped the effect of the initial sorcery. Time froze as he met my gaze, and I swear, there was both sadness and regret in that look. Then he was gone, torn away by the remaining stones and bodies.

All across the approach, the former sea of humanity was turning into a waterfall of debris, humans, and corpses. I'd seen avalanches before. But I had never seen anything as cruel and bloody as this.

Below us, the human army was rushing to part and escape the horrid effects of the tumbling, crushing forms. The huge shield covering the entire range blinked and burst in seconds. Along with that, their last chance at survival disappeared. Once they reached the edge of the mountain, they poured out into the air to tumble hundreds of feet down to a lower ledge and certain death.

The chaos was complete. The few soldiers on the battlements who weren't completely enthralled with watching the gory scenery were sniping away at the few enemies who managed to make it to the relative safety of our defenses. They lasted only minutes.

Then, for a blessed moment, there was silence. Silence as we watched the rain pour down the now slippery, unscarred surface of the steep stretch leading up to our defenses. Soon, it would be washed clean of all the blood and filth. As for my mind, that was a different thing. This was going to come up in some of my nightmares.

CHAPTER TWENTY-SEVEN

"Courage is willingness to take the risk once you know the odds. Optimistic overconfidence means you are taking the risk because you don't know the odds. It's a big difference." —Daniel Kahneman

Silence reigned over the mountainside. Then, it was broken by cheering. Howls, roars, and hollering rang out into the open air as our people celebrated the simple joy of having survived and beaten back the enemy with almost no losses on our side.

"Well done, everybody. Especially our shamans. You were the key to this. Everybody who leveled up, I recommend you spend what you've earned right away. It will likely be a while before they recuperate from this, but they *will* be back. They've come this far and know there is no easy escape. There's no way that they're giving up now."

I was right. They did come. An hour later, the enemies started making their way up the now almost flawless, even incline that was made slippery and even more dangerous with the freezing rain summoned by our mages. Cursing inside my mind, I turned to Timothy again. "Bastards. They're sending the non-humans."

Timothy looked downslope with a crestfallen sensation. "Yeah. But they aren't just letting them loose and trusting them. Look."

"Motherfuckers." The non-humans were climbing carefully in their thousands, navigating the start of the slippery, coverless area in one large, formationless multitude. On either side, a few adventurous climbers were also attempting to scale the mountain itself, ostensibly to get at us from above. I didn't envy them the attempt. Creziel had prepared the sides personally. That in itself wasn't the problem. The problem was what was following them.

Right behind the uneven ranks of the non-humans, archer companies followed at a slower pace. Rank after rank of the companies, they must hold every single human archer left in the army. I believed I could see mages at the front, trying to work on the soil to make it easier to ascend. That wasn't the infuriating point, though. It was how their bows were readied and aimed... straight at the backs of the Secondary.

Timothy looked like he was trembling. "They are really leading them forward at bowpoint? I wanted to kill them before, but now, I feel more like wholesale slaughter! Stuff to make Jeffrey Dahmer blanch."

I fumed. "It's that one-armed bastard and the dwarf. I swear, I regret killing Caliga now. She might have been more competent than these bastards, but at least she had a hint of a conscience." I rubbed the ridge over an eye, glared down over the incoming forces. "None of the scouts report spotting either of the pricks in-person among the archers, though. They aren't taking any chances at all." I took a deep breath, focused on what I *could* do something about. "All right, Tim. I know we were planning to save the doors for an ambush or something. Should we... deviate from the plan? Just a bit?"

He looked at me with mock surprise. "You're suggesting we abandon our carefully laid plans simply to appease your humanity? Do you really think you can convince me that's a good idea?" He snorted. "Of course we should. If you hadn't said anything yourself, I would have kicked you."

"But... you're..." I waved a claw right through his shoulder. "immaterial... much like your sense of humor!"

The well-dressed ghost snorted. "You're such an ass. Now, let's flip the situation on those dirty assholes."

"I know I said that I was probably not going to address you again. Turns out, I was wrong." I looked at the multitudes of non-humans climbing toward us. I had plenty of time to observe them over the past weeks, but in this valuable moment right before everything was going to blow up, I found myself investigating them with intense concentration, as if trying to cement their existence.

They weren't as varied in race as I'd believed weeks ago, in that first, chaotic battle. In fact, there were only around five races represented in numbers. The most numerous ones were those most humanoid in aspect, like the lithe, cat-like light infantry who were scrambling up the mountainside with ease.

Others, like the massive, werewolf-like humanoids were muscled enough they looked like they were walking on plane ground. Viperkin. Some insectile humanoids. What looked like Ethium. There weren't that many different races represented. They just *looked* very varied, because all groups were mixed. Apparently, segregation wasn't a thing *inside* the Secondary. Other races were present outside of the most common ones, too, like an armored pair of fighters that looked more like humanoid peacocks, but only as the occasional outlier.

At this point, the first non-humans had climbed around halfway up the ascent toward the battlements. They made good time. Five more minutes, and they would be here. Obviously, it was made quite a lot easier by the lack of attacks from our side. I glanced at my soldiers standing ready and saw more than one clenching weapons in death grips. They did *not* like the idea of standing inactive, while armed enemies approached. Well. Time to roll the dice.

"This, however, promises to be my last message to the

Secondary. You know the truth, by now. The bows at your back speak volumes that are hard to deny. The humans will see you dead, one way or the other. Therefore, if we talk again, it will not be with you as part of the Nefren Empire, but at our side."

I gave the signal and, on either side of our battlements, a Shadow Door swung open, revealing the illusion that had kept them hidden until now. "This is my offer. Flee the humans. Join our side, as allies. We will protect you, and make you part of our world. As equals. Or continue, and we will have to fight you... as the humans' slaves."

The world held its breath then, as the cohesion in the human army was tested... and finally broke. In seconds, the first non-humans started streaming up the treacherous stretch like a furred, scaled, or feathered wave. Cries of relief rang out, and some even flung their shields or weapons away as they climbed, slithered, or half-ran.

"They're doing it, Tim. They're actually doing it. They're joining us, man!"

"I know, you scaly mountain! It's the best! That asshole dwarf must be fuming." He grimaced. "Oof. Not everybody, though. Look, there's a group that decided they wanted to stay with the humans."

Timothy was right. One large clump of non-humans on the right flank had stopped, weapons in hand, and were trying to stop t,hose who tried to move past them. Shouts rang out, and moments later, non-humans spilled the blood of their own.

It wasn't an isolated experience either. All across their numbers, smaller groups either tried to stop their own running for the welcoming entrances, or simply stayed put, deciding to go with a neutral approach—not hindering their own, but not trying to join them, either. Still, compared to the people who actually tried to join us, they were very much in the minority. One in eight, at most.

Timothy grinned, but there was a manic glean to it. "Sooo. O mighty scale-bird and ruler. Did we ever cover exactly how we can tell whether they're trying to join us or just rushing to attack, because we were kind enough to open the doors?"

I was glad there were no mirrors nearby. I did *not* need to know exactly how goofy I looked right then and there. Because, of course, we didn't. An armed non-human defecting and one attacking would look pretty much the same. It *felt* like they were joining us, but... I cleared my throat. "Bear with me a moment." Then, I stretched my senses outward, trying to take in the emotions coming from outside.

My Mental Power and Control, boosted by the powers of the Blessing of Deyra, were through the roof by now. I could pretty much read the room in a second, which did make my public speaking quite a bit easier. But what was coming toward us was nothing as simple as a crowd. These were people moving on the edge of death, who knew full well that they might die before the hour had passed.

Their emotions were strong, coming in waves. But did the elation reaching from them stem from the sudden possibility of survival or from being able to escape their oppressors? Hope. Sure. Could work both ways, too. Defiance? That was promising. Bloodlust? Less so. One of the strongest emotions, coming from all sides, though... I turned back to Timothy, frowning. "I... *think* we're good."

"Think?"

"Yeah. I'm taking in their feelings. It isn't what you'd call an exact science. But *the* strongest feeling coming from them pretty much feels like a middle finger. And I doubt it's raised at us."

He chuckled nervously, then started laughing. "Mood!"

"What?"

"That's a whole-ass mood!" He raised two triumphant middle fingers at the humans. "That's right! We're all agreed. The finger to you, you bastards!"

Maybe the leaders of the human army were able to sense emotions, too. I didn't know if that was just a dragon thing or something one could be trained to learn. However, it was frighteningly obvious to spot when they realized that the Secondary wasn't going to fight, but were jumping ship. Because the humans opened fire on them.

For the hindmost ranks of the non-humans, it was a slaughter. They were mowed down by waves of arrows. The archer companies were maybe half as many as the non-humans, but they were right behind them, with the entire rise spread out ahead of them like a shooting gallery. Some of the groups of the Secondary who had decided to fight their brethren or at least ignore our promise of safety waved frantically in the attempt to stop their perceived allies from attacking. They died with the others.

The forces farther up the incline were a bit better off. With the added height, the archers had a limited distance, and the foremost two-thirds of their forces, still several thousand in numbers, were speeding up, realizing that their lives were being threatened by their former allies. All over the approach, non-humans fought to reach us, sometimes struggling among themselves to come first. Every other second, one of them would fall, rushing down the slippery slope and inevitably tear others down with him.

"Fliers! Attack the humans right now! Beware their retaliation—we just need to distract them!" Above us, the Imps and other fliers went airborne. I roared with glee to see them joined by a half dozen of the fliers formerly from the human army. Three of the millipede-like monsters and three spitters followed them aloft. They must have finally made a breakthrough in their training.

I turned back to the glowing form. "There must be something more we can do. Tim. Ideas, except for the two of us charging in?"

He shook his head with a grim expression. "They're outside the reach of our spellcasters, even if we had something ready that might help them. We have the Gallery of Illusions, but they are too far down for it to have an effect." His eyes narrowed in hatred. "Poor bastards. I hope those who fall at least take some of the damn archers with them."

I growled and dug my claws into the stone of the fortifications in frustration. Silently, I agreed with him. Maybe some of the falling and dying soldiers could start another wave and tear apart their ranks, stopping the attacks that way. Except, that would have been too easy, of course. When the sliding non-humans, living or dying, came closer to the following archers, they met a shield of force and were slanted to the side, falling in an inglorious mix of dead and dying people to pass right past the formations of the humans.

Now the human companies started moving. Ignoring the multitudes of crying, hurting humanoids hurtling past then and straight toward the edge of the mountain, they began marching up the incline again. This time around, they must have been doing something magical, because their climbing speed increased, making it look like they were marching up a small hill instead of a forty-five degree climb. Our Imps and other flying fighters were getting hits in here and there, but it was not enough to cause a difference. Their shields were *strong.*

"It must be the damn mages. They're doing something to the mountainside, or their feet or... I don't *know!"* Timothy sounded like he wanted to strangle somebody. "They're going to catch up to them and kill them all."

I'd gone numb. The time for being upset was past. "It doesn't matter what they're doing. What matters is that their ranks are getting into range now."

I addressed all our forces. My mental voice sounded emotionless, clinical. "All ranged fighters and spellcasters. Shoot at will. Target the humans only. Pour it on them."

In seconds, the sky was shrouded with our attacks. Letting my gaze slide over our battlements, we weren't the only ones influenced by what we were seeing. Voices spewed, shouted, and cursed, words filled with outrage and hatred, reflected on their visages. I looked intently at the front rank, willing their shields to break apart so we could slaughter them and save the Secondary.

Except it didn't. The bloody thing held, and only the ballista bolts looked like they were making any impressions on the shield.

I cursed. It felt like all I did today was curse the humans, but... it felt like the thing to do. "They must have brought every single remaining spellcaster. That, or the damn dwarf is there. But I'm not seeing him." Focused on my troops, I continued. "Keep up the attacks. Ahzel. You and I are going to join the fliers. We go to break through their protection."

It was stupid as all hell. I knew that. I wasn't a bloody Red, able to shrug off arrows like they were raindrops, or Creive, able to unleash lightning among their kind. A concentrated wave of arrows would be able to take me down, hardened scales or not. There were weak places—eyes, tendons, the lighter tissue of my wings—that didn't take damage well.

That was even disregarding how some of the enemies were bound to have horrible feats of their own. Still, it needed to be done. If their shields weren't breaking down, we had to act, to make sure the archer companies didn't slaughter the Secondary and reach the battlements intact.

With those thoughts fixed in my mind, I didn't waste any time, flung myself out into the air, and beat my wings, climbing higher. I'd show them who was in charge here.

Wasting no time, I tried to affix a Shadow Whorl in the middle of the central human formation. It wouldn't cover the entire formation, but should be able to disrupt their coherence. Except, it was repelled by a magical shield. Dammit! Okay, so they had some magical shields. That didn't mean the dwarf was there. We would see in a moment. I rose even farther, distancing myself against the backdrop of the dark clouds that continually poured a near-frozen rain down on the attackers.

Then I wrapped myself in shadows, cast an illusion on top of that, and willed myself to disappear before turning back, readying myself for an attack.

There was no way the illusion would hold up against the number of high-level enemies. I knew that. I was merely trying to postpone the moment they spotted me, to avoid the worst concentrated waves of attack. It worked. I came in at an angle from behind, aiming at the necks of the central company.

Only a few soldiers were looking my way, for a very good reason. The mountainside was lit up. From everywhere in the sky, the Imps, Ahzel, and other fliers spewed elemental damage and aerial attacks down upon the intruders. Farther back, I spotted a handful of the flying beasts formerly from the human forces flying to the attack on our side. I joined them, breathing my Weakening Fog down on the climbing soldiers. To no effect whatsoever.

"Goddammit. Evade. Evade." I commanded the fliers, as I myself flew away, dodging and weaving. I spotted an Imp, who slammed head-first into a mid-air collision with the shield, but managed to take off again, looking rather shell-shocked. But, surprisingly, the humans didn't fire back.

Then, I got it. I could have slapped myself. They would have to lower the shields in order for their own physical or magical attacks to get out, of course. I veered again. "They're staying defensive. Keep attacking for as long as the shields are in place and—"

That was how far I got. The color of the magical shields faded into nothingness. The ranks of archers paused their climb, raised their bows and, as one, let loose.

"Evade!" My mental shout rang out again, as I closed my wings, wind roaring against me as I let myself drop like a stone toward the ground.

I needn't have bothered, though. The humans didn't aim at us. Their arrows flew in one direction. Uphill. At the undefended backs of the nonhumans. After two volleys, they hefted their bows and started trotting upward again, even as new bodies started sliding downhill.

What the hell were they planning? Were the humans that hell-bent on revenge on the poor non-humans, for daring to jump ship? Unleashing another Weakening Fog to no visible effect, I rose higher in the air, trying to get a more coherent overview.

314

The scene was as grisly as I could have expected. The bodies of the dead and injured flowed in a steady stream downhill, shunted aside to move farther down the mountain and out into oblivion. Some tried to hold on, fight to avoid other fallen, or avoid the incoming bodies, knowing full well that the alternative was death. A few wounded realized the futility of their struggles as they slid toward the humans, flung themselves at their shields in an attempt to buy some semblance of revenge with their final moments. To no avail.

Farther up, the first non-humans were starting to enter the Shadow Doors. Inside the door, tight ramps led up to the battlements. Some of our melee fighters stood ready, guiding them up the ramp and then into the tunnel behind, toward safety.

On the ramparts, the few fighters without ranged weapons looked on anxiously, watching the spectacle. A few cheered on the Secondary. Some cried out in horror.

Timothy flew by me, stunning missiles slamming out from his translucent form. Around him, Imps unleashed their fury at the archers, too, while everybody on the ramparts attacked with all they had. With a rare few exceptions, neither spells nor missiles impacted with the enemies, who kept marching uphill.

Some of the archer companies on the edges were having a harder time of things, humans dropping wounded ever so often. But this central company was holding strong. If their shields held out, I couldn't see how we might stop them. At least half of the remaining non-humans were in danger of being caught up with. I couldn't even spot the bloody mages who were keeping the bastards safe.

What was worse, farther down the mountain, new companies of the remaining human forces were starting to move, too. From this distance, it looked like somebody had kicked an ant hill, and everything was in motion. Whatever they were planning, they were throwing everything into it.

But finally, they had gotten in range. Whatever they were using to defend themselves, I'd tear it apart now. I took in the Gallery of Illusions, placed at the very center of the battlefield.

The construction stretched for 300 x 300 feet, placed in the perfect center of the incline. It was by no means large enough to affect all the incoming companies, but the central archer companies on the mountainside would soon lose their precious shields and cohesion. With the mental equivalent of flicking a switch, I turned the Gallery of Illusion into the active position and grinned.

The archer companies practically imploded. From one moment to the other, their cohesion disappeared, along with their shields. Soldiers yelled, screamed, started defending against imaginary foes and, in some cases, actually attacking each other. The shields went down, too.

I commanded, "Attack! Now! Their shields are down!" and dove myself to unleash a Weakening Fog on the west-most company of the lot, while Ahzel did similarly to the east. Now, my attack did work. Humans stumbled, fell to the ground, or were visibly weakened.

Alone, I might not have been able to take them down until they regained their control and cohesion. But I was far from alone. Within seconds, their ranks were riddled with missiles from everywhere, as our entire defense and every flier let loose on them. Soon, the central part of the mountainside was filled with human corpses sliding down toward the following infantry.

However, one company still stood in the area. The central archer company remained untouched and still climbed, ignoring the effects of the Gallery of Illusions, ignoring our ranged attacks and everything!

Arthor was the one who spotted him. He was still camped out with Creziel and every single one of the shamans on top of the battlements. They had strict orders not to spend their mana attacking, however. Their role in the battle was clear. They were supposed to do everything they could to ensure that nobody was able to break the hardened, enchanted rock and force their way *through* the ramparts. Except, here his mental voice was, ringing out toward me across the battlefield, completely panicked. "He is there. The dwarf is there! I can feel his strength through the soil!"

"What?" I let my eyes flow over the formation again. There was nothing to be seen there, at all. All were archers, all humans. In fact... "Goddammit. It must be some type of illusion. Arthor. Hold the shamans ready to defend the walls."

I thought quickly, then turned my attention outward. We were still hurting the outer companies, whose shields were far less efficient than those of the central company, but whatever the dwarf was planning, we needed to stop it! "Everybody. Focus your fire on the central formation. Kill those, and we win."

For the next few moments, the central company was partially obscured by the rain of missiles flying down at them. The ballistas kept firing, as well, and suddenly the vision of the company shimmered and was replaced by a very different one. These weren't archers. They were shieldbearers, one and all, surrounding a central core of spellcasters and... yeah, that damn dwarf, Hair Growth and Lord Nerve Damage.

With our entire army focusing its attention on them, their magical shields were starting to wilt and fail. One after one, they died, reigniting again moments later, only to sputter out again under the next barrage. But one, large, central shield never died entirely. It flickered under the hardest attacks and gave out in areas, but stayed strong. I had no doubt whose it was. At least they didn't keep firing arrows at the fleeing non-humans. Instead, they started veering to the left and increased their pace.

But why the hell would the spellcasters even expose themselves like that? Caught out in front of the walls, we'd be able to slaughter them before the rest of their army came to back them up. Their shields were starting to die right now, there was no way they'd hold out another ten minutes.

Then, my eyes slid from the rapidly climbing shieldbearers to the non-humans they were swiftly catching up on... and onward, to the Shadow Door, where the soldiers of the Secondary were being herded through in ones and twos. The open Shadow Door. The open door which had several thousand non-humans fighting and struggling to get in.

I've made my share of hard decisions. I used to agonize over firing people. Then, lately, I've had my share of moral dilemmas and life-and-death situations to ponder over. Trying to face reality and not shy away from doing what has to be done. But the decision I made right then and there was one of the hardest I've ever made, and there was nothing I could do to soften the blow or in any way diminish what I was doing—condemning thousands of thinking people to their death. Still, I did it.

"Close the northern Shadow Door!" I wondered if others could hear the fury in my mental voice.

The door didn't close. Any one of my minions would be able to close the door, but you needed to touch it physically. Non-humans were still streaming through the opening on both sides. They vastly outnumbered my people near the door, too, bedraggled and winded though they may be.

Right at their heels followed the dwarf and his damn spell-casters.

I repeated myself. "You need to close the northern Shadow Door *now!* The humans don't need to take the wall. If they can barricade the tunnel and keep it open, they have direct entry, and ranged attacks won't do us any good against him in there. Unless you act now, this battle is *lost!*"

Then they got it. Panicked cries rang out as my minions ran to obey the order. The door on my left remained open. On that side, most of the human forces had been eliminated. What few attackers were still standing were following the non-humans at a distance, taking potshots at the fleeing defectors. They were nowhere near to catching up, though. On my right, however... a clamor rang out from within the tunnel, followed by screams of pain and fear. I abandoned my attacks on the speeding company and wheeled to return and help them close the door.

A sigh of relief escaped my throat as a distant groaning of stone over stone announced that the door was starting to close. Then it stopped again. My heart sank.

I dove and looked into the half-closed Shadow Door. From within, a blue shimmer met my gaze. It was... ice. A large block of ice, summoned into being, blocking the door from being closed. I said to myself, softly. "Oh no."

Then, the active part of me took over, and commands poured from me. We needed to take the dwarf spellcaster down before they made it to the safety of the tunnel. Only then would we be able to close the Shadow Door and maintain our defense of the mountainside against them. Only then would we be able to survive.

CHAPTER TWENTY-EIGHT

We failed. Horribly. We rained down destruction upon their heads, unleashing every single skill, cooldown, and feat we had to bring to bear, while our forces were boosted by the Outposts and their strength was being debuffed.

Our Shadow Towers kept pouring abuse down on them. The mountainside was one disturbing obstacle course from the constant flow of downed, dead, and dying humans sliding down the slippery surface to be tossed into the open air below. Desperate, we even attacked through the tunnel, Roth and Koa'tem leading a charge that should be made eternal in song. Our Imps dove and dodged, weaving through openings between arrows that shouldn't be physically possible.

Still, we failed. The shield bearers surrounding the dwarf fell in droves to protect him and the remaining spellcasters. When they reached the non-humans milling around the opening, beating on the block of ice holding the Shadow Door open, the spellcasters unleashed a slaughter that made me nauseated to think about. Within seconds after that, they were right in there, barricaded inside the tunnel, behind the magical shield of the dwarf. Ever so slowly, his army was working its way up the mountainside to join him and continue onward to attack Fire Peak.

We made them pay. Oh, we made them pay. While Hargren was in the tunnel, he couldn't protect his army outside, and they only had the rare remaining squad mage to rely on for protection. This meant little faced with our wrath and combined attacks. I had also, just in case, added a handful of Shadow Traps to the inside of the corridor, and I could tell when they engaged, their see-through tentacles tearing into the enemies.

But, as before, they were simply too many. This time, they didn't even have to kill us. They just had to survive. So, they struggled up the mountain, figuring out the reach of the Gallery of illusions under a rain of death. All too soon, and at a terrible cost, their soldiers started reaching their leaders. Minutes later, they started emerging from the other side of the tunnel. Once they managed that, we were forced to pull back or risk being caught on the battlements, cut off from our escape. Once again, we were on the run. Back to Fire Peak.

My mind was reeling. This was utter crap! Our clever preparations had backfired horribly, because we–I–wanted to take the chance and rescue the Secondary. Sure, many had made it in, but... the thoughts of the slaughter happening right outside our battlements threw my gut into chaos. Even more was to come. We'd whittled their numbers down, again and again, but we remained outnumbered. Without the mountain to protect us, we'd be screwed. But... I needed to focus. Focus! What could I use in this situation?

I stumbled on next to my racing minions. I had taken the rear guard, trying to ensure that the hindmost of our people didn't get butchered before reaching the relative safety of the city walls. Behind us, humans roared, leading into a charge, defying the onslaught from the Imps hovering above, protecting our rear with constant firebolts. I halted, spat a Weakening Fog at them and watched their ranks slow down, unable to keep up our pace. Then I started running again.

Lost. Fuck that. We hadn't lost yet. I refused to believe that!

Yes, we were reeling, reacting to whatever was happening. I almost stumbled, realizing... so were they. There was no way they could have planned for the way the battle had evolved. They were just doing better than we were. So, we could still turn this around. Also... they were right at our heels. We might be able to use that!

"Dimodeus." I sent the message as I ran, as tight and controlled as I could. "You said some of the Dworgen wanted to earn their freedom? They have their chance now. It's risky. Odds are they'll die. But, if they make it, they'll be off the hook. For good." I gave him the details, as fast and concise as I could. Then, I took to the air.

I kept in place, guarding the rear of our forces. However, I needed the chance to take in the situation. Needed to see where *he* was. The answer was "right there." Less than half a mile behind us, protected by shield bearers and two surviving spell casters, the dwarf strode onward.

Imperious. Deadly. Certain in his success and our downfall. Well, I'd be damned if that happened on my watch. Spewing another breath attack at the following forces, I turned back toward the city and kept myself relatively steady, as I dove into the minimap.

Excellent. In their haste to take us down, the human forces still hadn't managed to take down all the Shadow Towers. Hell, why would they? With the tunnels behind the Shadow Doors leading straight to the exit tunnels, they circumvented the area that the towers were able to fire upon entirely.

They might not even realize they were there until later. Heh. Well, now I could use it against them. I hovered above my forces, while I mentally moved every single Shadow Tower to where they would shortly be needed. Then, I deactivated each and every one of them. Phase one complete.

I sent out orders left and right. Despite our defeat, we hadn't suffered bad losses. In fact, we had managed an impressive degree of coherence, even as we retreated. Our Clencher riders joined us, helping us keep their forces off our backs by harrying anybody who came too close on our heels.

There would be praise aplenty to go around... if we made it through this. For now, I ensured that all our people hopefully made it into place in time... then I prepared a surprise to teach that bastard a couple of lessons. My people made it back to Fire Peak, but I remained, floating above the city gates, making the necessary preparations before touching down and, with a dive and a final breath attack at my pursuit, roared and retreated into the city.

The Dworgen ran to meet me right near the gates as our forces were fleeing the other way. Good. Somehow, Dimodeus had told them in time. I explained what I needed. As they started racing for the gates, I sent a mental message, spreading it far and wide enough that anybody inside the crater, including our enemies, would be able to hear it. "Close the gates. You stupid bastards. Didn't you see what they did? We need to close it *now!*"

Behind our forces, the Dworgen were the only ones who remained outside. They started pushing on the massive, elaborate city gates, fumbling as the weight of it apparently became too much for them. Then, they waited for more of their kind to join them and help. Half a minute later, the following human armies had drawn in close, but they were finally enough to start pushing the huge city gates closed. Except, they didn't make it.

The Dworgen paused, confused, as the doors refused to close further. They looked at each other, at the near-blinding glow of the magical block of ice holding the doors open, at the oncoming enemies... then they ran for the far reaches of the cavern in the attempt to escape the armies.

I silently wished them luck as the enemies followed. They had done what we needed.

Now, the humans entered Fire Peak.

We kept retreating, while the humans poured into the city. At my order, we gathered in the central plaza. It was fitting that we should finish things here, I guess. Where Selys used to lay down her judgements and dispense her "wisdom" upon the masses of the city, we would attempt to end this, once and for all, ensuring that the human army failed in their onslaught.

As the enemies drew farther into the city, they reformed, redrew their ranks and formations, and started to proceed more slowly. Beyond them, their forces stretched on in one long column reaching all the way back to the battlements. They just didn't stop coming.

We pulled away from them now, giving ourselves the time to get ready. In the central plaza of the city, our forces met. The lines were drawn. I glanced around me, and, in the middle of everything, found a moment of peace. Honestly, if this was how things should end... I didn't really mind.

On every side, I had friends and stout supporters ready to throw their lives on the line. The Talpi, constantly there for me. Crawls, ugly, but tough, grasping weapons and oversized shields in their strong hands. The Imps, hovering, raving to go on the offensive. Every other race of the city was represented, weapons in hand, ready to throw their worst at the invaders. There, on the ground below us... I paused at the realization. I hadn't *known*.

The tiles were there. In their hundreds. The pictograms stared up at us, depicting every single feat option known to us, and the unfolding of the selections as one grew and leveled. I felt a touch of warmth spread inside me. This was what we were fighting for. Freedom... and free knowledge. The future of our people was writ large, right below our feet.

On the far side of the courtyard, the Key of the North and Lord Verneth stood tall, as the human formations spread into the plaza. They were clearly raving to go, ready to finally unleash their frustrations on the people of the city. Lining up opposite of our forces, they clearly waited for the signal to go.

I checked over the minimap one more time. About a third of the remaining human forces, two to two and a half thousand perhaps, had made it into the city, with more streaming through the gates every second. Yes. It was time.

I stepped forward, Timothy at my side. The dwarf on his side did the same, along with the one-armed bastard. They were again surrounded by the blue sheen of their shield. Of course. They were in charge of the gates. Why maintain a shield over the gates, when the battle would be met here? We met in the center of the courtyard.

The dwarf's arrogant smirk was so damn punchable. I wasn't sure how it was possible for somebody of his stature to look down on me, but he managed. "I have been looking forward to this."

I growled under my breath. "I'm not so sure that you'll think the same two minutes from now."

"Threats? How very predictable from a monster of your kind. I would rethink my strategy if I were you, though. If you want us to spare any of your precious monsters, you had better start groveling, beast."

I snorted. "Not happening. Honestly, it's not like you've given us any chance to believe that you would even keep your promise. I pity the soldiers of the Secondary. They believed your lies, and look what happened to them."

He waved a hand dismissively. "If only they had remained loyal and known their place, they might have made it. But they will be easily replaced. They're nothing but monsters. Like your beasts. Still, the chance of survival and a life in service is better than instant death, would you not agree?"

"Gee, and you wonder why we're not jumping at the chance to join your side. See, I had the idea that I'd rather give you a counteroffer."

The dwarf leered now, magic building between his hands. "Counteroffer? Really? That would require that you have anything worth offering that I cannot take for myself."

"I do, at that." I sent a message to my people to prepare. Then I concentrated. I found the spot in the system I needed and pressed [Activate Fire Web]. All around the city, the fire shield sprang to life and cut off the entirety of Fire Peak from the rest of the army. "How does your survival sound?"

Shouts rang out from their army as they spotted the flames. It enveloped the entire city in flames, bathing everything in a hellish glow. If Selys were to be trusted, it would be able to run for a day or two before running out.

"What did you do?" His tone suddenly did a one-eighty, belligerence replaced by surprise, even shock. He looked everywhere around him, eyes growing wider as he suddenly noticed the edges of the courtyard growing packed. The news had spread, and the people of Fire Peak were slowly rushing in, as were some of the former Secondary, I noticed.

"I turned the tables on you. About that offer. Right now, you have about a third of your army with you, inside the city. You are surrounded by our armies, you will not be able to fight your way out, and we have the constructions of Deyra to aid us, while you have... nothing. So. Are we going to discuss your surrender?"

I honestly didn't expect him to accept the offer. Heh. It's not like I would have, in his place. Again, shadow dragons. We didn't have the best of reps. But, I had to admit his complete lack of reticence as he threw back his head and roared for his troops to attack.

Unfortunately for him, that gave me the time to access the minimap and activate every single Shadow Tower that adorned the buildings surrounding the entire Victory plaza. Even as the leading ranks of the humans rushed onward, their numbers started dropping on the edges, as the towers started firing their debilitating payload.

It was not an easy battle. We had them outmaneuvered and outnumbered. Our Illusion Defense ruined their vision and confused their cohesion, and our Outposts weakened their forces while boosting ours. Even so, these veteran human soldiers had finally made it to where they could get their hands on us, and they weren't going to give up without a battle. On top of that, the dwarf spellcaster finally went entirely on the offensive, giving up the attempt at defending his people to unleash elemental hell on everybody and everything.

Still, the outcome was decided from the start. With every Weakening Fog, every frost attack by Ahzel, every debilitating bolt by a Shadow Tower, their forces were weakened, while the avenues leading to the plaza were congested with the number of fighters who wanted nothing more than finally taking those damn invaders down.

We fought smart, melee fighters fighting defensively, while the rest of us let ranged attacks rain down upon them. The buildings on all sides of the plaza were packed with people from Fire Peak tossing down missiles on the humans. Weapons, rocks, anything.

Those not among my original minions didn't do as well. Too many of them fell, taking the chance to earn power for themselves and getting cut down by the human fighters who had plenty of levels and attributes on them.

He held up longer than he should, by all rights, have been able to. However, at long last, his mana drained, and the leeching powers of my breath weapon and the Shadow Towers started taking effect. In the end, he fell, stabbed, run through, and torn down by a half-dozen defenders at the same time.

I stood there, staring down on the lifeless form of the former Key of the North, watching as, on all sides, the few remaining humans threw down their weapons and surrendered. We just needed to finish these last opponents, then we'd be able to take on the remaining enemies. Leaderless and bereft of spellcasters, their numerical superiority wouldn't matter as much. Hopefully.

One single person still stood tall, despite everything, bleeding profusely from a nasty cut on his forehead. Lord Verneth grinned defiantly, ignoring the situation. "What are you waiting for, you damn animal? Come at me, already."

I sneered. "Why? Do you really want to die that much? Surrender. *Our* forces don't kill people just because they're the wrong race."

He snorted, stumbled slightly as he moved forward, raising

his hammer against me. "I'm done anyway. Captured by an animal. Twice. I am going to lose everything I have."

"Listen, you moron. You already *have* lost. Why even think about that?"

He started laughing. Deep, belly-wracking snorts of laughter that sounded suspiciously like sobs. "Hargren never said?" His smile was completely bereft of actual humor, resembling a viper more than anything else. "Why did you think he was in such a hurry? We got a messenger from the Empire. With Galica gone, and the rest of the leadership dead? We were being replaced. The stupid dwarf wanted to earn all the glory for himself. As did I."

"Wait. That means... they are sending others?"

His eyes were empty. He looked like he had already checked out. "They're already arriving. They sent word by spell earlier in the day. They are arriving under illusion, to not spoil the surprise.. Enjoy your last moments alive. Once that shield drops, you will be slaughtered. They are sending the First Shield. I only... I only wished, I would be here to see you die." With a hate-filled yell, he raised the hammer one last time and stumbled onward.

I met him head-on. Moments later, his dead body hit the floor.

Inside the fire shield, the human army was defeated. We were leveling up, celebrating our victory and survival. We had done it, and now, it was time for us to heal and prepare to chase the rest of the bastards out of our mountain!

We got half an hour. Then our plans and dreams were smashed to bits. Outside the fire shield, flying creatures were appearing from thin air, illusions fading as they could see they were unnecessary. Setting down inside the crater, they landed to unload the new leaders. They kept coming, unloading strong, well-rested riders in a steady stream, and the leaderless, half-broken army rallied around them.

I almost dropped the fire shield right then in order to take the fight to them. But then I started inspecting their soldiers. Lord Verneth had been right.

I have no clue how much time I lost. I slipped from soldier to soldier inside the minimap, investigating their levels, their attributes. I was aghast. I only stopped when I realized I was probably looking at the same enemies I had already Inspected. Most of them were above Level 30.

There were sorcerers. Fighters. One of them, a mountain of a man in full plate armor, was Level 52. The one ordering them all about, a solemn-looking graybeard with a much-used tower shield... didn't register. For the first time ever, my Inspect failed to work inside the mountain, even though I held the Blessing.

Did that mean he was ten levels higher than I was? Twenty? Twice my level?

I observed, as they landed safely outside the raging inferno of the fire shield and slowly started arranging their defenses to their advantage. With a sinking feeling, I closed the minimap and went to inform my people.

We had won... and we had lost.

CHAPTER TWENTY-NINE

"You walk along the Streets at Night shouting, It's Twelve O'clock and All's well.
I said what if it is not all well, and he said, You bloody find another street." – Terry Pratchett, Guards, Guards

The morning sun was hazy, hard to see through the thin layer of clouds. It made the scene feel unreal, like it was just an illusion. I had looked forward to getting out of the mountain again, for sure. Not exactly like this, but... yeah.

We fled through the mountain. Not all of us. Not by any means. A lot of people wanted to fight against the humans, hide out deeper down in the tunnels, and strike back against them. The Aberrants stayed. So did Ahzel. A lot of the inhabitants from Fire Peak, as well. They spread out, using the Corren tunnels to go to where they wanted to go. I was so damn proud of them. The humans had so many levels on them, but they were going to fight back tooth and nail to force these interlopers back out again.

Not that the humans were going to find a place they could just take over and enjoy from day one. No. In the single day we'd had before the shield fell, we'd looted the place of everything worth having, littered it with traps, poisoned the water reservoir, and emptied the hoard. They were going to find a lot of empty buildings and not much else. Of course, we'd collapsed the tunnels and burst open the Blessing behind us. We weren't going to allow them to find our escape route and gain access to Deyra's gifts, just like that.

I couldn't fight down the wave of pride that washed through me. Sure, we had lost. That had smarted for a good while, I wouldn't deny that. But we had faced up against everything the Nefren Empire had to throw against us, and we'd survived. We had eradicated *two* of the Nefren Empire's main armies and emerged stronger. I didn't care that there were still maybe a quarter of their original number left in the Fourth. With what we'd subjected them to, that army was history.

Somehow, even with everything we'd suffered through, they put their lives in my claws. I swore to myself that I wouldn't rest until I had secured a future for my people. Heh. Besides, as long as we were alive, we had a chance. Below me, fires were blooming into being as we were readying food for the evening.

I moved among them all, heart swelling. There was sadness there, a lot of loss, but also hope. To my surprise, there was also endless kindness, beyond what I would have expected. The people of the Secondary were officially lost, tossed into something they could never have foreseen or prepared for, through no fault of their own.

They believed that they were fleeing for a better place, only to be tossed into a situation as fugitives from their former allies. But among their huddled, defeated forms, my people moved. At some camp fires they shared what limited provisions we had, used their magics or skills to improve the situations of the non-humans. Sometimes, they just sat down and talked.

I saw them before me. My council. My most trusted people, all hard at work managing the situation and ensuring that nobody was left by themselves. And just like that, I knew. This wasn't insurmountable. It was a setback. It was a challenge. It was a struggle to be had. But we were up to the task. With these friends, this family around me, there was nothing that we couldn't handle.

I spread my mental voice far and wide, for everybody to hear. "The humans are entering Fire Peak right now. They think us beaten, defeated, fleeing. They have never been more wrong. I walk among you now, and I don't see defeat. I see people who are ready to make a life for themselves.

"The humans might believe that they have won. *But we are not done.* You heed those notifications, those levels you've gained and see them for what they are. Victory! Heed them well and choose wisely which attributes and feats you can choose. Ask our experts for aid in choosing. Because we are not lost. We know exactly where we're going.

"Out there, we have scouted another Blessing, another place where we can grow strong, which the humans do not know. Once we're ready? We will build our strength, gather our resources, and take our mountain back! With the humans ousted, we will finally be able to take up our rightful place as the masters of the wastes." Head held high, I watched them pridefully as they cheered to shake the mountain.

ABOUT LARS MACHMÜLLER

Lars Machmüller lives in Denmark with his wife and three kids. Family comes first, and as such, he spends a lot of time perfecting the art of packed lunches, cleaning food off the floor and delivering kids to and from school, kindergarten, playdates and whatnot.

Whenever somebody is *not* crawling on his shoulders, he dedicates every waking moment attempting to exorcise all those LitRPG plot bunnies that keep finding a place to live within his skull.

Whatever little time remains, he distributes evenly between his towering to-be-read pile, his trusty PC, and music.

Connect with Lars:
LarsM-Writes.com
Instagram.com/LarsMachmuller
Facebook.com/groups/357145749698735
Patreon.com/Moulder666
Mailchi.mp/94863280f513/Cranky-Chronicler

ABOUT MOUNTAINDALE PRESS

Dakota and Danielle Krout, a husband and wife team, strive to create as well as publish excellent fantasy and science fiction novels. Self-publishing *The Divine Dungeon: Dungeon Born* in 2016 transformed their careers from Dakota's military and programming background and Danielle's Ph.D. in pharmacology to President and CEO, respectively, of a small press. Their goal is to share their success with other authors and provide captivating fiction to readers with the purpose of solidifying Mountaindale Press as the place 'Where Fantasy Transforms Reality.'

Connect with Mountaindale Press:
MountaindalePress.com
Facebook.com/MountaindalePress
Twitter.com/_Mountaindale
Instagram.com/MountaindalePress

MOUNTAINDALE PRESS TITLES
GameLit and LitRPG

The Completionist Chronicles,
The Divine Dungeon,
Full Murderhobo, and
Year of the Sword by Dakota Krout

Metier Apocalypse by Frank G. Albelo

Arcana Unlocked by Gregory Blackburn

A Touch of Power by Jay Boyce

Red Mage and
Farming Livia by Xander Boyce

Ether Collapse and
Ether Flows by Ryan DeBruyn

Dr. Druid by Maxwell Farmer

Bloodgames by Christian J. Gilliland

Unbound by Nicoli Gonnella

Threads of Fate by Michael Head

Lion's Lineage by Rohan Hublikar and Dakota Krout

Wolfman Warlock by James Hunter and Dakota Krout

Axe Druid,
Mephisto's Magic Online, and
High Table Hijinks by Christopher Johns

Skeleton in Space by Andries Louws

Dragon Core Chronicles by Lars Machmüller

Chronicles of Ethan by John L. Monk

Pixel Dust and
Necrotic Apocalypse by David Petrie

Viceroy's Pride by Cale Plamann

Henchman by Carl Stubblefield

Artorian's Archives by Dennis Vanderkerken and Dakota Krout

Vaudevillain by Alex Wolf